a Whisper *at* Midnight

DARCY BURKE

USA TODAY BESTSELLING AUTHOR

OLIVERHEBERBOOKS

For my dear friend David

CHAPTER 1

London, March 1868

Two days ago, aspiring investigator Miss Matilda Wren received a request to assist with a sensitive case for a woman who wished to divorce her husband. Initially thrilled to have the opportunity for another paid investigation, Tilda was then shocked to see the identity of her new client: the former fiancée of her friend and associate, Lord Ravenhurst.

Rather, Hadrian, as he'd bade her to call him at their last meeting, which had also been two days ago. She hadn't known about the investigation with his former fiancée until after he'd left her grandmother's house where he'd taken tea with them. And she wouldn't tell him.

The reason for the dissolution of their betrothal was both embarrassing and upsetting to Hadrian. He'd caught his fiancée in a compromising position. She and Hadrian had parted ways, and she'd married the man Hadrian had seen her kissing.

Tilda would not be responsible for bringing the woman back

into his life or even his awareness. Indeed, she wasn't entirely certain she wanted to help this person, given her treatment of Hadrian, but Tilda needed the employment.

She lived in her grandmother's household and managed the finances, which had recently improved from absolutely dire to uncomfortably sufficient. Her grandmother's solicitor had found an account of funds that had been "lost" in the transition between solicitors. It wasn't a great sum, but it permitted them to support the newest member of their household—Tilda's grandfather's cousin's butler who'd been displaced by the cousin's death.

It also ensured they could afford her grandmother's medicine for her aching hands, so she could keep up with her beloved embroidery. The money also encouraged more restful sleep for Tilda, and for that, she was extremely grateful. Still, she was frugal and committed to making sure their circumstances did not reach a dire state ever again.

For that reason, she would accept this assignment to assist Hadrian's former fiancée.

Taking a deep breath, Tilda stepped into the outer office of Mr. Forrest, the barrister who had requested her assistance and for whom she'd worked on several occasions. His clerk, Mr. Clarence, looked up from his desk and removed his spectacles. Setting them down, he smiled at her as he stood. "Good afternoon, Miss Wren. What a pleasure to see you."

"Indeed, good afternoon, Mr. Clarence." Tilda nodded warmly at the wiry man. In his early fifties, he had thinning gray hair and sharp, assessing brown eyes.

"Go right in, Miss Wren. Mr. Forrest is expecting you."

Tilda stepped through the open doorway into the barrister's spacious office. It was more like a small library, with bookcases lining two of the walls. He stood from behind his large oak desk and gestured toward the seating area near the hearth.

The barrister was a bear of a man who would have been suited for the Metropolitan Police. He possessed a thick, rugged build and kind blue eyes that were at odds with his imposing presence. His chin was somewhat long and tended to jut when he was contemplating something, which was quite often in his work.

"Welcome, Miss Wren," he said with his usual engaging smile. "I'm delighted you are able to assist. This matter is quite sensitive."

"I understand." Tilda perched on the chair she usually sat in when Mr. Forrest summoned her to work on a case. "Your client is seeking a divorce on the grounds of cruelty and adultery?"

"Yes. Mrs. Chambers also says Mr. Chambers has stolen some of her jewelry and sold it, but once they wed, it became his property. She has no recourse there." His tone was perfunctory, but there was a sympathetic gleam in his eyes.

Though it was perfectly legal for Mr. Chambers to do as he wished with his wife's jewelry, Tilda would do her best to find it. But would Mrs. Chambers pay Tilda to do that investigative work? It was not part of her assignment from Mr. Forrest, and Tilda couldn't afford to work for free.

Tilda couldn't help feeling curious about this woman who'd once been betrothed to Hadrian. He'd said he was glad to have avoided an unhappy marriage, but he hadn't mentioned his feelings toward Mrs. Chambers. Had he loved her? He'd indicated he was now content to be a bachelor, but was that due to not wanting his heart broken again?

Tilda wouldn't want to take that risk a second time. In truth, she didn't even want to take it a first time. For a woman, marriage meant losing her independence. That was far too high a price to pay, and for what? Whilst Tilda had seen a happy marriage firsthand, that of her grandparents, she'd spent far more time with an unhappy one, that of her parents. She'd long ago decided that she preferred to make her own way without having to rely on anyone else.

She was more than pleased to live as a spinster and build a

reputation for conducting investigations. She'd already solved the murder of her grandfather's cousin, as well as other murders that had been related—with Hadrian's help.

Shaking thoughts of Hadrian from her mind, she focused on the barrister and the matter at hand. "What information do you have for me to begin?"

"Regarding the cruelty, Mrs. Chambers says her husband pushes and grabs her with force regularly. She has bruises, but I did not ask to see them." He inclined his head toward Tilda. "I will leave that to you."

That was one of her primary roles when conducting these investigations for Mr. Forrest. Tilda would note any wounds or marks on the woman's body and write an affidavit detailing what she observed. They would then file a report with the Metropolitan Police.

"I will call on her as soon as possible," Tilda said. "Is there a time that is convenient, so I won't encounter her husband?" Presumably, Mrs. Chambers would not want to meet with Tilda while Mr. Chambers was at home.

Mr. Forrest's mouth lifted in a brief smile. "As it happens, Mrs. Chambers would like you to call on her this afternoon— number twenty Catherine Place. Are you able to go there directly?"

That was a very nice street. Hadrian's former fiancée had married well. "Certainly." Tilda stood, eager to begin her investigation.

The barrister also stood. "Excellent. I look forward to your report."

Tilda nodded and then saw herself out. After acknowledging the clerk once more, she made her way outside where she shortly caught a hack to Catherine Place.

Alighting, she surveyed the façade of the fashionable brick-and-stone terrace with its wrought-iron balcony on the first floor. She took a deep breath as she walked up the short stone stairs to the front door and knocked. A moment later, a stout butler answered.

Tilda smiled. "Good afternoon, I am Miss Wren. I believe Mrs. Chambers is expecting me."

"Indeed." He opened the door wider for her to step into the marble-tiled entrance hall. "If you'll follow me."

The butler led her into the staircase hall and up the stairs. While the furnishings appeared well made and elegant, the interior was not as grand as Tilda had anticipated. There weren't many paintings on the walls, and the décor was minimal. Perhaps her expectations had been somewhat tainted by her recent visit to the excessively opulent Northumberland House where she'd attended an event with Hadrian several days ago.

In truth, she felt far more comfortable here than somewhere like Northumberland House or Hadrian's residence, Ravenhurst House. She was not at all used to excess, even if her mother had often spent money that Tilda had later realized they didn't have. Her mother liked nice things—clothing and accessories, linens, and furnishings. When Tilda's father died, there'd been debt that her mother had accumulated, which Tilda's grandfather had resolved, in part by selling many of those furnishings. That experience was a primary reason that Tilda refused to take on debt and chose to live as economically as possible.

Tilda refocused her thoughts as the butler took her to the drawing room. A woman—Mrs. Chambers, presumably—stood from a chair in the central seating area. Actually, it was the only seating area, though there were a few chairs scattered about the perimeter of the room and a chaise in one corner. Mrs. Chambers nodded toward the butler, who departed, then fixed her attention on Tilda.

"Good afternoon, I am Miss Wren," Tilda said, walking farther into the room to join her new client.

"I'm so pleased you've come," Mrs. Chambers said, her answering smile tentative and perhaps a trifle nervous. She was beautiful, with chocolate-brown hair and wide, amber-brown eyes. Delicate brows arched prettily, and her cheekbones were high and defined. Small, pink bow-shaped lips pursed gently as she gestured to another chair. Tilda could see why Hadrian would have been attracted to her. Assuming he had been. They hadn't discussed that either, and there was absolutely no reason they should.

Mrs. Chambers' gaze moved over Tilda and did not immediately focus on her. It was a slight reaction, but Tilda understood that her garb was outdated and that a woman like Mrs. Chambers might judge Tilda by her appearance.

"Would you care to sit?" Mrs. Chambers asked.

"Thank you." Tilda lowered herself onto the cushion, then she removed a notebook and pencil from her reticule. "I will take notes whilst we talk," she said. "Mr. Forrest has told me about your situation. I am sorry you are in a position where you feel dissolving your marriage is your only option. I know that cannot have been easy for you to decide."

"It was not, particularly when so many people told me not to wed him," Mrs. Chambers said bitterly, her expression one of angry defeat.

Tilda knew Hadrian had caught Mrs. Chambers kissing her current husband. Had Chambers coerced her? Would she have preferred to wed Hadrian but realized she could not after he'd witnessed her in a compromising position?

While those were interesting questions, Tilda needed to make sure she was adhering to the investigation and not satisfying her personal curiosity. "Why was that?"

Mrs. Chambers exhaled, her features drawing down into a near pout. "It's a tedious story. Suffice it to say I was seduced by Louis and ended up with little choice in the matter. How I wish things had gone differently."

Overall, that was a vague recounting of whatever had happened, particularly since Mrs. Chambers didn't know that

Tilda was aware of how things *could* have gone. Tilda decided it was worthwhile to learn how her client's marriage had started and progressed to where it was now. "Did you not want to marry him?"

Taking a moment to respond, Mrs. Chambers seemed to have difficulty finding the words. "I did. However, I was fooled by him. I was swept up by his flattery and passion. That had seemed important to me."

"You say you were fooled," Tilda said. "Can I assume that flattery and passion did not continue?"

"They did not," Mrs. Chambers replied firmly. "After several months, perhaps a year, I sensed his disinterest. Over time, that turned into dislike and our relationship became rather contentious. I think we both regret marrying one another, unfortunately."

"I'm sorry you regret your marriage." Regardless of how Tilda might feel about Mrs. Chambers throwing Hadrian over for her husband, she had great sympathy for a woman who felt trapped. Who *was* trapped. "You do know how difficult it is to obtain a divorce, even now?"

"I do," Mrs. Chambers said with a nod. "But I must try. Perhaps then my family will forgive me and welcome me back. Though I don't hold much hope. They will likely shun me again, this time because I divorced."

Tilda's pity for the woman increased, and she decided she would help her, despite Mrs. Chambers' history with Hadrian. "I will also hope they embrace you," Tilda said. "The life of a divorced woman is difficult. Do you have a plan for what you will do if you are successful?" She didn't add *if your family doesn't welcome you back*, but that was the second part of that question.

"Not really." She regarded Tilda with a fiery gaze. "He should have to provide me with a settlement, shouldn't he? That is only fair since he received my dowry, not to mention the way he has treated me. He is unfaithful and he is … rough." She dipped her head down to look at her lap.

"I'm sorry to hear that," Tilda said. "Mr. Forrest did tell me about those things, but I am here to gather the specific details. Do you want to talk about Mr. Chambers' infidelity first, or would you prefer to show me how he's hurt you?"

Mrs. Chambers' shoulders twitched. "Mr. Forrest said you would look at the bruises on my arms. Louis grabs me roughly and throws me down or pushes me. I have a cut on my head from the last time. I grazed the edge of a dresser before I hit the floor." She lifted her hands to her dark hair and gingerly felt along the front left quadrant of her head. "Here." She pulled her hair apart.

Tilda stood and went to look down at the exposed part of the woman's scalp. There was a small, scabbed wound. "I see it. When did this happen?"

"Four days ago," Mrs. Chambers replied.

Retaking her seat, Tilda wrote down the date the injury occurred and asked Mrs. Chambers to detail exactly what had happened. She waited expectantly as Mrs. Chambers lowered her hands to her lap.

She fidgeted her fingers a moment before meeting Tilda's gaze. "I'd finally confronted him about his infidelity. I asked with whom he was having a liaison, but he only laughed at me and accused me of doing the same, which is ludicrous."

Was it? Mrs. Chambers had been unfaithful to the man to whom she was betrothed.

Tilda would not make judgments. At least not yet. She was merely collecting information—and she could not trust that everything Mrs. Chambers said was the truth even if it was sympathetic. It was certainly only Mrs. Chambers' perspective. "Why do you suspect his betrayal?"

"As I mentioned before, he grew disinterested in me within a year of marrying. He began to be absent more and more, particularly in the evenings. I would wait for him in his chamber, but I would fall asleep as he typically returned quite late. He was often drunk and sometimes smelled of perfume. He was never interested in lying with me those nights, so I would return to my chamber. We have not shared a bed in nearly three years."

After making notes, Tilda looked over at Mrs. Chambers. "Let us discuss your suspicions of his infidelity. Do you suspect a specific woman, or does he carry on with a variety of women?"

"I think he visits a house of prostitutes or whatever they are called." Mrs. Chambers sniffed. "However, the perfume I have smelled recently seemed expensive. I thought perhaps he had a mistress."

As men often did, Tilda mused. "Did you recognize the perfume?" It would be difficult to find someone based on fragrance alone, particularly if it wasn't specially created for a single person.

Mrs. Chambers shook her head. "It might have been floral? I confess I didn't pay close attention to the specific fragrance."

Tilda sought to confirm an important detail. "You don't have any children from the marriage?" Mr. Forrest hadn't mentioned any, and he would have, but Tilda wanted to make sure.

"No, thank goodness. I would not be able to seek a divorce in that case. It would be too difficult for the children." She sniffed again and pressed her lips tightly together as if she were trying to contain her emotions. "I know it's not helpful that I can't prove he is being unfaithful, but hopefully you can." Her expression was expectant.

"That is my job," Tilda said in what she hoped was a reassuring tone. "Can you provide me with any information as to where he goes at night?"

"He belongs to Arthur's." Mrs. Chambers frowned at Tilda. "But he wouldn't meet any women there."

"No, but someone there might know where he goes after the club," Tilda said, not that she would be permitted to go inside and ask. If Hadrian were assisting her again, he could do so, but she could not involve him in this matter. She'd have to find another way. "Is there anywhere else your husband goes?"

"I don't know." Mrs. Chambers wrung her hands before flattening them atop her lap. "He rarely tells me anything anymore. He supposedly works a great deal. He is opening a drapery shop with his partner, Edgar Pollard."

Tilda wrote the name down. "Can you provide his address as well as where this shop is located?"

Mrs. Chambers gave her the man's residential direction, but did not know the location of the shop, just that she thought it was on Oxford Street. "I should know where the shop is," Mrs. Chambers said almost sheepishly. "However, I'm afraid I don't pay much attention to what Louis says about his business endeavors, nor does he want me asking about them."

Their relationship sounded rather horrid. Tilda gave her a sympathetic nod. "I'll find out where the shop is located."

"Did Mr. Forrest also tell you about Louis stealing my jewelry?" Mrs. Chambers asked.

"He did. I'd like to know when you realized items were missing, as well as a description of each one. Then I can publish a list in the newspaper. That may help us find them if they've been sold."

"Does that mean you believe me?" Mrs. Chambers' eyes were wide. "I didn't think Mr. Forrest did. Or perhaps he simply didn't care. He said my jewelry became my husband's property when we wed, but surely Louis can't just take heirlooms that have been in my family for generations without my permission."

"I'm afraid he can, but that doesn't mean I can't find them for you," Tilda said. "However, since this is not part of the investigation I was hired by Mr. Forrest to conduct, I'm afraid you must hire me directly to search for your jewelry. Do you wish to do that?"

"I do." There was a note of hesitation in Mrs. Chambers' voice. "I just ... have very little pin money left, and Louis doesn't give me much anymore. I've borrowed the money to pay Mr. Forrest from a friend. Could I pay you by selling one of the pieces of jewelry after you find it?"

Tilda couldn't really afford to do that. "My only concern is that if I can't find any of it, I will not be paid for my time."

"Of course. I'm sure my friend can lend me some additional funds." Mrs. Chambers gave her an imploring look. "Please say you'll find my jewelry."

"I would be happy to, provided you can pay me," Tilda said with an encouraging smile. "Are you certain your friend will loan you more money? I'm afraid I can't work without compensation." While that was true, Tilda found herself wanting to help Mrs. Chambers anyway.

"I understand." Mrs. Chambers' brow was deeply furrowed. "I will speak with my friend as soon as possible. I suppose we can wait to discuss the matter until I've paid you."

Tilda hated that she couldn't just agree to help her. The woman was in distress. "Please go ahead and tell me why you think your husband would take your jewelry."

Perhaps Tilda was being foolish, but she would trust that Mrs. Chambers would obtain the necessary funds. Tilda simply couldn't say *no*, not when the woman's heirlooms had gone missing.

Mrs. Chambers shrugged gently. "I'm not sure, but perhaps he sold it to gain more money for his business venture. Or he gave it to his paramour—my jewelry began to disappear in December, and that's when I first smelled that perfume." Her lip curled, and Tilda saw a deep anger behind the woman's expression.

Tilda wrote down Mrs. Chambers' suppositions and then recorded a detailed description of the missing items as well as when they'd disappeared from her jewelry box. Looking up from her notepad, Tilda asked, "Is there anything else I should know?"

"I can't think of anything just now. I should show you the

bruises on my arms." Mrs. Chambers rose. "We'll go to my chamber."

Tilda stood and followed her from the room. They went to the back corner of the first floor where Mrs. Chambers led her into a pretty bedchamber decorated in bright florals with a small seating area near the hearth. There was also a dressing area in the corner with a screen and a table with a mirror.

A maid came into the chamber through a narrow door in the opposite corner that was barely visible in the wainscoting and floral wallpaper. A few years younger than Tilda and Mrs. Chambers, she had round cheeks and hazel eyes. She wore a modest dark-blue gown and a white cap atop her dark-brown hair. The maid cast a nervous look toward Tilda as she entered.

"This is Clara," Mrs. Chambers said. "I told her to listen for me as I will need her help to undress." She moved behind the screen, and the maid followed her.

Tilda took the opportunity to look about the room. "Where is your jewelry box?"

"I finally hid it after the garnet necklace went missing a week or so ago," Mrs. Chambers replied. "I still have some pieces left, and I refuse to allow him to steal any more. I should have hidden it after the first time." She sounded bitter, and Tilda didn't blame her.

Mrs. Chambers emerged from behind the screen. She'd removed her gown but still wore her petticoats and corset.

Tilda stepped toward her client and studied her left arm. There were faint bruises around the upper portion. She cocked her head to see the backside, and Mrs. Chambers rotated her arm in response. "Thank you," Tilda murmured.

The bruises did look like those that would be caused by fingers digging harshly into the flesh. Tilda wrote down her observations then moved to the right arm where she saw similar bruises.

"Are there more?" Tilda asked.

"Not at the moment. I had one on my shoulder when he pushed me, but that was more than a week ago, and it's faded." She presented her right shoulder, and Tilda could see a very faint swath of yellow.

"I see the remnants," Tilda said before recording it in her notebook. "Thank you, Mrs. Chambers. You can dress now."

The woman retreated behind the dressing screen with the maid, and Tilda walked about the room. "How did those injuries occur?"

"The bruises on my arms came from an argument we had three days ago after dinner. I'd asked if he took my garnet necklace. I'd also asked him about the other jewelry when it went missing, but he always said he wasn't to blame. Still, I wanted to ask him anyway—just to let him know that I know he did it." She sounded angry and defiant.

Tilda appreciated the woman wanting to stand up for herself but wondered if it was worth the trouble. "Was he violent with you those other times you asked?"

"No. This violent behavior is relatively new."

"When did that start?" Tilda asked as she wrote in her notebook.

"I suppose in December. He's threatened me in the past, but he didn't get rough."

"Can you tell me what happened with the bruise on your shoulder?"

"I was in his study downstairs. He doesn't like for me to go in there." Mrs. Chambers emerged from behind the screen. "He told me to leave and pushed me. I hit the edge of the doorframe."

Tilda noted what the woman said. "Can you take me to the study and show me where he pushed you?"

"Of course." Mrs. Chambers started for the door as the maid came from behind the screen. She kept her head down as she walked to the door in the corner and departed.

Mrs. Chambers led Tilda back downstairs to a masculine

room at the back of the house. She nodded toward a closed door. "My husband's bedchamber is through there."

Tilda nodded before looking about the room. There was a desk, a seating area, and several bookcases. "Where did he push you?"

"Against that doorframe," Mrs. Chambers said, indicating the doorway from a small sitting room into the study.

Noting the location of the violence, Tilda wrote it in her notebook, then she startled as the door to the bedchamber opened.

A tall, lean gentlemen filled the doorway, his small eyes narrowing at Tilda and Mrs. Chambers. His dark, wiry hair was a bit disheveled, and his stock was crooked.

"What the bloody hell are you doing in here?" the man thundered.

Tilda noted that Mrs. Chambers flinched, but she didn't move otherwise. This man had to be her husband.

"Why aren't you at the shop?" Mrs. Chambers asked, her voice tinged with apprehension.

"Who the hell is she?" Mr. Chambers asked his wife, though he pinned his angry stare on Tilda.

Summoning a placid smile, Tilda replied, "Mrs. Chambers has enlisted me to assist her with some refurbishment ideas, and I'm afraid I insisted she show me the library. I do want to ensure I don't introduce a style that doesn't compliment the entire house." Tilda closed her notebook.

Mr. Chambers stepped into the library and moved his attention to his wife. The nostrils of his long, sharp nose flared. "Refurbishment? What nonsense is this? There is no money for that whilst I have invested in this new venture. Nothing needs refurbishment anyway, and certainly not directed by someone in such outdated fashion." His gaze swept over Tilda with open distaste before returning to his wife. "You are the epitome of wastefulness, my dear."

Mrs. Chambers' shoulders twitched. "You're the wastrel, not me."

Tilda again saw the woman's defiance but hoped Mrs. Chambers would not pay a price for it.

Mr. Chambers' gaze simmered with fury. Tilda noted that he clenched his hands into fists briefly. She was torn between wanting to beat a hasty retreat from the house and not wishing to leave her client alone with her husband.

"I need to return to the shop," Mr. Chambers bit out. He grimaced briefly and brushed his hand over his abdomen, which Tilda found odd. Then he snapped his attention to Tilda. "I don't wish to see you here again. There will be no refurbishment." He stormed out of the study, striding between them and jamming his shoulder against his wife's as he passed.

Tilda moved to the woman's side. "Are you all right?"

Mrs. Chambers nodded even as she rubbed her shoulder where he'd bumped into her. "I'm fine. I think he must have had too much to drink again last night. He's been feeling poorly of late because he indulges too excessively." She wrinkled her nose in distaste.

"I can stay for a while if you'd like," Tilda offered earnestly.

"That won't be necessary. He's gone now."

Tilda frowned. "He will return, however. Do you have somewhere you can stay?" Tilda was truly worried for the woman's safety. "You could stay at a hotel, even," Tilda suggested, though it seemed money was an issue given what Chambers had just said. And if he was stealing his wife's jewelry, that might indicate financial hardship.

"I'll consider it, thank you." Mrs. Chambers smiled, but the lines around her mouth revealed the agitation behind it.

"I'll look in on you tomorrow, if you don't mind," Tilda said.

"Thank you." Mrs. Chambers guided her from the study and to the entrance hall. "I appreciate your help. My situation has become untenable. I can't continue like this." Her eyes held an almost wild glint.

"I understand," Tilda said, hoping to soothe the woman. "We'll move toward a divorce with due haste. Just try to keep to yourself and be safe."

As Tilda left the house, she couldn't quite shake the feeling that something bad was going to happen. She would do her best to ensure it did not.

CHAPTER 2

*H*adrian Becket, the Earl of Ravenhurst, stepped from his coach and surveyed the house in front of him. It was one of the larger homes on the street, with a pleasing stone façade accented with wrought iron. His former fiancée, now Mrs. Beryl Chambers, had come out well enough, it seemed, despite throwing him over for her current husband, a self-important, arrogant ass if Hadrian had ever met one.

Oddly enough, Hadrian had encountered him last night. One of Hadrian's colleagues had convinced him to go to his club where Louis Chambers was a member.

Despite the passage of time, Hadrian was still baffled as to why Beryl had preferred Chambers. She'd said she was in love, but Hadrian just couldn't see any redeeming qualities in the man. He was loud, obnoxious, and utterly unaware of his irritating behavior.

Hadrian had to admit he'd felt a measure of relief after catching her in Chambers' arms at that ball. Well, following the initial flash of anger and betrayal.

He and Beryl had parted ways, and she'd wed Chambers. Hadrian had moved on. Alone.

But now he was here because she'd sent him a somewhat succinct letter yesterday begging him to call on her today. She'd said she was in dire need of his advice and perhaps assistance. She'd ended it by saying if he'd ever cared for her at all, he would come.

So, here he was. That she had requested his help and he'd later encountered her husband was a curious coincidence.

"What's that there?" his coachman, Leach, asked in his typical gruff tone. He inclined his head toward a wagon in front of the next house.

"That is the Metropolitan Police," Hadrian replied with a slight frown. He hoped there was nothing amiss next door.

The sight of the wagon brought Tilda to mind. It had been just a week since he'd last seen such a wagon. The police had taken away the heinous criminal they'd caught after conducting a thorough and rather intense investigation.

He'd seen Tilda a few days ago, but he missed her already. He supposed that was normal since they'd been in each other's company every day for a couple of weeks. Honestly, it seemed they'd known each other much longer. They'd fallen into a pleasing friendship—odd for a man and a woman—as they'd worked together.

He also missed the fact that she was the only person who knew of the strange new ability he'd acquired after nearly dying two months ago following an attack in which he was stabbed. He'd hit his head on the pavement, and now he saw visions and felt sensations when he touched certain objects or even people. It had proven rather useful in their investigation.

However, it was also quite frustrating as the ability caused Hadrian to suffer painful headaches, and he had no control over whether it worked or how. He could touch an object or a person and feel nothing. Then, ten minutes later, he could touch it or them again and a vision would flicker in his mind.

What he had learned, so far, was that the "gift"—he sometimes thought of it as a curse for a variety of reasons, not the least of which was the potential that he was going mad—did not seem to work with objects or people he knew well. When his valet touched him, Hadrian did not see any visions, nor did he feel any sensations.

It also hadn't seemed to work with someone who was dead, which he'd surmised after he and Tilda had discovered a corpse. Hadrian had been able to see the man's memories before but had stopped being able to do so after he'd died.

However, he'd later seen a vision when touching something that had belonged to someone who had been dead for some time. That made Hadrian think the length of time someone had been deceased mattered. Or perhaps it was just that his ability was changing over time. Honestly, he never knew what to expect, except the accompanying headaches.

Thankfully, Hadrian was not affected when he touched objects in his own home. Being assaulted with the feelings or memories of other people in his household, or people who had once lived in his house, such as his father, would be unsettling.

The best defense against Hadrian's newfound ability was to keep his gloves on, for then he couldn't be bothered with it. He approached the front door and rapped on the wood, eager to learn why Beryl had summoned him.

A moment later, the door flew open. The butler, an average-sized fellow in his middle fifties with a stout frame, his eyes wide and his round face pale, regarded Hadrian with surprise. But there was something else in the man's gaze—agitation or perhaps even apprehension.

"Good morning," Hadrian said slowly as he handed the butler his card. "I'm here to see Mrs. Chambers."

The butler glanced down at the card before inclining his head toward Hadrian. "Your lordship. She did mention that you may be calling. However, I'm afraid the household is in the midst of a tragedy, and it may be best if you call another time."

Tragedy? And the Metropolitan Police wagon was on the street. "Are the police here?" Hadrian's curiosity about Beryl's note climbed.

"Yes. They arrived a short while ago." The butler sounded most distraught.

"Allow me to help," Hadrian said calmly. He walked into the entrance hall, and the butler had no choice but to close the door behind him. "I'm an old friend of Mrs. Chambers, and since she requested my presence, I am sure I can provide assistance. Where is she?"

The butler pursed his lips, his rather wide forehead creasing. "In the study, my lord, with the police. But it's a … sensitive situation."

Hadrian gave the man an encouraging nod. "Is the study through here?" Hadrian moved toward the archway at the rear of the entrance hall.

"Yes, my lord." The butler hastened past him into the staircase hall and then into a sitting room where he turned to the left.

Voices carried from the room they were about to enter, presumably the study. The butler stepped to the side after crossing the threshold. There was one constable speaking with Beryl. Her cheeks and nose were red as if she'd been crying.

"Beryl?" Hadrian said tentatively as he approached them.

"Oh, Hadrian!" Beryl practically leapt upon him, throwing her arms around his neck. Her body quivered against his.

Surprised by her embrace, Hadrian loosely held her, awkwardness warring with the overwhelming sense of unease. Something was very wrong.

The constable cleared his throat, and Hadrian separated himself from Beryl. She sniffed and dabbed a handkerchief to her eyes.

Hadrian addressed the constable. "Good morning, I'm Lord Ravenhurst."

"He's a friend of mine," Beryl said. She clasped Hadrian's arm tightly, her fingers digging through his coat. "Louis has been murdered. The maid found him this morning."

Hadrian's pulse quickened. This was not what he'd been expecting. How strange that he'd just seen the man last night.

And Beryl's note had arrived yesterday. Apparently, she'd begged Hadrian to come hours before her husband had been found murdered. What the devil was going on?

"I'm so sorry, Beryl," Hadrian murmured as he patted her hand. Thankfully, she loosened her grip, though she did not release him.

"I'm just glad you're here," she said with another sniff.

A man stepped out of the next room. "Did I hear Lord Ravenhurst has arrived?" Inspector Samuel Teague regarded Hadrian. In his middle thirties, the inspector was of average height and build. He was also not wearing his usual police uniform of a blue coat and helmet.

"Teague," Hadrian said, surprised to see him here, though he should not have been. "Where is your uniform?"

"I was promoted to the Detective Branch after finding justice for that missing young woman." He referred to the investigation that Tilda and Hadrian had completed, and on which Teague had provided assistance. "It just happened two days ago, in fact. I'd planned to inform you and Miss Wren." Teague sent him an earnestly appreciative look.

Whilst Teague had been of great help in apprehending the culprit, the majority of the investigative work had been done by Tilda and Hadrian. Still, Hadrian was glad to see the man had been promoted to Detective Inspector. "Congratulations," he said warmly. "You rightly deserve it."

"Thank you. How is it you are here?"

"I'm an old friend of Mrs. Chambers," Hadrian replied. He did not add that she'd requested his presence. He wanted to gather more information before he offered any himself.

Teague's features darkened. "Her husband has been murdered."

Hadrian inclined his head toward the doorway that Teague was standing near. "In there?"

"That's his bedchamber," Beryl responded. Her eyes filled with tears. "I can't believe he's dead." She took her hand from Hadrian's arm and clapped it over her mouth as a sob wracked her frame.

"Do you mind if I look?" Hadrian asked, though in truth, he was more interested in touching something to see if he could glean anything about what had happened. His ability had allowed him to see the memories of the man who'd tried to kill him. Perhaps he'd see those that belonged to Chambers' murderer, and perhaps identify the killer. Not that Hadrian could share his findings with Teague, for then he'd have to reveal his "gift," and the inspector would likely insist he seek medical help.

Teague's auburn brows rose. "We are collecting evidence."

"I could help," Hadrian offered. "You know I'm of some use in that area."

The detective inspector grunted in response. "You can stand at the doorway."

"Good enough," Hadrian said benignly. He could likely inch his way inside. Before he went to look at the bedchamber, he met Beryl's gaze. "Is someone bringing you tea? Perhaps you should sit."

"I don't think I can. I'm too distressed." She shook her head, closing her eyes tightly.

"It's going to be all right," Hadrian murmured. He felt a pull to stay and comfort Beryl, but he was also eager to see what he might learn from the bedchamber.

Hadrian glanced toward the young constable who stood nearby. He held a notebook and had likely been asking Beryl questions. Surreptitiously removing his gloves and stuffing them in his coat pocket, Hadrian walked to the bedchamber and stood in the doorway.

A large, four-poster bed dominated the room. The window hangings had been pulled open to let in the morning light. There were also a few lanterns about the room providing plenty of illumination.

The bedclothes were drawn back to reveal the body of Louis Chambers. He wore a night shirt, the front of which was stained a dark brown-red.

Another constable was writing in a notebook, or perhaps drawing. Teague was poking about the room, looking in corners and under furniture.

"How was he killed?" Hadrian asked.

"Stabbed through the heart," Teague replied. "I'm looking for the knife—without luck so far."

Hadrian touched the doorframe with his bare hand, his breath halting as he hoped for a sensation or a vision.

Nothing.

"Would you like help looking?" Hadrian offered.

"This is a police matter," Teague said as he dropped to his knees and bent to search under the bed. "I need a bloody lantern."

Hadrian moved quickly, swiping one from a dresser and bringing it to where Teague was crouched. Just before he set the lantern on the floor beside the detective inspector, a vision flashed in Hadrian's mind: he saw a hearth. There was an accompanying sensation of feeling tired, as if he hadn't slept long enough. Hadrian presumed he was seeing and feeling the memories of a retainer who'd touched the lantern at some point.

Teague frowned up at him. "You weren't supposed to come in."

"Apologies, I was only helping." Hadrian clasped the post of the bed as he pivoted to return to the doorway.

Chambers' face flashed in Hadrian's mind. The man was

laughing. Then his eyes narrowed seductively. Hadrian felt a rush of desire, but the sensation didn't belong to him. It came from whoever's memory he was seeing. Chambers reached out, and Hadrian felt as though he were being pulled. He saw an outstretched hand that was decidedly feminine clutching Chambers' fingers. Chambers fell back on the bed, and Hadrian landed atop him.

Hadrian blinked, and the vision disappeared, thank goodness. Hadrian wasn't sure he'd wanted to see—or feel—what would happen next. But he could guess. Whoever's memory Hadrian had seen was a woman Chambers had taken to bed.

Hadrian had to assume it was Beryl. He didn't particularly care to see his former fiancée's memories, and he definitely didn't want to feel her emotions.

"How do you know Mrs. Chambers?" Teague asked as he looked under the bed.

Hadrian, rattled and head aching from the vision, was grateful for the interruption to his thoughts and moved back to the doorway. "She was my fiancée."

Teague banged his head on the underside of the bed, then he swore rather colorfully. He came out from beneath the bed and massaged his scalp as he stood. "You might have mentioned that association when you arrived. Have you learned nothing about investigations and sharing information to solve crimes?"

"I wasn't hiding anything," Hadrian said. "This is a shock."

"Is it shocking to you?" Teague asked, his brown eyes narrowing. "Since you're still friendly with your former fiancée?"

"It's shocking because a man was murdered in his bed. And I am *somewhat* friendly with Mrs. Chambers," Hadrian said vaguely. He would need to tell Teague about the note she'd sent him as it may pertain to his investigation. Why was he hesitating? Because he wanted to know more about the situation before he said or did anything that might incriminate Beryl. She'd sent Hadrian a rather desperate note, and then her husband had been killed. He couldn't help wondering what the connection might be.

Wait, did Hadrian think she'd killed her husband? No, he couldn't fathom it, actually.

Teague's gaze hadn't moved from Hadrian. "Why didn't you marry her?"

"We were not a love match," Hadrian said.

"Mrs. Chambers, I am so sorry." The feminine voice carried to Hadrian in the bedchamber from the study. He knew that voice. His pulse picked up speed and a rush of anticipation spread through him. The pain in his head lessened, as if driven away by his excitement.

Hadrian turned and went into the study. His gaze fell on Tilda, and he couldn't help the smile that teased his mouth. She looked lovely, her reddish-blonde hair neatly coiled beneath her smart green hat. Her green gaze was fixed on Mrs. Chambers.

Wait. What in the bloody hell was Tilda even doing here?

He stepped toward them. "Tilda, what a surprise to see you here." He watched her eyes flash with her own surprise, then she cocked her head in a manner that indicated an awkwardness to the situation.

"I am working on an investigation involving Mrs. Chambers," Tilda said, her heart-shaped face reflecting concern and perhaps a touch of hesitation. "I'm surprised to see *you* here."

"I invited him," Mrs. Chambers said quietly.

Both Tilda and Hadrian swept their gazes toward her.

Mrs. Chambers went on, keeping her voice low. "I was going to ask for his help in finding a place to stay, as you suggested, Miss Wren. That was before. Before what happened to Louis."

Why was Tilda suggesting Beryl leave her home? Hadrian looked from Beryl to Tilda.

"What are you investigating?" Hadrian also spoke softly.

"I wanted to divorce Louis," Beryl whispered.

Hadrian's insides went hollow for a moment. She wanted to divorce her husband, and now the man was dead.

"Does Detective Inspector Teague know that?" Hadrian asked.

Tilda snapped her attention to Hadrian. "Teague is here? And he's a Detective Inspector now?"

Hadrian nodded. "He was just promoted to the Detective Branch two days ago. He's in the bedchamber." He glanced toward the constable who was eyeing them suspiciously. "Perhaps we should postpone this conversation."

"Yes," Tilda murmured. "The butler told me Mr. Chambers had been murdered. Do you know what happened?"

"Stabbed in the heart," Hadrian replied.

A sob caught in Beryl's throat. She pressed her handkerchief to her mouth as a few more tears leaked from her eyes. "Clara found him when she went in to stoke the coals this morning. She's quite distraught."

"Clara is the maid?" Hadrian asked, and Beryl nodded.

Tilda looked at Beryl with sympathy. "Then you sent for the police?"

"Yes. I do think I need to sit down. And drink the tea you mentioned, Hadrian."

"Of course," he said. "I'll go downstairs and fetch some."

"I'll come with you." Tilda gently put her hand to Beryl's arm and guided Beryl to a table and into a chair. "We'll be back with tea directly."

Tilda strode from the study, and Hadrian followed. When they were in the sitting room, she turned her head to give him an arch look.

"What?" Hadrian said.

Tilda moved to open a door in the corner that led to the servants' stairs down to the kitchen. "This is not where I imagined I would encounter you next."

"Nor is it where I expected to see you. You're helping Beryl secure a divorce?"

Tilda explained how the barrister who sometimes hired her to assist with divorce cases had employed her to work with Beryl. "I called on her yesterday to obtain information. She had bruises and spoke of her husband's physical abuse and menacing behavior." They reached the bottom. Tilda turned to face him. "I told her I would return today to see how she's faring. I was worried about her being here with Chambers. That is why I suggested she find another place to reside for the time being—for her own safety. Apparently, she turned to you for help with that." Tilda's curiosity was evident, but then she was the most curious person he'd ever met.

Hadrian had no idea Beryl's life had taken such a turn. "I didn't realize Chambers was hurting her." He felt a surge of fury toward the man who'd stolen his fiancée. "But Beryl and I have not remained close since dissolving our betrothal. I've only seen her a few times over the years and never on purpose."

He hadn't wanted to maintain even a friendship with her, though he'd been cordial despite the embarrassment that had come from a broken engagement. Perhaps that was because his anger had so quickly become relief after Beryl had chosen to wed Chambers instead of Hadrian.

Early in their courtship he'd experienced a thrilling flutter in his chest—the one he'd felt upstairs when he'd seen Tilda—but it had faded during their betrothal. He'd mistaken that for love and was glad he'd avoided marriage to Beryl.

"You're angry," Tilda noted, drawing him back to the present.

"I'm upset that Beryl has been mistreated. As are you, I gather."

"Yes," Tilda said with a nod. "But I do not have a history with her as you do. She asked you to call on her despite not remaining friendly?"

He nodded. "She sent a note yesterday, which I did find odd."

"What did the note say?" Tilda asked, clearly in the throes of her investigation.

"She requested I call on her because she was in dire need of my help."

"Did that concern you?" Tilda concluded.

"Yes, particularly because we haven't been close. I couldn't imagine why she would be writing to me for help." Hadrian smiled at her. "I found myself very curious, which I think you understand."

She returned his smile. "I do." Her features smoothed. "Has Teague questioned you yet?"

"He was busy searching Chambers' bedchamber," Hadrian replied. "I told him of my betrothal to Beryl."

Her gaze turned sympathetic. "That could not have been easy to discuss. I am sorry that history is being revisited."

"It's particularly odd because I encountered Chambers last night."

Tilda's brows shot up. "Where?"

"A club called Arthur's. I am not a member, but I accompanied a colleague who invited me."

"Did you speak with Chambers?"

Hadrian recalled their encounter and the discomfort as well as surprise that he'd felt. Tilda was right that this wasn't easy. He would prefer to leave the past alone, especially the chapter that pertained to Beryl and her husband. However, after hiding his ability from Tilda when they'd become acquainted, he'd promised that he would be completely honest with her going forward.

He grimaced as he responded. "That is not how I would characterize it. Chambers yelled at me from across the room. He was a boisterous, gregarious fellow, but not in a charming way." The man was most disagreeable in Hadrian's experience, albeit limited.

"You didn't like him?" Her eyes briefly shuttered. "I'm sorry. I know you caught him with Beryl whilst you were betrothed to her. Of *course* you didn't like him."

"I barely knew him," Hadrian gritted out, his jaw clenched. "I found him annoying, as do most people, including my colleague —Sir Godfrey Hammersmith."

"What happened when Chambers yelled at you?" she asked.

Hadrian summoned the incident in his mind and decided to start from the beginning. "When I arrived, Chambers was standing in the main reception room with a few other gentlemen. They were talking and drinking. I recognized Chambers immediately and hoped we would not meet. However, Chambers saw me. He called across the room and then approached me. He did not appear pleased to see me and demanded to know what I was doing there." He frowned as he recalled the burst of irritation he'd felt at Chambers' behavior. "I believe his words were, 'What the bloody hell are you doing in my club?'"

Tilda grimaced. "That must have been awkward. Why would he greet you in such a manner?"

Hadrian shrugged. "I don't know. I've only met him on a few occasions, and I can't remember the last time I saw him. We don't move in the same circles."

"I can't imagine you would want to after his behavior with your fiancée," Tilda observed softly. "What happened next?"

"I think he was drunk," Hadrian said. "After his obnoxious greeting, he said I would not enjoy Arthur's, that I would be happier at my priggish club for pompous arses, since I was one. Pardon my vulgarity; those were his exact words. Then, one of the men Chambers had been speaking to came to pull him away. Sir Godfrey and I moved to another part of the club."

"You didn't want to leave?" Tilda asked.

"I did, but also didn't want to abandon Sir Godfrey. We went upstairs to a quieter room and drank port. I left about an hour after I arrived. Thankfully, I did not encounter Chambers again."

"Teague will want to hear about this encounter," Tilda said. "Did you go straight home after leaving the club?"

Hadrian narrowed his eyes at her. "Do you think I may have gone somewhere else?"

"I think you should have an alibi," she replied evenly.

Her words chilled Hadrian. "You can't think I would kill Chambers."

"I don't, but you have a motive."

Alarm pricked Hadrian's neck, making him feel hot and agitated. "What would that be?"

"Jealousy. Revenge. Anger after the way Chambers treated you at the club."

"I've been treated worse," Hadrian replied with a snort. "And I am not jealous, nor do I have any reason to seek revenge."

Tilda again looked at him with sympathy, but he didn't like it. "Chambers stole your fiancée. You caught them in a compromising position."

"Yes, but in the end, everything worked out as it should," he said coolly. Tilda was right that it wasn't easy to revisit this. In fact, he preferred not to.

"You weren't … heartbroken?" Tilda asked, her brow creasing. "Forgive me, I assumed you were marrying her because you loved her."

Hadrian exhaled. "Must we delve into the specifics? I was not heartbroken. I was relieved. After I was done being angry. It was an embarrassing situation." Now more than ever, Hadrian couldn't understand why Beryl would choose Chambers over him.

"I understand. I won't pry any further, but Teague might, so you should be prepared for that."

Hadrian shook out his shoulders in an effort to clear his agitation. "Aren't we supposed to be fetching tea for Beryl?"

"Yes, let us speak with the cook." She preceded him into the kitchen where three women stood around a table. Two were in their forties, one of whom wore an apron, whilst the third, garbed in a dark-blue gown, was young—younger than Tilda.

The woman with the apron looked toward Hadrian and Tilda first, then the other two followed suit. "Can I help you?" the woman in the apron asked.

"That's Miss Wren," the young woman said. A white cap sat atop her dark-brown hair, and Hadrian assumed she was the maid.

The other two women reacted faintly to this revelation, as if they knew of Tilda but hadn't yet met her.

"Good morning, Clara," Tilda said with a brief smile as she walked toward them. Hadrian followed her. "I'm sorry about Mr. Chambers."

The maid looked down, and the other two exchanged glances. There seemed to be a wealth of communication in what they didn't say.

When no one said anything in response, Tilda said, "Mrs. Chambers would like tea."

"I'll take it up," the woman in the apron said. She fetched a pot from the warming stove.

The other older woman—she looked to be the eldest of the three, perhaps nearing fifty—also wore a white cap, which covered her severely styled gray-and-sable hair. Her brown eyes were sharp and assessing as they surveyed Hadrian and Tilda. "I am Mrs. Blank, the housekeeper. This is Mrs. Dunning, our cook." She pinned her attention on Tilda. "I believe you met Clara yesterday."

"I did," Tilda said with a nod. "I'm pleased to make your acquaintances as well. This is Lord Ravenhurst."

All three retainers showed a reaction—including the cook who'd just picked up the tray—but the young maid's was by far the most revealing. Her jaw dropped before she snapped it closed and averted her eyes.

"Have you heard his name before?" Tilda asked.

Hadrian wasn't at all surprised that she'd noticed the maid's reaction, nor that she'd questioned her about it.

Clara nodded, but it was the housekeeper, Mrs. Blank, who spoke. "We know who his lordship is." She cast an enigmatic look toward Hadrian that piqued his curiosity. What did they know?

"Mrs. Chambers has mentioned him?" Tilda prodded.

"And Mr. Chambers," Clara replied.

Mrs. Blank pursed her lips at the maid but said nothing. The cook sniffed as she departed with the tea tray.

Now Hadrian was even more curious. Why were they discussing Hadrian years after Beryl had decided to wed Chambers? He didn't like it, particularly since it involved him in this situation.

"Mr. Chambers discussed his lordship?" Tilda asked. "How peculiar as they are not friends."

"He's only mentioned him a few times," Clara mumbled.

The butler entered the kitchen from a corridor that led toward the front of the house. He looked toward Hadrian and Tilda. "Your lordship. Miss Wren." Then he moved his gaze to the young maid. "Clara, it is your turn to speak with the constable."

Clara took a deep breath and chewed her lip.

"Don't fret," Mrs. Blank said. "Just answer his questions." She gave the young woman a direct stare, and again, Hadrian had the sense that there was silent communication.

The maid hurried toward the doorway the constable had come through and disappeared into the corridor.

"The constable has been interviewing all of you?" Tilda asked.

"Yes," Mrs. Blank replied. "He's asking us if we'd noticed any evidence of someone breaking into the house, but everything was as it should be this morning. Except for Mr. Chambers, of course."

"Not everything," Oswald noted. "What about the missing kitchen knife?"

Hadrian snapped his attention to the butler and noticed Tilda did the same. "There's a knife missing?" Tilda asked.

"Mrs. Dunning noticed it was gone this morning," Oswald replied.

"Do you need anything?" Mrs. Blank asked, her expression expectant.

"No. We came to ask about the tea." Tilda smiled at the house-keeper. "We'll leave you to it." She turned and slightly inclined her head toward the door to the stairs whilst meeting Hadrian's eyes.

He accompanied her from the kitchen, and they climbed the stairs to the landing on the ground floor. The door to the sitting room was ajar.

"I can tell that you wanted to interview the retainers," Hadrian said. "I am very curious as to why Chambers is mentioning me after all this time."

She turned to face him, her features shadowed in the dim space for there was only a single candle burning in a sconce. "We are not conducting an investigation. I was hired to assist with a divorce, and that is no longer necessary."

"But we make a good team," Hadrian said with a smile. "I was hoping we'd have a reason to work together again, and here we are at the scene of a murder."

Mrs. Dunning opened the door wider from the sitting room and stopped short upon seeing them.

"Pardon us," Tilda said, as she moved past the cook into the sitting room. Hadrian followed her, and the cook went into the stairwell.

Tilda's gaze followed the cook's movements. "Mrs. Dunning, I understand one of your knives is missing."

The cook pivoted, her eyes narrowing slightly. "Yes, but I didn't use it to kill Mr. Chambers. I already spoke to the consta-ble." There was a glimmer of apprehension in her gaze.

"When was the last time you used it?" Tilda asked.

"Yesterday morning when I butchered a guinea fowl. I cleaned the knife and returned it to the block. This morning, it was gone." The cook put her hand on her hip. "Why are you asking?"

"I'm an investigator," Tilda said.

"I thought you were investigating Mr. Chambers so Mrs. Chambers could get a divorce." Mrs. Dunning sounded skeptical.

"I was." Tilda gave the woman a benign smile and said nothing else. The cook went downstairs.

Hadrian closed the door to the servants' stairwell. "Do you have the sense the retainers are holding something back?"

"Perhaps. They seem guarded—the cook and the housekeeper anyway." She glanced at Hadrian's hands. "You aren't wearing gloves. Have you been able to see or feel anything helpful?"

"In fact, I had a vision in Chambers' bedchamber."

"Teague allowed you inside?" she asked.

"Not really. But he needed a light to see under the bed, so I provided him with a lantern." He didn't bother telling her about the vision that had provoked, but he shared what he'd seen when he touched the bed, including the feelings of desire the woman had felt.

Tilda's cheeks tinged faintly pink. "How odd for you to have to feel such things. Which hand of hers did you see?"

Hadrian thought back. "The left." Details were so important, revelatory even, and Tilda was always focused on them.

"Was there a ring on her finger?"

"No." It wasn't Beryl then. She wore a wedding ring on her left hand.

"Then it was not Mrs. Chambers. Although, I wouldn't have guessed it to be her. She hasn't shared her husband's bed in nearly three years. Though I suppose you could be seeing a memory from years ago. We know that's possible."

Indeed it was, as Hadrian had seen memories going back more than thirty years. "Chambers *was* a philanderer as well as cruel then."

"Mrs. Chambers believes he was having an affair, and she will need to prove adultery to have any hope of securing a divorce." Tilda glanced toward the study. "Not that she needs a divorce any longer."

If Hadrian could be a potential suspect, so could Beryl. In fact, she'd be a greater one than him, probably. "I don't think Beryl killed him." The words fell from him before he realized he meant to say them.

Tilda snapped her gaze to his. "Why not? It doesn't seem you know her very well."

"I knew her once, and I would not have betrothed myself to a murderess."

"I doubt you intended to marry an unfaithful woman either," Tilda said wryly.

"Your point is well made." Though it rankled him. "Beryl may not be the most faithful person I've known, but she is not a killer."

A man came from the stairwell they'd just left. He glanced at Tilda and Hadrian but didn't stop. He appeared to be in a hurry, his face flushed as he strode into the study.

Hadrian exchanged a glance with Tilda, and they wordlessly followed the unknown man.

"How did he die?" the unknown man, who was tall and lanky, his dark hair falling over his forehead, asked Teague.

Beryl stood nearby, fidgeting her hands at her waist. "This is my husband's valet, Massey."

"We will need to ask you some questions," Teague said to the valet.

"I need to see Mr. Chambers first," the valet insisted.

Beryl moved to touch the valet's arm. "Massey, he is gone."

The valet shook her hand from him and turned his head to direct his glower at her. "I'm sure you're thrilled." His lip curled.

Hadrian stepped toward the valet. "There's no call for such behavior in this moment. It's a sad and shocking time for all."

Massey looked Hadrian up and down. "Who the devil are you?"

"Ravenhurst," Hadrian replied succinctly.

The valet's dark eyes popped, and his jaw dropped briefly. "*You?*"

"Do you know the earl?" Teague asked, his brow creasing with interest.

"Mr. Chambers said he saw Ravenhurst at his club last night."

Teague snapped his gaze—now angry—at Hadrian. "You saw Chambers last night?" He glanced at the valet. "Pardon me, Massey, but I must interrogate Lord Ravenhurst first."

CHAPTER 3

*T*ilda watched Hadrian's eye twitch at the word "interrogate." Was he angry? She was trying to think if she'd ever seen him truly angry and didn't think she had. He typically controlled his emotions quite well.

Teague turned to Mrs. Chambers. "Is there somewhere I can take Ravenhurst to talk privately?"

"The parlor. It's off the entrance hall," the widow said.

Meeting Hadrian's eyes, Teague inclined his head toward the door. "Please excuse us," he said to Mrs. Chambers. Then he looked to the valet. "Massey, I will speak with you when I return."

Hadrian glanced toward Tilda, then he strode from the study with Teague following behind. Tilda went after them. When they reached the entrance hall, Teague turned and frowned at her.

"I didn't invite you," Teague said, sounding quite cross. He was generally an amiable fellow, and they'd formed a good rapport as Tilda and Hadrian had worked to solve the case of who had stabbed Hadrian.

"Nevertheless, I am here," Tilda said with a vague smile. "Do you really object to my presence? Hadrian will tell me everything you discuss."

"Very well." Teague nodded, and they all went into the parlor.

Hadrian arched a dark brow at Tilda. Though he appeared annoyed, he was still quite handsome, with his square jaw and sculptured brow. His blue eyes were fringed with long, dark lashes that any woman—besides Tilda—would envy.

"Do you mind my being here?" she asked.

"Not at all. As you said, I would tell you everything anyway." He shifted his gaze to the detective inspector. "Just as I will tell Teague all he wants to know."

"*Everything*," Teague said. "I want to know everything, starting with where and when you saw Chambers last night. Be specific."

Hadrian related the events at Arthur's in much the same way he'd told them to Tilda earlier.

"You've no idea why Chambers behaved in that manner with you?" Teague asked, echoing Tilda's question.

"I do not."

Teague grunted. "Tell me about your betrothal to Mrs. Chambers and why you didn't marry."

Hadrian's jaw tensed. "We were betrothed four years ago. I caught Beryl in Chambers' arms at a ball. We decided not to wed, and she went on to marry Chambers." He spoke in a clipped tone. Tilda was sorry he had to bring this up again.

"I suppose I can understand why you didn't readily offer those details," Teague said. "Still, you should have told me."

"Forgive me if I didn't care to explain how I was betrayed," Hadrian replied icily. "I prefer not to discuss it."

Teague's expression was wary, assessing. "Back to last night, what happened when you left the club?"

"My coachman drove me home. We arrived shortly before midnight."

"I or one of the constables will need to speak with him."

"He's outside," Hadrian said, gesturing toward the window that faced the street.

Teague nodded. "Did you remain at home, or did you leave again?"

"I retired to my bedchamber." Hadrian gave Teague a stern stare. "My valet can corroborate that."

"Can he also confirm you were in your bedchamber all night?" Teague asked.

Hadrian pressed his lips together, appearing beleaguered. "I sleep alone, so no, he cannot confirm that. He woke me at eight this morning and I was still in my bed. Does that help?"

Tilda heard his irritation and sarcasm. She didn't think it helped at all but refrained from saying so.

Teague had watched Hadrian intently whilst he spoke and didn't react to Hadrian's frustration. "Have you had any interaction with Chambers—or Mrs. Chambers—since they wed?"

"I've encountered Beryl a time or two but not intentionally. Which is why I was quite shocked to receive a letter from her yesterday asking me to call on her. She said it was a dire matter and that if I'd ever cared for her, I would come."

He hadn't shared the details of the letter's language with Tilda before. She hadn't realized Mrs. Chambers was prone to being emotional.

"I will need the letter," Teague said. "I assume you still have it."

Hadrian nodded. "I will bring it to Scotland Yard later, if you like."

"I would, thank you." Teague contemplated Hadrian a moment. "So, you received this letter from Mrs. Chambers after all this time, and you decided to come here. Upon arriving, you discovered her husband is dead."

"It's incredibly shocking." Hadrian glanced at Tilda. "I was also surprised to learn from Tilda that Beryl wanted to divorce her husband."

Teague looked to Tilda. "I haven't yet sat down to speak with Mrs. Chambers at length, so I was not aware of this. How do you know?"

"I work for the barrister she hired," Tilda replied. "I called here yesterday to meet with her." She went on to disclose all she'd learned the day before, including Beryl's bruises, the missing jewelry, and her husband's potential affair.

"That is all deeply concerning," Teague said. "Chambers doesn't sound like a particularly pleasant fellow."

"No," Tilda agreed. "I met him briefly yesterday, and he was most disagreeable. To hide the purpose of my visit, I said I was here to help with refurbishment. That made him very angry as he said there was no money for that. He bumped into Mrs. Chambers on his way out, and while that may sound innocuous, he did so violently. I do not believe it was an accident."

"I would say Mrs. Chambers is better off without him," Teague said with a dark frown. "Which makes her a suspect."

Tilda did not respond to that but glanced at Hadrian, whose expression was somewhat dour. Addressing Teague once more, she said, "I've already published a list of the missing jewelry in a few newspapers."

"Do let me know if you hear anything, please," Teague said. "I appreciate you sharing this information. What will become of your investigation now?"

"Since Mrs. Chambers is no longer in need of a divorce, my work is concluded. Except for searching for the jewelry. That was a separate endeavor."

Teague nodded. "I was afraid you were going to tell me that you plan to investigate Chambers' murder."

Tilda wished she was, but she could not afford to work without being paid. "I have not been hired to do so. But would you have a problem with that?" It sounded as if he might.

"As detective inspector, conducting this investigation is my job now," he said. "This case will have my full attention until I've found the murderer."

"I am glad to hear it," Tilda said with smile. "Congratulations to you. The Metropolitan Police are lucky to have you in this role."

Teague smiled in response. "Thank you, Miss Wren. If you think of anything else that would help our investigation, I hope you'll let me know."

"Of course. I'm sure you'll try to determine whether Mr. Chambers had a paramour, and if so, who she could be. You'll also want to look into the drapery shop he was opening with a man named Edgar Pollard."

"I did hear mention of the shop," Teague said. "I believe the butler said someone should notify his partner." He turned to Hadrian. "Do you have anything else to share?"

Hadrian shook his head. "I've told you everything. I'll deliver Beryl's letter later today."

"Thank you. I am sorry for the discomfort this situation may have caused you. I don't mean to offend." He turned toward the door. "I must go interview Massey. I would ask that you delay your departure for a short while, as I would like to send a constable outside to speak with your coachman."

"Of course," Hadrian replied.

Teague left, and Hadrian turned to face Tilda. "Am I a suspect now?"

"He didn't say, but he's at least gathering all the information he can, which includes your alibi. I would do the same."

"But you are not, because this is not your investigation." Hadrian studied her a moment. "Do you wish that it was?"

"There is no point in wishing," Tilda said brusquely—because she would dearly love to. "I can't afford to work without payment, and Mrs. Chambers no longer needs my services to obtain a divorce." Tilda frowned slightly. "It's convenient that her husband is dead. I know you said she would never kill him, but I do think Teague will focus his investigation on her. *I* would, at least for the moment."

"In that case, she needs someone to find the truth. You must investigate. I'll hire you on her behalf." Hadrian had hired her for their last investigation, which had started as a search for the man who'd stabbed him.

"You can't keep paying me to conduct investigations."

He arched a dark brow. "Isn't that what you do?" His tone was wry, and Tilda had to keep from rolling her eyes.

"Yes, but last time you had a personal stake because you were nearly killed." Tilda cocked her head. "Unless, you also have a personal stake in this investigation?"

"I do if Teague considers me a suspect."

Tilda saw the constable walk through the entrance hall on his way outside, presumably to interview Leach about Hadrian's departure from Arthur's last night. "The constable just went out," she said.

Hadrian glanced at the window. "Even if Teague doesn't consider me a suspect, I am still under investigation." He met Tilda's gaze. "As such, I want to hire you to prove someone else committed the murder."

She couldn't find fault with that, even if she didn't really want to take money from him again now that they were friends. She could also not deny the fact that she was most eager to investigate this murder—almost as eager as she was to ensure Hadrian wasn't harmed by the investigation. To be accused of murder would be an ugly affair, and it was already bad enough that he had to revisit the aborted betrothal in his past. "Are you serious about hiring me?"

He smiled. "Quite. You are now officially on the case. If you agree. Please agree."

Tilda wanted to make sure he knew what he was asking her to do. "What if I find that Beryl killed her husband?"

He met her gaze with an intense stare. "I trust that you will discover the truth, whatever it is."

Glad to hear him say that, Tilda inclined her head. "Yes, I will investigate this for you." He smiled in relief, and she knew she'd made the right decision to help him. "I want to see what else I can learn here. Let us return to the study."

"Allow me to escort you," he said pleasantly. And they were now officially back in the roles they'd occupied during their last investigation. Or were they?

Tilda had started toward the entrance hall but turned to face him. "Are you planning to assist me as before?"

"Won't my cursed gift be of use to you? I also hope I contribute to the investigation with my intellect."

"Both are useful," Tilda replied as she turned toward the entrance hall. "I would see Mrs. Chambers before we go. I need to speak with her about the missing jewelry and whether she wants me to continue looking for it."

Hadrian followed her into the entrance hall. "Is her missing jewelry now part of the murder investigation?"

Tilda paused. "It is indeed." Now she needn't worry about whether Mrs. Chambers would pay her. Since Hadrian was now funding the investigation, that would include Tilda's pursuit of the missing heirlooms.

As they walked together to the study, Tilda was aware of Hadrian's proximity. She caught his scent, a distinctive cologne he wore. It was pleasing, though she could not detect the individual fragrances within it. Hadrian likely could, and not because he'd purchased it, but because he had a nose for such things.

She *had* missed seeing him, even though it had barely been a week since they'd concluded their investigation. Now, they were doing it again. She couldn't deny it was thrilling.

Her father had been a police sergeant on the verge of promotion to the Detective Branch when he'd been killed as he encountered a theft taking place. He'd taught Tilda everything she knew about observing situations and people, as well as how to solve problems and find answers. If she'd been able, she would have joined the police herself.

As they entered the sitting room, Hadrian waved at her to

stop. He crept toward the door to the study and motioned for her to move in front of him. Putting his finger to his lips, he inclined his head toward the doorway.

Tilda listened and made out the conversation between Teague and the valet.

"Mr. Chambers returned from his club around midnight," Massey said. "I undressed him and took my leave. It was my regular night off. Each fortnight I have a night to myself."

"Then why were you here so late?" Teague asked.

"Mr. Chambers prefers I'm here to help him undress and take care of his clothing. In exchange, he does not expect me to return until mid-morning."

"And where do you go?"

There was an extended silence before the valet answered. "Is that important?"

"We need everyone to provide an alibi."

Another silence before Massey said something Tilda couldn't make out.

"Pardon?" Teague said.

Again, Massey spoke, but Tilda still couldn't hear what he said.

"I see," Teague replied slowly. "I understand your concern. I am not here to punish anyone for anything other than the murder of your employer. However, I may need the name of the … establishment you went to so that I may confirm your alibi. I will not record the location in the report. When you left the house last night, Mr. Chambers was alive?"

There was another silence. Perhaps the valet had nodded.

"Forgive the indelicacy of my next question," Teague said. "Were you aware of Mr. Chambers having a liaison?"

"It is not my place to notice such things." The valet sounded almost nonchalant. "I know Mr. Chambers was unhappy in his marriage and that his wife had refused him access to her bed."

That was not what Mrs. Chambers had told Tilda. However, she needed to consider the possibility that her client had lied.

"You have no idea who your employer's paramour may have been?" Teague prodded.

"As I said, I do not pay attention to such things. I *can* say that Mrs. Chambers was having an affair."

"You knew about her having an affair but not her husband," Teague noted. It didn't sound like a question. "With whom is she having a liaison?"

"I am not certain."

"Do you have suspicions?" Teague prodded.

"Mr. Chambers often mentioned his wife's infidelity. Just last night, he speculated it was likely Ravenhurst."

Tilda heard Hadrian's intake of breath behind her. She turned her head and gave him a quelling look.

"What was his evidence for making that claim?" Teague asked.

"He didn't say. You haven't asked, but I would not be surprised to learn that Mrs. Chambers killed him."

"Why is that?"

"She did not care for her husband at all," the valet said with disdain. "They fought a great deal."

"What did they fight about?"

"Most often, it was money. Mrs. Chambers is a spendthrift. Her reckless purchasing and running up debts were a cause of great stress to Mr. Chambers. He was always taking her to task over it, and she would grow angry. She was also not supportive of his investment in the drapery shop, which angered him. He was trying to improve their financial situation by becoming a man of business."

"I see," Teague said.

"May I see Mr. Chambers now?" Massey asked, his voice sounding a bit hollow.

"Yes. I don't have any more questions for the moment. We will need to take the body for the inquest tomorrow. You can come with me into the bedchamber, but you may not touch *anything*. Is that clear?"

The constable who'd gone outside returned. He eyed Tilda and Hadrian before proceeding into the study.

Tilda moved away from the doorway, and Hadrian followed her. "I don't believe for a moment that a valet wouldn't be aware of his employer having an affair. I've never had a valet, or a personal maid, but wouldn't they know if their employer had entertained someone who wasn't their spouse in their bedchamber? And we know Chambers did that because of the vision you saw."

"I would be surprised if a valet *didn't* know, particularly given Massey's awareness of what's happening in this household between his employer and his wife."

Massey strode from the study, his gaze falling briefly on Tilda and Hadrian before he continued into the sitting room. Tilda craned her neck to watch him pass through the open doorway to the servants' stairwell.

"You're still here," Teague said, drawing them to turn toward the study where he stood in the doorway. "My constable says you were likely eavesdropping on my interview with the valet."

"I was looking for Mrs. Chambers," Tilda said, purposely not responding to Teague's comment. "I must speak with her to conclude our business before I leave."

"I'm here." Mrs. Chambers stepped into the sitting room. She'd pinned a black bow to her bodice.

"I'll let you go first," Teague said. "Then you can be on your way." He smiled benignly, but Tilda could tell he was eager for them to go, lest they continue to eavesdrop on his interrogations. Which they'd absolutely done, and which Tilda would do again if given the chance.

"Inspector, do you know when the inquest will be?" Tilda asked. "I imagine you will want Hadrian to be there."

"He will be summoned," Teague confirmed. "As will you, since you have information pertaining to Mrs. Chambers seeking a divorce from her husband. I've no doubt the coroner will determine Chambers was murdered, and he will conduct an inquest to aid us in solving the crime."

"Must I go as well?" Mrs. Chambers asked, her voice sounding small, her features creased with concern.

"You will also be summoned," Teague said. "You are a suspect as well as a witness."

Mrs. Chambers' amber-brown eyes rounded, and her face went completely white before she crumpled toward the floor.

CHAPTER 4

*H*adrian rushed to catch Beryl before she hit the floor. Sweeping her into his arms, he saw that her lashes were already fluttering.

"Take her to the parlor," Tilda suggested.

"I didn't mean for that to happen," Teague said, his brows plummeting with concern.

Hadrian continued toward the parlor where he laid Beryl onto the settee, propping a pillow between her head and the arm of the settee. She was still pale, her lips parted and her long, dark lashes curling against her ivory flesh.

He felt badly for her. Not just for losing her husband, which was horrible, but because she'd apparently been mistreated by him. Again, he wondered if she regretted choosing Chambers over Hadrian.

A part of him hoped she did. Her behavior had caused him embarrassment and upset. He found he was upset again, after all this time, especially now that he knew what a blackguard Chambers was. That Beryl had preferred someone like him to Hadrian stung his pride.

He reminded himself that he was pleased with how things had

turned out. After seeing them together, he hadn't wanted to marry her—first out of anger, and then because he realized he hadn't ever loved her. And apparently love was important to Hadrian.

Before he could follow that thought, Beryl's eyes fluttered open. It took her a moment to focus on Hadrian. "What happened?"

"You fainted," Hadrian said.

"Do I need to fetch smelling salts?" Tilda asked as she entered the parlor. Her gaze fell on Beryl. "I suppose not."

Teague stood behind Tilda, his concern evident in his expression. "Is she all right?"

"She'll be fine," Hadrian replied. "We'll take care of her."

Visibly relaxing, Teague nodded. "My apologies, Mrs. Chambers. I should have been more circumspect with my speech."

"Thank you," Beryl said quietly without looking at Teague. The inspector inclined his head toward Hadrian, then returned to the back of the house.

Beryl worked to sit up. "Does that inspector really think I murdered my husband?"

Hadrian helped her to a sitting position, then he sat down beside her. "He didn't say that. He said you were a suspect."

"Try not to fret," Tilda said. "It is usual for the spouse of a murdered person to be suspected of the crime."

"That may be, but it is most distressing." Beryl rubbed her fingers over her furrowed brow. "I didn't kill Louis."

"You did want to divorce him, however," Hadrian said.

Beryl turned her head toward him. "I was going to tell you about that today when you came. I'm so glad you did. I wasn't sure if you would."

"Your note conveyed your urgent need."

"Desperation, you mean," Beryl said with a trace of humor.

"Why did you write to me of all people?" Hadrian asked.

"When Miss Wren suggested I find somewhere to stay for my

own safety, I immediately thought of you. You always made me feel safe." Beryl met Hadrian's gaze with a faint smile. "I couldn't very well write to my parents. Nothing has changed between us since I wed Louis. I do have a friend I could ask, but she is already helping me in other ways." She glanced toward Tilda, who'd perched on a chair across from the settee. "How are the two of you acquainted?"

"I hired Tilda for an investigation," Hadrian replied. He didn't want to explain the specifics just now. He also wasn't sure how he felt about what Beryl had said. He was glad that he made her feel safe, but that wasn't his responsibility—they were not close.

"What a coincidence," Beryl said.

"Indeed," Tilda murmured. "Regarding my investigation into helping you secure a divorce, that is no longer necessary."

"That is true." Beryl shook her head. "I still can't quite believe I'm free."

Hadrian was glad Teague hadn't accompanied them. He would likely interpret her comment poorly.

Beryl fixed her gaze on Tilda. "What of my missing jewelry? You will still conduct that investigation, won't you?"

"I have already had the list of items published in a few news-papers. Hopefully, someone will contact Mr. Forrest with infor-mation." Tilda paused briefly.

"Why not you?" Beryl asked. "He didn't seem to think I could recover my heirlooms."

"I've arranged for him to be the liaison," Tilda replied. "Because I don't have an office to field inquiries."

Hadrian wondered if she wanted that someday.

"I haven't yet spoken to my friend about borrowing more money," Beryl said to Tilda. "However, now that Louis is dead, I should be able to pay for your services from the household account." Beryl smiled, appearing relieved. But then she grimaced. "Except I don't know how to access those funds.

Perhaps you might help me, Hadrian?" She batted her lashes, and Hadrian clenched his jaw.

"I will help you," Hadrian replied. Doing so would allow him to assess Chambers' financial situation which would be helpful to Tilda's investigation.

Beryl exhaled. "Thank you. Louis did not keep me informed about our finances. He said it wasn't my business. He gave me pin money every quarter, but the amount has steadily decreased since we wed, particularly in the last several months. My wardrobe is woefully unprepared for the Season, not that we attend many gatherings. Still, I try to look my best."

Beryl looked quite fashionable. Hadrian flicked a glance toward Tilda, whose wardrobe was sinfully out-of-date. He hoped she would be able to improve upon that now that she and her grandmother had some extra funds. Hadrian had supplied the funds to a solicitor who'd handled Tilda's grandmother's finances, but they didn't know. Tilda never would have accepted the gift from Hadrian, especially not after he'd already compensated her for her investigative work.

"Now I will need black gowns," Beryl said with great agitation, her features creased with worry. "How am I to do that when I can't leave the house since I am newly widowed?"

"Perhaps your friend can help you?" Tilda suggested.

"I will ask her. She lives next door—Mrs. Styles-Rowdon." Beryl shook her head. "One would think it would be easy for me to obtain new gowns easily since my husband is opening a drapery shop."

Tilda's gaze narrowed slightly and shrewdly. "You will likely have a stake in the business since your husband was investing."

Beryl's eyes lit. "I hadn't considered that. I honestly know nothing about the endeavor." Beryl shook her head. "Louis didn't want me to. I feel so foolish."

Hadrian gently touched her arm. "Do not judge yourself harshly. We will speak with his partner."

Beryl relaxed, her entire frame settling against the back of the settee. "Thank you, Hadrian. I am so grateful for your presence." She looked to Tilda. "And yours, Miss Wren, or may I call you Tilda as Hadrian does? How lucky I am that you know one another and can work together to help me."

Tilda's brow arched as she darted a look at him. He wondered if she was thinking the same thing he was—that Tilda was working to help *him*. Still, he didn't think Tilda's investigation would lead to discovering that Beryl killed her husband. In that way, he supposed Tilda was helping her too.

"Tilda is fine," Tilda replied, perhaps a bit tightly. "I can help you best by collecting information. Can you tell me about last night? When did you last see your husband?"

Beryl squeezed her hands together. "At dinner. Louis was in a very disagreeable mood." She gave Tilda a wary look. "You saw him yesterday. He was like that but worse."

"That must have been difficult," Tilda said softly. "When did he arrive home? For the second time, that is."

"I think it was around half seven," Beryl replied after hesitating a moment. "We typically have dinner at eight. Then he's off to his club or wherever he goes afterward. He was late to dinner. I didn't say anything about that, but he tried to goad me into an argument."

"In what way?" Tilda asked.

"He is often late, particularly since he partnered with Mr. Pollard. I used to comment on it, but I stopped several months ago because he never apologized and always grew angry. Last night, he wanted to know why I wasn't badgering him. He seemed more agitated than usual."

Hadrian thought of how Chambers had behaved with him last night at the club. "He was often agitated?"

"Of late, I would say he was irritable. There were also many nights when he didn't come home for dinner at all." Beryl looked away from both Tilda and Hadrian. "Honestly, that was nice."

"Did anything happen at dinner?" Tilda asked.

Giving her head a shake, Beryl met Tilda's gaze. "He told me again that he wasn't going to pay for any refurbishment and asked why I would even have someone here to discuss such a thing. I apologized and said it wouldn't happen again. Then I tried to ask about the financial situation. I was very gentle. I tried to be, anyway. I asked if he'd put too much into the shop." She paused to take a breath. "That was when he became particularly angry. He said that was none of my concern. Then he stormed out."

Tilda scratched the pencil across her notebook and then looked up, leaning slightly forward. "What time was that?"

"Before the last course was served, so before nine."

"And was that the last time you saw him?" Tilda asked, her eyes narrowing slightly. Her expression was one of engagement but also deep thought. Hadrian had seen it on her many times, and he knew she was noting every detail Beryl said.

"Yes," Beryl said with a nod. "I finished dinner, then I had a bath and read a book until I retired, probably just after eleven. Clara would know for sure."

"After you retired last night, did you hear anything odd down-stairs?" Tilda asked.

"The inspector asked if I heard any loud noises or perhaps shouting." Beryl sucked in a breath and brushed her hands along her skirt. "I didn't hear a thing. It's so upsetting to think that someone was down here ... *killing* Louis. And I slept through the entire event. I often take a sleeping tonic, and I sleep like the dead." She grimaced and murmured, "Poor choice of words."

Hadrian touched her arm again, but this time he let his finger-tips rest against her sleeve a moment. It occurred to him then that he could take her bare hand in his. Would he see or sense something? There was only one way to find out.

He moved his hand down her arm and clasped her hand. She turned her face toward him, her eyes open now. She appeared surprised but also grateful. Her hand closed around his. He braced himself in case he saw a vision or felt something from her touch, but there was nothing.

"I know this is upsetting for you," Hadrian said. "And I'm sorry you'll have to go through it all again tomorrow." He tried to sense something from touching her, but there was still nothing, so he released her hand.

"It will be worth it if they can find who killed him. I wonder if I need to be afraid to stay here." Beryl looked to Tilda.

"I don't think you need to be afraid," Tilda said firmly. "Whoever killed Louis did so and left without troubling any of the rest of you."

Beryl sniffed. "I think the killer must be someone Louis knew. Perhaps someone *I* know. I do think it could have been his paramour, whoever she is."

"You said Clara found Louis in his bed?" Tilda asked.

Beryl nodded. "Each morning after waking, I have a small repast in my room—tea and toast, or the like. I was in the midst of that when I heard Clara scream. She goes into Louis's bedchamber each morning to stoke or light the coals in his hearth. That was when she found him. I ran downstairs upon hearing her."

Tilda looked at her with sympathy. "Did you go into his bedchamber?"

"Yes. The butler and housekeeper were also there, as was the cook. Mrs. Dunning—the cook—was consoling poor Clara."

"Is that the entirety of your staff? Along with your husband's valet," Tilda added. At Beryl's nod, she went on. "Have you a lady's maid?"

"I did, but she left nearly a fortnight ago." Beryl's lip curled faintly. "Louis said that Clara could fill Farrow's role of lady's maid in addition to her other duties. The housekeeper also took on additional tasks that Clara had been performing before my maid departed."

Tilda's fair brows drew together. "Why did your maid—Farrow, is it?—leave?"

"Yes, Farrow. I don't know." Beryl shrugged. "She resigned her post rather suddenly. I'd no idea she was thinking of leaving. Thankfully, she waited to do so until the day after the last dinner party we hosted. Still, it was most inconsiderate of her to resign without notice." Beryl looked at Hadrian. "Why would it matter why my maid left?"

Before he could answer, Tilda spoke. "I find it's best to gather as much information as possible, even things that may seem unrelated or unimportant." A placid smile lifted her lips briefly. "Who sent for the police?"

"That was Oswald, the butler."

Tilda's brow furrowed, then she took a deep breath, her features smoothing. "I do have a question that may be a little upsetting for you, Mrs. Chambers, and I apologize. I know you said Mr. Chambers accused you of having an affair. Was that, by chance, true?"

Beryl's cheeks flushed pink. "Why would you ask such a thing?"

"Because I must, even if I suspect the answer is *no*."

Beryl gripped her hands more tightly together. "Louis was horrid, but I would never be disloyal."

Except she had been. With Chambers when she was betrothed to Hadrian. His gaze met Tilda's briefly. She seemed to be thinking the same thing.

Hadrian realized he could not entirely trust Beryl, even if he wanted to. She'd long ago demonstrated her infidelity, and it was likely that had not changed. That made him wonder what else she may be lying about.

He glanced toward the doorway, half expecting to see Teague standing there expectantly. He transferred his gaze to Tilda. "Should we leave soon?"

"Yes," Tilda said with a nod.

Beryl put her hand on his sleeve. "You can't go. I have questions about the inquest."

"We can come here beforehand tomorrow," Tilda suggested. "Perhaps we can talk to everyone and put your mind at ease."

Hadrian suspected Tilda wanted to interview everyone. Doing so while preparing them for the inquest was rather ingenious.

Beryl's features relaxed, but there was still an edge of tension in her posture. "That would be most helpful, thank you." She looked at them both earnestly. "I was hoping I might impose on you to complete a couple of errands for me. I require a black hat and a few pairs of black gloves. Would you be able to fetch those from my milliner? Flanders on Regent Street."

Tilda looked to Hadrian. He lifted a shoulder as he replied to Beryl. "We'd be happy to help. What is the other errand?"

"I'm in need of more sleeping tonic," she said almost sheepishly. "I find I need it most nights, and I'm afraid tonight I will have much difficulty sleeping. You must visit my druggist, Newbold, in Leicester Place. Mrs. Styles-Rowdon recommended him. You'll find him a bit thorny, but his sleeping tonic has done wonders for me. I've an account there, as well as at Flanders," Beryl added.

"We can fetch that as well," Tilda said kindly. "And we'll bring everything back here later."

Beryl's frame slumped gently against the back of the settee. "Thank you." She turned her head toward Hadrian. "I could not have borne this day without you."

"I'm glad we could help in your time of need."

Beryl turned to Tilda. "Thank you as well. You'll let Mr. Forrest know there is no need for a divorce?" She stood, and Hadrian leapt to his feet.

"I will." Tilda rose. "I hope you can find some rest."

Beryl departed the parlor.

Tilda fixed her gaze on Hadrian. "Did you see anything when you touched her?"

"No. I wish I could understand this bloody ability so that I may control it." He exhaled. "I am sorry it has not been helpful to you today."

"It's all right," she said with a smile. "I am glad you are not suffering a headache."

"Are you looking forward to visiting her druggist and milliner?" Hadrian asked.

Tilda's mouth quirked up. "Of course."

"You can also speak with Leach before we leave. So you can ascertain my alibi," he added.

"I will, but I know you didn't kill Chambers."

"Thank you for that," he said softly, grateful for her faith in him.

"I can't believe I missed your coach when I arrived," Tilda said as they walked to the entrance hall.

"Leach may have taken a turn around the block to keep the horses fresh. Are you ready?"

"Yes." Hadrian pulled his gloves from his pocket and drew them on. He opened the door, and they stepped outside into the cool March day.

The coachman inclined his head toward Tilda. "Good morning, Miss Wren. It's a pleasure to see you."

"I am also pleased to see you, Leach," she said with a smile.

Hadrian pursued his goal of providing an alibi. "Leach, what time did you drive me home from the club last night?"

"It was just after eleven, my lord. Just as I told the constable."

"And we went directly home," Hadrian said, flicking a glance at Tilda.

Leach looked at him as if he'd knocked his head again. "Yes. I told the constable that too."

Hadrian smiled at Tilda. "Satisfied?"

"Yes, but I took you at your word."

"I'm sorry to hear your friend's husband died," Leach said with concern.

"You will hear more about this unfortunate situation as Miss Wren will be investigating, and I will be providing assistance once more."

"Can't say I'm sorry to see more of Miss Wren," Leach said, extending a warm smile to Tilda as he opened the door to the coach.

"Thank you, Leach, you are most kind." Tilda climbed into the vehicle.

"Tilda, do you mind if we stop by Ravenhurst House to fetch the letter that Beryl sent me?"

"Not at all," she replied.

Hadrian instructed Leach to drive them to the druggist in Leicester Place after Ravenhurst House, then climbed into the coach. Tilda had taken the forward-facing seat, which he'd insisted she do when they'd first become acquainted. He was glad to see she hadn't forgotten.

As Hadrian settled against the squab, he reveled in the comfort of being with Tilda and in the anticipation of working with her again.

"We are partner investigators once more," he said.

She inclined her head. "Indeed we are, though I am sorry it's necessary. I truly wish you hadn't been drawn into this situation with Mrs. Chambers."

"You may as well call her Beryl since she's to call you Tilda," he noted wryly. "I confess I wish I hadn't been drawn into this matter either. I was quite content to not see or deal with Beryl or her husband again."

"Was it terrible for you when the betrothal was dissolved?"

"If you're asking whether there was a scandal, yes, though it could have been much worse. No one knew about them embracing at the ball. Miraculously, I seem to have been the only witness."

Tilda cocked her head. "Then why was there a scandal? I am not well-versed in Society."

"Because we ended the betrothal. That is generally not done. Once a couple is engaged to marry, they are allowed to be more familiar with one another, and a woman may suffer because of that."

"Of course, the woman would suffer," Tilda said with a faint cluck of her tongue. "I can't imagine Beryl was unaffected?"

"Since she married, she fared better than most women."

"They are ruined?" Tilda made a noise in her throat that was rather unladylike. "How horrible that a woman—or a man—can't have a change of heart. Surely, it's better to do that before the wedding than after." Her brows drew together. "I hope it wasn't terribly taxing for you. I'm going to do my best to make sure this doesn't draw you into another scandal." Her gaze locked with his, and he saw her commitment clearly.

His pulse quickened. "Thank you."

"I will do my utmost to solve this case as quickly and as quietly as possible."

"If anyone can, it's you."

CHAPTER 5

Tilda remained in the coach as Hadrian dashed into Ravenhurst House to fetch the letter from Beryl. Hadrian's home was jaw-droppingly large. She'd visited him once before and had done her best to keep from goggling at the stateliness of his home. Set back from the street, it boasted six columns across the front of its gleaming white façade and a tidy garden with sunny daffodils, which Tilda adored.

It was a stark reminder of their difference in station, just as their conversation prior to arriving had been. Tilda hadn't asked for the specifics regarding the scandal surrounding his broken betrothal, but she could imagine there had been a great deal of gossip. Had it affected his work or his social life? Had he been evicted from his club? Perhaps the news had appeared in the paper. Or multiple papers.

How awful to have one's life sensationalized.

She'd meant what she'd told him about solving the case as quickly as possible and keeping the scandal at bay. She didn't want to think what would happen if people knew that Scotland Yard considered him, the Earl of Ravenhurst, a suspect in the murder of the man who'd stolen his fiancée.

Hadrian returned to the coach, and he offered her a folded piece of parchment. "Do you want to read it?"

"I suppose." Tilda opened the letter and read the brief scrawl of handwriting.

My dear Hadrian,

Beryl's use of "my dear" made Tilda want to roll her eyes.

I hope this letter finds you well. I am sure you are surprised to receive this, but I didn't know where else to turn. I am in dire need of your advice and perhaps assistance with an urgent matter. Please call on me tomorrow. If you ever cared for me, you will come.

Most sincerely,
Beryl

"I'm not surprised you did as she asked," Tilda said, refolding the letter and handing it back to him. "This sounds rather desperate."

Hadrian slipped the parchment into an inner pocket of his coat just over his breast. "That was the word she used."

"I'm surprised you aren't angry with her for dragging you into this."

"She couldn't know that her husband would be killed. Anyway, I'm glad it allows me to work with you."

Heat unfurled in Tilda's belly. She looked out the window and tried not to think of the deepening connection between her and Hadrian.

Instead, she addressed what he'd said about Beryl not knowing her husband would be killed. "What if Beryl did know her husband would die?"

"Because she was planning to kill him?" Hadrian asked.

Tilda looked back at him. "It's possible. It's also possible she wrote you that *desperate* letter in order to involve you—a likely suspect—in the matter."

Hadrian sucked in a breath. "I do not like thinking that is possible."

"At this point, we must assume anything is," Tilda said gently.

A deep frown etched his features. "I hope that does not include me as the murderer."

"No, I don't assume that." Tilda could not. But why was she allowed to discount him as a suspect because of what she thought she knew of him, yet he wasn't supposed to do the same with someone he knew and had once cared about?

A short while later, they arrived in Leicester Place. Leach opened the door, and Hadrian climbed out and then helped Tilda to the pavement. They'd stopped in front of the druggist.

The shop appeared small and somewhat dingy. The front window could have benefitted from a thorough cleaning, as could the sign which read *F. Newbold, Druggist.*

Hadrian opened the door, and she preceded him into the dim interior. A counter stretched across the shop. Behind it were shelves teeming with bottles of various size and shape. Surveying the labels—those she could make out—Tilda noticed he sold poisons in addition to medicine, which was not unusual.

A small, thin man shuffled from the back of the shop. Wispy white hair covered the sides of his head while the top was bald.

"Good afternoon, Mr. Newbold?" Hadrian asked.

"Yes," the druggist replied. "May I help you?"

"I hope so," Hadrian said affably. "I've come to fetch a sleeping tonic for my friend, Mrs. Louis Chambers. I'm Lord Ravenhurst."

Newbold's nostrils flared, then he flicked a glance at Tilda. "Is this Lady Ravenhurst?"

"No," Tilda said quickly. She did not want to be mistaken as anyone's wife, not even Hadrian's. More importantly, she didn't want to *be* anyone's wife. "I am also a friend of Mrs. Chambers.

We've come in her stead because there's been a terrible tragedy." She looked to Hadrian so that he could reveal the news.

The druggist shifted his gaze to Hadrian in expectation.

"I'm afraid Mr. Chambers has died," Hadrian said with a grimace. "Mrs. Chambers requires the tonic so that she can be assured of sleep tonight."

The lines in Newbold's face had deepened. He shook his head. "How terrible for her. Please convey my condolences. I have the tonic she prefers just over here." He shuffled to a shelf and moved a stool so that he could stand on it and retrieve the bottle. It was one of many just like it. Looking at the quantity compared to other items, Tilda would say the tonic was a popular product.

Newbold returned to the counter and set the bottle down in front of Hadrian. "Will you be paying for that?"

"Mrs. Chambers said she has an account," Hadrian said. "Can you add it to that?"

"Of course," Newbold snapped, seeming aggrieved by the question.

"He asked because it is our understanding that Mrs. Chambers may have a debt with you," Tilda said with a benign smile. "Perhaps you could tell us how much so that we may convey that to her." Tilda wanted to know how much Beryl owed.

The druggist's nostrils flared. "That is none of your concern. My clients rely on my discretion."

"I am assisting Mrs. Chambers with her finances," Hadrian put in. He spoke with authority, sounding very much like an earl. "I'm sure you understand what a tragedy this is and how deeply she is affected. We are merely trying to support her in every way we can."

"I'll send a bill to her, and then she can decide who to share it with," Newbold said stubbornly.

Hadrian picked up the bottle of tonic. "That would be most helpful. Thank you, Mr. Newbold."

"Thank you," Tilda added before preceding Hadrian from the shop.

When they were both outside, and the door had swung closed, Tilda threw a glower toward the shop. "'Thorny' was an accurate description that Beryl provided."

"Indeed it was. I'm sorry you weren't able to learn anything."

"Hopefully our visit to the milliner will be more helpful," she said as they walked to the coach.

Hadrian directed Leach to the milliner on Regent Street, and they were shortly on their way once again. "I am anxious to look at Chambers' finances," he said. "Was he really struggling, or was he trying to control his wife's spending?"

"Just to be controlling, you mean?" Tilda asked, thinking that aligned with the man she'd met briefly the day before.

"That or Beryl *is* a spendthrift as the valet indicated."

"It could be both," Tilda noted. "I think the one thing we can say for certain is that their marriage was not a happy one. I witnessed that myself yesterday. He spoke harshly to Beryl, and she did the same to him, though less so. Then, as he left the room, he walked by Beryl and used his arm to bump into her. I don't think he hurt her, but it was a physical message. Seeing that and the bruises on Beryl's arms, I have no trouble believing he was violent toward her."

Hadrian's features darkened. "I hate thinking that is how things ended up for her after choosing him over me."

"And yet you're relieved that she did so," Tilda pointed out.

"Yes, and that makes me a little uncomfortable because she would have been better off with me." Hadrian leaned back against the squab.

"What drew you to her in the first place?" Tilda had given in to her curiosity which had been piqued during their conversation on the way to Ravenhurst House, but she worried she was being intrusive. "You don't have to answer that. I understand it may be unpleasant for you to discuss that time."

"Not unpleasant, but perhaps a bit embarrassing, which is how I felt with Teague earlier. With you, however, I am not bothered at all." His eyes met hers, and Tilda felt that surprising warmth again. When would it stop surprising her?

"I am not sure I could have offered to help someone who had treated me so poorly." If Tilda's fiancé had carried on with someone else, she would have been furious and doubted that emotion would lessen over time.

Hadrian shrugged. "I met Beryl at a ball. She was somewhat of a wallflower, and I made a point of dancing with one or two on such occasions. Honestly, they were usually far more interesting than the young women who were more popular. I liked Beryl because she seemed genuine. She found London Society intimidating but wanted to make her parents proud by securing a good marriage."

"She's also very pretty," Tilda noted.

"Yes. I can admit that an attractive woman will usually draw my notice," he said sardonically.

Tilda wondered if he saw her that way but quickly put the thought from her mind. Why would she want him to find her attractive? That would only complicate their association. Never mind that she found him arrestingly handsome.

Hadrian continued, "Beryl was young, and her family was pushing her to wed me, I think. She never proclaimed to love me, nor I her, so it wasn't as if we were a romantic match. She did say she loved Chambers, however, so that is why I feel badly for her. She married for love and things turned out quite poorly."

Further proof that marriage was a risk that often didn't meet one's expectations. Tilda was glad for Hadrian that he'd avoided it. She also admired his support of the woman who'd caused him considerable aggravation. "You are a very kind man."

The coach came to a stop, and Tilda looked out the window to see they were in front of Flanders Millinery. They departed the coach and went into the shop, which was much larger than the druggist's. It was also far tidier, and the front windows were filled with fashionable accessories on display.

There were a few ladies in the shop perusing the items. A girl of sixteen or seventeen greeted them with a pretty smile. She was dressed smartly and wore a small, charming hat despite being indoors. Tilda presumed she was wearing something made in the shop.

The girl perused Tilda's unfashionable gown, one of her brows ticking gently upward. "Welcome to Flanders."

"Good afternoon," Tilda said, ignoring the flash of self-awareness that came from knowing her dated wardrobe could not compare with that of her companion—an esteemed earl. Her lack of current fashionable clothing hadn't ever bothered her much. Until she'd begun moving about with Hadrian. Now she felt out of place. She did not care for the sensation and pushed it away. "Is Mr. Flanders available? We would like to speak with him about a delicate and urgent matter."

The girl's brown eyes rounded slightly. "He is my father. I'll fetch him." She hurried behind the counter and through a doorway.

"Should I remove my gloves and try to touch something?" Hadrian whispered.

Tilda turned her head toward him. "It might be strange for you to do so. I suppose if you can see an opportunity, you may as well. Though I have to think you'll see visions from any number of customers."

"That is certainly possible. Perhaps I'll have the chance to shake Mr. Flanders' hand and that may reveal something about Beryl."

Tilda noted there was another woman working in the shop, at least she appeared to be as she spoke with a pair of women much older than her. They all wore hats, but the younger one didn't carry a reticule, leading Tilda to believe she was an employee and not a customer.

"Flanders seems to run a very nice shop," Hadrian observed. "Not that I have much experience with millinery."

"It's lovely," Tilda agreed. "Though I have never been here. Shopping on Regent Street is above my economic ability. Even if it wasn't, I have never been one to thrive on shopping."

"You are a most efficient person," Hadrian observed with a faint smile. "I can't imagine you buying anything you don't specifically need."

"Indeed. Why bother?" she asked with a shrug. Though sometimes need and want were intertwined. One might need something but also want that something to be of a certain quality that one could not afford. Tilda was used to settling. Still, perhaps it would be nice to purchase something at a place like Flanders someday.

Miss Flanders returned and said her father would see them in the private sitting room. She guided them to a doorway beside the counter, opening the door so they could move into a well-appointed room with a settee and several chairs. There was also a tall mirror in one corner, and Tilda thought he must use this room for certain customers who wished to shop in privacy.

A man came in through the other door, his narrow features drawn with concern. "Good afternoon, I am Flanders. My daughter said you needed to speak with me. Would you care to sit?"

Tilda and Hadrian exchanged a glance, then sat together on the settee. Mr. Flanders took a chair opposite them, and his daughter lingered near the door she'd closed that led to the shop.

Hadrian looked to Tilda who gave him a slight nod. "I'm Lord Ravenhurst, and this is Miss Wren. We have come on behalf of Mrs. Louis Chambers, our dear friend." Tilda winced inwardly at the word *dear*, for that wasn't remotely true. Still, saying that could help their cause. "I'm sorry to report that her husband has died. We are here to obtain mourning accessories for her."

Miss Flanders let out a sob before clapping her hand over her mouth. Tears ran down her cheeks as her shoulders shook. Tilda felt sorry for her. She must know Beryl very well.

"How can that be?" Flanders said, aghast. He was not crying, but he looked stricken, his face going pale. "We just saw Mrs. Chambers a few days ago, and all was well. At least, she didn't mention that her husband was ill."

Hadrian glanced at Tilda again and she gave him another nod. May as well tell them the truth. It wasn't a secret, though it was distressing, which was why she hadn't told the druggist Chambers had been murdered. But the druggist also hadn't seemed this affected.

"I'm sorry to be indelicate," Hadrian said gently, casting a sympathetic look toward Miss Flanders. "I'm afraid Mr. Chambers was murdered."

As Miss Flanders' sobs grew louder, Mr. Flanders sent her a worried glance. "Please forgive my daughter. She is rather fond of Mrs. Chambers, as she comes in about once each week. We've come to know her well. I'm most distraught to hear of this misfortune. How is Mrs. Chambers?"

"In shock, as you can imagine," Tilda said. "Which is why we've offered to take care of certain things for her, such as ensuring she has appropriate mourning accessories."

Mr. Flanders sniffed. "You are good friends. I know just what she needs. Please allow me to fetch some items from the shop. My daughter can bring tea if you'd like."

"That won't be necessary," Tilda replied. "But thank you for your kindness."

Nodding, Mr. Flanders stood and then went to his daughter. He whispered something, then dropped a kiss on her head before going into the shop and closing the door behind him.

The simple act of a father consoling his daughter made Tilda's heart clench. She missed her father so very much. Being without him these past eleven years had been difficult, but she'd managed to persevere. However, seeing Mr. Flanders and his daughter together reminded her of just how much she'd lost. Emotion surged in her chest, and she took a deep breath to keep it at bay.

Hadrian angled himself toward Tilda. "I forgot to ask if I should pay for the items."

"Mrs. Chambers has an account," Miss Flanders said as she dabbed at her eyes with a handkerchief. "Though she hasn't made a payment in some time, and my father told me just yesterday that we really oughtn't let her purchase more items without doing so."

"I can certainly pay for the accessories," Hadrian said with a comforting smile. "You like Mrs. Chambers a great deal, don't you?"

Miss Flanders nodded. "She has a wonderful eye for fashion. My mother died a few years ago, and Mrs. Chambers has given me good advice about ... womanly things."

Tilda was glad Beryl had been helpful to this young woman. She was also eager to see what else Miss Flanders might share. "Did you also know Mr. Chambers?"

"No." Miss Flanders' nose wrinkled. "Mrs. Chambers said he wasn't very nice. She was always telling me to be careful around men, that I must not fall for their pretty words or excessive charm. She said she wished she'd never married him," the young woman added in a whisper as if she were imparting a secret.

Tilda and Hadrian exchanged another look. "We will be sure to convey your condolences to Mrs. Chambers," Hadrian said.

"Oh, yes," Miss Flanders said with a jolt. "I should have said that immediately. I'm terribly shocked by this news. Please tell her that I am thinking of her and hope she is well."

Mr. Flanders returned then, coming through the door where his daughter stood. He looked to her. "Elinor, I've set some things behind the counter. Will you box them up for Lord Ravenhurst and Miss Wren?"

"Yes, Papa." Miss Flanders disappeared through the door, and her father closed it behind her.

"I can pay you for the items," Hadrian said. "How much?"

Mr. Flanders waved his hand. "I wouldn't hear of it. These are gifts to Mrs. Chambers, as one of our best customers. Please tell her how sorry we are for her loss."

"We will do that," Tilda said, rising from the settee. Hadrian stood beside her.

"I am curious what will happen with her husband's new shop," Mr. Flanders said. "Without one of the partners, will it even open?"

Tilda jumped on the opportunity to discuss Chambers' business venture. "I wondered the same thing. Do you know where the shop is located?"

"Not far from here. Just west of Regent's Circus on Oxford Street. They've done a great deal of refurbishment. It looks to be most elegant. I have stopped in a few times."

"You are acquainted with Mr. Chambers then?" Hadrian asked.

"Somewhat. He was eager to show off the store. I could see he was quite proud of it. But his partner, Pollard, is a bit of an ass, if you'll pardon me for saying so." Flanders' features pinched in distaste. "I've known him for some time. His uncle owns a drapery warehouse in Cheapside, and I've purchased from him on occasion. Pollard worked there—or used to. I'm not sure he has time for that now that he's opening this shop with Chambers. Also, his wife worked for a friend of mine, Madame Ousset, as a seamstress for many years. Until she married Pollard."

"What has influenced your opinion of Mr. Pollard?" Tilda asked.

"Do you mean, why do I think he's an ass?" Flanders snorted. "He saw me as a competitor, which I found surprising at first. I thought they were just opening a clothing store, but Pollard said it's to be much larger with a wide array of offerings. I believe he's modeling the shop after Harding, Howell & Company." Flanders moved closer to them and kept his voice low, though it wasn't as if anyone would overhear him. "I sensed conflict between Pollard and Chambers over the shop. When you said Chambers had been murdered, my first thought was that Pollard must have done it. Did he?"

"The police have not yet arrested anyone for the crime," Tilda said.

"There is to be an inquest tomorrow," Hadrian added.

Flanders' thin, dark brows climbed his forehead briefly. "Indeed? I may try to attend, if only to find out what happened. So devastating." He clucked his tongue and cast his eyes toward the floor.

"We thank you for your time," Hadrian said. "And for your generosity."

"It's the least I can do," Flanders said with a brief smile. He moved to open the door to the shop for them. "Elinor will have Mrs. Chambers' things for you at the counter."

"Thank you," Tilda said before making her way to the counter where Miss Flanders was boxing up the rest of the items.

The young woman looked over the counter at Tilda with a sad expression. She gestured to the round box tied with ribbon. "Those are two hats, one with a thick veil that she can remove if necessary." She set another box next to it. "Here are three pairs of black gloves as well as some handkerchiefs. Those are white, but they are embroidered with black designs. Please tell her I will pray for her every night."

Hadrian picked up the boxes. "We will. Thank you, Miss Flanders."

"Yes, thank you." Tilda gave the young woman a warm smile. "Your kindheartedness will serve you well."

They took their leave, and Tilda immediately asked if they could go to the drapery shop next to hopefully speak with Pollard. Hadrian grinned in response, saying he was eager to do so, then gave Leach the direction to the shop.

Inside the coach, Hadrian set the boxes next to him on the rear-facing seat.

"You could sit beside me if you are crowded," Tilda suggested as the coach began moving. "Or if you would simply prefer to face forward. There is plenty of room." She understood why they'd sat opposite each other for the entirety of their acquaintance, but now that they were friends, did it matter? Then again, it was sometimes easier to conduct conversations facing one another.

"I am fine where I am for now," Hadrian replied. "But I will keep your kind invitation in mind." His eyes glowed with something she couldn't define and decided she was probably better off not discerning.

"It's too bad you weren't able to shake Flanders' hand," Tilda noted.

"Perhaps I'll have more luck at our next stop."

Tilda was still pleased with what they'd been able to learn from the milliner. "Mr. Flanders' comments regarding Pollard and the shop he was to open with Chambers were most interesting," she noted.

"Yes. It was very helpful of him to offer such information." The coach stopped, and Hadrian met her gaze. "Shall we see if Pollard is a murderer?"

CHAPTER 6

*H*adrian and Tilda walked to the door of the shop, but it was locked. The windows were covered so they could not see inside. He knocked loudly.

"I hope someone is here," Tilda said, her lips pursing briefly. "I've a good many questions for Mr. Pollard."

So did Hadrian. He knocked again for good measure.

After a long moment, the door opened to reveal a man of slight stature and dark, wiry hair. He wore glasses and an extremely harassed expression, his mouth set into a deep frown, and his hazel eyes narrowed. "Yes?" he snapped.

"Good afternoon," Hadrian said pleasantly. "I'm Lord Ravenhurst, and I'm looking for Mr. Pollard."

"I am Pollard," the man said, his features relaxing only the slightest amount. "What can I help you with?"

Hadrian inclined his head toward Tilda. "This is Miss Matilda Wren. We've come to speak with you about Mr. Louis Chambers. Have the police been here today?" Hadrian wasn't sure if Teague would have had time to come yet due to all he was busy with regarding the murder.

Pollard's brows shot up as his eyes rounded for a scant moment. "Why would the police come?"

He seemed surprised, Hadrian noted, though he could be pretending. "May we step inside to speak with you? It's a rather sensitive matter."

"I suppose." He still sounded annoyed, though less so as he opened the door wider to allow them entry.

Tilda took her hand from Hadrian's arm and preceded him into the shop. It was quite large with several distinct areas. They couldn't even see the entirety of the store as it appeared to continue upstairs given the wide staircase at the center.

Pollard closed the door. "Please get right to the point of your visit. I'm very busy, and my partner has decided not to show up again this morning. Hopefully you know where he is since he is the reason you're here."

Again? Was he often missing?

Hadrian glanced at Tilda, and she wordlessly encouraged him to deliver the news. "I'm sorry to tell you that your partner, Mr. Chambers, was found dead this morning. He was stabbed."

"Bloody hell," Pollard muttered, his jaw dropping briefly before he snapped it closed and put his hand over his mouth. He shook his head, blinking. Then he paced away from them and back. "He's dead? That is … shocking. Who killed him?"

"The police have not determined that yet. There is to be an inquest into the death tomorrow, but I'm certain it will be declared a murder." Hadrian looked for an opportunity to surreptitiously remove his glove in the hope that he could touch something in the shop. He should have tried to shake the man's hand when they arrived.

Pollard fixed his gaze on them. "How terrible for his wife. Is she all right?"

"She is in shock, but she is managing," Hadrian said.

"Is she a suspect?" Pollard asked. "They were both quite unhappy. Chambers told me on several occasions he wished he'd never married her. In fact, just a few days ago, he said he was considering divorce."

Hadrian exchanged a look with Tilda, but before they could say anything, Pollard went on.

The man's dark, thick brows gathered as he studied them with a dubious expression. "How do you both know Mr. and Mrs. Chambers, and why are you delivering this news instead of the police?"

"I am an old friend of Mrs. Chambers," Hadrian said.

Before Hadrian could explain that Tilda was investigating the matter, Pollard nodded vigorously. "Of course. Ravenhurst. I'd forgotten you were once engaged to marry Mrs. Chambers. I'm surprised you've maintained your friendship."

There was a sarcastic edge to his tone that Hadrian didn't care for. Indeed, his initial impression of Pollard was not favorable.

Tilda gave the man a cool smile. "I am investigating the murder. How did you know about Lord Ravenhurst?"

Pollard sized Tilda up briefly, as if he were trying to determine whether she was capable of investigating a murder. "Chambers has mentioned him several times." He sent an apologetic look to Hadrian. "He didn't have anything particularly nice to say, I'm afraid."

"How odd since we hardly knew each other at all." Hadrian didn't bother cloaking his irritation.

Standing beside him, Tilda inched closer so she could gently jab him with her elbow. "How will Chambers' death impact your shop opening?" She looked about the space.

"Honestly, it will make things much easier." Pollard shook out his shoulders and nearly smiled. "He was not as engaged as he ought to have been—as he once was. And he was not able to provide the financial support that he promised."

"In what way?" Tilda asked.

"We have a written agreement for our partnership, and he's required to provide certain monetary amounts at various stages.

He's been late in making those payments the past several months, which has delayed the work that needed to be done. We should be opening the shop next week, but we are still several weeks away." Pollard spoke bitterly, his eyes flashing. The contention that Flanders had mentioned was evident.

"Do you have the entire investment now?" Hadrian asked.

"No, and I suppose I never will." Pollard put his hands on his hips and looked about the not-quite-finished shop. In addition to work that needed to be done, the cases were mostly empty of items to sell. "It's good that I have been speaking with another potential investor, though Louis didn't want me to do that. He was very angry." Pollard locked his eyes with Tilda. "Do not think I killed him over our disagreements. I did not."

"I am not making any conclusions," Tilda said evenly. "I am merely collecting information, and I greatly appreciate your candor. What else did you disagree about besides finances?"

"That was the prime reason for our conflict, though we ultimately had different visions for the store. I have always said I wanted a department store that would expand. Louis never thought big enough." Pollard scoffed. "He imagined we would simply sell dresses and add men's clothing later. I want customers to walk into Pollard and Chambers and be able to meet every one of their clothing needs, including shoes and boots."

"How did you and Mr. Chambers decide to go into business together?" Tilda asked.

Pollard exhaled. "Louis had been looking for a way to distinguish himself. His older brother inherited their father's engineering firm, and Louis didn't have the skill for that anyway. His younger brother is a curate. Louis didn't have anything, and then he suddenly had a wife, which I don't think he really wanted." He shrugged. "We were friends at our club, and one night after drinking too much, I told him of my dream to open a department store. My uncle owns a drapery warehouse, and I'd been working for him. He would be able to supply the materials for the shop at an exceptionally reasonable price, and my wife is an accomplished dressmaker."

"Is she making everything for the store?" Tilda asked in astonishment.

"Of course not. She has hired seamstresses, tailors, and milliners who are already working on items that will be here in the store when we open. We'd hoped to hire a cobbler, but there hasn't been money for that." Pollard's eyes narrowed with anger again. "This is why it was so important for Louis to make his payments on time, and he did not."

Tilda nodded sympathetically. "I can understand your frustration. Are you in debt with the store?"

Pollard frowned at her. "I think you are overstepping now."

"I'm sure the police will ask the same question, and you'll be obliged to answer them," she said with a placid smile. "No matter."

"Yes, my uncle has loaned me money as well as provided material in advance of payment," Pollard said tersely. "I was expecting a payment from Louis this week. It was already late, but he promised that he would have it by yesterday."

"Which he did not," Hadrian said, thinking that another nonpayment of funds Chambers was obligated to pay was as good a motive for murder as anything else.

"Was he missing again yesterday?" Tilda asked Pollard. "You indicated that happens often."

"He was here, but he came in late, which he does most days recently. He says he is ill." Pollard's lip curled slightly. "I suspect he's just drinking too much. I deeply regret partnering with him." He shook his head.

"You mentioned you were speaking to another investor," Tilda noted. "Will he be taking Chambers' place in the partnership now that he is dead?"

Pollard thought for a moment. "I suppose he could. I am sorry

Louis is dead, but this is a boon for me. Perhaps now I can launch the store as planned, albeit late."

"Who is this new partner?" Hadrian asked.

"I'd rather not say, as nothing is in writing yet," Pollard said, notching his chin up. "I've already helped you enough, I think. If the police want to come calling, let them."

The door to the shop opened, and Detective Inspector Teague entered along with two constables. Hadrian stifled a smile at the man's impeccable timing.

Teague looked from Tilda to Hadrian. "I should be surprised to find you here, yet I am not." He settled his gaze on Pollard. "I'm Detective Inspector Teague from the Metropolitan Police."

"Lord Ravenhurst and Miss Wren told me what happened to Louis," Pollard said. "I'm sorry to hear it."

Teague looked around the shop. "I'm afraid you're going to have to repeat whatever you told them."

"I'm happy to help." Pollard gestured toward the stairs. "I've a sitting area in my private office where we can speak if you prefer. Though it's on the second floor."

"Wherever is convenient to you," Teague said. "First, however, excuse me for a moment whilst I have a word with Ravenhurst and Miss Wren." He inclined his head toward the door.

The detective inspector led them outside and closed the door, leaving the constables inside with Pollard. He focused on Tilda, his mouth tipping into a slight frown. "I thought you said you were not investigating this matter."

"Ravenhurst has hired me to find the murderer," Tilda said. "I am eager to prove his innocence."

Teague addressed Hadrian. "I dispatched a constable to Ravenhurst House to speak with your retainers about when you returned home last night and your activities overnight."

Hadrian hoped none of the neighbors observed the constable arriving as that would generate curiosity and specula- tion. Already, the possibility of becoming gossip fodder was present. "Splendid." He didn't bother keeping the sarcasm from his tone.

"Since I've encountered you here, I hope you'll allow me to ask about something that came up in my interview with the valet. Perhaps you already know what I'm going to ask."

Because Hadrian and Tilda had eavesdropped, he had a good idea. "No, I am not having an affair with Beryl." The notion was repellent. "I would never behave in that manner with someone who is married." Or betrothed.

"If I ask my next question as to whether you may have plotted with Mrs. Chambers to kill her husband, you would answer in the negative?"

Hadrian glowered at Teague. He liked and respected the man, but he could not help feeling offended. "Unequivocally."

Tilda sent Hadrian an encouraging glance before fixing her attention on Teague. "I would share information as we did in our last case, but I understand you may not wish to do that since you are officially assigned to this."

Teague had not been assigned to the matters that Tilda and Hadrian had investigated surrounding Hadrian's stabbing. Another, almost certainly corrupt, investigator had tried to bury the investigation into Hadrian's attack, likely paid by the man who'd been behind it, though they hadn't been able to prove that. That investigator, Padgett, had retired from the police.

Though he hadn't been directed to work on those matters, Teague had suspected something was awry and had worked on his own time to aid Tilda and Hadrian with the investigation. He'd also been instrumental in helping them capture the criminal. But this was a different situation, and Hadrian wasn't sure what the man would do.

Teague exhaled. "I can't work with a private investigator. However, between us, I will gladly accept your assistance."

"And will you aid my investigation?" Tilda asked, her brow arched.

The inspector grimaced. "I'm sure you're aware that the Metropolitan Police would not approve of that, particularly since you are a woman."

"Never mind the daughter of a highly respected sergeant who died in uniform," Hadrian said with a measure of heat.

Tilda deeply appreciated Hadrian's defense of her father. But she knew the police did not care who she was. Keeping her attention on Teague, she said, "I understand. My primary goal is ensuring Hadrian's innocence is proven and that his involvement in this situation is not sensationalized. I know you must investigate all suspects, but Hadrian does not have a strong motive. You'd do better to focus on Beryl Chambers or even Mr. Pollard. He has much to gain from Louis Chambers' death, which you will learn when you conduct your interview."

Hadrian stifled a smile. She would make Teague work to learn the specifics.

"I'd prefer that nothing to do with this investigation is sensationalized," Teague said. "Let us work to solve the crime as quickly as possible, shall we?"

Tilda nodded in agreement. "That is precisely what brought me here to Pollard's shop. I would appreciate if you would share who Pollard's new partner may be. He wouldn't tell us that."

Teague's brows climbed. "A new partner? I am most anxious to speak with him. I will see you tomorrow at the inquest."

Hadrian removed Beryl's letter from his coat pocket and handed it to Teague. "Here is the letter Beryl sent me yesterday."

"Thank you, Ravenhurst." Teague tucked it into his own coat. A faint grimace creased his features briefly. "I hope you understand that I am only doing my job by investigating your connection to Louis Chambers."

"I do," Hadrian said. "I don't have to like it, however."

"Can't imagine I would either." Teague waved at them before returning to the shop.

Hadrian frowned at the door. "I should have shaken Pollard's hand when I arrived. And I didn't have a chance to remove my gloves to touch anything."

"Perhaps you can try the door," Tilda suggested.

Quickly removing his right glove, Hadrian stepped to the door and put his hand to the wood. Nothing came to him, so he moved his hand around slowly. He focused his mind on seeing or feeling something and wished he had some control over this power.

A vision rose, foggy at first, but then Hadrian recognized the shop. There were two men talking together—Pollard and someone Hadrian had never seen before. He was younger than Pollard, and younger than Hadrian. Hadrian could only see him in profile, but he had dark hair and a long nose. The image dissolved, and Hadrian moved his hand slightly, willing it to return. How he wished he could hear what was happening in his visions, but that had never happened.

Withdrawing his hand, he turned with a frustrated grunt.

Tilda was watching him intently. "You saw something?"

"Briefly. Pollard was in the shop speaking with a dark-haired young man, but I've no idea who." He pressed his fingers to his temple as a dull ache spread across his forehead. "They were talking, but I can never hear anything, which is bloody annoying."

"I'm sorry. But at least you saw something. Perhaps we've yet to meet this young man. Will you be able to recognize him if we do?"

"I'm not sure. I only saw his profile. He had a long nose, so perhaps that will help identify him." He glanced toward his coach. "Shall we be on our way to Beryl's?"

"I suppose we should, though it's too bad we can't listen to Teague interrogate Pollard." She walked with Hadrian to the coach. "There are times I sincerely wish I was a member of the Metropolitan Police."

Leach opened the door, and Tilda climbed inside. Hadrian confirmed with Leach that they were going to Beryl's house next, then followed Tilda into the coach. He decided to take her suggestion and sat next to her on the forward-facing seat.

Her features registered surprise.

"You don't mind?" he asked, though she'd invited him to do so earlier.

"I encouraged you, if you recall," she replied with a smile. "It only makes sense with Beryl's items on the other seat."

Did that mean he should only sit next to her if they were transporting items? Hell, why was he dwelling on this so much? It was a seating arrangement not a declaration of affection.

And yet perhaps it was. Or at least the deepening of their friendship.

He certainly felt different sitting beside her. The coach felt … smaller. More intimate. Did she sense that too? He wasn't going to ask. Instead, he would simply enjoy this shift.

Perhaps, though, he ought to inject a bit of levity. "You don't plan to elbow me again, do you?" Hadrian smiled.

The coach moved forward as Tilda looked over at him, a glint of humor in her gaze. "I was afraid you were becoming upset, or at least bothered by Pollard's disclosure about what Chambers said about you. I didn't want you to prevent Pollard from talking to us."

"I admit I was irritated." Hadrian looked straight ahead. "I should not have been. I just don't understand Chambers' hatred of me."

"It does seem as though he had strong feelings against you," Tilda mused. "And what did Pollard mean about Chambers not really wanting a wife?"

Hadrian turned his head toward Tilda. "That was interesting, wasn't it? I wonder if Beryl knows that."

"Do you think Chambers would have confessed that to her?" Tilda sounded dubious.

"Perhaps in the heat of an argument. But I'm not sure I want to ask her about it in case she doesn't know."

Tilda lifted a shoulder. "It's entirely possible Pollard was mistaken or exaggerating." She was quiet a moment, her gaze fixed across the coach as she pondered something. Finally, she said, "If it's true that Chambers didn't want to marry Beryl, and she knew, it would explain the conflict in their marriage."

"It also strengthens her motive to kill him," Hadrian said with a frown.

"Perhaps, but it doesn't make sense to me that she would pursue a divorce whilst also planning to kill him. Unless she was trying to make it look as though she hadn't killed him."

Hadrian blew out a breath as he crossed his arms over his chest. "I suppose that's possible. If so, she's a very accomplished liar and actor. I quite believed her distress today. And I was persuaded by her letter."

"I believed her too," Tilda said. "Though her upset could be due to the fact that she killed her husband in a fit of passion. But she would have had to fetch a knife from the kitchen—if the missing knife is the murder weapon—and stab her husband in his bed, and that does not support a sudden, uncontrollable rage that could lead to murder. Perhaps it was a little of both—unplanned and then quickly executed."

"She certainly had plenty of reason to be angry with him, let alone outright despise him."

Tilda was quiet a moment, then said, "You are right that she had several reasons for hating her husband. She thinks he stole her jewelry, he's said awful things to her and has treated her violently, and she believes he is having an affair."

"We know all that to be true, except the jewelry," Hadrian remarked.

"Thanks to your visions, yes. Would you mind having a vision about the missing jewelry so we can confirm that?" she asked with a smile.

Hadrian chuckled. "I shall endeavor to do so. How many pieces went missing?"

"Nine in total," Tilda replied. "A set of three pieces disappeared before Christmas and the last ones in recent weeks."

"That's a long stretch of thievery," Hadrian remarked. "I suppose Chambers may have had to continually sell things of value in order to make the necessary payments to Pollard for the shop."

The coach slowed as they approached Beryl's house.

"You think Chambers sold Beryl's jewelry to a pawnbroker to gain the funds he needed? If so, I hope that the pawnbroker will see the published list and come forward with information that will help us."

Us. Hadrian smiled at how they were a team once more.

The coach came to a stop, and Hadrian grabbed the items they'd fetched for Beryl from the opposite seat. He followed Tilda from the coach, and Hadrian noted that a yew wreath dressed with black ribbon had already been placed upon the door of the house.

Oswald greeted them quite soberly. "Mrs. Chambers has a guest at the moment."

"We'll wait to speak with her," Hadrian said.

"This way, if you please." The butler led them into the parlor they'd occupied earlier in the day.

"Thank you," Tilda said to the butler before he departed. She waited a moment before turning to Hadrian. "It's too bad we can't just go 'wait' in Chambers' bedchamber. I should like to look at it closely myself."

"What do you hope to find?"

"Any number of things, but a clue as to the identity of his paramour would be most helpful. As would any clues having to do with Beryl's missing jewelry." Tilda removed her gloves and tucked them into her reticule. "There, now you can remove your gloves, and it won't look strange."

Hadrian set the boxes and sleeping draught on a table, then he removed his gloves. "You don't think it odd that we would call on someone without our gloves on?"

Tilda shrugged. "Perhaps, but we are 'dear' friends of the person upon whom we are calling, aren't we? Rather, you are anyway."

"Clever," Hadrian replied with a chuckle.

Voices carried into the parlor, and both Tilda and Hadrian turned toward the doorway into the entrance hall from whence they'd come. A moment later, Beryl appeared. A gentleman was with her. He was tall, dark-haired, and his nose was rather long.

The man turned his head slightly toward Beryl so that Hadrian saw his profile. Hadrian sucked in a breath and, without thinking, grasped Tilda's hand.

The contact of her skin against his sent a delicious tremor through him. And it had absolutely nothing to do with a vision. Touching her felt altogether different than that. It was ... invigorating.

He was only sorry that the timing wasn't different, for it was the first time he'd touched her like that, and he wanted to savor it. Instead, he was overcome with a rush of excitement at the identity of the man with Beryl.

Tilda swung her head to look at him, her brows dipping and her eyes bright with curiosity.

"That's him," Hadrian whispered. "The man I saw in the vision —in the shop with Pollard. What the devil is he doing here?"

CHAPTER 7

*T*he moment Hadrian clasped Tilda's hand, her body reacted in a very peculiar manner. She tensed, but it wasn't due to tension. Anticipation sparked and spread through her. The feel of his bare hand in her bare hand was almost … electric. It also felt shockingly *right*. And Tilda wasn't at all sure what that meant.

Then he'd begun to whisper, his words coming fast and urgent. She heard his excitement and worked to keep her features still. This man with Beryl had been in Hadrian's vision at Pollard's shop.

He looked to be about Tilda's age of twenty-five and was tall, though not as tall as Hadrian, who was a couple inches over six feet. His hair was dark and his nose long, just as Hadrian had described him from the vision he'd seen. But there was also something familiar about the man that Tilda couldn't quite grasp.

Beryl's attention fell on Tilda and Hadrian. Her gaze fell to their joined hands. Hadrian released Tilda at precisely the same moment she loosened her grip. She clasped her hands at her waist and tried not to notice that her palm was still tingling where he'd touched her.

"You've returned," Beryl said. She briefly turned her head to the man at her side. "Allow me to present Lord Ravenhurst and Miss Wren."

"I'm pleased to make your acquaintance," the man said, though he didn't smile. "I'm Oliver Chambers. Louis was my older brother."

That was why he looked familiar. Tilda saw it now—his face was the same shape as his brother's, and the nose was identical. The younger Chambers had more hair than his brother had possessed, and it waved back from his face. His eyes were also gray instead of brown, and they weren't as cold. Then again, Oliver Chambers wasn't currently glowering or spewing insults at anyone.

Chambers went on. "I came to pay my respects to my sister-in-law."

"That is most kind of you," Hadrian said. "Please allow us to offer our deepest condolences on the loss of your brother."

Us? Tilda wasn't sure why he was speaking on behalf of her. They were a business partnership, not a romantic couple or family or anything else that should provoke him to include her in his sentiments. She wanted to set the disturbance aside, but it continued to needle the back of her mind.

"Yes, I'm very sorry for your loss," Tilda said.

Chambers shook his head in a manner that seemed to indicate he was trying to clear it of something. "I'm rather shocked. A detective inspector came to tell me earlier, and I hastened here to see Beryl." He looked over at her with a slight frown. "Such a tragedy to lose one's husband so young."

Beryl only glanced at him before looking at the floor for a moment.

"Don't you have another brother?" Tilda asked. Where was he? Why hadn't he accompanied his brother on this condolence call?

"Yes, but Daniel did not take the news well. He shut himself in his study with a bottle of brandy, I believe." The younger Chambers brother grimaced. "I should return to him."

"You reside together?" Tilda asked, knowing she was treading the line between genial conversation and unsuitable curiosity, particularly in this time of shock and grief.

"For the time being. I just returned to London in December."

"He was a curate in Kent," Beryl said. "But he decided the religious life didn't suit him."

Chambers turned and put his hand on Beryl's upper arm, then pressed a kiss to her cheek. "I'll see you tomorrow."

"Will you be coming to the inquest?" Tilda asked, again risking being overly inquisitive. She had to be since it was her job.

"Yes, I planned to go in support of Beryl," Chambers replied. He looked to Hadrian. "I'm pleased that she has your support as well. I'll bid you good day." He inclined his head and went to the door.

When he was gone, Beryl wasted no time in asking if they'd brought the sleeping draught.

"Yes, and we also brought some accessories from Flanders," Hadrian said. "I will fetch them from the parlor."

Whilst he went to retrieve the items, Tilda asked Beryl how she was feeling. "Were you able to get some rest?"

"Not really," Beryl said, and indeed she did not appear rested. There were lines around her eyes and mouth, and she was still somewhat pale. "I did lie down for a while, but then Oliver arrived. I am so glad he called."

"You are close with your brothers-in-law?" Tilda asked.

"Just Oliver. He has always been very kind and considerate, things Louis turned out not to be. Their older brother, Daniel, is rather stoic. He's difficult to know." Beryl's brows arched briefly. "I am surprised at how badly he took the news. I never credited him for having an excess of sentiment about anything."

Hadrian returned with the boxes and the draught, which sat

atop them. "Mr. Flanders gifted you the hats and gloves in the boxes. He and his daughter were distraught to hear of your husband's passing."

Beryl put her fingers to her mouth for a moment and blinked, appearing to have to subdue her emotions. Finally, she said, "How thoughtful of them. I hope dear Elinor wasn't too upset. She is a sweet-natured girl."

"She felt badly for you," Tilda said gently. "And sends her condolences."

"I will write them a note to be delivered along with a funeral invitation. Oliver is taking care of ordering those, though we can't print them until I know when we can have the funeral." Beryl wrung her hands. "The inspector couldn't tell me when Louis's body will be returned."

"It shouldn't be more than a few days," Tilda said.

"I'm glad you are both here to help. Hadrian, I located the household ledger if you're still willing to review it for me."

"Of course," Hadrian replied. "On that note, I hope you won't mind my asking, but do you owe money to the druggist and the milliner?"

Beryl inhaled. "Did they tell you that?"

"No," Tilda said. "Hadrian is only trying to help, and he'll need to know if you have outstanding debts."

Pink stained Beryl's cheeks. "I don't know how much I owe, but I haven't made payments to them recently because Louis had cut my allowance."

Tilda felt badly for the woman because she had no control over her finances, which meant she had no real autonomy at all. "It seems your husband may have been struggling financially."

"Which explains why he stole my jewelry," Beryl said with a flash of irritation.

"Are you certain *he* stole it?" Tilda asked carefully. "I know you think he did, but have you any evidence that it was him?"

Beryl opened her mouth, then closed it again, pressing her lips together. "I don't have evidence. Isn't it your job to find it?"

"Yes," Hadrian said quickly. "However, Tilda can only do her job with the information that is available to her. Your belief that your husband stole your jewelry doesn't particularly help her in any meaningful way." He spoke kindly, and Beryl nodded.

"I've told her everything I know," Beryl said.

"Is it possible someone else stole the items?" Hadrian asked. "Perhaps one of your retainers? I hate to make that suggestion, but I think you must consider it."

Beryl's gaze flew to him, her eyes widening. "None of them would do such a thing."

"What about the maid who left your household suddenly?" Tilda asked.

"Farrow would not have stolen from me." Beryl looked upward, her features creasing with concentration. "I just realized that nothing has gone missing since she left." She sounded defeated, which Tilda could understand. It would be terrible to think someone you trusted had stolen from you. It might also be that Beryl was disappointed to learn that the culprit might not have been her despised husband.

"Do you know where I can find Farrow? Also, her first name would be helpful." Tilda would track her down.

"Martha, but I have no idea where she could be. I believe she once told me that her family lived in Stepney. Perhaps you could find them?"

"I will try." Tilda gave her an encouraging smile. "I would like to speak with your staff. Possibly whilst Hadrian reviews your accounts?"

Beryl nodded. "Yes, please talk to Clara. She is nervous about the inquest tomorrow."

"I'd be happy to," Tilda replied.

"She's in her chamber at the moment. I can take you up there." Beryl looked at the items Hadrian held. "Let me take those too.

You can go to the study whilst I escort Tilda upstairs to speak with Clara." She smiled at him as she took the boxes. The bottle of the tonic balancing on top wobbled.

Hadrian plucked it up and tucked it into the top box. "That will ensure it doesn't fall as you go up the stairs."

Beryl's gaze softened as she smiled at Hadrian. "You are so thoughtful. The ledger is on Louis's desk." She turned toward the staircase hall.

Tilda exchanged a look with Hadrian. She wanted to speak with Clara alone. "Beryl, you should join Hadrian in the study. I'm sure he'll have questions about the ledger."

Hadrian nodded. "Yes, that would be most helpful."

Beryl looked back over her shoulder. "Of course. I'll be down directly." She turned once more.

Tilda smiled at Hadrian and barely whispered, "Thank you."

"Good luck," he replied softly before Tilda followed Beryl. They did not stop at the first floor or the second. They climbed to the uppermost floor with its lower ceilings and narrow corridor.

Beryl glanced back at Tilda over her shoulder. "Clara's room is at the end."

When they reached her door, Beryl knocked softly. "Clara, Miss Wren has returned. Is now a good time for you to speak with her?"

"Yes," came the reply. The door opened a moment later to reveal Clara. She fidgeted with her skirt, and her eyes were downcast.

Tilda felt sorry for her. Finding her employer dead had to be a shock. "Shall I come in?" Tilda asked, giving the young maid a gentle smile.

Beryl held the boxes slightly toward the maid. "Clara, the milliner sent black hats and gloves for me. Wasn't that kind of him? When you're feeling up to it, you can come down and unpack them. I know how much you like it when I have new things."

"I will, Mrs. Chambers," Clara said, and Beryl departed.

Tilda closed the door. "I understand you're a bit apprehensive about the inquest tomorrow."

The maid did appear worried, but also dubious, as if she wasn't sure if she ought to trust Tilda. She gestured to the chair she'd vacated. "You can sit, if you like."

"Thank you," Tilda said. "Where will you sit?"

"I can sit on the bed." Clara went to perch on the edge, her position that of a bird ready to take flight.

Tilda angled the chair toward Clara and sat down. "There is nothing to fear from the inquest. The coroner will ask the witnesses questions. And a jury will determine the cause of death."

"But I will be questioned." Clara chewed her lip. "I received a summons."

"Don't be nervous." Tilda gave her an encouraging smile. "Just answer the questions. Can you do that?"

Clara nodded. "I already answered the constable's questions earlier. Will they be like that?"

"Yes. Even more reason not to be nervous. You've already done this. Would you like me to ask some questions so you can feel comfortable?"

"Would you?" When Tilda nodded, the maid asked, "How do you know so much about this?"

"My father worked for the Metropolitan Police, and I am an investigator."

Clara looked at her with admiration. "I didn't know a woman could do that."

"Most people don't think they can," Tilda said sardonically. "However, I work for a barrister who knows I am capable, and I'm starting to work as a private investigator on my own." Never mind that all her clients so far had been the Earl of Ravenhurst. "Are you ready to answer some questions?"

Clara squared her shoulders and looked Tilda in the eye. "Yes."

Tilda smiled. "That is an excellent way to present yourself—with confidence and enthusiasm. Now, when did you come to work here in the Chambers' household?"

"Six years ago, when I was seventeen. I worked in the scullery for a few months, then became the maid when the other one left."

"You were the only maid?" Tilda asked.

"Until Mr. Chambers married, and he hired a lady's maid for Mrs. Chambers."

"That was Martha Farrow who resigned her post? Then you became Mrs. Chambers' maid?"

"Yes, though I still complete most of my regular duties as well."

Tilda was glad for the chance to speak with her about the maid who'd left. "Did you know Farrow well?"

Clara clasped her hands in her lap, her body seeming to tense. "We weren't close, but we talked and laughed together."

"Do you know why she left?"

The maid shook her head. "It happened rather quickly. She told me she was leaving and was gone the next day."

"Was there anything that occurred that might have prompted her to leave?" Tilda asked. "Perhaps she was unhappy here?"

Clara's gaze shifted, and she chewed her lip again, indicating she was agitated, or so Tilda had gathered based on her behavior. "She didn't say so. Massey seemed to know her better. You could ask him."

Tilda made a note to do so. "I will. Do you know where Farrow is employed now?"

"No, but Massey might. Or you could ask her family. Her father does something with the law in Stepney."

"Is he a barrister or a solicitor?"

Clara lifted her hand and gestured with enthusiasm. "A solicitor, I think."

Tilda beamed at her. "Clara, you are doing very well."

A smile lit Clara's face. "Thank you. I am feeling much better. In spite of everything."

"Would it be all right if I asked you a few more questions?" Tilda asked.

"Yes, please, this is helpful."

"Excellent." Tilda smoothed her hands over her lap. "You are aware of Mrs. Chambers' jewelry going missing." Tilda knew she was because Beryl had talked about it yesterday when Clara was in the room.

Clara's brow creased. "She is very upset about it."

"I would be too," Tilda said. "She thinks Mr. Chambers stole it, but nothing more has gone missing since Farrow left. Do you think it's possible she took the jewelry?"

"I suppose it's possible." Clara frowned. "I really couldn't say."

"That's all right." Tilda gave her a reassuring nod. "Can you tell me about Mr. and Mrs. Chambers? In your opinion, how did they get on?"

"Not terribly well. They argued, and Mr. Chambers sometimes grabbed Mrs. Chambers or pushed her."

"Did you witness him doing any of that?"

Clara shook her head. "I didn't, but Farrow told me not long before she left that she'd recently seen Mr. Chambers push Mrs. Chambers down into a chair."

Tilda already wanted to interview Martha Farrow, but now it was absolutely necessary. Perhaps she'd also been summoned to the inquest. If not, Tilda would find her. And she had a place to start in Stepney with her family.

"Was it difficult working here knowing that about Mr. Chambers?" Tilda asked.

Clara hesitated. When she answered, she spoke in a near whisper. "I wasn't sure I believed that was true. Mr. Chambers hired me to this position, and I am loyal to him." She pressed her lips together tightly as if she was trying to keep from saying more. Her jaw tightened.

"I can understand that," Tilda said gently.

"But then I saw the bruises." Clara met Tilda's gaze with a fiery anger. "I didn't realize he could be that cruel. He was always very kind to me. Or what I thought was kind." She looked away. A tear fell from her eye, but she quickly brushed it away.

Tilda had a bad feeling about what she might learn next. "How was he kind to you?"

Clara looked back at Tilda but then shifted her gaze to her lap. "He made me feel … special. My mother had died just before I came to work here, and my father left us a long time ago. I was alone, but he made sure I felt cherished."

Cherished? "Like your father would have made you feel?" Except Louis Chambers was perhaps a decade older than Clara at best.

It took Clara a moment to respond. "No. Not like a father."

Tilda tamped down her revulsion at what Clara might reveal. "Was he … intimate with you?"

Clara nodded. She wiped her cheeks and kept her head down. "Mrs. Chambers doesn't know. She'd throw me out without a reference."

"Your affair continued until Mr. Chambers died?" Tilda wanted to make sure she understood.

Snapping her head up, Clara goggled at Tilda. "*No.* That stopped when they wed. I refused to lie with him after that, though he did try to persuade me to do so."

"He ultimately left you alone?"

"I am sure he had other women." Clara looked down once more and plucked at her skirt. "I think he sometimes took Martha to his bed, but I'm not certain."

Martha became more and more interesting. Tilda dearly

wanted to know why she'd left and whether she'd taken any of Beryl's jewelry with her.

"Do you know about any of the other women?" Tilda asked. "Someone who was perhaps his paramour and might wear perfume?"

Clara's forehead squeezed. "I can't think of anyone, but I would not be surprised. I feel so foolish thinking he was such a kind man for so many years. Then, when I began to care for Mrs. Chambers, I could see the evidence of his abuse. She is better off without him," she added fiercely, surprising Tilda with her vehemence.

"Thank you for sharing that with me, Clara. I would advise you to only share what you know tomorrow. The coroner doesn't need to hear your opinions." Especially not when they might draw attention to Clara as a suspect. Although, perhaps she ought to be.

"I'll remember that," Clara said eagerly. "Thank you for helping me. But please don't tell Mrs. Chambers about how things were before she married Mr. Chambers."

Tilda looked at the maid with sympathy. "It will likely come out at the inquest. I'm sorry. Perhaps it would be better if you told her beforehand, so she isn't surprised."

Clara paled. "I couldn't," she breathed.

"Would you like me to tell her?"

"She'll toss me out." Clara appeared stricken, almost panicked. "Probably without a reference."

"I hope not, but if she does, I'll do my best to help you find a new position." Tilda sought to soothe the maid but also meant what she said—provided Clara had not been involved in Chambers' murder. "Will you trust me to help you?"

Clara nodded. "I suppose I don't have any choice."

Tilda reached over and touched Clara's hand, prompting the maid to meet her gaze. "I promise I will do everything I can to make sure you have a position—either here or somewhere else.

Perhaps Mrs. Chambers won't turn you out. It's not as if you carried on with him after they were wed."

Hoping to distract the young woman from worrying, Tilda returned to discussing the inquest. "The coroner will also ask you about finding Mr. Chambers this morning. You don't need to go through that again with me. I'm sure it was most upsetting."

"It was." Clara wiped her brow. "I was expecting to find a mess but not like that." She shuddered.

Tilda's curiosity got the better of her, as it often did. "What sort of mess were you expecting?"

"Mr. Chambers had been drinking excessively the last several weeks." Clara wrinkled her nose. "His chamber pot was disgusting."

"Vomit?" Tilda wanted specifics, as unpleasant as they were.

"And the night soil was just …" Clara made a face. "Forgive me. He was very ill from drink."

Tilda nodded. "I think I understand. I'm sure you won't miss that."

Clara actually smiled. "No, I will not."

Tilda stood. "A hearty repast and a good night's sleep will do wonders for you." She moved toward the door. "I'll be here tomorrow and will go to the inquest with Mrs. Chambers. If you have more questions for me, you can ask me then."

"Thank you," Clara said.

Tilda took her leave, closing the door behind her and hesitating a moment in the corridor. It seemed there were two new suspects: Clara and Martha Farrow. There was also more evidence that Louis Chambers was despicable. He'd preyed on a young retainer in his household. Perhaps two, if Martha Farrow had also warmed his bed.

When a murder victim was loathsome and disliked or even hated by a great many people, the list of those who would be pleased by his death was long.

Tilda had a great deal of work to do.

CHAPTER 8

*H*adrian walked into the study and immediately saw the ledger on the desk. However, he ignored it and went straight to the bedchamber, opening the door slowly lest it creak and alert someone he was going into the room.

The chamber was dark, the curtains drawn. It was in much the same condition as it had been that morning. Even the bloodied linens were still on the bed. He supposed that was understandable. The household had undergone a great shock.

Hadrian wasn't sure how much time he had, so he moved quickly. Well, as fast as he could when he was trying to coax his mind to see a vision. He wished he knew how this bloody power worked. Would it be easier if he knew what he was trying to see? Or at least whose memories he wanted to glimpse?

Perhaps he should think of Beryl, except he didn't want to see any intimate moments between her and Chambers. Perhaps he ought to think of her being angry, so that he could see their discord instead. That was what he was most interested in.

Except without being able to hear what was being said, would it really be helpful? He thought back to the visions that had been most integral to the case he'd solved with Tilda recently.

It was the visions in which he'd been able to recognize the people who were involved. Then he and Tilda could question them and gain more information. The most helpful vision was when he'd identified the killer, but that had been because there were multiple people present. Hadrian had been able to see the murderer in the memory of another person. He realized that had been the first instance he'd seen the memories of someone who was dead.

Hadrian hadn't been able to see or feel anything from the corpse they'd found—and Hadrian *had* seen that man's memories when he'd been alive. Hadrian also hadn't been able to see the memories of Tilda's grandfather's cousin who had recently died. What was the difference? Was it because the one man had been dead longer? Or was it that he hadn't been murdered as the others had been? Hadrian really wished this ability had come with a handbook.

Perhaps the ability would change over time, particularly as Hadrian learned to manage it. *If* he could learn to do so.

Hadrian went to the bed and touched the headboard. Nothing came to him. He moved around the bed, gliding his hands over the bedclothes, careful to avoid any blood, and the posts as well as the draperies. Still nothing.

He should not have been surprised. Perhaps he wouldn't see Chambers' memories because he had very recently died, or he'd been murdered. Or perhaps both.

Pausing at the post where he'd seen the vision from the paramour's perspective earlier, he pressed his hands to the carved wood. He didn't particularly want to see memories of her engaged in sexual acts with Chambers, but he couldn't control that.

He focused on what he'd seen earlier. The vision rose in his mind—or was it just his memory of the vision? Pain sparked in his temple. Then it *was* a vision, apparently.

But it wasn't quite what he'd seen before. Chambers looked

slightly different. His hair was longer. And his position on the bed was different. He was fully reclined, his lips spread in a lazy smile. Whoever's memory Hadrian was seeing, the woman put her hands on his bare chest. Recalling Tilda's question about a ring on the woman's hand, he saw that there wasn't one. But these hands were different from the ones he'd seen earlier. They were rougher, the nails short and blunt.

Hadrian realized the first memory had been of someone from a higher status than what he was seeing now.

Chambers' head suddenly turned toward the door. And Hadrian was now looking at the door. It was closed. The woman scrambled from the bed, dragging something with her—clothing, he realized. He saw a white cap and a dark-blue garment.

Hadrian's perspective changed with her movements. She flattened herself onto the floor and slid under the bed. Hadrian was overwhelmed with fear and anxiety. He concluded that someone was about to enter the chamber, and she did not want to be caught in Chambers' bed.

"Hadrian?"

Damn. He hadn't been paying attention to how long he was in here, and now Beryl was in the study.

He massaged his hand across his forehead as the pain blossomed. This headache would take a while to dissipate, he feared.

Turning, he started toward the door but felt a bit wobbly. He grazed his hand along the back of a chair to steady himself. Another vision flashed in his mind. A woman stood before him. She was dressed as a maid, her dark-blonde hair pinned up beneath a white cap. Pretty, with plump lips and sultry, heavy-lidded eyes, she was not familiar to Hadrian.

A hand gestured before him. It belonged to whoever's memory he was seeing. The wrist was feminine. And she wore a wedding ring studded with garnets.

Pain streaked through his head once more. He forced himself

to release the chair, to end the vision and because he needed to leave the bedchamber.

He took several deep breaths as he made his way to the study. "Beryl, my apologies. I'm afraid I couldn't help looking in the bedchamber." He closed the door behind him, his head throbbing.

She stood near the desk. "Why?"

"I suppose I wanted to see if there was anything that might help the investigation."

"You want to help the inspector?" Beryl asked, aghast. "But he thinks I'm guilty."

"I don't know that he does," Hadrian said. "But I understand how it feels to be investigated. Teague also sees me as a suspect."

Beryl scoffed. "That's ridiculous."

"I've hired Miss Wren again to find Louis's killer."

"Were you helping her then by searching Louis's bedchamber?"

"I was," Hadrian replied. "Though I am sure she'll want to look for herself when she's finished with the maid."

Beryl cocked her head. "If she's going to search it anyway, why would you bother? Are you helping with her investigation?"

"Yes. We made a good team when we worked together before."

"But I thought you hired her to investigate *for* you." She appeared confused.

"I did, and I also provided assistance." He wasn't going to explain that he provided a valuable resource for Tilda. "In this case, she's glad for my help since you and I have known each other several years."

"We have not known each other well," Beryl said, sounding perhaps regretful. "At least not since I ... married Louis. I am sorry for that," she added softly. "If I could go back, I would not have allowed him to woo me to break things off with you."

There was Hadrian's answer. "I'm sorry you have regrets. But I thought you loved him."

"I thought I did. He made me feel very ... wanted. Not that

you didn't. It's just … he was so persistent and … ardent." She seemed to be choosing her words very carefully. Was she trying to say Hadrian had not felt as passionately toward her as Chambers had? Looking back, she was right. Hadrian hadn't been ardent at all.

But Hadrian didn't want to upset her in the midst of her current ordeal. "I am sorry for the way things ended." That wasn't entirely true since he was quite relieved they hadn't married. Though it was better than saying he regretted becoming betrothed to her, which was the real truth. He'd made a mistake, and she'd managed to correct it with her betrayal. How cold that sounded.

"I suppose one could say we didn't know each other all that well when we were betrothed," she said. "I confess that I was intimidated by you."

"Why?"

She shrugged. "At first, it was just because you are an earl. I never imagined I could attract the interest of someone like you. As we became acquainted, I could see you were different than the other men on the Marriage Mart. You are sophisticated and intelligent. Most of all, you seemed genuinely interested in knowing me."

"I *was* genuinely interested," Hadrian said. Thinking back on her behavior then, he could see how she was shy and hesitant at first. She'd lacked the confidence that Tilda possessed. Now he wondered what had attracted him to Beryl in the first place.

He'd found her attractive, and he'd liked that she wasn't from London. He'd been sought after on the Marriage Mart, mostly for his title, but Beryl hadn't worked to gain his attention. He'd seen her at a few balls, and no one had danced with her. In those days, he went out of his way to dance with the wallflowers. Even if he decided he wasn't interested in courting them, they would at least be seen dancing with an earl. Some people cared a great deal about such things.

"You aren't intimidated anymore, I hope," he added with a smile.

"No. If I can suffer marriage to Louis, I am made of the sternest stuff, I think."

Hadrian sobered. "I am truly sorry for all you've endured. I had no idea he was so beastly."

"Nor did I, or I would not have married him, would I?" she asked wryly. "Still, I am sorry he died and in such a ghastly manner. I know a divorce would have been difficult, or perhaps even impossible, but that was what I hoped to achieve. If I'd wanted to kill him, why would I bother with hiring a barrister?"

"You don't have to convince me," Hadrian said, lifting his hand. Though hadn't he begun to consider that she could be guilty of the crime?

Still, he *believed* she was innocent. Or that she'd been motivated by desperation or some sense of self-defense—he and Tilda had even discussed that.

Perhaps he couldn't bring himself to acknowledge that he would betroth himself to a killer. Except he *had* betrothed himself to someone capable of betrayal.

Hadrian pushed that thought away. "Shall we look at the ledger?"

"Yes." Beryl pivoted toward the desk. "I confess I only glanced at it to make sure it was the correct book."

Hadrian sat at the desk, and she took the chair beside it. His head still ached, and he massaged his forehead as he opened the ledger.

After reviewing several pages, he quickly deduced that each page contained entries for a given month. There were the usual household records, though they seemed inconsistent with the retainers' payments, detailed by person some months and then grouped together in others.

Beryl's quarterly allowance was documented, and Hadrian could see how it had decreased in the last year. Starting in

August, there were payments to Pollard. They were the same for three months, then diminished in November and December. This lessening amount matched what Pollard had told them.

December also contained an entry for "Oliver."

Hadrian glanced at Beryl. "Why did Louis give his brother twenty pounds?" That was a large sum for someone to part with who was struggling financially.

"I don't know." Beryl shrugged, her gaze dipping to the ledger. "Perhaps he wanted to help Oliver after he'd left his post in Kent."

Hadrian turned to January and saw that there was no entry for Pollard that month. Nor was there one in February. His accounting since the new year was slipshod. There was income in January—his "quarterly interest"—but there was hardly any money left at the start of March. Looking back, Hadrian could not see where all the money had gone. It appeared some payments had not been recorded or had been entered with the wrong amount. Whatever the reason, there didn't seem to be much money at present.

Beryl leaned close to him. "What is it? You're frowning."

Hadrian turned his head toward her and was shocked to see her face just scant inches from his. He could see the golden flecks in her amber-brown eyes. He'd forgotten they were there, but now he was transported back to when he'd held her in his arms and kissed her. That seemed a lifetime ago. He hadn't thought of her in that way in a very long time. And he found he couldn't think of her that way now, nor did he want to.

A sound from the doorway made them both turn their heads. Tilda stood there, her features serene, her green eyes leveled on them. "I hope I'm not interrupting."

"Not at all." Hadrian stood. He felt distinctly uncomfortable, as if he'd been the one caught in a compromising position, which was silly.

First of all, there was nothing between him and Beryl. Secondly, Tilda wouldn't be upset if there were. Or would she?

Hadrian froze for a moment. Did he have burgeoning romantic feelings toward Tilda?

He might.

Shaking himself internally, Hadrian decided it was far too early to think such things. They hadn't even been acquainted for a month.

"How did your conversation with Clara go?" Beryl rose from her chair. "Did you put her mind at ease?"

"Somewhat, at least." Tilda moved farther into the room. "I know this is extremely trying. For all of you."

Beryl glanced down at the floor. "Yes," she murmured.

The butler appeared in the doorway. "Mrs. Chambers, you've a guest. Mrs. Styles-Rowdon is here with her maid and an array of black garments. For now, they are in the parlor."

Eyes widening with something akin to glee, Beryl smiled. "Wonderful, thank you, Oswald. Please tell her I'll be there directly."

The butler inclined his head before departing.

"That is your neighbor?" Tilda asked.

"Yes. You should come meet her," Beryl said with enthusiasm.

Tilda sent Beryl an expectant look. "Do you mind if I take a few minutes to peruse the bedchamber first? I should like to conduct my own investigation of where your husband died. It won't take long."

"I don't mind at all," Beryl said, stepping toward the doorway that the butler had just vacated. "Hadrian said you would want to do that. I appreciate any help you can offer in proving my innocence." She moved her gaze to Hadrian, her features softening slightly. "Just as I am deeply grateful for your assistance. I couldn't do this without you."

Beryl left the study, and Tilda speared Hadrian with a dubious stare. "Did you tell her I was going to prove she is innocent? That is not what you hired me to do."

"I said you would find the killer, and we would both be found innocent. Or something to that effect. I wanted her to let us search the bedchamber. I was in there when she arrived."

Tilda's brow shot up. "Were you? And did you learn anything? You must have—you're massaging your temple," she said with a frown.

Hadrian hadn't even realized he'd put his hand to his head. "I've a headache."

"What did you see?"

"Do you want to hear about the visions first or the ledger?"

"Did you say visions, plural?" She held up her hand. "Tell me about the ledger. I've always preferred to save the best things for last." She started toward the bedchamber.

He followed her. "Why is that?"

She shrugged. "I like the anticipation, I suppose? Or perhaps I have always preferred to do harder or less interesting things first so that I can enjoy what I really want."

Hadrian grinned. "I am precisely the same way. I always studied Latin before anything else." He shuddered as he recalled working to somewhat master the language.

"I know only a smattering of Latin. And a little more French." She faced him when they were inside the bedchamber. There was a wistful glint in her gaze. "I would have loved to learn languages. I tried, but I had no one with whom to practice speaking them."

"I can help you with French. My Greek and Latin are far less impressive, and I can't really speak either."

She laughed softly. "When you find someone with whom to speak Latin outside of a university, I will be most impressed." She turned and began searching the room, starting with the small table near the door. It held a single drawer, which she opened. "Tell me about the ledger."

Hadrian watched as she surveyed the contents, then closed the drawer firmly. "Chambers made payments to Pollard at the same amount for three months starting in August, then lesser amounts for two months. By January, Pollard had disappeared from the ledger."

Tilda glanced at him as she continued her search, moving to the hearth where she looked behind and under the clock that sat atop the mantel. "What do you suppose happened to cause Chambers to reduce payments to Pollard?"

"I've no idea, but Louis made a payment of twenty pounds to his brother Oliver in December. There's no indication as to why. Beryl supposed it was to help Oliver after he left his post as curate in Kent."

Pausing briefly, Tilda put her hand on her hip as she looked toward Hadrian. "Twenty pounds is a great deal for someone who was apparently short on funds."

"I came to the same conclusion," Hadrian said. "As of March, there isn't much left in the household account—definitely not enough to meet the expenses."

"How fortunate you are paying for the investigation into her missing jewelry as part of the murder inquiry," Tilda noted. "Always coming to the rescue."

"For you, yes." He was eager to help anyone. Except it was somehow different with Tilda—and he knew it.

Breaking their eye contact, Tilda moved to a dresser on the other side of the hearth situated in the corner of the bedchamber. She opened drawers and moved the contents about. She closed the drawer and went to the bed where she wrinkled her nose. "I wonder when they plan to launder the bedclothes."

"I'm sure they're all distracted and overwhelmed with grief."

"Yes, I suppose," she murmured. She moved the pillows and the bedclothes about, careful not to touch any of the blood-stained areas.

"Are you looking for anything in particular?" he asked.

"No," she replied crisply. "I suppose I am looking for the knife that was used to stab him, but a good investigator does not search with an end goal in mind. That is an excellent way to miss something. It is far better to look with open curiosity for whatever you may find."

"Did your father teach you that?" he asked softly. He knew how much the man had meant to her and how much he'd taught her about investigation.

Hunched over the bed, she turned her head and met his gaze, but only briefly. "Yes." She straightened. "What did you see in here earlier? With your ability, I mean."

"I knew what you meant," he said wryly. "The first vision was similar to the other one I had with the woman and Chambers. He was inviting her to his bed, but it wasn't the same woman."

Tilda looked at him shrewdly. "How do you know?"

"Because of what you asked me regarding her hands, I paid close attention. No wedding ring, and the nails were short and blunt, the hands roughened. She was not of the same economic class as the first woman I saw."

Tilda's nostrils flared, and he could see that this interested her. "Well done, Hadrian. Did you see anything else that might point to her identity?"

"I did, in fact," Hadrian was eager to see her reaction. "She and Chambers were interrupted. I could sense her fear and anxiety. She leapt off the bed and scurried underneath to hide, grabbing some clothing as she went. I made out a white cap and a dark-blue garment. I believe she was a maid."

Tilda's eyes gleamed with excitement. "That is very helpful. I learned in my conversation with Clara that she was intimate with Chambers before he wed Beryl."

Hadrian didn't know Clara's age, but he judged her to be younger than Tilda, who was twenty-five. "She had to have been quite young."

"Just seventeen when she joined the household," Tilda confirmed. "Chambers' treatment of her is appalling."

"I did not think my opinion of him could sink lower, but it

has." Hadrian was glad he wouldn't ever see the man again. "You think I was seeing Clara in his bed?"

"Perhaps. What was your second vision?"

"It came when I touched that chair." He considered putting his hand on the back of it once more, but the pain in his head had only just started to lessen.

"It's no wonder your head was hurting after two visions. Does it still ache?" Her worry was evident in her tone and her expression.

"Yes, but it's improving. Slowly." He was pleased she'd asked. "I appreciate your concern. When I touched the chair, I saw a woman—a maid, I believe. She wore a cap and a dark-blue dress, like the one Clara wears. But this maid's hair was blonde. She was quite attractive."

"You didn't recognize her?" Tilda asked.

"I did not."

Tilda's expression became contemplative, her eyes narrowing slightly. "I wonder if it was the maid who resigned her post recently—Martha Farrow. I spoke with Clara about her, but she wasn't able to tell me much, such as why she left. I wonder if it's possible that she was the maid in Chambers' bed."

"He was having an affair with her too?" Hadrian was thoroughly disgusted by the dead man.

"I don't know, but given what we know of Chambers, it seems possible." Tilda spoke with an edge of derision. She refocused on Hadrian. "Do you have any idea whose memory you were seeing when you touched the chair?"

Hadrian shook his head. "No, but the person gestured, and I saw a woman's left hand and wrist. She wore a garnet-studded wedding band."

Admiration sparked in Tilda's gaze. "Hadrian, this is excellent information."

Whilst he was pleased by her reaction, he could not escape his own frustration—that only *he* could see what had happened. And through a wholly bizarre and inexplicable manner. "Except it only exists in my mind's eye. It's not proof we can use."

"No, but we've no reason not to trust what you see. It hasn't led us wrong yet."

That was true. It bolstered Hadrian's confidence whilst also making him wonder if the visions might mislead them someday. He hoped not. And he certainly hoped not now.

Tilda looked around the room in resignation. "I think we're finished here. Is it possible the maid you saw in the second vision was the same as the woman who crawled under the bed with her garments?"

"It seems more than possible. Do you know what Martha Farrow looked like?"

"No, but we can ask Beryl," Tilda said with a sly, brief smile. "I am quite eager to find Miss Farrow. Clara says her father is a solicitor in Stepney. I am hopeful we can find her through him. Alas, that will have to wait until tomorrow. I need to go home to my grandmother. She will wonder where I've been all day. I didn't tell her when I would return, but she may be growing slightly concerned."

"I can convey you home now, if you like."

"Thank you, I would appreciate that." She glanced away. "Unless there is a reason you need to stay here? I can take a hack."

He wondered again if she felt a touch of jealousy. "There is no need for me to remain. We can depart at your convenience."

Tilda moved to the doorway and turned to look back over the room, her eyes seeming to scrutinize every space. "Where does he dress? There is no clothing in here. The dresser held linens and some accessories. Is there a separate chamber?"

Hadrian looked at the corners of the wall behind the bed's headboard. A faint line in the dark-bronze-colored wallpaper drew his eye in the corner to the right of the bed—the same side of the bed on which he still stood. He walked to the wall and saw the release in the top of the wainscoting. He pressed the lever, and the door swung inward.

"Here's his dressing room."

"Brilliant," Tilda said with a smile, which Hadrian was delighted to see. She came around the bed and Hadrian waited for her to precede him into the newly revealed chamber. "Can you grab the lantern?"

Hadrian went to the mantel to fetch the lantern that had been left burning and brought it to the dressing room. Inside, there was a table with a mirror and a stool, along with an armoire and a tall dresser as well as a tub. There were also implements for the valet to do his job. Where *was* the valet? Perhaps he was upstairs in his chamber as the maid had been in hers.

Moving to the opposite side of the small chamber, Hadrian located another door. It led to a servants' staircase. "This is how the valet accesses his chamber from upstairs." He saw another door and moving to open it, he found the dining room. There were stairs down to the kitchen as well, which made sense.

He returned to the dressing room where Tilda was searching the table, opening drawers and looking beneath it. Pausing at the threshold from the servants' corridor, he braced his hand on the doorjamb. "There's a servants' staircase with access to the dining room as well as to the kitchen and the upper floors."

Hadrian grimaced as another pain shot through his temple. The vision rose fast and strong, a memory of the dressing chamber. A lantern burned low on the dressing table. The light from it glinted off the blade in the hand of the person this memory belonged to …

Gasping as a sharper pain tore through his head, Hadrian released the door.

Tilda was at his side, her hand on his arm. "Are you all right?" she asked softly.

Hadrian blinked to see her gaze was full of concern. He

nodded but winced as that only made his head hurt more. "I don't know whose memory I saw, but it was the killer, I think."

Tilda sucked in a breath. "Why do you think that?"

"Because they were holding a knife," he said darkly. "They came in through this door. And no, I didn't see the hand because they were wearing a dark glove. The vision was also too fast. And too painful." He cupped his hand to his forehead and tried to take a deep breath.

"You need to sit." She guided him to a stool and gently pushed him down, not that he needed much assistance. Sitting sounded rather necessary.

"Thank you," he rasped, his head pounding. Even if Tilda hadn't wanted to leave soon, he would ask to do so. "I ought to go home, I think."

"In a moment. You need to right yourself first. Can I fetch you anything? Water? Brandy? A cool cloth?"

All of those would probably help, but for now he was fine just sitting here with her. Tilda's company was most soothing.

He started to shake his head. "Dammit," he breathed. "I can't shake my head in these moments, and I always seem to forget."

"This spell seems worse than usual. Perhaps because you were already in pain. You need to put your gloves back on."

"Yes. Thankfully I stopped myself from nodding that time." He smiled, and even that added to his discomfort. He pulled his gloves from his pocket and donned them.

Tilda studied the door a moment. "The killer came in here, passed through the dressing chamber into Chambers' room, and killed him. He—or she—brought the knife, meaning they'd planned to kill him." She looked to Hadrian. "Was it a kitchen knife?"

"I think so, yes."

"Why come in this way and not through the study?" Tilda asked. "Unless they were a servant."

"That seems to make the most sense." Hadrian was having a

hard time thinking through his worsening headache. He'd no idea why some visions impacted him more adversely than others. All he could discern was that this one had been fast and strong. Perhaps those kinds of visions caused more pain. They also tended to be the most helpful.

He groaned. "Let us take our leave." He started to rise, and Tilda took his arm.

"Let me help you," she said, guiding him back into the bedchamber. She closed the door behind them.

"Thank you. I am very glad you know about this terrible affliction of mine. It is good to have at least one person I can lean upon." He tried another smile, but it was weak. "Literally," he added.

"I am sorry it affects you in this way." Her tone was low and deep with concern.

They walked through the study and made their way to the entrance hall, where they came face-to-face with Beryl and an exceptionally attractive woman in her early-thirties with gleaming blonde hair and the most exquisite heart-shaped face. Her blue eyes sparkled with a pleasing spirit that instantly made one want to befriend her. Or perhaps take her to bed.

Hadrian made that observation objectively. He was not attracted to her in that way. But he imagined many gentlemen were.

"There you are," Beryl said. "I was waiting for you to come so I could introduce you to Mrs. Styles-Rowdon." She turned her head toward the stunning woman. "Gillian, this is Lord Raven-hurst and Miss Wren."

"Ravenhurst," Mrs. Styles-Rowdon murmured. She almost sounded as if she were purring. "What a pleasure to make your acquaintance. Beryl has told me all about you." She smiled allur-ingly. Flirtatiously, even. Then she moved her gaze to Tilda. "And Miss Wren, I'm equally delighted to meet you. Beryl has told me you are helping her, and I am so glad a woman has come to her aid. She says you're an investigator. I confess I am agog. How absolutely wonderful!" She spoke with great animation, her hands moving and her features creasing with genuine interest.

"It's a pleasure to meet you too," Tilda said. "I'm happy I can be of service to Beryl. Now, you must excuse us, for we need to be on our way." She looked to Beryl. "We'll see you tomorrow before the inquest."

"Thank you. With you and my new widow's weeds from Gillian, I will be ready to face the coroner." Beryl smiled, but there was an underlying tenseness to her expression.

"I'll be there too," Mrs. Styles-Rowdon said. "For moral support. You need all the help and friends you can have at this time."

Beryl sniffed. "Thank you, Gillian. Could I trouble you to bring a batch of your cinnamon biscuits? It's been too long since I've had any."

Gillian gave Beryl a warm, sympathetic smile. "Of course, my dear."

Hadrian and Tilda bid them farewell and left. The cool breeze outside eased Hadrian's headache. He closed his eyes briefly as Tilda guided him toward the coach.

"Are you going to be all right?" she asked quietly.

"Yes. Don't say anything in front of Leach. I don't need my staff worrying over me."

"But it's fine for me to do so?" Her query was dry, her eyes glinting with humor.

"More than," he said as they reached the coach. He met her gaze and saw a surprising heat in her eyes—a warmth he felt too.

Then she looked away as Leach opened the door and she climbed inside. Hadrian followed her and situated himself on the seat beside her. He settled back against the seat and closed his eyes immediately.

Tilda sucked in a breath. "Blast."

He opened his eyes. "What's wrong?"

"I forgot to ask Beryl what Martha Farrow looked like." Her mouth turned into a deep frown. "I'll ask her tomorrow." Still, she looked very disappointed.

"We can go back," Hadrian offered, though he was rather eager to go home.

Tilda shook her head vehemently. "Absolutely not. I didn't think to ask her because I was concerned for you, and that worry has not lessened. You must rest," she added gently. "Close your eyes again."

"Thank you," he murmured, once again soothed by her.

As the coach rumbled along, Hadrian tried to think of the case and all they'd learned over the course of this incredibly busy day. But he only wanted to absorb the energy and warmth of the woman beside him and imagine her beautiful green eyes watching him with concern.

And wonder what may come in the future.

CHAPTER 9

*A*fter fetching her hat and gloves from her chamber on the first floor, Tilda went downstairs to await Hadrian. The inquest would begin at one o'clock that afternoon, and he would arrive to fetch Tilda at eleven. Tilda wanted to be sure they had time to answer any questions or soothe anyone's nerves at Beryl's house before they went to the Crown and Sceptre, the pub where the inquest would take place.

Tilda's grandmother was seated near the window in the parlor at the front of the house, taking advantage of the morning light to read a magazine. Half-moon glasses perched on her delicate nose. She looked up when Tilda walked in and smiled, the lines around her mouth deepening. "Lord Ravenhurst is due to arrive shortly?"

Last night, Tilda had told her grandmother about Louis Chambers' death and that she'd been hired to investigate the matter. However, she did not reveal that Hadrian was her client because she didn't want to share that he was a suspect. Instead, she'd explained that Hadrian was once again assisting her, which was true.

"Yes." Tilda set her gloves on a table and pinned her hat to her

hair. "Did I get that right?" she asked her grandmother. Sometimes when she donned a hat without the aid of a mirror, she set
it off-center or too far forward. Or too far back. Tilda was not as
adept with feminine tasks as someone like Beryl probably was.

Grandmama removed her glasses and surveyed Tilda. "A little
to the left. Your right, I suppose," she added with a chuckle.
Pursing her lips briefly, she ran her gaze over Tilda once more.
"You really do need a new gown or two. I know you say we can't
afford that right now, but I believe you must prioritize your
wardrobe, particularly since you are working with the earl again.
What a coincidence that is."

Tilda made the adjustment to her hat whilst ignoring her
grandmother's comments about purchasing new garments. They
probably could afford at least one gown, but she did not need to
spend the money.

Instead, she responded to her grandmother's comment about
Hadrian. "It is somewhat of a coincidence, yes." She had not told
her grandmother that Hadrian had once been betrothed to Beryl.
Rather, she'd offered the explanation that Hadrian had used on
several occasions—he and Beryl were old friends.

"Well, I am glad for it," Grandmama said with great satisfac-
tion. "I like the earl very much. I'm quite looking forward to
seeing him again. As is everyone, I think. Look, here's Mrs. Acorn
waiting for his arrival." She sent the housekeeper, who'd just
entered the parlor, a cheeky grin.

"I came to see if you wanted tea," Mrs. Acorn said, smoothing
her hands over her apron.

Tilda hid a smile. She knew everyone in the household liked
Hadrian. Just as she also knew that her grandmother and Mrs.
Acorn, in particular, hoped there might be something more than
a professional partnership between Tilda and Hadrian, despite
Tilda assuring them both there was not.

There was friendship and nothing more. Except the recurring
feelings of anticipation and excitement Tilda experienced when

she thought of him, or the jolts of heat and attraction that shot through her, such as when he'd taken her hand yesterday.

She was rescued from further contemplation by the arrival of his coach outside on the street. "He's here."

"I'm coming," Vaughn called from the entrance hall. The butler was just a year younger than Tilda's grandmother, but a lifetime of service had hunched his back. However, since he was exceedingly tall, he still towered over most people. He moved more slowly than Grandmama, his shuffling gait now a familiar sound. He worked hard, finding endless things to do to contribute to the household since joining them just a fortnight or so earlier. He'd been butler to Tilda's grandfather's cousin, whose murder she and Hadrian had solved. Instead of retirement, he'd made it clear he preferred to continue working. And so he was.

Tilda suspected it wasn't so much a desire to work but to be a part of something akin to a family, a place where he was needed and appreciated. She could understand that. After her father had died and it was just her and her mother, Tilda hadn't felt like she belonged. She'd never been as close to her mother, and when she decided to remarry, Tilda had jumped at the chance to move in with her grandmother instead of joining her mother and her new husband in Birmingham. Now she had only to tolerate visits with her mother and stepfather once or twice each year.

"Good morning, Lord Ravenhurst," Vaughn greeted from the entrance hall. "It's a delight to see you."

"I'm very pleased to see you as well, Vaughn," Hadrian replied. Tilda could hear the warmth in his voice from the parlor. "No lasting ill effects from that knock on your head?"

Vaughn had been the victim of a housebreaker before relocating from his former household to Tilda's grandmother's. He'd suffered a mild concussion, but he hadn't managed to remain in bed for the prescribed week.

"None at all," Vaughn said proudly.

"Glad to hear it." Hadrian appeared in the doorway. His gaze landed on Tilda first, and he smiled, then he looked to her grand-mother and the housekeeper. "Good morning, ladies. I hope I am not disturbing you too early."

"Of course not," Grandmama replied. "We were expecting you."

Tilda kept from rolling her eyes. Hadrian wasn't here to see all of them.

"I trust you are doing well?" Hadrian asked. He shifted his gaze to the housekeeper next. "And you, Mrs. Acorn."

"Yes, thank you, my lord," Mrs. Acorn murmured with a faint blush.

Tilda realized he had them all under some ridiculous spell that only a handsome member of the peerage could cast. For some reason, this bothered her today.

Or perhaps it wasn't that at all. Perhaps she was still faintly annoyed from yesterday when she'd walked into Chambers' study and seen Hadrian and Beryl together. They'd appeared intimate, and Tilda felt as though she were intrud-ing. Seeing them like that had provoked an agitating twist in Tilda's gut.

Hadrian said he was relieved to have avoided marrying Beryl, but perhaps his sentiments were changing. Tilda did not have time for such ridiculous meanderings in her mind. She needed to focus on the investigation at hand.

She realized Hadrian was chatting idly with her grandmother. Pulling on her gloves, Tilda waited for a break in the conversa-tion, then suggested they should go. She looked to her grand-mother. "I am not sure when I will return."

"I hope all goes well," Grandmama said. "I won't worry, espe-cially since you are with his lordship." She sent a grateful smile to the earl.

Now Tilda did gently roll her eyes. She did not need the earl to protect her, especially not when she was only going to an inquest.

So far. Who knew what the rest of the day would hold? Yesterday had taken them on quite a quest.

Everyone bade goodbye to Hadrian. Tilda's grandmother encouraged him to return any time for a social call. Hadrian said he would.

Hadrian sat across from her in the coach instead of beside her. Was that because he didn't want to be close to her? Perhaps things *were* changing between him and Beryl.

Tilda pushed the irritating thought aside. "I hope you are feeling better today."

"I am, thank you," he said with a smile. "I had a much-needed glass of brandy and restorative bath when I returned home. A wonderful dinner and a restful night's sleep has put me back to rights."

"Perhaps you should only allow yourself to have one vision per day," Tilda suggested. She didn't like him suffering.

"How will I manage that?" he asked with a light laugh. "This ability is beyond my control."

"Can't you simply put your gloves on after you have a vision? Then you won't have another."

He blew out a breath. "I suppose I could, but I don't like the notion of not seeing something that might be helpful. If I'd put my gloves on yesterday after the first vision, I would not have seen the killer enter the dressing room."

Tilda didn't like that part either, but she didn't want him to cause damage to himself. "It *is* helpful, but at what cost? Your health and well-being are vitally important."

He smiled. "Your concern is well-received. How about I agree to be careful going forward? If my head is troubling me over-much, as it was yesterday, I will don my gloves."

"You must do what you think is best," she said. "Just know that I am paying attention."

Hadrian touched his chest. "I am thrilled to have you watching over me."

Tilda wanted to speak with him about Clara. "I think it's important that Clara's past intimacy with Chambers is revealed at the inquest. Clara is worried how Beryl will react to this information and fears she'll be dismissed. Have you any idea what Beryl will do when she finds out?"

"I don't. It happened before Beryl married him, so perhaps she won't be too upset," Hadrian said. "Not to mention the fact that Clara was preyed upon by Chambers. I'm not sure I would blame her for what happened."

"I promised I will help her if Beryl throws her out. Clara doesn't have any family."

Hadrian frowned. "That's a shame. I will help too, if necessary. Speaking of family, I wondered if you might want to search for the other maid's father in Stepney after the inquest."

Tilda smiled. "I do, in fact. You know me too well."

"I think I may." He winked at her, and Tilda's insides did a joyful flip. "Should you tell Beryl about this before the inquest so she isn't surprised?"

"I suppose that would be best. Do you mind being with me when I tell her?"

"Not at all. I am eager to be of assistance to you." He leaned slightly forward as he met her gaze. "That is my job."

They arrived at Beryl's house. Leach opened the door and Hadrian stepped out. He then assisted Tilda to the ground. She'd grown accustomed to him touching her, always with his gloves on, in this perfunctory manner. But since he'd grabbed her bare hand yesterday—neither of them wearing gloves—this somehow felt different. She felt a brief frisson, a reminder of the electricity that had arced between them.

When they reached the door, Teague opened it.

Tilda blinked at him in surprise. She couldn't imagine why he was acting as butler. Where was Oswald? "Has something happened?"

"Come in," Teague said rather somberly. "Everyone is downstairs in the kitchen, including Mrs. Chambers. She's gone down to deliver the bad news I just gave her."

Tilda had stepped into the entrance hall whilst Teague held the door, and Hadrian had followed.

"What news is this?" Hadrian asked.

Teague closed the door. "We found Martha Farrow—the maid who resigned her post here about a fortnight ago."

Tilda tensed for the bad part of that news and feared the worst. "I don't suppose she'll be attending the inquest today?"

Shaking his head, Teague frowned. "She fell over a stair rail last night, tumbling three stories to her death."

~

Hadrian exchanged surprised looks with Tilda before frowning at Teague. "That is rather shocking. Where did this happen?"

"At the house where she was lodging in Spitalfields," Teague replied. "Her death was reported to the local branch, and I learned of it this morning."

"That is unfortunate," Tilda said softly. "Was she murdered?"

"As in pushed? She doesn't appear to have been," Teague said. "But there were no witnesses. Still, I have asked for a coroner to review her body and decide if there should be an inquest. I find it suspicious that she worked in this household where a murder was committed until recently when she resigned suddenly."

Tilda nodded. "I agree. I was hoping to find her after the inquest. Clara told me that Miss Farrow's father is a solicitor in Stepney. I'd intended to start there."

Teague's brows lifted. "Is he? All I know so far about Miss Farrow is that she has been lodging with a family called Jefford in Flower and Dean Street since leaving the Chambers' household. I haven't had time to speak with the lodging house owner yet, but I've sent a constable to conduct interviews as he can." He fixed his gaze on Tilda. "What were you hoping to learn from Miss Farrow?"

"Primarily, why she left. It seems that no jewelry has gone missing since her departure."

"You think she was stealing Mrs. Chambers' jewelry?" Teague asked.

Tilda lifted a shoulder. "I'm only collecting information at this point. I have not yet made any deductions. There is something else you should know. Louis Chambers was intimate with Clara Hicks, the maid, when she began working here six years ago. That continued until he wed Beryl."

Teague's mouth twisted into a brief expression of disgust. "Does Clara harbor ill will toward Chambers?"

"Not with regard to their relationship, as far as I could tell," Tilda replied. "However, Clara was upset to learn of Chambers' abuse of Beryl. She said Beryl was better off without him."

"Well, I think many of us can probably come to the same conclusion. Chambers was not a pleasant man. The number of people who wouldn't mind his death continues to grow." Teague blew out a breath. "Thank you for sharing that with me. I don't suppose there is anything else you learned that you think I should know?"

In the interest of moving himself further down the list of people who weren't upset about Chambers' death, Hadrian would have liked to tell Teague what he'd seen in his visions, but he could not. Instead, he and Tilda would work to find evidence to support what he'd seen. He could, however, share what he'd learned from the ledgers. "I looked through Louis Chambers' ledger yesterday."

"Ah, yes, so did one of the constables," Teague said with a nod. "I'm aware of the payments to Pollard and then lack of payments."

"And of the payment of twenty pounds to Oliver Chambers?" Hadrian asked.

"Yes. He is the new investor in Pollard's drapery shop."

Hadrian exchanged a look with Tilda. "Did Pollard tell you that yesterday?"

"Reluctantly," Teague said wryly. "When I asked why he was hesitant to share this news, he said he was worried it would cast suspicion on Oliver. Pollard went on to say that Oliver had approached him weeks ago with an offer to join in the business. Oliver knew his brother wasn't holding up his financial promises —Pollard explained that Louis hadn't been keeping up with his investment."

"I am most curious as to why Chambers was suddenly unable to continue his payments to Pollard," Tilda remarked.

"And why did he give his brother Oliver twenty pounds?" Hadrian mused. "Beryl thinks it was perhaps due to Oliver leaving his job as a curate. Louis may have just wanted to help him."

Teague stroked his jaw. "How did Louis Chambers even come up with twenty pounds when he was failing to meet his financial commitment to Pollard?"

"I think I know where he was getting the money," Tilda said. "Mrs. Chambers is missing nine pieces of jewelry. They began to disappear in December. She believes her husband stole them." Frowning, Tilda added, "Though if he was stealing them and selling them, why wasn't he then paying Pollard?"

Teague inclined his head. "A very good question. Presumably, he partnered with Pollard knowing he had the money to invest."

"Unless he didn't. Perhaps he was gambling to make money?" Hadrian suggested.

"That is possible," Tilda said vaguely. "I would like to better understand Chambers' financial situation—how he spent money and how much he had to begin with."

"His father founded a successful engineering firm," Hadrian said. "He was the second son of a large landowner in Hertford-shire. From what I understand, they have considerable wealth."

Teague scrutinized him a moment. "How do you know all that?"

"I was curious who my fiancée chose to marry instead of me," he responded with more derision than he probably ought.

"If Chambers' family has a great deal of money, why was he struggling to pay Pollard?" Teague asked. "I'll speak to his brothers. I have not yet interviewed them as thoroughly as I would like. The elder brother, Daniel, was too upset. And now the inquest is upon us. I should get to the pub. I'll see you there soon."

Teague departed, leaving Tilda and Hadrian in the entrance hall. "That's a shame about the maid," Hadrian said quietly.

"Yes," Tilda agreed. "I am most eager to visit the lodging house where she died."

Beryl walked into the entrance hall. She wore a modest black gown. "I didn't realize you'd arrived." Her nose and eyes were red.

"Teague let us in," Hadrian said. "We're so sorry to hear about your former maid."

"It's so shocking, especially after Louis." Beryl dabbed a handkerchief to her nose and sniffed.

Tilda looked at Beryl with sympathy. "I wonder if we might move to the parlor. I'm afraid I have more news to share."

Beryl blinked away tears. "I'm not sure I can withstand anything else."

"You will hear it at the inquest," Hadrian said gently. "We thought it may be best if you learned of it beforehand. No one has died," Hadrian added, hoping to reassure her.

They went into the parlor and Beryl sank onto the settee. Hadrian sat beside her and gave her an encouraging smile, then looked to Tilda who took a chair opposite them.

Tilda fixed her attention on Beryl. "When I spoke with Clara yesterday, she told me she and your husband had an intimate relationship before he married you."

Beryl stared at her. "Before?"

"Yes, and not since," Tilda said firmly. "Still, she is worried you will dismiss her."

"I'm—" Beryl shook her head. "I don't know what I am."

"Clara is quite loyal to you," Tilda said.

"Is she? I always thought she admired Louis." Beryl scoffed. "She seemed to."

"She may have, but when she learned of his abuse toward you and saw it for herself, she became your staunch supporter. She told me you are better off without him."

Beryl sniffed again. "I suppose that's nice."

There was a knock on the door. Beryl looked toward the entrance hall.

"I haven't seen Oswald return," Hadrian said. Their settee faced the entrance hall, and Hadrian hadn't noted the butler at all. "I'll answer the door."

Hadrian stood and made his way to the front door. Opening it, he was surprised to see a constable. Hadrian recognized him as one of the men who'd been at Beryl's house the previous day with Teague.

"Lord Ravenhurst, I'm to inform you and everyone in the household that the inquest has been postponed until Monday. Same time and place."

"Why?" Hadrian's blood was suddenly pumping faster. This seemed a significant change.

"I can't say, my lord. Will you deliver the message?"

"I will, thank you." Hadrian closed the door and returned to the parlor. Pressing his lips together, he met Tilda's gaze. "That was one of the constables who was here yesterday. The inquest has been postponed until Monday."

Tilda shot to her feet. "I heard you ask why but nothing else. What did he say?"

"That he couldn't say why."

Frowning, Tilda rushed to the entrance hall. Hadrian followed her, watching as she opened the door and stepped outside. She looked down the street where the constable was striding in the direction of the pub where the inquest was to be held.

"Do you want to go after him?" Hadrian asked.

"No." She exhaled, then turned back and stepped into the house.

Hadrian closed the door. "Why would they postpone the inquest? Does that happen often?"

"I don't know the answer to either of those questions. I'm inclined to seek Teague out and ask him, but we've other matters to investigate first." She looked up at him with firm determination.

It seemed to Hadrian she had a plan. "The lodging house in Spitalfields?"

She nodded. "Let us be on our way."

"We need to inform the household about the inquest," Hadrian noted.

Beryl appeared in the doorway to the parlor. "I'll tell everyone about the inquest being postponed. Though I don't know where Massey is. I don't believe he slept here last night, and no one has seen him."

"Does anyone know where he goes when he has his free nights?" Tilda asked.

Hadrian wished they'd been able to hear that part of Massey's conversation with Teague yesterday.

"He always said he was visiting family, but I don't know who or where that is," Beryl replied. Her expression turned sad once more. "Farrow would have known. They were rather friendly."

But Farrow was now dead. Her demise was proving to be a problem for their investigation, and Hadrian had to think that made her death even more interesting, if not suspicious.

Another knock on the door prompted them all to turn. Hadrian moved to answer it once more. This time, it was Beryl's elegant neighbor, Mrs. Styles-Rowdon. She smiled at Hadrian.

"Lord Ravenhurst, how lovely to see you." She carried a round tin with a landscape on the lid.

"Gillian, the inquest has been postponed until Monday!" Beryl said with some distress.

Mrs. Styles-Rowdon's features collapsed into a pout. "How stressful." She moved past Hadrian and gave the tin to Beryl. "It's good I brought cinnamon biscuits. Why has it been moved?"

Beryl's features smoothed slightly as she clutched the tin to her chest. "We don't know."

"And here, we rushed to alter your gown," Mrs. Styles-Rowdon said with a tsking sound. "Ah well, you look beautiful anyway, and that is something to be thankful for," she added with a warm, encouraging smile.

Hadrian was glad Beryl had such a good, supportive friend.

"If we hear why the inquest was postponed, we'll let you know." Hadrian suddenly recalled that they hadn't yet asked for a description of Martha Farrow. "Beryl, can you tell me what Martha Farrow looked like?"

Beryl's brow creased. "She had blonde hair and was very pretty. When I hired her after marrying Louis, he said she was too beautiful to be a maid. Why did you want to know that?"

Hadrian was certain the woman he'd seen in the vision from the chair was Martha Farrow. And she was probably the maid who'd been in Louis's bed, then had to scramble beneath it.

"I was only curious," he said vaguely. "We will take our leave now."

Beryl gave him a faint smile. "Thank you, Hadrian."

"Yes, thank you, Lord Ravenhurst," Mrs. Styles-Rowdon said enthusiastically. "You are a bright light in this dark time."

Hadrian opened the door for Tilda, and they departed.

As they walked toward his coach, she glanced over at him, murmuring, "A bright light in a dark time."

"That was a trifle amusing."

"She was flirting with you, I think," Tilda said.

"What? No. That would be inappropriate. It's a … dark time."

Tilda arched a brow at him, her eyes glinting with a hint of mirth that quickly disappeared as her features sobered. "Do you think Martha Farrow was the maid you saw in your visions?"

"I do."

"Let us be on our way to Spitalfields." Tilda pressed her lips together. "I'm not at all sure Martha Farrow's fall was an accident."

CHAPTER 10

Flower and Dean Street in Spitalfields was a noisy, run-down street that immediately put Hadrian on alert. He'd known it wasn't a nice area, but he hadn't been prepared for the filth and stench.

He looked over at Tilda as the coach slowed. "How do you suppose the daughter of a solicitor who'd worked as a maid in the west end found her way here?"

"Perhaps she didn't have much money when she left the Chambers' household. Though, if so, why would she resign in the first place? I wonder if it was not her choice to leave."

"Everyone in the household said she resigned," Hadrian noted.

Tilda met his gaze. "Everyone but her and Louis Chambers, neither of whom we can ask."

"Good point." Hadrian wondered why they had slowed. He rapped on the roof, and Leach pulled to the side of the road and stopped.

A moment later, the door opened to reveal Leach standing outside the coach.

"Why were we moving so slowly?" Hadrian asked.

"There are a few goats in the lane, my lord."

"Goats?" Tilda asked with a faint smirk. "I suppose we can get out here. We need to find the Jeffords' lodging house."

"I don't suppose you have your pistol with you?" Hadrian asked her.

"I do not." Her golden brows lifted. "I thought I would be spending my day at an inquest."

"Take mine, my lord," Leach said before disappearing for a moment. When he returned, he handed Hadrian the pistol he kept beneath his seat.

"What if you need it?" Hadrian asked.

Leach lifted a shoulder. "I'll manage. Better for you and Miss Wren to have it."

"Thank you, Leach." Hadrian tucked the weapon into his coat, then stepped out of the coach. He helped Tilda down and looked about. "Now what?"

"We ask someone where the Jeffords' lodging house is located." She surveyed his clothing and frowned. "I wish you didn't look so wealthy."

Hadrian barked out a laugh. "Perhaps I should keep a thread-bare coat in the coach."

"Not a bad idea," Tilda said, surprising Hadrian.

"I was joking."

"Were you? Well, you should consider it. Let me do the talking. Just arrange your expression into something unpleasant."

"What does that mean? Should I appear angry?"

She surveyed him, cocking her head. "Forbidding, I think. Is there anything you can do to make yourself unattractive?"

His blood heated because she found him attractive. He stuck his jaw out and narrowed his eyes. "How's this?"

"There's no hope of making you hard to look at," she said with a sigh. "But this will do. Cross your arms over your chest and try to appear intimidating." She spun about and began walking.

He hurried to fall into step beside her. Before he could ask what she meant to do, she approached a pair of women standing in a doorway.

Tilda grinned at them. "Afternoon, ladies," Tilda said in her Cockney accent, which Hadrian had heard a couple of weeks ago when they'd gone to a tavern in the east end in search of the man who'd stabbed him.

The two women eyed her dubiously. Their clothing was worn and shabby but also revealing. Their upper bosoms were quite exposed. Hadrian supposed they were prostitutes.

"I'm lookin' for the Jeffords' lodgin' 'ouse," Tilda said. "You know it?"

"Aye, it's up there, mayhap five or six 'ouses. It 'as a 'ook, because it used to be a butcher," one of them said with a nod of her head in the direction of the lodging house. "What do you want with it?"

"Someone died there last night," the other one said with rounded eyes.

Tilda stepped toward them. "I'd 'eard that." She'd lowered her voice. "What do you know of it?"

"She were a lodger," the first woman said. She sniffed and wiped her hand over her nose. "Might know more if you want to pay for it." She looked toward Hadrian with a glint of interest. Then she raked him with her gaze before licking her lower lip. "Though I might tell you in exchange for a tumble."

Had she just offered to give them information if Hadrian would lie with her? He would do as Tilda had said and let her speak, but it was difficult not to decline the woman's suggestion.

Tilda handed the woman a coin. "'E's not for barter. Besides, 'e's a clumsy dolt. Stole those clothes off a drunken gent and nearly got 'imself caught."

Hadrian quashed a smile. She was really too good at this.

"What do you know of the lodger?" Tilda prompted.

The woman squinted at the coin before tucking it into her

bodice. "Showed up 'ere a fortnight ago or so. Kept to 'erself, but I could see she was carryin'."

Tilda's nostrils flared. "She was with child?"

"Looked to be. I can spot 'em." The prostitute tapped her face next to her right eye. "I see everythin'."

"What else did ye see?" Tilda asked. "Anyone visit 'er?"

The prostitute put her hand on her hip and her gaze turned skeptical. "Why do you want to know?"

"She worked with a friend o' mine, and I said I'd try to find out what 'appened to 'er." Tilda spoke casually, as if she weren't hungry for every piece of information she could gather. But Hadrian knew differently.

"Told you everythin' I saw," the prostitute said, her focus moving past them. "Fancy coach you got there." She narrowed her eyes at Hadrian. "You steal that too?"

"Belongs to me employer," Tilda snapped. She grabbed Hadrian's arm and turned, stalking quickly to the coach.

She paused at the door and spoke to Leach. "We're going up the street about five houses. You'll let us out again, but then you'll need to keep moving. This coach is drawing too much attention."

"I can't leave you here," Leach said as he cast a glance toward the prostitutes who were watching them with interest.

"You'll give us fifteen minutes and return. We'll be sure to be done by then." Tilda took his hand and stepped into the coach.

Leach looked at Hadrian in question. "You heard her." He followed Tilda inside and sat down beside her. The coach began moving almost immediately. Leach was in a hurry, and Hadrian was grateful for that. He wanted to minimize their time here in Flower and Dean Street.

Hadrian looked over at Tilda. "You are frighteningly good at transforming into a different person entirely. You could have a career on the stage."

"But there is no investigation in that career," she said with a smile. "I hope you weren't too offended by the prostitute's proposal."

"Not at all. I was too preoccupied with my surprise."

Tilda laughed lightly as the coach came to a stop. "I'd like to confirm Martha's pregnancy with the lodging house owner if we can."

Leach opened the door, and Hadrian climbed down. He helped Tilda out and said to Leach that they'd see him in a quarter hour.

As the coach pulled away, Hadrian felt a slight nip of anxiety. He turned to the house with Tilda. "Is this it?"

She inclined her head toward the hook hanging near the door. "Looks to be."

"Do I still need to look intimidating?" he asked.

"No, your name should take care of that. Just be yourself—the Earl of Ravenhurst. Say you are asking after Martha because she used to work in your household."

He nodded. "Who are you then?"

She straightened her shoulders, her attention on the house, a brick-and-timber structure in need of maintenance. "Your housekeeper."

"Why not my wife?"

Tilda snapped her gaze to his, her lips pursing. She glanced down at herself. "My garments are not as fine as yours. I look more like your housekeeper than your wife."

Hadrian wanted to argue, but it was true. Her gown was of a decent quality, but it was outmoded and not at all something a young countess would be wearing. He exhaled in frustration. He didn't like that they looked as though they didn't belong together. "Mrs. Wren, then."

They walked to the door, and he knocked. A moment later, it opened to reveal a woman in her middle thirties. She wore an apron and a cap atop a pinned-up mass of frizzy dark hair. Her gaze moved over them, lingering on Hadrian before narrowing her eyes. "What do ye want?"

"I'm inquiring about the lodger who died here last night," Hadrian said. "I am Lord Ravenhurst, and Miss Farrow once worked in my household."

The woman's eyes widened. "Do ye want to come in, your lordship?"

Hadrian gave her a mild smile. "If you don't mind. This is my housekeeper, Mrs. Wren."

The woman closed the door after they moved into the dim entrance hall. "I'm Mrs. Jefford. We feel badly about what 'appened to Miss Farrow, but it weren't our fault. She must 'ave tripped. Ye know 'ow it can be when you're carryin' a babe. You can be clumsy sometimes." Her eyes rounded once more. "You likely *don't* know that."

"Had she married then?" Tilda asked. "She was unwed when she worked for us."

Mrs. Jefford shook her head. "Not that I know. She were by 'erself. Couple people visited 'er though, and one were a man. 'E could 'ave been the father, I suppose."

"Did you know his name?" Hadrian asked, wondering if it could have been Chambers.

"No. 'E only came one time that I saw."

"Can you describe what he looked like?" Tilda gave her a soft smile. "One of our footmen liked Miss Farrow a great deal. I believe they saw each other after she left our household."

"'E were tall and dressed in dark clothes. 'Is 'air flopped in front." Mrs. Jefford motioned over her forehead with her hand.

Hadrian immediately thought of Chambers' valet, Massey.

"That doesn't sound like our footman," Tilda said. "Did anyone else visit Miss Farrow?"

"A woman, but she wore a veil, so I can't tell you what she looked like. She came twice. That I know of. I didn't see 'er the second time, but my daughter said she saw 'er 'ere last night."

Hadrian's pulse quickened. Perhaps there had been a witness to Miss Farrow's fall.

"Was that around when Miss Farrow fell?" Tilda asked.

Mrs. Jefford shrugged. "I don't know. We didn't 'ear anything as we were eatin' dinner downstairs. My daughter saw the woman in the veil arrive as she was coming down to eat. We didn't find Miss Farrow until later. She was lyin' in the stairwell in a pool of blood." Mrs. Jefford pivoted and motioned through a doorway. Hadrian could see the stairs.

"Would you mind if we went to her room?" Tilda asked, her features set with deep concern. "I'm hoping to find something I can give to her parents."

"The constable who was 'ere said not to let anyone up there." Mrs. Jefford sounded as though she could perhaps be persuaded otherwise.

Hadrian took a couple coins from his pocket and handed them to her. "We would be greatly obliged."

Mrs. Jefford immediately pocketed the coins. "Top floor, first door on the left."

"Thank you, Mrs. Jefford," Tilda said with a grateful smile before walking into the stairwell.

Hadrian followed her and paused to look at the floor where Martha Farrow would have landed. Whatever mess had been created had been cleaned.

"There's some blood here," Tilda said, leaning down.

Not thoroughly cleaned then.

Hadrian joined her and saw the smudge of blood on the floorboards. "Such a shame, especially as she was with child."

Tilda straightened. "I am quite eager to know who the father was, but I'm afraid I can guess since we know she was working in the Chambers household until recently."

"And it's likely she was sharing Louis Chambers' bed," Hadrian said, loathing the man even more than he had before. "The man was truly despicable."

"Particularly if he was aware of the child. Perhaps she told him, and he evicted her from the household. Let us look in

Martha's room."

Hadrian followed Tilda, pausing at the first and second landings to look down. When they reached the third one—the top—he stood there a moment. "That's a terrifying fall."

Tilda looked over the rail and grimaced. "Yes. And how did it happen? I'm not sure I believe Mrs. Jefford's claim of clumsiness. This rail seems high enough that Martha wouldn't have fallen over it by accident."

"Do you think she may have been pushed?"

Tilda moved closer to it and touched the wood. The railing moved.

Gasping, Tilda jumped back just as Hadrian curled his arm around her waist, pulling her against his chest. She was breathing heavily—as was he.

They stood like that a moment, long enough for Hadrian to realize he needed to let her go. But also to acknowledge that she seemed content to be in his arms. Likely because she was terrified.

"I see how Martha may have fallen," Tilda said breathlessly. "And why Mrs. Jefford would want to say they weren't at fault since that railing is not secure."

They eased apart, and Hadrian asked, "Are you all right?"

"I feel a little unsteady," she replied. "I think I'll stand over here." She moved away from the railing to the opening of a short corridor with two doors on either side. These had likely been servants' quarters when the house was built decades before.

Whipping off his glove, Hadrian made sure he was not too close to the railing before touching it gingerly. He was hoping for a sensation or a vision, but there was nothing.

He cautiously wiggled the railing, ascertaining how loose it was. He was surprised it hadn't come free when Martha had fallen.

Or had it?

He moved to where it was attached to the wall and again gave it a rattle. It separated from the wall, and he released it, stepping back. "I think this may have broken and has since been repaired —though quite shoddily. Perhaps Mr. Jefford sought to improve the state of the railing so he wouldn't be blamed for Martha's death."

"Well, he did a rather poor job," Tilda remarked as she turned toward the door Mrs. Jefford had indicated. Pushing open the door, she walked into the room.

The chamber was small, with a low ceiling and a minimum of furniture. There was a narrow bed, a chair and tiny table, and a dresser with three drawers. Rather, it had space for three, but there were only two present.

"I suppose you should touch something, but please be mindful of how many visions you allow," Tilda warned.

Hadrian appreciated her concern, but he wasn't sure if he'd even be able to sense any of Martha's memories since she was newly dead—*if* that was a parameter of his unpredictable ability. What he did know—or thought he knew—was that whatever he touched with his bare skin also had to have touched the other person's bare skin in order for him to see their memories. Rather, to have a *chance* to see them. With this infernal ability, nothing was guaranteed, except the accompanying headache.

Whilst Tilda looked through the shabby dresser, he touched the door. Nothing.

He moved farther into the room and ran his hand over the back of the single chair. Still nothing.

"Hadrian." Tilda sounded almost breathless. "I found one of Beryl's missing pieces of jewelry."

Pivoting, Hadrian moved to her side. She held a brooch shaped like a flower made of what looked to be diamonds and topaz with emeralds for the leaves. It was stunning. "You're certain that belonged to Beryl?"

"It matches the description she gave me." She looked at Hadrian. "Teague said he dispatched a constable here, but if he searched the room, why would this still be here?"

"Perhaps the constable hasn't come yet. Or at least, he hasn't searched this room. Could they have been busy with the inquest and other matters?"

"That's possible, but I don't think we should leave it here." She held it out to him. "You should touch it."

Hadrian took the brooch, and for the first time, he felt a warm sensation in his hand. "That's odd."

"What?" Tilda asked, again sounding exhilarated. He realized he loved that tone of hers.

A vision began to unfurl in his mind. "One moment," he breathed, immersing himself in what he saw so that the room around him, including Tilda, faded.

He saw Louis Chambers, his face set into deep, tension-filled lines. His thick brows were drawn over his eyes which were fixed on someone—whoever's memory Hadrian was experiencing. His lips moved, so Hadrian deduced he was speaking to someone.

Chambers handed the brooch to the person. Hadrian looked at the hand—it was a woman's and had the same blunt nails and work-roughened skin as the woman in the second vision he'd seen in Chambers' bed.

A wave of anger rattled Hadrian along with a sense of injustice. He felt intense outrage toward Chambers.

Pain filtered through Hadrian's head, and the vision began to dissipate. Tilda returned to his vision, her green eyes caressing him with both concern and her indefatigable curiosity.

Fixing on her somehow made the ache in his head more bearable. He took a deep breath, realizing he'd been holding it.

"What did you see?" she asked softly.

"Louis Chambers. He looked unhappy or agitated. Perhaps both. He spoke to whoever's memory this was, but of course I couldn't hear what he said. I should probably learn to read lips," he quipped.

Tilda's features eased into a smile. "Perhaps. Do you think you were seeing Martha's memory?"

"I can't say, but he handed her the brooch. I know it was a woman's memory because of the hand. And the hand looked similar. It may have been the same as the one I saw yesterday belonging to the maid who'd been in his bed and then had to hide under it."

"We wondered if that could be Martha," Tilda said in a low voice. "Does this confirm it?"

"My suspicion is stronger, but I am not certain." Hadrian felt a wave of frustration with this infernal power. "I'm inclined to think it wasn't since she very recently died, and I haven't ever been able to see the memory of someone who only just passed." He gave the brooch back to Tilda. "Whoever it was felt angry and as if they were being done wrong—whatever was happening seemed unjust to them. The strangest thing was that I felt a warmth in my hand before the vision came. That has never happened before."

"Perhaps it signifies you are now able to see the memories of those who are newly deceased." Tilda shrugged. "Just a suggestion."

"In the absence of instructions on how this power works, suggestions are all I have," he said drily.

"Let us consider for a moment that you *were* seeing Martha's memory." Tilda's gaze lost focus on him as her mind worked. "You said the person felt angry and wronged. Martha was with child. If she'd told Chambers about it and his response was to toss her out, she would feel those things."

"Yet, he also gave her a very expensive brooch, so he didn't completely ignore her plight. That does nothing to improve my opinion of him, however."

"Nor mine." She tucked the brooch into her reticule. "We should go. I fear we are nearly at our quarter-hour limit." She preceded him from the room, and he closed the door behind them.

As they approached the stairs, Hadrian thought of how he'd caught Tilda in his arms when the railing had moved. What if she'd lost her balance? A shudder tore through him. It was a thoroughly terrifying thought, and one he did not wish to entertain. Better to think of how she'd felt in his embrace, of her feminine, slightly floral scent.

On the way downstairs, Tilda asked, "Did Mrs. Jefford's description of Martha's male visitor remind you of Massey?"

"It did. I'm sure you're anxious to speak with him."

"I am, though I don't know where to find him. I think we must go to Scotland Yard and find Teague. Hopefully, he will tell us where we can find Massey, as well as why the inquest was postponed."

"Should we give him the brooch too?" Hadrian asked as they neared the ground floor.

"Probably, though I wonder if we should keep it in case you can try to feel something else from it in the future." She looked over at him as they walked toward the front door. "You held on to that ring for a long time, and it was useful to you."

She was referring to the ring that Hadrian had removed from the hand of the man who'd stabbed him. He hadn't realized he'd had it at first, and when his valet had given it to him days later, Hadrian's strange power had awakened. Touching that ring had given him his first vision.

Hadrian hadn't meant to withhold the ring from the police, but when they'd decided his attack had been perpetrated by a footpad and Hadrian's vision had told him that was not the case, he'd held onto it. "If we keep the brooch and give it to Teague at a later time, I don't think he'll be pleased." Hadrian opened the door for her, and they stepped outside.

"No, he won't." Tilda sighed. "We'll give it to him. I can hope doing so will persuade him to share what he can about Massey and the inquest."

Hadrian was glad to see his coach coming toward them.

"Excellent timing, Leach," he murmured.

After instructing the coachman to take them to Scotland Yard, Hadrian helped Tilda into the coach. He sat beside her on the forward-facing seat, and they were quickly on their way.

"That was a most helpful excursion," Tilda said. "I find myself feeling quite sorry for Martha Farrow."

"I do as well. But we still don't know if her death was an accident or not."

Tilda looked over at him, her eyes gleaming vibrantly. "We need to find the woman in the veil."

CHAPTER 11

*I*t was mid-afternoon when they arrived at Scotland Yard. Hadrian escorted Tilda into the building, and she asked if Detective Inspector Teague was available.

A constable showed them to Teague's office where the inspector was seated behind his desk. He wiped his mouth with a napkin and stood as they entered.

"I was just finishing lunch," Teague said. "Busy day, and I'm only here for a short while."

Tilda moved to stand near his desk. "We're sorry to disturb you, but we've just visited the Jeffords' boarding house in Spitalfields."

"I take it you've something to share?" Teague said.

"Yes, but first I'd like to know why the inquest was postponed," Tilda replied. "Did something happen?"

Teague tossed his napkin onto the desk next to a greasy paper wrapping that had likely once contained his lunch. "All I can say is that the coroner decided to do a more thorough post-mortem examination."

"What prompted that?" Hadrian asked.

"I repeat that this is all I can tell you," Teague replied, looking pointedly at both of them. "What did you learn in Spitalfields?"

Tilda removed the brooch from her reticule. "We found this in Martha Farrow's room. Did your constable miss it?" She held the piece out on her palm.

A scowl twisted Teague's features momentarily. "The constable hasn't been there yet. We were shorthanded, and I needed a pair of men to search the Chambers' house again from top to bottom."

Tilda would have wagered the search had something to do with the additional post-mortem examination but didn't ask. She could visit Beryl and hopefully find out what had taken place.

Teague picked up the brooch from Tilda's palm. "Where did you find this?"

"In a dresser drawer. It belongs to Beryl Chambers," Tilda said.

"You're sure?" Teague asked, his brows arching.

"It matches the description of one of the missing items and was the last of the pieces to disappear—just before Martha Farrow left the household."

"It would appear she stole it then."

Tilda couldn't tell him that Martha hadn't stolen it, that Chambers had given it to her. However, Martha would have recognized it as belonging to Beryl. Not returning it to her was as good as stealing.

Teague turned the brooch over in his hand. "But why hasn't she sold it? She could have used the funds to stay somewhere far nicer and safer than Flower and Dean Street."

Tilda lifted a shoulder. "Perhaps she'd planned to do so and just hadn't yet." Except why wait? And since she hadn't sold it, she must have had other funds to pay for her lodging the past several days.

"Did you learn anything else?" Teague asked.

Tilda wasn't sure she wanted to tell him more, not when he

was withholding information about why the inquest was postponed.

Teague must have sensed her hesitation. He glanced toward Hadrian who stood beside her. "If your goal is to convince me of Ravenhurst's innocence, you should share any information with me that would help with that endeavor."

"Does the inquest postponement have anything to do with Hadrian?" Tilda asked.

"Not that I am aware of, but this is an ongoing investigation." He gave her a direct stare, his brown eyes fixed on her. "I have not yet learned anything that has proven Ravenhurst was involved in Chambers' murder. If you have information that would help my investigation, I would appreciate you sharing it."

"We interviewed Mrs. Jefford," Tilda said finally. "As well as a pair of local women. All of them said Martha was carrying a child."

"Bloody hell," Teague whispered. "Was the father with her?"

"No, we suspect Chambers sired the babe," Tilda said. "It just makes sense given what we know of him." And definitely not because Hadrian had seen a vision that seemed to indicate Martha Farrow had shared Chambers' bed. She glanced at Hadrian who gave her an almost imperceptible nod.

"I agree it makes sense," Teague said. "Too bad we can't question Miss Farrow." He shook his head.

"And doesn't that make you suspect her death was not an accident?" Tilda asked.

"It's definitely suspicious. However, now that we know she was with child and that Chambers may have fathered the babe, we must also consider that she may have had motive to kill him."

Tilda had thought so too. "I'd like to speak with her family at least."

"You can try, but her father doesn't have much to say about her. I called on him in Arbour Square earlier. He's a solicitor at the Thames Magistrate Court."

Hadrian crossed his arms over his chest as his brows pitched low over his eyes. "How on earth does his daughter end up as a maid and then living in a shoddy boarding house in one of London's worst rookeries?"

Teague frowned. "She was expelled from her house at the age of sixteen because she was with child."

Tilda wondered what had happened to that babe. Martha hadn't had a child when she'd worked in the Chambers' household. "How terrible for her to be turned out by her own family," Tilda said quietly.

"Her father has not softened over the years. He showed no sadness for her death and even indicated he wanted to leave her to a pauper's grave. However, his wife insisted they bury her in a plot."

Tilda wished things had turned out differently for the young woman. And she was determined to find justice for Martha if she'd been pushed over that stair railing. She decided to tell Teague about the veiled woman—they needed all the help they could manage if they wanted to find her. "Mrs. Jefford said that Martha had two visitors. Once was a woman in a veil who called at least twice, including last evening. She arrived as they were about to have dinner, and Mrs. Jefford did not see when the woman departed."

Teague arched a sardonic brow. "A woman in a veil? That's not suspicious. Who was the second visitor?"

"We think it was Massey based on Mrs. Jefford's description," Hadrian replied.

"Well, that is interesting," Teague said slowly, his gaze focused somewhere on the wall behind them as he appeared to be contemplating this latest bit of information.

"I'd like to speak to Massey, but he did not sleep at Beryl's house last night, nor was he there this morning," Tilda said. "I don't suppose you would tell us where we may find him? I suspect he's wherever he spends the nights he is not at the Chambers' house."

Teague hesitated, and Tilda began to grow frustrated. She'd shared a great deal of information with the man. "It's rather sensitive," Teague said at last.

Hadrian uncrossed his arms. "In what way?"

"He spends his free nights at a brothel called the Cock and Hen on Craven Street near Charing Cross." Teague pinned them both with an intense stare. "It is not a typical brothel. He didn't say what he does there, but I know they cater to a variety of tastes." He focused on Hadrian. "You can't take Miss Wren there."

"I decide where I go, Inspector," Tilda said crossly.

Hadrian gave Teague a cool smile. "You heard her."

Teague nodded as he exhaled. "Why do you think Massey visited Miss Farrow?"

"They were friends, according to Beryl," Tilda replied. "Friends who could have conspired to kill their employer."

"Massey is not a suspect," Teague noted. "Unless you've deduced something I have not." He sounded dubious.

"Not yet," Tilda said with a smile. "My suspects are Beryl, Pollard, Oliver Chambers, and Martha Farrow. Do our lists match?"

"I would add Lord Ravenhurst." He cast Hadrian an apologetic glance.

Tilda saw Hadrian scowl from the corner of her eye. "I have eliminated him as a suspect. He does not have a strong enough motive, and I believe he was at home all night when Chambers was murdered."

Teague's brows slanted down. "Chambers apparently despised him and stole Ravenhurst's fiancée. You don't think that is enough motivation?"

"We've no idea why Chambers disliked Hadrian so much, and Hadrian certainly didn't return the sentiment. He hardly thought of the man at all and definitely didn't hold a grudge over losing

Beryl to him. Indeed, Hadrian had decided he and Beryl didn't suit, so Chambers, in fact, did him a favor." Tilda didn't clarify when Hadrian had made that decision, and it sounded as though he'd done so perhaps even whilst they were still betrothed. In fact, she had no issue with Teague interpreting it that way.

"I see. Well, that is helpful to know. I am still not ready to remove Ravenhurst from my list of suspects."

Tilda hardened her gaze upon Teague. "So long as you also consider that it would benefit the killer if focus was directed at Ravenhurst, who is innocent."

Teague inclined his head as he moved from behind his desk. "I understand. Now I must be on my way to Spitalfields to take an official report from Mr. and Mrs. Jefford."

"We'll leave you to it," Hadrian said.

"Thank you for the brooch." Teague gestured toward Tilda with the piece of jewelry.

"We'll see you at the inquest on Monday," she replied.

They left Teague's office, and Tilda couldn't help feeling slightly frustrated. When they were outside and walking toward Hadrian's coach, she finally said, "I am trying to think of why the coroner would postpone the inquest to conduct a more thorough post-mortem examination. What prompted him to do that? Or was he instructed to do that by someone else?"

"Who would have done that?" Hadrian asked.

"I've no idea. Coroners are often self-important, or so my father used to say. So, it's perhaps more likely that the decision came from him. I just want to know *why*."

They arrived at the coach, and Hadrian pivoted to face her. "I appreciate what you said to Teague about me being innocent."

"I do trust him to be thorough in his investigation," she said. "But I also felt the need to point out that there is focus on you when there needn't be. You did not have a relationship with Beryl, and you did not wish Louis Chambers ill."

He gave her a faint smile laced with understanding. "I'm sorry you're aggravated."

Tilda worked to push her annoyance aside and focus on what she could do to continue her investigation. "At least we can go question Massey now."

Hadrian's brow puckered, and his mouth tipped into a slight frown. "We've already survived one threatening environment today, should we really enter another?"

"Craven Street won't be as bad as Flower and Dean," Tilda said with a smile.

"Perhaps not, but the Cock and Hen may not be an appropriate place for you to visit." He spoke cautiously, probably because he knew Tilda would disagree.

"I don't care about such things," she said perhaps a bit too sternly. "Particularly when I am conducting an investigation. Though in truth, I've no reason to visit a place like that when I am not." She met his gaze and held it a moment. "Please don't worry. You can take Leach's pistol again if it will make you feel better."

"I will," Hadrian said before informing Leach of their destination.

"Happy to give you the pistol when we arrive, my lord," he said with an affable nod before handing Tilda into the coach.

"Thank you, Leach." She settled herself on the forward-facing seat as Hadrian sat down beside her.

As they began moving, Hadrian asked, "Is there any place you wouldn't go in the effort of solving a crime?"

"Nothing comes to mind, but I suppose it would depend on the specific situation. For example, I am not sure I would have ventured to Flower and Dean Street after dark. At least, not without fetching my pistol first."

"Perhaps I should start carrying a pistol," Hadrian said.

"Don't feel as though you need to. I am quite capable of seeing after myself."

Hadrian looked over at her, his eyes dark and somewhat intense. "I will always protect you, whether you think it's necessary or not. And don't think to debate me." He shifted his gaze forward, and Tilda regarded his handsome profile. The set of his jaw told her he was quite serious about keeping her safe.

Tilda wouldn't quarrel with that. "I do think if I can manage an evening at Northumberland House, as we did recently, the Cock and Hen will be easy."

This lightened Hadrian's expression, and he laughed. "I don't think they are comparable, but I understand your point. You are willing to venture wherever necessary to conduct your investigation." He inclined his head. "I'm just glad you're allowing me to come along."

~

The Cock and Hen appeared to be a somewhat respectable establishment. It was at least in better condition and tidier than most of what they'd seen earlier in Spitalfields.

Leach parked the coach across the street, and once again gave Hadrian his pistol.

Tilda took Hadrian's arm as they made their way to the brothel, which looked rather like a tavern. It even had a common area with a bar. There were no customers, however, perhaps due to it being afternoon.

A middle-aged woman came from behind the bar and greeted them, her expression cautious. She wore an elaborate hairstyle that looked as though it were from another era but was also quite flattering. The color was a vibrant red, which made Hadrian think it was likely a wig. Her features were painted with cosmetics, and her lips were scarlet.

"Good afternoon," she said with a dark, husky voice. "How can I help you?"

Hadrian wasn't sure what to say, so he left the response to Tilda.

Smiling, Tilda inclined her head at the woman. "Good afternoon. We are looking for a young man called Massey."

The woman fluttered her lashes and gave them a patient half smile. "What makes you think you'd find him here?"

"We know he is here," Tilda replied. "If you would tell him that Lord Ravenhurst and Miss Wren wish to speak with him, we would be most obliged."

Surprise flickered across the woman's features at the mention of a nobleman. She dipped a brief curtsey to Hadrian. "Your lordship. Your need to speak with Massey must be urgent if you decided to come here. Why don't you follow me to the sitting room, so you aren't seen in the common area? I'm Mrs. Longbotham." She led them to a doorway at the back of the common room into a short corridor and then into a room on the right, gesturing for Tilda and Hadrian to go in before her.

Windowless, the room was covered in mirrors and several bright lanterns ensured there was plenty of light. The furniture was boldly colored with red, orange, and a brilliant blue.

"Wait here, and I'll see if Massey wishes to receive you." Mrs. Longbotham turned from the doorway in a rustle of dark-bronze silk.

"Should we sit?" Hadrian asked.

"You can if you wish, but I'll wait to see if Massey arrives," Tilda said. "Rather, if he *receives* us." She waggled her brows.

"Mrs. Longbotham seems rather formal for an establishment such as this," Hadrian noted. She was dressed for an evening out, she'd curtsied to Hadrian, and she'd behaved as if they were paying a call at someone's residence. "Her hair was rather astonishing, though I do suspect it is a wig."

Tilda arched her brow at him briefly as she took a step toward him, so they were rather close. "You do realize that Mrs. Longbotham isn't a woman," she whispered.

Hadrian blinked. "Indeed? I found her attractive."

"She is," Tilda replied in agreement. "At least in my estimation."

"But she is not a she," Hadrian said despite visual evidence to the contrary. She certainly looked like a woman.

"Teague did say the Cock and Hen catered to a variety of tastes." Tilda kept her voice low and looked toward the doorway. "I wonder if Massey will be dressed as a woman."

Hadrian tried to imagine that and found he could. "I daresay he would also be attractive. Now I am wondering how I might look in a gown."

Tilda surveyed him, her eyes moving over him from his boots to his hat. Heat pricked through him under the heady weight of her perusal. She looked abruptly away from him and took several steps toward the center of the room as her gaze moved around the space. He wondered if she'd felt the same blistering warmth.

A moment later, Massey entered the room. He eyed them both with considerable wariness. "How did you find me here?"

Tilda faced him. "Detective Inspector Teague told us."

Massey's face lost a bit of color. "What else did he tell you?"

"That this is where you spend your evenings off," Tilda replied. "However, we are not here to trouble you about that. We have come to speak with you about Martha Farrow. You are aware she has died?"

The valet moved to the nearest seat—a chair with a red-and-orange floral pattern—and sank down as he covered his mouth.

Hadrian felt a surge of sympathy for the young man, as it seemed he had not known.

"I'm sorry," Tilda said, moving closer to Massey and perching on a chair near his. "I should have revealed that information in a more sensitive manner." She glanced up at Hadrian with a light grimace.

Joining them in the seating area, Hadrian sat in a third chair and angled himself toward Massey. "Please take all the time you need to acclimate yourself to this news. We understand from Beryl—Mrs. Chambers—that you and Miss Farrow were friends."

Massey pulled a handkerchief from his pocket and dabbed at his eyes. "We were. She was …" He cut himself off before saying whatever he'd meant to. He lifted his gaze to look at each of them. "Is that why the inquest was postponed? I went to the pub as I was summoned to do but learned it would take place on Monday instead."

"We aren't sure why it was delayed," Tilda said. "We learned of Miss Farrow's death just this morning when we arrived at the Chambers' house."

"I haven't gone there today." Massey wiped his nose. "I fetched some belongings yesterday. I didn't think I should remain there now that my employer is gone."

"But you could, I'm sure," Hadrian said. "Why would you think you needed to leave?"

"Mrs. Chambers doesn't care for me, and the feeling is mutual." Massey's lips pursed but he blinked the expression away before regarding them intently. "How did Martha die?"

"She fell over the railing at the house where she was lodging in Spitalfields," Tilda said gently. "Did you visit her there recently?"

Massey's gaze turned wary once more.

Tilda clasped her hands in her lap. "We know you did. We also know that Martha was expecting a child."

Nodding, Massey dabbed the handkerchief to his eyes once more.

"Was your employer the babe's father?" Tilda asked.

Massey sucked in a breath. "How did you know?"

Tilda exchanged a brief look with Hadrian. They could not reveal his visions, of course. "I wasn't certain, but I appreciate you confirming that," she said with a soft smile. "Do you know why she resigned her post?"

"You already know the answer to that," Massey said. "She was with child. She couldn't stay there."

Hadrian thought of the visions he'd had, particularly of how the woman who'd received the brooch from Louis Chambers had felt. Martha Farrow was likely that woman, and she'd felt as though she'd been wronged. "But was leaving entirely her decision?"

"No," Massey whispered. "She didn't want to lose her position, which meant she couldn't have the babe. She asked Mr. Chambers for money to take care of it, but he said he wouldn't help her and that she had to leave. She refused, so he gave her one of Mrs. Chambers' brooches and told her to sell it. He also offered to give her a reference."

Hadrian wondered why Martha hadn't sold the brooch.

Tilda gave the valet an encouraging smile. "We appreciate your telling us this, Massey. I found the brooch in Martha's room at the lodging house. Have you any idea why she didn't sell it?"

Massey rubbed his palms along his thighs in an agitated manner. "She tried, but the pawnbroker accused her of stealing it. He said someone like her wouldn't have something that nice, and he would fetch the police." The valet gave them a mournful look. "She was just trying to do what she could to survive. I know you'll think she was foolish to lie with Mr. Chambers, but Martha thought she loved him. Her family had turned her out. She only wanted to be loved."

"I'm sorry she struggled," Hadrian said.

"When and why did you visit her at the lodging house?" Tilda asked.

"She sent me a note asking me to come, saying she needed money. I took her what I could. That was last Sunday."

"Then you were aware of Mr. Chambers' infidelity?" Tilda prompted. "You indicated to Detective Inspector Teague that you were not."

Massey's face flushed. "How could I not be?" His brows

pitched in anger. "Mr. Chambers treated Martha horribly. After he turned her out, he lamented to me about what a strumpet she was and how she'd lured him to her bed. It's as if he thought I wasn't aware of what went on here." His lip curled, and his eyes were darkly furious.

"Why did you lie about that to the inspector?" Tilda asked.

Massey shrugged as some of the vitriol left his expression. "I suppose I was trying to protect Martha. I don't think she would kill anyone, but if the inspector knew she was carrying Mr. Chambers' child and that he'd turned her out, I can't imagine it would have looked good for her."

"I understand protecting a friend." Tilda darted a glance at Hadrian.

"Also, Mr. Chambers always told me to mind my own business as I expected others to mind theirs. I was not in the habit of sharing his secrets." His gaze darted away for a moment. "As you have likely deduced, I have my own secrets I prefer to keep hidden."

Hadrian wasn't entirely sure what Massey's specific secret was, nor was it his business. "Why were you so loyal to a man that you clearly dislike? Particularly after he died?"

The valet's nostrils flared as he regarded them once more. "I had a good position. Chambers allowed me an entire night to myself once a fortnight. Do you know how difficult that is for someone in service to have? I can't imagine you do." His gaze lingered on Hadrian.

Massey was silent a moment, his features stoic. "Chambers would taunt me sometimes, saying it would be a shame if I ran into trouble whilst I was enjoying my night off. When he tossed Martha out, she warned me that Chambers would turn on me too if the need arose." His eyes simmered with anger. "And before you ask—I didn't kill him."

"You said that Beryl did," Tilda said. "Why do you think that?"

"She was just as bad as he was. They were horrid to one

another—shouting at one another and harming each other. She beat him with her hairbrush once, left red welts on his neck."

Hadrian clenched his jaw lest he gasp. This was shocking to hear.

Tilda glanced at him before looking back to Massey. "Was she also unfaithful?"

"Yes, I told the inspector that." He looked at Hadrian. "I thought she was likely having an affair with you, given the way Chambers went on about you."

"It is definitely not me," Hadrian said sharply, keeping his anger in check.

Tilda touched Hadrian's arm. "It was not Lord Ravenhurst. He was not in contact with Mrs. Chambers until she asked him for help the day before her husband was killed. Have you any other suspicions as to who her lover might be?"

Massey shook his head. "She wasn't conducting any liaisons in the house, unlike her idiot husband."

"Was Chambers carrying on with anyone besides the two maids?" Tilda asked.

"Not in the house." Massey hesitated. "Though I did wonder if he'd had someone in his bed on one of the nights that I was gone last month. I smelled perfume on the linens—a strong floral scent, roses perhaps."

Tilda recalled Beryl telling her about smelling perfume when they'd met the first time. "That is helpful—thank you, Massey. Can you tell us anything more about Martha? We are trying to determine if her death was truly an accident. It seems coincidental that she would die the day after Mr. Chambers."

Massey shook his head. "I've told you everything." His chin dipped, and he looked at his lap. "Martha wasn't a bad person. She was a good friend to me. She knew my secret and kept it."

"I am sorry Martha is no longer here for you," Tilda said softly.

Massey sniffed and lifted his head, blinking away his emotion.

"I'm just glad to be away from that household. I confess that Mr. Chambers had become difficult to work for. He'd been drinking excessively and was often ill the past fortnight or more. I was weary of cleaning up after him." He grimaced. "I do wish I had a reference from him. Though I worry no one will want to hire me after what happened to my employer."

Hadrian understood that this was a scandal, and that it may negatively impact Massey as well as the other retainers. "Perhaps I can help by offering my own recommendation."

"Why would you do that?" Massey asked dubiously, his gaze narrowed.

"You should not suffer because your employer was murdered," Hadrian said simply.

"That is incredibly kind of you, my lord." Massey's voice was small, his eyes grateful.

"I have one more question for you," Tilda said. "A woman in a veil was seen at Martha's lodgings the night she died. Have you any idea who else would visit her?"

Massey's brow creased, and he pushed his hair back from his forehead. "A woman in a veil? No one from the Chambers' household would have visited her. I was the only one who liked her. The housekeeper, cook, and Oswald are thick as thieves and never really took to the rest of us. They were already working in the house when Chambers assumed the lease."

"What about Clara? She's been with the household for some time. Did you know her well?"

"Chambers hired her on the year after I started. She was very timid and eager to please, which Chambers took advantage of." His mouth twisted with disdain briefly. "I was glad when she stopped sharing his bed after he wed—and relieved that Chambers didn't press her to continue. But we never became close."

Tilda cocked her head. "Did Chambers pressure her to begin with?"

"I don't know."

"Do you think she could have killed Chambers?" Tilda asked.

"That would shock me, but then I don't know her very well."

"You don't know me either, yet you think I would have an affair with another man's wife," Hadrian said, knowing he sounded sour. However, his life and reputation were at risk. "It would be helpful to me if you stopped reiterating that lie."

Massey looked pained. "I do apologize, my lord. It's clear Mr. Chambers didn't care for you, and I should have realized he was more concerned with denigrating you than speaking the truth. I'll understand if you would rather not help me as I search for a new position."

"I will help you," Hadrian replied. "I am not one to hold a grudge. I am not sure, however, if you'll find a position where you can be gone overnight on a regular basis, but I will hold out hope for you. Have you considered employment where you are not in service? You could work in a gentleman's club, perhaps."

Surprise flickered in Massey's gaze. "I had not considered that."

"You may need to make some … adjustments if you took that path. You would not want to be seen living in an establishment like this."

Massey nodded. "I understand."

Tilda had one more question. "Did anyone ask you to say that his lordship was carrying on with Mrs. Chambers?"

The valet shook his head. "No. It was something Mr. Chambers said." He twisted his lips. "And I repeated the lie thinking it was true." He sent another apologetic look toward Hadrian.

"Thank you, Massey," Tilda said with a kind smile as she rose. "You've been very helpful. We'll see you at the inquest on Monday."

Hadrian stood, and the valet did as well.

"I'm sorry for what I said about you," Massey said to Hadrian before looking at Tilda. "Who do you think killed Mr. Chambers?"

"I don't know yet," Tilda replied. "But we will find the truth."

They took their leave, and when they were outside, Hadrian escorted Tilda across the street to the coach. "I am rather hungry," he said. "I don't suppose you'd care to join me for a repast at the pub up there?" He gestured toward the Strand.

"I should return home to my grandmother, but I confess I am hungry too. Let us have a quick meal, and we'll review what we know, including our latest suspect."

Hadrian arched a brow at her. "Who is that?"

"Massey, of course."

CHAPTER 12

*A*fter informing Leach they would be dining at the pub, Tilda took Hadrian's arm for the short walk. "How do we know if this is any different than the Cock and Hen?" she asked.

"You make a good observation. I suppose we will find out." He waggled his brows at her.

They entered the River's Edge and Tilda immediately saw that it was not like the Cock and Hen. There was a dining room where several tables were occupied.

In short order, they were seated at a table and ordered a light repast, including wine, which was delivered with alacrity.

Hadrian offered a toast. "To making progress with our investigation."

Tilda tapped her glass to his. "I will toast to that, but I am still bothered about the postponement of the inquest."

After sipping his wine, Hadrian set the glass down with a slight frown. "It is agitating not to know why, isn't it?"

"Quite." She took a second small sip of wine, then put her glass on the table. "I fear we won't know until Monday." After eyeing him a moment, she said, "You were very kind to offer to help Massey, particularly after he contributed to your being a suspect in Chambers' death."

"I am just glad he won't be repeating that nonsense at the inquest."

"Still, you didn't have to offer your assistance." Not that Tilda was surprised. Hadrian had often demonstrated his concern for others.

"I worry that the retainers in the Chambers' household will suffer through no fault of their own."

"Provided they are all innocent of any participation in Chambers' death," Tilda noted.

"Yes, of course," Hadrian said. "This is a scandal, and it may be difficult for them to find employment. I don't mind helping them if they need it."

"Are all earls as kind as you?" Tilda asked bemusedly.

Hadrian laughed. "I couldn't say."

Their food arrived, and Tilda immersed her thoughts in the investigation whilst she ate her steak-and-kidney pie. She was nearly halfway through it before Hadrian broke the silence.

"I can practically hear you thinking," he said with a smile. "What brilliant deductions are you making now?"

"None. I am trying to make sense of all we know. I confess I am slightly stuck on Martha and how she fits into Chambers' murder—or *if* she does. Her death could simply be an accident."

"But the timing is bizarre," Hadrian noted.

"Perhaps I am spending too much time thinking about Martha," Tilda said. "Let us return to Louis's murder and what we know about that. We know the killer likely entered his bedchamber through his dressing room—and brought the knife with him."

"Or her," Hadrian noted. "Pity no one has found the knife."

"I do wonder if it was the one missing from the kitchen," she mused. "I keep thinking of people's motives and what would have pushed them to fetch a knife from the kitchen to kill Chambers.

It would not have been an act of sudden passion where the killer grabbed whatever weapon was available. They planned to kill him."

"Since there was no evidence of anyone breaking into the Chambers' home, it does seem as though it may have been someone in the household," Hadrian said.

Tilda smiled. "You are beginning to sound like an investigator."

"Thank you. I've an excellent instructor." He lifted his glass once more and took a sip.

Tilda took another bite of pie. After swallowing, she said, "Using that theory, our primary suspects would be Beryl and all the retainers. That leaves you and Pollard out."

"Well, we know I didn't do it."

"Of course. But I don't think we can discount Pollard yet. Especially since we don't know why the inquest was postponed. I must presume there is evidence of which we are unaware."

"Let us focus on the retainers for now," Hadrian said. "Massey didn't think Clara would have done it."

"I'm not sure he's reliable. He lied about you having an affair with Beryl—or at least he misled Teague. He also has a strong motive. Chambers knew his secret and had threatened to expose Massey. He'd also treated Martha, whom Massey liked, poorly."

"What of the cook, housekeeper, and butler?"

Tilda picked up her wineglass. "I am not aware of any specific motives they may have. Unless they simply didn't like Chambers. He seemed to be rather disagreeable." She sipped her wine.

"That is a diplomatic way of putting it," Hadrian said drily. "He was a blackguard."

Setting her glass down a touch harder than she meant to, Tilda sloshed a bit of wine on her hand. She wiped it away with her napkin. "There is also Oliver Chambers. He wanted to invest in the drapery store, but his brother was possibly standing in his way."

Hadrian cocked his head. "That seems a flimsy reason to kill one's brother. But then I can't think of a good reason to kill anyone, unless it's to defend oneself—or someone they care about." He looked directly at Tilda as he added the last part, and she wondered if he was thinking of how he'd fought to defend her from the murderer they'd apprehended with Teague's help.

They fell silent for a moment as they finished their meals. Hadrian spoke next, saying that there likely wasn't much to be done tomorrow since it was Sunday.

"I would very much like to speak with Oliver as well as the oldest Chambers brother, as well as Pollard," Tilda said. "However, I don't think any of them would care to be bothered on a Sunday."

Hadrian gave her a wry look. "Probably not. It's just as well there's not much to do tomorrow as I will be having tea with my mother for our fortnightly appointment."

"It's an 'appointment'?" Tilda asked with a chuckle.

"It's *required*." Hadrian exhaled. "Since I was stabbed, she is keen to make sure I am doing well. It is a mother's responsibility, I suppose."

Tilda wasn't sure she agreed. At least, she didn't think it was a responsibility her own mother would adhere to. "That's nice that she cares so much."

"It's also her opportunity to pester me about marriage again. I've an heir to beget, you see." He leaned forward and whispered as if it were a secret, "I've a cousin who can inherit, so it's really not important."

Tilda had thought it was vitally important for peers to ensure their legacy, but who was she to question such a thing?

They finished their dinner and prepared to depart. Hadrian held her chair as she rose. "Shall I fetch you for the inquest on Monday?"

She looked over her shoulder at him with a smile. "Yes, thank you."

Hadrian paid for their meal, and as they made their way to the door, his hand grazed the small of Tilda's back. A pleasant shiver danced along her spine.

She thought of earlier, when he'd caught her in his arms at the lodging house. When the jolt of fear had passed, she'd become very aware of his strength and heat. The sensation had surpassed comfort and sent her somewhere she'd never been—a place where she yearned for more of his touch. Of his care.

The thought troubled her. She didn't want that from someone, especially a man. She could comfort and care for herself.

When Hadrian settled himself beside her in the coach, that awareness returned. He was close enough that she could occasionally detect his masculine scent, and it was annoyingly stirring.

It seemed they were becoming closer each time they were together. Was that bad?

Yes.

Their closeness could not move beyond friendship. Tilda wasn't interested in romance, not that Hadrian was suggesting that. She liked how things were between them, and she would do her best to keep them that way.

∼

*H*adrian was pleased that his mother had spent the first part of their fortnightly tea discussing his sisters and their children. Having her attention on them instead of him always put him at ease. Which made him wonder why her desire for him to wed bothered him so much. Was it because he'd tried once already, and the experience had ended disappointingly? He acknowledged that the end of his betrothal to Beryl had soured him. But he also hadn't spent much time thinking about it. Now that Beryl had reentered his life, he supposed it was natural for him to think about marriage and why he wasn't pursuing it.

Was he really going to allow what had happened four years ago with Beryl and Chambers to prevent him from taking a wife? And it wasn't just about fulfilling his duty, which he ought to consider even if he said otherwise. What about the potential for love and a family? Did he really not want that?

"Oh!" his mother said, startling him from his thoughts as he lifted his teacup to his lips. "I can't believe I didn't mention this straightaway. I read about Louis Chambers' death. What a horrid business!"

After swallowing a sip of tea, Hadrian set his cup down on the saucer. "Quite." He considered telling her he was providing assistance to Beryl, but his mother had been very upset when they'd ended their betrothal. Hadrian didn't wish to bring any of that up.

"I'm so concerned for Beryl," his mother went on. "She must be devastated. I will send a note and perhaps call on her when she is feeling up to it." The dowager countess fixed her blue eyes, which were exactly like Hadrian's, on him. "You should do the same. I'm sure she'd be pleased to hear from you."

Damn. If Hadrian didn't reveal that he was already involved in the investigation and his mother found out, she would be angry with him for keeping that from her. That was a risk he was willing to take. "Er, probably." Hadrian squirmed in his chair.

"I liked her very much," his mother went on, clucking her tongue. "I was so disappointed when you didn't wed. And now look how things have ended up. I'm sure she regrets not marrying you." She gave Hadrian an expectant look. Was she hoping he would say he felt the same?

"We were not suited," Hadrian said, glad he hadn't told her that he'd not only seen Beryl but was a suspect in Louis's murder.

"I think you were more upset by that dissolution than you ever let on," his mother said with a probing stare. "Why else would you not have courted or married since? Perhaps when Beryl's mourning period is over, you can try again."

Hadrian had picked up his teacup and was relieved he hadn't taken a drink, for he would have choked on the liquid. Before he could respond to that outrageous suggestion, his butler, Collier, entered the drawing room.

"My lord, Miss Wren has arrived and requests an audience."

"Did you invite her to join us for tea as I suggested?" the dowager countess asked. She'd met Tilda a fortnight ago when she was last here.

Blast. How was he to explain Tilda's presence without mentioning the investigation they were working on? The one where she was working to prove he was innocent of killing Beryl's husband. Could he really hope to keep it secret from her?

"I did not." He exhaled. "As it happens, Miss Wren is conducting an investigation into Chambers' death, and I am assisting her." He would leave out the part about him being a suspect, for his mother would only worry unnecessarily.

Hadrian looked at Collier, who was standing in the doorway, his features a mask of disinterest. "Please show Miss Wren up."

Inclining his head in silent response, the butler pivoted and departed.

"You must have spoken to Beryl. Why wouldn't you say so?" The dowager countess pursed her lips at him.

"I didn't want to discuss the matter with you." Hadrian spoke with an edge, hoping it would deter her from prodding further.

"Because you didn't want to talk about Beryl or your missed opportunity at marriage," his mother said with considerable exasperation.

"It was not a 'missed opportunity.'"

His mother took a drink of tea and fumed at him over the edge of the cup. "You have avoided discussing marriage since then."

Hadrian tried to avoid discussing it, but his mother continued to ensure they did. "It hasn't interested me, and it still doesn't."

Throwing her hands up, she made a sound low in her throat. "You can be so very frustrating on this matter. You need an heir. Do you want your cousin to inherit?" She didn't wait for his reply as she barreled onward. "If only your brother hadn't died. I'm sure he would be wed by now. Then I needn't worry about you."

Hadrian's insides twisted. His mother rarely mentioned her youngest child, Gabriel, but when she did, he never failed to react viscerally. Gabriel's death in India just a year after their father had died had been a blow to the family.

Indeed, Hadrian *knew* Gabriel would be married by now. He'd written to Hadrian before he'd become ill saying he'd fallen in love and hoped to marry, if her family would permit it. Hadrian had never told his mother about it, thinking the knowledge would only make her sadder about losing her child.

Hadrian realized Tilda was standing just inside the threshold of the drawing room, clutching her reticule. Fine lines creased her forehead, revealing her concern. Had she heard what his mother had said about Gabriel? Hadrian hadn't ever discussed his youngest sibling with Tilda.

Standing, Hadrian welcomed Tilda. "Please, come join us."

Tilda walked hesitantly toward the table near the windows where his mother was still seated. "Good afternoon, Lady Ravenhurst."

"Good afternoon, Miss Wren. How pleasant to see you again. I understand you're helping dear Beryl Chambers with the great tragedy that has befallen her."

That was not what Hadrian had said at all. He'd said they were investigating. He gritted his teeth.

"I am," Tilda replied with a nod. "In fact, I've come to speak to … Lord Ravenhurst about a development. I'm sorry to interrupt." Had she been about to refer to him by his given name? Hadrian was glad she had not, for that would have piqued his mother's curiosity to no end.

Tilda must have important news to share. Hadrian's pulse ticked up, and he hoped his mother would realize she ought to go. However, that seemed unlikely. She was likely annoyed that their tea had been disturbed.

"You are more than welcome," his mother said with enthusiasm.

A maid entered with another tea setting and deposited it on the table before taking her leave.

"Thank you," Tilda said as she took one of the empty chairs at the table, which put her between Hadrian and his mother.

The dowager countess poured Tilda's tea as Hadrian retook his seat. He hoped his mother would leave soon, for he was anxious to hear Tilda's news.

"I am fascinated that you are a private investigator," his mother said whilst stirring sugar into her tea. "What an awful situation for Beryl." His mother wrinkled her nose as if she were smelling the worst sort of offal. "I can't imagine why you'd want to involve yourself in something so unpleasant."

"I enjoy investigative work, my lady," Tilda said pleasantly. "My father was a sergeant with the Metropolitan Police."

"Ah yes, Hadrian had mentioned that. And that your grandfather was a well-known magistrate. Still, you don't find a … murder to be distasteful?"

"I find murder to be abominable, which is why I am eager to bring the responsible party to justice," Tilda said evenly.

"That is most … enterprising of you. What does your family think of you doing that?"

"My grandmother, with whom I live, is very proud of me," Tilda said simply.

The dowager countess smiled. "That's lovely." She picked up her cup to finish her tea. "Well, I suppose I will be on my way so you can discuss whatever it is you need to discuss."

Hadrian rose. "Delightful to see you, Mother, as always." He moved to hold her chair as she stood.

"I'll see you soon, dear. Please give Beryl my very best."

"I'll do that." Hadrian escorted his mother to the doorway, then bussed her cheek.

"Miss Wren." His mother waved her fingers at Tilda before departing.

Hadrian returned to the table where Tilda was watching him with interest. "You must have something important to share."

"In a moment," she said. "Your mother seems fond of Beryl. Was she disappointed when you and she didn't wed?"

"Yes, but I don't know that it had anything to do with the bride in particular. She just wants me to marry."

"I did hear that she wants you to have an heir." Tilda gave him a gentle, understanding look. "That must induce stress for you."

"Somewhat, but I have mostly learned to ignore her."

"I didn't know you had a brother," she said, confirming that she'd heard all that.

He lifted a shoulder. "I don't speak of him often. He died of cholera five years ago in India. My father had died the year before, so it was a difficult time, particularly for my mother."

"Were you and your brother close?"

"When we were younger. He was still a boy when I went off to school." Hadrian frowned at his teacup. He wished they'd been close, especially since their father had been so cold. But Hadrian had been focused on his own life and growing up. He couldn't wait to leave home. "I'd looked forward to when we might grow closer in adulthood." But they would never have that chance.

"I'm sorry," Tilda said softly. "I don't know what it's like to have siblings, let alone lose them."

Hadrian blinked a few times, then straightened. "You did not come here to be weighed down by melancholy. What news do you bring? I am most anxious to hear."

She'd taken another sip of tea and now set her cup back in the saucer. Her gaze met his, and for the first time since her arrival, he saw deep concern. It made him apprehensive. Had she engaged in conversation to postpone whatever it was she needed to say?

"Teague called on me earlier. He had information to share. Apparently, Louis Chambers consulted with a solicitor about divorcing Beryl. The solicitor said Louis was certain she was having an affair." She paused, and now she looked apprehensive. "With you."

Hadrian swore under his breath.

"I heard that," Tilda said mildly.

"My apologies," Hadrian murmured. "Is Teague coming to interrogate me?"

She shook her head. "He already did so the other day. I just thought you should know of this development."

Hadrian was both relieved and pleased that she would come to tell him.

She laid her bare hand atop the table. "I am sorry you keep getting dragged back into this mess."

"Why does Chambers keep telling everyone that I was having an affair with his wife? Is it because he appears to have been holding a grudge against me for some perceived slight?"

"It is noticeable," Tilda said with a slight frown. "Perhaps the reason behind Chambers' hatred of you *is* important. I apologize for discounting it."

"I think I will visit Arthur's tonight and make some inquiries amongst Chambers' friends." He sent her an apologetic look. "I'm sorry you can't accompany me."

"Can you go without being a member?" Tilda asked. "I realize your title has extraordinary privilege, but surely it doesn't extend to that."

"I will go with my colleague who invited me the other night," Hadrian replied. "Provided he is able."

"I regret I cannot come along." She frowned with disappointment.

Hadrian was sorry too. "Perhaps you could dress as a man."

Tilda smirked. "I don't think I'd make a passable gentleman."

"I disagree. You've demonstrated your ability to affect a Cockney accent with ease and blend in at a tavern in the east end as well as in a horrible rookery. Why not a gentleman from Mayfair? If you wore a hat and did not remove it, you could fool people."

"I think it would be more complicated than that," Tilda said with a chuckle. "Too bad we can't consult with Mrs. Longbotham at the Cock and Hen. Perhaps she could help disguise me."

Hadrian thought that was a brilliant idea. "Why not? Let's go there now."

"Dressing as a man may not be Mrs. Longbotham's forte," she said wryly. "I suppose we could try. I would very much like to accompany you to Arthur's. My only hesitation is what would happen if I was discovered. I would hate to cause trouble for you or your friend, whose membership could be at stake."

"If we keep to the shadows and corners, I daresay the ploy could succeed. Do we have the courage?"

"Or foolhardiness?" she asked with a laugh.

"Perhaps a little of both." Hadrian smiled with a lift of his shoulder.

"You don't need to accompany me to the Cock and Hen," Tilda said. "I can take a hack and then you can pick me up later to go to the club, assuming your friend agrees to take us."

"Thank you for reminding me that I must dash off a note to him. I can have Leach deliver it whilst we are at the Cock and Hen." He watched faint lines form between her brows. "I would feel better if you allowed me to join you." He didn't like thinking of her in a brothel by herself, even if they had already made the acquaintance of multiple people in residence.

She gave him a patient smile. "I am an investigator and able to manage such things. I believe you even complimented my ability to blend in with others. Furthermore, I've been taking care of myself for years. Long before I met you."

Yes, she was a capable, independent woman. He admired that very much about her, even if a part of him wanted her to need him. Perhaps just a little.

"All right," he said in defeat. "You don't need me. May I come anyway?"

Tilda laughed. "I suppose you may."

"Excellent." Hadrian smiled in relief. "Now, excuse me a moment whilst I quickly draft a note to Sir Godfrey to ask if we may accompany him to the club. I'll have Leach deliver it whilst we are at the Cock and Hen." He went to a small writing desk in the corner and quickly scratched out a note.

"Ready?" he asked.

Tilda nodded, and they left the drawing room. "I do apologize for intruding on your tea with your mother," she said.

"You've no need to apologize." Hadrian smiled briefly. "But don't be surprised if I invite you properly for our next one or the one after. My mother will not forget that you have arrived during two of our appointed meetings. Nor will she soon forget that you are investigating a *murder*."

"I hope she doesn't think poorly of me for that."

"She will not," Hadrian said firmly. "It is simply something she could never understand—a woman investigating such a thing."

"Then you must ensure she doesn't find out I've visited a brothel. Or that I'm going there a second time."

Hadrian barked a laugh. "I don't want her to know *I've* visited a brothel. I won't be divulging any of our investigative secrets to her or anyone else."

She looked over at him as they reached the entrance hall. "And that is why we make a good team."

CHAPTER 13

*M*rs. Longbotham had been absolutely delighted to help Tilda and Hadrian with their endeavor to disguise Tilda as a man so she could gain entry to Arthur's. It turned out, there were, in fact, a few women who dressed as men at the Cock and Hen, and one of them was present and eager to transform Tilda into a gentleman. They'd made arrangements to return after dinner—via an unmarked door tucked behind a column on the façade—as they would not be going to Arthur's until about ten o'clock.

Hadrian had then taken Tilda home so she could dine with her grandmother. Later, Tilda had explained that she had investigative work to do with Hadrian, who'd returned to fetch her. It was notable and perhaps slightly vexing that her grandmother wasn't worried in the slightest that Tilda was going out at night to make inquiries with Hadrian. If she'd gone by herself, however, Grandmama would certainly have voiced her concern.

Back at the Cock and Hen, Tilda became Mr. William Taylor. They'd chosen a simple, innocuous name—hopefully something completely forgettable. Donning the man's costume, Tilda looked far more fashionable than she did as herself. But the key to her transformation was the hair, which included a wig, beard, and mustache, which they affixed with an adhesive used in the theatre. When they emerged sometime later, they'd done so as Lord Ravenhurst and Mr. Taylor.

They were shortly on their way to Arthur's where they would meet Sir Godfrey, who'd been delighted that Hadrian wanted to return, particularly after the way Louis Chambers had behaved the other night. He was also eager to meet Hadrian's friend who was visiting from Somerset—the shy and quiet Mr. Taylor.

"You make a more than passable gentleman," Hadrian said as the coach rolled toward St. James.

"Thank you." Tilda pitched her voice low. "I don't know how long I'll be able to bear this beard. It's not particularly comfortable."

"We won't stay long—an hour at most. I just hope the men that I saw with Chambers are present."

They arrived at Arthur's and met Sir Godfrey in the vestibule. Short of stature with a thick mop of light-brown hair, Sir Godfrey appeared to be in his mid-thirties. He greeted Hadrian warmly and was eager to make Mr. Taylor's acquaintance.

"We appreciate you allowing us to accompany you this evening whilst Taylor is in town," Hadrian said.

"My pleasure. I'm surprised you didn't take him to one of your clubs," Sir Godfrey noted with a chuckle.

Hadrian inclined his head. "I plan to do so later. Forgive us if we don't stay overly long."

Tilda tried not to appear too interested in her surroundings, but the fact that she was inside a gentleman's club was an entirely thrilling experience. To see what women were excluded from was both irritating and fascinating.

They moved from the vestibule into a large reception room. Hadrian leaned toward her as they walked. "This was where Chambers yelled out to me."

"In front of so many people?" she whispered back, keeping her voice low so Sir Godfrey, who was walking in front of them, would not overhear.

"There were more people here on Thursday."

Tilda looked about, taking in the elegant chandeliers and grand stone staircase. "Do you see any of his friends?"

"Not as of yet. But there are other rooms."

"Didn't you say you went upstairs?" she asked.

Sir Godfrey paused and turned around. "We could go into the library or to the drawing room upstairs. Have you any preference? There's also the billiard room."

"Perhaps we could have a tour," Tilda suggested in her masculine voice.

Hadrian sent her an admiring look. "Excellent idea."

"Then let us begin with the billiard room as it's just through here," Sir Godfrey said with a smile. "I confess it's my favorite room in the club."

"Is it?" Hadrian asked as they walked toward an archway that led to—presumably—the billiard room. "You should have told me so last time. I would have joined you in a game."

"Perhaps tonight then." Sir Godfrey led them into the billiard room where there were four tables.

Tilda grabbed Hadrian's arm before they could follow Sir Godfrey to an empty table. She released him before the usual warmth she felt from touching him could distract her. "I don't know how to play."

"You don't need to."

"What about the tour? I don't want to be stuck in here. We need to find Louis's friends if we can."

Hadrian's gaze had been moving about the room as they spoke. Now his features arrested as his eyes locked on a gentleman on the other side. "That is one of them," Hadrian whispered.

The gentleman seemed to notice Hadrian as well. His features were impassive, but he pivoted and moved toward another doorway.

"Damn, he's leaving," Hadrian said.

"I'll go after him," Tilda started toward the doorway, but Hadrian touched her arm briefly. "Is that wise?"

She arched a brow at him. "Don't interrupt my work, Lord Ravenhurst," she said in a deep, teasing tone.

He briefly presented his palms to her, a faint smile quirking his mouth. "A thousand apologies."

"Just stay here with Sir Godfrey, so I can find you when I'm finished. I've no desire to go wandering about the club on my own." She hastened to the doorway where the man had disappeared.

Finding herself in a small sitting room, she saw that the gentleman Hadrian had pointed out was standing at a bar speaking with a liveried employee. Tilda milled about the room for a moment while watching him. The employee gave him a drink, and Tilda moved to join him.

"What are you drinking?" she asked.

The gentleman, who was a few inches taller than Tilda, looked down at her with dark-brown eyes glinting with curiosity. "Scotch whisky."

Tilda looked to the employee. "I'll have the same. I'm here with Sir Godfrey." Hadrian had explained that anything they ate or drank would be added to his account. Tilda didn't like having someone else pay for things, but Hadrian assured her Sir Godfrey was happy to do so. Furthermore, he was more than financially able.

"I saw you with Ravenhurst," the man said, his tone as probing as his gaze.

Happy to use his curiosity to her advantage, Tilda nodded. "Are you surprised to see him here after the other night?"

"Were you here?" the man asked. "That was quite a scene."

"I was not, but I heard about it," Tilda replied as she accepted her drink. She thanked the employee and turned away from him toward the room. "I'm Taylor," she said to the man.

"Kirkham," he replied with a nod.

They moved away from the bar. "You know Ravenhurst well then?" Kirkham asked.

"Well enough. Do you know him?"

Kirkham shook his head. "Not personally. I know Chambers though." He grimaced. "*Knew* him. Can't believe he was killed not long after that. Makes one wonder about Ravenhurst."

Tilda tamped down the flash of ire the man's ridiculous comment provoked. "Wonder what?" She wanted to hear him say it.

"You know." Kirkham gave her a meaningful look. "Perhaps he was angry enough at the way Chambers embarrassed him that he decided to ensure it never happened again."

"I didn't think he was particularly embarrassed about the other night. It was more that he was confused as to why Chambers had behaved so obnoxiously toward him."

"It's not necessarily what happened the other night," Kirkham said as if he were imparting a secret. "But what happened a few years back—when Chambers stole Ravenhurst's fiancée."

Tilda shrugged. "Ravenhurst wasn't too troubled by it, actually. He didn't bear any ill will toward Chambers. In fact, he found Chambers' vitriol toward him quite puzzling, if not irrational. As you pointed out, Ravenhurst is the one who ought to have been angry."

Kirkham nodded slowly, then sipped his whisky, seeming to ponder what Tilda said. "You're right that Ravenhurst didn't seem upset the other night. He simply walked away. Chambers, however, went on and on about what a sneaky bastard the earl was, though now that I think of it, he didn't offer any examples."

"You've no idea why Chambers despised Ravenhurst? His grudge seems odd."

"I haven't a clue, but you could ask his brother, Daniel. He's also a member, though we haven't seen him since Louis died," Kirkham said. He gave her a somewhat sheepish look. "In all honesty, Chambers—Louis, I mean—was a blowhard. We found him entertaining, but only in small amounts. He could become quite tiresome, particularly with his bragging about women. I felt sorry for his wife because he never once mentioned her. Though he often commented that marriage was a bore."

What an ass, Tilda thought.

She finally took a sip of the whisky. She had to fight to hide her reaction. She hadn't ever had the fiery brew, and it burned a path down her throat. Her eyes stung for a moment.

When she could speak, she said, "I'd heard of his reputation with women. Did he tell you about his current mistress?" Tilda hoped she wasn't walking headfirst into a corner. She was all but certain he had a paramour.

"Oh, yes," Kirkham rolled his eyes. "He spoke of her endlessly. She is apparently 'the most beautiful and intoxicating female to ever draw breath.' He would tell us about the gifts he bought her —perfume, jewelry, a fur-lined cloak. He even showed us a set of rubies before he gave them to her."

The mention of perfume had made Tilda's breath catch, then the rubies had stalled it completely. "A set, as in a necklace, bracelet, and earrings?"

Kirkham sipped his whisky again. "Yes. Looked as though it had belonged in his family perhaps. The case was older and a bit worn."

Tilda was certain he was talking about the first pieces of jewelry that had disappeared from Beryl's chamber. "Makes one wonder who the woman is." Tilda held her breath again, waiting to see if Kirkham might know.

"He never said. But last Thursday he mentioned that he may be divorcing his wife, which led us to believe that whoever the mistress is, he could marry her. Why else would he bother with a divorce?"

Indeed.

Tilda lifted her glass to her mouth as though she were going to take a sip but only pretended to. A small bit of the whisky wetted her lips, and she gingerly licked it off. The flavor wasn't terrible. She just wasn't going to take another drink here where she might choke on its heat.

"Still a shame that he's dead," Kirkham said.

"Quite."

Kirkham's eyes took on an excited gleam. "There's to be an inquest tomorrow. A couple friends and I thought we might attend. You should come along since you're interested in Chambers."

"I am not able to, unfortunately," Tilda said.

"Shame, but you'll be able to read about it in the papers." His brows twitched as he smirked. "Might have to place a wager on the likely killer."

"Who would that be?" If he said Hadrian, Tilda would be hard-pressed not to kick him in the most debilitating place.

"Don't know yet," Kirkham replied with a contemplative look. "Ask me again after the inquest." He grinned.

Tilda nodded vaguely. "Pleasure speaking with you, Kirkham. Please excuse me." She took her leave, making her way back to the billiard room.

Hadrian and Sir Godfrey were engaged in a game of billiards. It was Hadrian's turn, and she watched as he knocked a white ball into a pocket.

"Well played, Ravenhurst," Sir Godfrey said with a smile. "I would suggest we play again, but I promised the next match to Ardmore." He inclined his head toward an older gentleman who was also watching.

"Quite all right," Hadrian said. "Perhaps I'll take Taylor on that tour of the club."

Sir Godfrey gave them a sheepish look. "I forgot about that. My apologies, I'm afraid I am too easily distracted by billiards."

Hadrian smiled. "Enjoy your game with Ardmore."

Nodding in appreciation, Sir Godfrey turned to the older gentleman.

Hadrian came toward Tilda, his gaze dipping to the glass in her hand. "Whisky?"

"Requesting it allowed me to move close enough to Kirkham to engage him in conversation."

"That's his name, Kirkham? How did it go?"

"It was most informative." She wrinkled her nose at the glass. "Though I am not sure if I care for whisky. I don't think I can drink more of it."

"I'll take it," he said with a laugh. His fingertips grazed hers, but whilst he had removed his gloves, she had not. He sipped the fiery brew and did not appear any worse off.

"That is clearly not your first time sampling whisky," she murmured.

"No," he said with a chuckle.

She glanced at his bare hand around the glass. "What happens when you touch that? Are you seeing any of my memories?"

His brow creased. "No. I've not ever seen a vision when I've touched something you have, or when I've touched you. Though I've done very little of the latter." His eyes glittered with … something. Was he thinking about touching her? Was he thinking he hadn't done it enough?

Or were those her own thoughts?

"What about someone else's thoughts?" she asked, keeping her voice down. "And what about touching other items here in the club or shaking someone's hand?"

"When I first grabbed the cue, I saw several flashes, but none of them were long or strong enough for me to discern anything."

"How did that affect your head?"

"I had a mild flash of pain, but it's gone now." He took another sip of whisky. She realized he was putting his lips where hers had been. Heat flushed through her, and she hoped her cheeks weren't turning pink, though the beard likely disguised it, thankfully.

She jerked her attention back to their discussion. "Such a strange power."

"And completely unreliable," he breathed. "Tell me about your conversation with Kirkham."

Tilda repeated what she'd learned regarding Louis Chambers' mistress, particularly his lavishing gifts on her, including the rubies that belonged to Beryl, and that Louis had mentioned divorce.

"Too bad Kirkham couldn't name the paramour," Hadrian said. "Did you happen to ask why Chambers hated me so much?"

"I did, and he had no idea. He was aware of Chambers' dislike of you, however."

"I think that was evident to everyone last Thursday," he noted sardonically.

Tilda wasn't sure she wanted to tell him about Kirkham wondering if Hadrian had killed Chambers or that tomorrow's inquest could turn into a spectacle where Hadrian's presence as a suspect would surely be reported upon.

His eyes narrowed slightly. "What aren't you telling me?"

Did he somehow know she was keeping something from him? Perhaps he was seeing something with the glass after all. But wouldn't he have told her?

"I can see you are hesitant," he said. "And concerned. You have these little pleats between your eyes." He lifted his hand, and for a moment, she thought he meant to touch her.

He must have thought so too, for he blinked and dropped his hand with alacrity.

She *was* keeping something from him. Apparently, he just knew her well. "Kirkham wondered if you'd been angry enough to kill Chambers."

Hadrian's nostrils flared and his jaw clenched. "I wasn't even angry the other night."

"I told him as much," Tilda said, eager to soothe his ire, which he was more than entitled to. "But then he pointed out that you were perhaps still upset about Chambers and Beryl. I disabused him of that notion, by the way."

Surprise flickered in Hadrian's eyes, and his features settled into mild amusement. "What did you say?"

She shrugged. "That you didn't hold a grudge and had no regrets. Or something to that effect."

"Thank you," he said softly, his gaze reflecting his deep appreciation.

Tilda did not allow herself to look into his eyes for too long. She glanced toward the billiards table where Sir Godfrey and Ardmore were playing. "I should also warn you that Kirkham and some of his friends will likely be at the inquest tomorrow. He sees it as entertainment, I believe."

"Spectacular," Hadrian muttered.

"One last thing," Tilda said. "Kirkham suggested we speak to Daniel Chambers about why Louis despised you. Apparently, he's a member here too, but he hasn't come in since Louis's death. Perhaps we can speak with him after the inquest tomorrow."

"I'd like to, if possible." He sipped more of the whisky. "We can go now, if you like."

"Yes, please." Tilda was pleased with how easily she'd moved about, but for the last few minutes, a gentleman across the billiard room had been staring at her off and on. "I'm concerned there's a man over there who may not be fooled by my disguise."

"I see. Then let us depart after we give our regards to Sir Godfrey."

A short while later, they were ensconced in Hadrian's coach. Tilda wished she could remove the hair stuck to her face, but that would have to wait until they returned to the Cock and Hen where she would return to her regular appearance.

"How did it feel to be inside a gentleman's club?" Hadrian asked with a smile.

"I confess I found it rather titillating, as well as annoying. Why can't women be allowed?"

"Some argue that they have their own clubs."

Tilda scoffed. "Not nearly as many or as varied."

Hadrian inclined his head. "And some men think women would ruin things."

"I daresay those men don't see women as their equal or as engaging individuals to, say, play billiards with."

"I don't agree with those men, by the way," Hadrian said. "You and I are the perfect example of how a man and woman can be friends and enjoy one another's company."

They were indeed.

CHAPTER 14

*H*adrian picked Tilda up at her grandmother's house on the way to the inquest. When they were settled in the coach, she turned slightly toward him on the seat.

"Have you considered that there will be reporters at the inquest?" she asked, her tone and expression somewhat tentative.

He appreciated her concern. "I did recall there were reporters waiting outside when we left the last inquest. I suppose I didn't spend time thinking about them being at this one." And why hadn't he? His presence at this inquest would draw notice because of his relationship to the victim and his wife.

He hadn't wanted to think about it.

Then last night, Tilda had mentioned what Kirkham had said. Now, he was preparing himself for a spectacle in which he would likely be named as a suspect in a murder. He could hardly wait for his mother to read those newspaper articles.

Actually, he was sorry she would read them. They would worry her unnecessarily. Perhaps he should have prepared her.

Tilda briefly clasped his forearm, her hand squeezing gently through the layers of his garments, which did not include a great-coat as the weather had decided, at least for today, that it was, in fact, spring. The sun shone in the sky whilst intermittent clouds puffed by like steam from a passing train.

"I'm sorry you've been troubled by all this," Tilda said.

"It will be over soon," he replied with a faint smile. "I hope."

The coach arrived at the Crown and Sceptre, the pub where the inquest was to be held. They were early, but there was still a group of people outside. Inquests tended to draw attention. People wanted to know what had happened in their neighborhood. Or they were perversely curious about the matter, like Kirkham who planned to attend for the amusement of it.

Leach opened the door, and Hadrian climbed down. He helped Tilda out, then offered his arm to her before they made their way to the door of the pub.

Several of the people milling about appeared to be onlookers, but a few carried notepads and writing implements. One of them, a long-faced man in his forties, spotted Hadrian and strode toward him and Tilda, blocking their passage.

"Lord Ravenhurst, are you a witness? You know Mrs. Chambers, don't you?"

The latter couldn't be a question so much as the reporter notifying Hadrian that he was aware of the past scandal. Irritation scalded Hadrian's insides, but he kept his features impassive.

"*Excuse* us, please," Tilda snapped, her eyes cold as she glowered at the reporter.

Her protection of him was astonishingly alluring.

"Who are you?" The reporter's gaze moved over Tilda, his face pinching as if he found her distasteful.

Hadrian wanted to knock him down. Instead, he elbowed the man as he guided Tilda past him. "Move."

Grasping the door, Hadrian pulled it open for Tilda. She took her hand from his arm and preceded him inside.

"Thank you," she said simply as they stepped farther into the common room.

Hadrian found her gaze and held it. "Thank *you*."

There were several people inside already, including what looked to be the coroner and jurors. Pollard was in attendance along with another gentleman and a woman. Massey stood in the corner, his expression dark.

The door opened behind them, and they pivoted. Teague and several constables strode in. Behind them, Oliver Chambers and another man, who had to be the eldest Chambers brother, entered. They were accompanied by a third man whom Hadrian recognized immediately.

He sucked in a breath and leaned toward Tilda. "That's Padgett."

"The inspector who oversaw the investigation into your stabbing?" Tilda whispered.

Hadrian nodded. "What the devil is he doing here?"

Padgett had gone out of his way to ensure no one properly investigated Hadrian's stabbing or that of another gentleman a week later in the same place. It seemed he was one of the members of the Metropolitan Police who chose to accept bribes to augment their salary. In exchange, he did things such as close investigations without properly conducting them. The villain who'd been behind Hadrian's stabbing had admitted to paying Padgett, but Padgett hadn't been prosecuted for accepting bribes. Instead, he'd been allowed to retire from the police.

Tilda's gaze followed the three men who moved together toward the seating area. "I wonder if he is now working as a private investigator."

"For the Chambers brothers?" Hadrian scowled.

"Perhaps."

Beryl arrived then. She wore black from head to toe, including a hat with a veil that completely covered her face. Hadrian may not have recognized her, except that her retainers were with her, along with Mrs. Styles-Rowdon.

The coroner asked everyone to take their seats whilst he

remained standing. Tilda and Hadrian sat in the second row of chairs behind Beryl and Mrs. Styles-Rowdon.

Introducing himself as Julius Graythorpe, the coroner addressed the room. "Mr. Louis Chambers was found dead in his bed this Thursday past of suspicious circumstances. We shall determine the cause of his death. Let us turn our attention to the deceased, who was stabbed in the chest four times."

He went on to describe the wound and the likely size of the blade that was used. "This sort of knife may be found in any kitchen. However, a knife was not discovered with the body.

"Upon review of the corpse, I noticed a bluish tinge to Mr. Chambers' fingertips as well as diminishment in his eyeballs. This prompted me to test for arsenic poisoning, and the results were positive."

Tilda gasped softly and leaned toward Hadrian. "That is why the inquest was postponed."

"But the stabbing killed him, didn't it?" Hadrian whispered.

"I would expect so, but the poisoning complicates matters." She shook her head, and they listened to the coroner continue. He estimated the time of death between midnight and three o'clock.

The coroner then called the first person to testify—Mrs. Louis Chambers. He started by asking her to lift her veil so that he may see her face.

Beryl did as instructed, and now Hadrian could view her profile from where he sat. The coroner first asked about her marriage to Louis and whether she was seeking a divorce. Beryl revealed Louis's treatment of her as well as her suspicion that he'd stolen several pieces of jewelry from her. She indicated that Tilda was helping her with the divorce.

Graythorpe asked about the night Louis was killed, as well as what happened the following morning. He then asked about her relationship to her former fiancé, Lord Ravenhurst.

Hadrian tensed. It wasn't as if he hadn't expected this, but it was still frustrating. No, it made him angry. Because he'd done nothing to warrant involvement in this matter.

Yet, he *was* involved because he'd had the misfortune to be betrothed to a woman who'd become tangled up with Louis Chambers, a man who'd apparently hated Hadrian and now, even in death, was causing him trouble.

Beryl told the coroner that she'd had little to no communication or interaction with Hadrian since they'd dissolved their engagement.

Graythorpe nodded vaguely. "Then why would you send him a letter the day before your husband was murdered asking for his help? Surely there were other people you could ask." He looked expectantly at Beryl.

"I had already asked for help from my friend and neighbor, Mrs. Styles-Rowdon." Beryl kept her chin up, but Hadrian thought she looked pale. "And I do not have family whom I can ask for anything."

"Multiple people have reported to the police that you were having a liaison with someone, and that person may have been Ravenhurst. Are either of those things true?"

"Of course not," she answered hastily as color rushed to her cheeks.

"Let us discuss the arsenic poisoning now," Graythorpe said. "Detective Inspector Teague found a bottle of arsenic in the pantry of your household. Did you have occasion to use it?"

It was usual for a household to have arsenic to poison vermin. Still, Hadrian exchanged a look with Tilda.

"No." Beryl glanced to her right where the members of her household were seated. "I'm sure Mrs. Blank or Mrs. Dunning may have done."

"I will ask them," Graythorpe replied. "Had your husband been ill?"

"Perhaps." Beryl lifted a shoulder. "I thought he was drinking too much and suffering the ill effects. Massey would likely know more about that." She flicked a look toward the valet, who was still standing in the corner.

Graythorpe then asked if Beryl had taken an insurance policy out on her husband. She replied that she had not. The coroner moved on to interview her retainers. The housekeeper and cook said they used arsenic to kill vermin. None could offer any information as to how Chambers had been poisoned.

Clara said she had cleaned up after Chambers being ill and also recounted how she'd found him dead in his bed. She also answered questions about her affair with Chambers and clearly didn't enjoy doing so. She shifted in her chair whilst flushing crimson the entire time.

Finally, it was Massey's turn to be questioned. It was evident he did not care for Beryl, and he repeated his belief that she was having an affair.

"You told Detective Inspector Teague that Chambers believed his wife's paramour to be Lord Ravenhurst?"

"I did, but I've no proof that was true," Massey said, much to Hadrian's relief. "Mr. Chambers seemed to have a deep dislike of the earl. I don't know why."

"What of Mr. Chambers' health?" Graythorpe asked next. "Did you notice he was ill?"

"Yes, but I also attributed it to his excessive alcohol consumption."

The coroner asked Massey to detail Chambers' symptoms, which sounded truly unpleasant. But how pleasant was an inquest supposed to be with a dead body laid out on a table? At least Chambers was covered with a cloth, and there were sprigs of lavender around the body.

As the coroner concluded his questioning of Massey, Hadrian realized that there'd been no discussion of Massey's secret—that he spent one night every fortnight at a brothel, and not an ordinary brothel at that—or that Chambers had threatened the valet with exposing his secret. Whilst Hadrian didn't want the man's private life laid bare, he couldn't help feeling that he didn't want his own past revealed either, particularly because it made Hadrian appear a suspect. Massey was also a suspect but did not appear to be since he wasn't questioned about his hidden behavior—of which Teague was aware. Why had Teague decided not to treat him as a suspect?

Tilda elbowed Hadrian gently. He turned his head to see her watching him intently. She nodded toward the coroner.

"Lord Ravenhurst?" Graythorpe asked, and Hadrian realized he'd been lost in his thoughts.

"Yes?" Hadrian stood.

"Thank you, my lord," Graythorpe said with a deferential smile. "Would you remain standing? Or you may take this chair." He gestured to an empty chair near the table.

"I'll stand," Hadrian said.

"How long have you known Mrs. Chambers?"

"About four years."

Graythorpe clasped his hands behind his back. "You courted her during the Season?"

"I did. And we became engaged to be married." Hadrian wanted to put this behind him as quickly as possible. "There was an unfortunate situation, and Mrs. Chambers and I decided we didn't suit."

"Because you caught Mrs. Chambers in an embrace with Mr. Louis Chambers, correct?" Graythorpe looked at him expectantly.

"Yes." Hadrian felt something brush his hand. He looked down and saw that it was Tilda. But she was already resting her hand back on her lap. Still, the brief, simple gesture eased his tension.

"Did you blame Chambers for the ruin of your betrothal?" Graythorpe asked.

Hadrian loathed having to answer this in such a public setting. It would undoubtedly hurt Beryl, but there was nothing Hadrian could do. "I mostly blamed Mrs. Chambers." He saw from the lower part of his eye that Beryl had turned her head toward him, but he kept his attention fixed on the coroner.

"Yet you came to help her when she asked," Graythorpe noted.

"I did. She sounded desperate, and I am not unkind."

"Is it possible you still have a romantic inclination toward Mrs. Chambers?"

Again, Hadrian disliked having to expose himself and his emotions in this manner. He rolled his shoulders. "It is not."

Graythorpe then asked Hadrian about what had happened at Arthur's the night before Chambers was killed. Hadrian relayed that, as well as his arrival at the Chambers' house the following day, including his shock at learning Chambers had been murdered.

"Shortly thereafter, Miss Matilda Wren arrived. The two of you work together to investigate crimes?"

"We have on one other occasion," Hadrian said. "I hired her to find Chambers' killer."

Graythorpe's brows drew together. "Why would you do that?"

"Because Miss Wren is a skilled investigator, and I believed she would find the murderer as quickly as possible."

The coroner's eyes narrowed, and Hadrian's neck bristled. "And you are working with her." It wasn't a question. "You have conducted yourself above reproach and have not sought to divert the investigation away from yourself?"

Hadrian's jaw clenched. "I always conduct myself with the utmost integrity, Mr. Graythorpe. Anyone will tell you that."

Graythorpe inclined his head. "Thank you, my lord. You may be seated."

Next, the corner asked Tilda to stand. She flicked a glance at Hadrian, and he couldn't detect even a modicum of nervousness or apprehension.

Over the next several minutes, she answered the coroner's questions about Beryl's intention to divorce her husband, as well as the jewelry that had gone missing and Tilda's efforts to find it.

He then questioned her about what she'd learned regarding Martha Farrow. Tilda answered everything openly and honestly.

When it seemed the coroner was finished, Tilda surprised him—and probably everyone in the room—by asking if she could pose a question of her own.

"That would be highly irregular, Miss Wren."

"Nevertheless, may I? The arsenic poisoning is a great surprise. Can you share how acute the poisoning was?"

"If you're asking whether the arsenic contributed to Mr. Chambers' death, it did not. Though if he'd continued to ingest it at the same levels, I expect he would have died from the poison in the near future." The corner pursed his lips. "You may be seated, Miss Wren."

Hadrian took that to mean that she was not to ask any further questions.

Next, Graythorpe questioned Pollard who provided an alibi for when Chambers had been murdered. Pollard had been at Arthur's until very late—or very early, depending on how one looked at it—with his cousin, whom he'd brought to the inquest. That was the gentleman who'd been standing with him earlier. And the woman was, apparently, Pollard's wife.

Finally, Graythorpe asked Daniel and Oliver Chambers if they would answer a few questions. The coroner queried Oliver about investing in the store with Pollard—which he'd also discussed with Pollard a few minutes earlier. They both indicated that Louis Chambers hadn't wanted to Oliver to invest.

When asked why, it was the eldest brother, Daniel, who responded. "Louis wanted to do something on his own. I inherited our father's engineering firm, and Oliver had pursued a career in the church. Until recently, that is."

Graythorpe addressed Oliver. "Was Louis upset with you for trying to intrude on his business plans?"

"Yes."

"And now you are benefitting from his death since you are, in fact, going to invest in Pollard's store."

"We have not yet finalized the arrangement," Oliver said quietly, his gaze focused on the floor.

The coroner looked toward Pollard once more. "Mr. Pollard, is it your intent to allow Mr. Oliver Chambers to invest?"

Pollard nodded. "Yes."

Graythorpe returned his attention to Oliver. "You will benefit from your brother's death."

"No, he would have made the investment anyhow," Daniel said, sounding angry. Hadrian couldn't see his face. "Louis was going to have to accept him."

"Why?" Graythorpe asked crisply.

Daniel frowned. "Because he was out of funds."

The coroner arched his brow. "How do you know that?"

"I know because I'd been giving him money periodically for years and recently stopped. I refused to watch him recklessly spend." He pressed his lips together, his expression one of frustration and sadness.

"Thank you, Mr. Chambers. And Mr. Chambers." Graythorpe turned his head to the jury. He asked if they needed to step out to deliberate or if they could come to a quick conclusion.

The jurors murmured amongst themselves and almost immediately returned their decision—Chambers had been murdered.

It wasn't shocking, but still people reacted, muttering and whispering.

The coroner thanked the jury, then urged the police to find the murderer as soon as possible, noting that they had an abundance of suspects. Graythorpe's gaze moved over those assembled, and for a brief moment his eyes connected with Hadrian's. Swallowing, Hadrian jerked his attention toward Teague who'd stepped forward.

"I am Detective Inspector Teague. If you know *anything* at all about Mr. Chambers, please speak to me. I will remain here for a short while. You may also visit me at Scotland Yard."

Everyone began to stand. Tilda clasped Hadrian's forearm briefly. He turned toward her. "You did well," she murmured. "I'm sorry you had to answer all that."

"It's all right. I look forward to when this is history once more." He gave her a small smile.

"I'd like to go to the Chambers' house," Tilda whispered. She glanced toward Beryl who was speaking to Mrs. Styles-Rowdon. "Do you think Beryl will mind?"

Hadrian understood what Tilda wanted to do. "You want to investigate the poisoning."

Her eyes gleamed with enthusiasm. "Yes. I would really like if Massey would come, but I'm not sure he will."

"Let's go ask him." Hadrian escorted her to Massey, who was trying to cut through the crowd toward the door. "Massey, wait," Hadrian called.

The valet paused, his features taut. "What is it?" He appeared impatient.

"I don't suppose you'd come to the Chambers' house with us?" Tilda asked. "I'd like to conduct some inquiries about this poisoning. In particular, I'd like to determine where it came from."

"Wouldn't it have been put into his food?" Massey looked toward the cook. "Seems like you should be speaking with Mrs. Dunning."

"I plan to," Tilda said. "I'd just hoped to speak to everyone who lived there. If you'd rather not come, I can ask you some questions now and then call on you at the Cock and Hen if I have further inquiries."

"I'll come to the house," Massey said, though he seemed annoyed. "I do need to fetch the rest of my things." He seemed hesitant. "I should also speak with Mrs. Chambers about making sure she'll continue to pay my wages. Though I am worried since Daniel Chambers indicated that his brother was out of funds."

"I will speak with her on your behalf," Hadrian offered. He hoped there were funds to pay the valet. Not to mention the rest of the staff. If not, he may talk to Daniel Chambers to see if he would ensure the retainers did not suffer because of Louis Chambers' financial recklessness. "Why don't you walk on ahead and pack up your things?" Hadrian suggested.

When the valet was gone, Hadrian and Tilda walked to where Beryl stood with Mrs. Styles-Rowdon.

"That wasn't so bad, was it?" Mrs. Styles-Rowdon said brightly. She wore an elegant purple ensemble adorned with a black sash at her waist.

Beryl had left her veil up for the remainder of the inquest. "I am glad it's over." She glanced at Hadrian with perhaps a touch of nervousness.

"I am also," Hadrian said. "Would you allow Tilda and me to accompany you back to your house?" It would be a short walk.

"Of course," Beryl replied.

Tilda smiled. "Thank you. I would like to speak with you and the staff about this poisoning business, as well as look around the house. Will that be all right?"

Beryl shook her head. "I can't believe he was poisoned. I suppose that was why he'd been ill. We had no idea." She seemed more surprised than sad, but Hadrian supposed that made sense. She'd made no secret that she disliked her husband and regretted marrying him. It was why she was a suspect.

And while Hadrian had a great deal of trouble believing she would have stabbed her husband, he somehow found it more believable that she might poison him. Did that mean he suspected she was guilty? Did that also mean multiple people had attempted to kill Chambers?

He wasn't sure, but *someone* had succeeded in killing Louis Chambers.

After today's inquest, he wasn't sure they were any closer to finding out who.

CHAPTER 15

*W*hen they stepped from the pub into the street, Tilda immediately wished they'd left through a back door. The number of reporters had increased, and several flocked toward Hadrian. Kirkham was also loitering about with a few gentlemen, and their attention focused on Hadrian.

Tilda clasped Hadrian's arm. "I know it's a short trip to Beryl's house, but perhaps we should take your coach."

"Lord Ravenhurst!" one of the reporters called. "Are you a suspect in the murder of Louis Chambers?"

"Were you having an affair with Chambers' wife?" another asked.

Hadrian tensed, and a muscle in his neck worked. "I don't want to leave Beryl to these jackals either. But I must tell Leach we're going to her house."

"He's going to move the coach. You may as well get in it," Tilda advised. "You go. I'll move Beryl and everyone else along." She didn't want to suggest Beryl go with him in the coach. That would only feed the rumors.

His eyes sparking with anger, Hadrian muttered something before hurrying to the coach. Tilda glared at the encroaching reporters and hastened to where Beryl and the others were already fending off several other reporters.

Tilda moved to Beryl's side. "You don't need to speak with them. Just walk quickly toward your house."

"What if they follow us?" Beryl asked, her features stricken.

"They wouldn't dare!" Mrs. Styles-Rowdon declared in horror.

Tilda was afraid they would. "Go. Quickly."

Mrs. Styles-Rowdon took Beryl's arm and steered her away. The retainers were already moving in the direction of Beryl's house.

Turning, Tilda took a deep breath and faced the press. "I will answer a question or two."

One of the reporters, a man who was perhaps a few years older than Tilda and garbed in a rather loud pair of orange plaid pants, squinted at her. "Who are you?"

"Miss Matilda Wren. I am investigating the matter of Louis Chambers' death."

The man swept his gaze over her and began to laugh. Thoroughly annoyed, Tilda glowered at him.

Someone else asked, "Why are you investigating?"

"I was hired to do so, and no, I will not reveal by whom," she said crisply.

"Who killed Chambers?" the reporter who'd laughed at her asked.

"The investigation by Scotland Yard is ongoing."

The journalist's expression soured. "You said you would answer questions, not evade them."

In truth, Tilda had only wanted to distract them from Hadrian and the others. Now that they were gone, she could also be on her way. She looked toward the door to the pub where Teague had just exited. "I'm sure *Detective Inspector Teague* will eagerly answer your questions."

She stressed Teague and his title, as she was certain the

reporter would be far more impressed with him. Judging by the speed with which the man in the obnoxious pants left to speak with Teague, she was not wrong.

Muttering the same curse Hadrian had a few moments earlier, Tilda pivoted and walked to Beryl's house. She moved quickly and noted that Hadrian was waiting for her at the door.

"Why did you linger?" he asked.

"I wanted to keep the reporters from following Beryl and her staff. I thought I would answer a few questions; however, it seems my role as an investigator is a matter of humor. So I directed them to Teague."

"Good." Hadrian frowned slightly. "Though I am sorry they did not take you seriously."

Tilda lifted a shoulder. "I should not have expected otherwise."

Hadrian held the door for her as she stepped into the entrance hall. The staff was still assembled, though Mrs. Styles-Rowdon was not present.

Mrs. Dunning, the cook, looked toward Tilda. She appeared to be a mixture of vexed and distraught, her features creased, and her dark brows drawn together. "I am most upset to think someone came to my pantry, pilfered the household arsenic, and used it to poison Mr. Chambers." During the inquest, Mrs. Dunning had testified that the amount of arsenic remaining in the bottle seemed to have decreased since she'd last used it, but that she couldn't be certain.

"It's ghastly," Mrs. Blank said with a fierce expression. She flicked a glance at Beryl, who was busy handing her hat, veil, and gloves to Clara.

"Someone in the household must have been poisoning Mr. Chambers," Oswald said. He also glanced toward Beryl.

Did they all think she was guilty?

Massey was nowhere to be seen, but then he'd walked ahead

of everyone when they'd left the pub. He was likely already upstairs gathering his things as Hadrian had suggested.

"I understand constables searched the house on Saturday after the inquest was canceled." Tilda wanted to know if they'd been aware of the arsenic poisoning before today, but it seemed they were not. "Did they not explain why?"

Mrs. Blank shook her head. "They only said they needed to do another search."

Mrs. Dunning frowned. "I did not realize they'd taken the arsenic from the pantry. But it's not something I use daily. Or even weekly sometimes."

"Does anyone have a notion as to how Mr. Chambers would have ingested the arsenic?" Tilda asked. "It doesn't smell or taste like anything, unfortunately, so it's possible you have had some too. Have any of you been ill?"

Clara glanced at Beryl whilst Beryl's features tensed.

"Clara, were you or Mrs. Chambers ill? Or Martha perhaps?" Hadrian asked.

"Mrs. Chambers was ill in January for a time. But she has been well for weeks."

Tilda looked to Beryl. "And were your symptoms similar to what was described at the inquest today?"

"Yes," Beryl whispered.

If Beryl had been poisoned, it would seem she was not then guilty of poisoning her husband. That wouldn't make sense.

Tilda looked at the retainers. "Was anyone else ill?"

They shook their heads.

"Can we be sure Mrs. Chambers was poisoned?" Mrs. Dunning wrung her hands. "Why would that have stopped?"

"Perhaps it was an accident," Hadrian suggested. "Is there any way arsenic could have found its way into something?"

"Absolutely not," Mrs. Blank responded as Mrs. Dunning turned pale. "Mrs. Dunning would never make such a mistake. Nor would she purchase tainted flour."

"Perhaps the food came from someplace else then," Tilda said gently. "Is that possible, Mrs. Dunning?"

Mrs. Dunning seemed to think a moment. "When they had their dinner parties, Mr. Chambers often brought in a few items, usually an extravagant cake or tart from somewhere. But everyone would have been ill." She frowned. "Though Mr. Chambers made sure only he was served any leftover cake or tart."

Tilda doubted the dessert had been poisoned because the cook was right—everyone who'd eaten it would have been ill. Except they would only have felt poorly for a brief period. If Chambers was ingesting all that remained, it was possible that he would have been sick longer. Still, it didn't support consistent illness, which seemed to have been the case.

Tilda continued her inquiry. "When was the last dinner party?"

"A fortnight before Mr. Chambers died," Mrs. Blank replied.

"That was just a few days after Martha left," Clara added. "I remember because it was the first time we had to prepare without her help."

Tilda wanted to know if these party desserts could be the culprit. "And the party before that?"

"They occurred monthly," Oswald said. "Though there were two in January. One on Epiphany and one a fortnight or so later."

These parties would easily have put a strain on Chambers' already faltering finances. Why would he continue to have them? Because he was completely reckless and apparently expected his older brother to bail him out.

Hadrian turned to her. "Is it possible the food from these parties contained arsenic?"

"It's possible, but I would find it surprising." Tilda looked to Mrs. Blank. "I would like you to write down the dates of the parties since Epiphany along with what items came from outside the house and from where. Please also indicate how much remained after the party and if you know how long it took Mr. Chambers to eat what was left."

The housekeeper nodded. "I'll do that straightaway."

Beryl addressed Mrs. Dunning. "I think we all require tea. I'll have mine in the parlor with his lordship and Miss Wren." She turned and walked into the parlor, and the retainers dispersed.

Tilda and Hadrian followed Beryl into the parlor where Beryl had already taken a seat on the settee.

"Beryl, if you would pardon us for a short while, I'd like to search Louis's bedchamber and study again." Tilda summoned her brightest smile and hoped Beryl wouldn't ask to join them. Having Hadrian try to see something with Beryl there could be troublesome.

"'Us'?" Beryl asked with a frown. She looked to Hadrian. "You're leaving me too?"

"Not for long," he said soothingly. "You do want us to find the truth?"

"I do, but I'm confused. And worried. You heard what Oswald said. Someone in the household was poisoning Louis. I don't think it was the cake from our parties. They come from a very nice and expensive bakery—Hosford's on Piccadilly. Louis had an account there." Beryl looked toward the doorway to the staircase hall through which everyone else had departed. "At this point, I suspect Clara," she whispered.

"Has something happened to make you think that?" Tilda asked.

Beryl shrugged. "She seems the likeliest person because of what Louis did to her when she first started working here. I confess I am uncomfortable with her now that I know of her behavior with him."

Tilda did not respond as she would have wished, which would be to tell Beryl that Clara's behavior was not her fault. She'd been young and taken advantage of by her employer. If anything, Beryl ought to have despised her husband even more.

"We'll be back soon," Tilda said before leaving the parlor and going to the study. She heard Hadrian following her.

When they reached the study, she turned to face Hadrian. "I don't anticipate finding anything since the constables have already searched and it was their second time doing so. Mostly, I just wanted you to touch things and see if you could determine where the poison came from." She grimaced. "I realize this is nearly as difficult as trying to find Beryl's missing jewelry."

"Except we already found one piece and know what happened to three others," Hadrian said with the optimism Tilda needed.

She smiled at him. "You're right. But don't touch anything until I motion for you to do so. I don't want you to become overwhelmed by a terrible headache from multiple visions again."

"I'll be careful. And I'll await your direction."

Hearing a noise in the bedchamber, they both turned in that direction. Hadrian moved toward the doorway just as Massey appeared. He carried a bag.

"Thank you for coming," Tilda said.

The valet must have come through the dressing room. "What is it you wish to speak with me about?"

Tilda reviewed what they'd learned from the other retainers. "Aside from the cakes and tarts from the dinner parties, can you think of anything Mr. Chambers ate or drank that did not come from the household?"

"No, though I must tell you that he often allowed me a small serving of those cakes, and I have not been ill. Why would someone risk poisoning the entire household?"

"I want to make sure Mr. Chambers wasn't ingesting something that was inadvertently poisoned," Tilda replied. "Some flours contain arsenic. It's to make them heavier so the seller can charge more. It's possible Mr. Chambers wasn't being poisoned on purpose. However, since you often ate those desserts, I think we can assume they were not poisoned."

"Could the poison have been in his liquor?" Massey asked. "He drank plenty of it."

"It could have been, but he likely would have noticed," Tilda said. "Arsenic dissolves in hot liquids, so it is usually found in tea or other hot dish or baked into food. If it had been in his liquor, he may have noticed its presence, at least the texture."

Massey nodded vaguely. "I can't think of anything he ate or drank that wasn't prepared here. I don't think Mrs. Dunning cared for him. Nor did Mrs. Blank or Oswald."

Hadrian arched a brow. "The list of people who liked him is rather short, I think."

"Is there anything else?" Massey asked.

"Not at the moment." Tilda eyed his bag. "All packed and ready to leave?"

"Hopefully never to return." The valet looked to Hadrian. "Have you spoken to Mrs. Chambers yet?"

"I have not, but I will," Hadrian said with a firm nod. "She is in the parlor."

Massey wrinkled his nose. "Then I shall leave through the downstairs. I suppose I should say goodbye to the others."

"Thank you," Tilda said. "I appreciate you coming. Will we be able to find you at the brothel?"

"For now. I must find a new position posthaste."

"I'll deliver a letter of recommendation to your address tomorrow," Hadrian said.

The valet blinked and offered a stiff bow. "Thank you, my lord." He grabbed his bag and departed with alacrity.

"He could not leave fast enough," Tilda noted. "We must consider that he may have been poisoning his employer, regardless of his insistence that he did not. I should think it would have been easy for him to add arsenic to tea." She turned to survey the study. "Let us search here first, then the dressing room. I am satisfied I searched the bedchamber thoroughly the other day."

They looked through every inch of the study and found

nothing out of the ordinary. And there was no food or anything related to food—just a cabinet with several kinds of liquor.

"You didn't ask me to touch anything," Hadrian said.

"There's nothing odd or suspicious. I wonder if you should go downstairs to the pantry and see if you can detect whether someone other than Mrs. Dunning or Mrs. Blank accessed it." Tilda blew out a breath. "Though without the arsenic itself, that may be pointless. I wish you could touch *that*."

They searched the dressing room next and again found nothing that provoked Tilda's curiosity or prompted her to ask Hadrian to touch anything. Frustrated, she told Hadrian they could return to the parlor.

As they walked from the study into the sitting room, they encountered Clara. She seemed to have been waiting and now flushed before looking away from them.

"Did you need something, Clara?" Tilda asked.

Clara hesitated. She worried her hands and chewed her lip. "I'm afraid," Clara whispered. "Someone poisoned Mr. Chambers. And stabbed him. I don't feel safe here."

Tilda felt sorry for the young woman. "Have you anywhere you can stay?"

"No." She took a stuttering breath. "I will manage. I didn't mean to bother you." She began to turn.

"Is there anything you aren't telling us, Clara?" Tilda asked.

"It's just … Mrs. Chambers has been acting strangely. She hasn't wanted me to help her very much since …" The maid's voice trailed off.

"Since her husband died?" Hadrian supplied.

Clara nodded. "She may just be upset with me because of what happened … before." She looked down at the floor.

"That could very well be," Tilda said kindly. "Try not to worry overmuch. It's a difficult time."

"That's what Mrs. Blank told me. She said I should feel fortu-nate to have a bit of a respite. It's true that we've all been working harder since Martha left." Clara brushed her hand over her nose and sniffed. "I'm sad about Martha too. Being here is difficult."

Tilda put her hand on Clara's shoulder. "I'm so sorry. Mrs. Blank is right. Take solace in this respite."

"Thank you, Miss Wren. You've been so kind." Clara smiled.

Removing her hand from Clara, Tilda asked, "Since you are here, can you tell me how long Mrs. Chambers has had the veil she wore today?"

"Mrs. Styles-Rowdon gave it to her when she brought the mourning clothes. She said she wore it after her husband died a few years ago."

"Thank you," Tilda said warmly.

Clara turned and went through the doorway to the servants' staircase.

Tilda pivoted to face Hadrian. "Why do you suppose Beryl is giving Clara a 'respite'?"

"It could be as Clara said. Or that Beryl is upset and needs time to herself."

"Or it could be that she's feeling guilty and doesn't want to be around the maid." Tilda frowned. "I don't know."

"Why did you ask about the veil?" Hadrian asked. "I confess seeing Beryl wear that earlier made me think of the woman who was seen visiting Martha."

"Precisely," Tilda said, glad that he'd also noticed that. "Clara says Mrs. Styles-Rowdon brought the veil on Friday. That was before the woman was seen with Martha later that night."

"But wasn't the veiled woman seen another time?" Hadrian asked.

Tilda frowned. "Still, it could have been Beryl. She may have already had a veil when Mrs. Styles-Rowdon offered hers and didn't want to say so."

Hadrian nodded vaguely. "Because she wouldn't want anyone to know if she'd been wearing it in Spitalfields to see Martha." He met Tilda's gaze. "Why would Beryl call on Martha? And why would she have pushed her to her death? Perhaps she'd discovered Martha's affair with her husband."

Tilda didn't think that was the reason. "Beryl would have been glad to have proof of her husband's infidelity, as it would have helped her pursuit of a divorce. I would say it makes more sense that Beryl was worried that Martha was aware of her poisoning Louis, so she called on her to find out. However, if Beryl was also being poisoned, it's unlikely she is the poisoner." Tilda paused and thought a moment. "I suppose it's possible that Beryl wasn't poisoned with arsenic—we can't know since her illness has resolved."

Hadrian grimaced faintly. "I confess I have an easier time believing Beryl might poison Louis as opposed to stabbing him."

"We should probably return to the parlor," Tilda said.

Upon arriving at the parlor, they had to stop short upon seeing that Beryl was not alone. She sat on the settee very close to her brother-in-law, Oliver Chambers, their heads bent together.

Oliver looked up and saw Tilda and Hadrian. He gently elbowed Beryl who also moved her gaze to the doorway.

Beryl straightened, angling her body toward Tilda and Hadrian. In doing so, she moved away from Oliver. Still, Tilda noted their closeness. Perhaps it was just that Oliver was comforting his brother's widow. Or there was a chance it was something else.

"Oliver came to see how I was faring after the inquest," Beryl said.

Hadrian inclined his head toward Oliver. "That's kind of you."

Tilda stepped into the parlor, and Hadrian followed her.

"We've decided to hold the funeral on Wednesday," Beryl said as Tilda and Hadrian sat opposite the settee in a pair of chairs. "Oliver has been kind enough to handle the cards."

"Detective Inspector Teague says the body will be delivered later today." Oliver's face was grim.

Tilda didn't really want to bother him amidst his grief, but she also didn't want to miss the opportunity to speak with him. "Mr. Chambers, would you mind if I asked you a few questions about Mr. Pollard and the shop?"

Oliver's dark eyes flickered with something—unease perhaps. "I suppose."

"I appreciate that," Tilda said with a supportive smile. "I imagine this is a difficult time. My primary goal is to find the person responsible for your brother's death."

"I understand. What do you want to know about Pollard?"

"Did you approach him about investing in the shop, or was it his idea?"

"It was my idea," Oliver replied. "When I decided the religious life didn't suit, I needed to find another occupation. I hadn't considered enterprise, but when my brother was struggling with making his payments, I offered to help. He wanted a loan, but I asked to become an investor."

Hadrian glanced at Tilda before asking, "You knew he wasn't making his payments to Pollard?"

"Daniel told me," Oliver said with a nod. "Daniel has always had to provide financial support to Louis over the years since our father died. Daniel told me that things became particularly dire a few months ago. He'd asked Daniel to help with the payments to Pollard. Daniel refused. He'd advised Louis not to invest in the shop in the first place."

"Why is that?" Tilda asked.

Oliver frowned. "Louis was never very good with money, and Daniel didn't think he'd be able to manage an investment like that. He was right, of course. Daniel offered to take over his finances and give him an allowance, but Louis refused."

"Presumably, Louis had some income," Hadrian said. "Otherwise, there would be no money at all to sustain the household or agree to an investment in the first place."

"Louis and I both have a quarterly income from investments

our father had made. Louis typically spent beyond that income, however."

"Did he have debts?" Hadrian asked.

"Yes, but Daniel knows more about that."

Beryl paled. "I didn't realize there were debts." She looked down at her lap. "I have debts too. At the milliner and druggist."

Oliver gave her a soothing pat on the hand. "I'm sure those are not substantial."

Tilda again noted their familiarity and wondered if Oliver might be Beryl's lover. "But your brother's debts *were* substantial?"

"I don't know the specifics. I would say you should ask Daniel, though I would not do so until after the funeral at least." Oliver grimaced faintly. "Louis's death has impacted him greatly. In some ways, I think he feels responsible, that he should have done more to protect Louis."

"From what?" Now that Tilda knew that Louis had debts, she wondered if Louis had owed money to unsavory lenders.

Oliver shrugged. "Probably from himself. If there was a bad decision to be made, Louis chose it." He glanced toward Beryl. "Except for marrying you."

"I don't think that ended up being a very good decision for either of us," she said quietly, her gaze still on her lap.

An uncomfortable silence reigned for a moment. Tilda looked to Hadrian and inclined her head toward the door to indicate they should go. He nodded, and they rose.

"I saw a man with you and your brother at the inquest," Hadrian said. "Padgett is his name."

"My brother hired him to investigate Louis's death." Oliver flicked a glance at Tilda.

Beryl looked at Hadrian. "He came here yesterday to speak with me. I was telling Oliver about it before you came in."

"Did Padgett indicate anything he was investigating in partic-ular?" Tilda asked.

Beryl shook her head. "I had the sense he thought I likely killed Louis." She shivered. "I didn't care for Padgett."

"I'm sorry he troubled you," Hadrian said. "We'll take our leave now."

Beryl gave him an expectant look. "You'll come to the funeral?"

Hadrian smiled. "Of course."

"And you're still searching for my missing jewelry?" Beryl asked Tilda.

Tilda felt Hadrian looking at her. She didn't want to tell Beryl about the rubies that Louis had given to his mistress—not yet anyway. Hopefully, Tilda would identify the woman and recover the jewels. Then she would tell Beryl what had happened, rather than add to her turmoil right now.

"I am," Tilda replied. "I will let you know if I am able to make any progress." She looked at Hadrian and again inclined her head slightly toward the door.

They said goodbye to Beryl and Oliver and took their leave. Outside, Tilda explained to Hadrian why she hadn't told Beryl about the rubies.

"That is probably the kindest thing at the moment," he said. "She doesn't need to be angry about her husband giving her jewelry to his mistress in addition to everything else."

"Agreed." Tilda thanked Leach as he helped her into the coach.

When Hadrian settled in beside her, she added, "I also didn't want to point out that she couldn't afford to pay me, yet I would do my best to find her jewelry anyway."

"I'm glad you're letting me pay you for your time."

"It isn't much," she said as the coach began moving. "You'll be paying me far more for the investigation into the murder, especially now that arsenic has been found."

He grinned at her. "And you're worth every shilling." He paused, his features sobering, before going on. "Did you have the feeling there may be a closer bond between Beryl and Oliver than just in-laws comforting one another?"

"I'm glad I wasn't alone in thinking that. I should like to know more about Louis's debts."

"Such as whether he may have owed someone who would have killed him over not being repaid?" he asked.

"Precisely. Though if that's the case, that means someone was poisoning Louis and someone else—a criminal—stabbed him." Tilda looked at Hadrian. "It's just such a coincidence that he was being poisoned and was then stabbed."

"Is it, when so many people had a motive to kill him?"

Tilda supposed not. "I should like to call on Pollard tomorrow. I would have also liked to speak with Daniel Chambers, but it seems we must wait until after the funeral."

"I will pick you up tomorrow morning at eleven, if that is acceptable," Hadrian offered.

"Indeed. Thank you."

"Damn, I forgot to speak with Beryl about Massey's employment," Hadrian said, crossing his arms over his chest with a deep frown.

"After listening to Oliver, there may not be money to pay him," Tilda said.

"That is a concern." Hadrian blew out a breath and uncrossed his arms. "Chambers was a right bastard."

"Don't let anyone else hear you say that," Tilda warned.

He turned his head to look at her, his features softening. His eyes were a dark blue in the dim light of the coach, and they glittered with a surprising intensity. "Thank you for your support today, particularly with the reporters."

"You don't deserve any of this trouble."

"I appreciate you saying that. This will pass. I just hope that happens soon."

"We're going to solve this case," Tilda vowed. She prayed it would be soon too.

CHAPTER 16

*T*ilda was ready when Hadrian arrived at eleven the following morning. She didn't want to waste a moment with him coming in to exchange pleasantries, though she knew her grandmother would be disappointed. Instead, she promised he would come in when he brought her back later in the day.

"Perhaps he will take tea with us," Grandmama suggested.

"Perhaps," Tilda said vaguely before kissing her grandmother's cheek. Vaughn held the door for her as she exited the house and hastened to the coach.

Hadrian had climbed down only to stop short upon seeing her. "You're ready to depart."

"We're eager to solve this case, aren't we?" Tilda replied with perhaps a touch of jovial impatience.

"We are indeed." Chuckling, he handed her into the coach.

When they arrived at the drapery shop, Hadrian removed his gloves before leaving the coach. "I will not miss an opportunity to perhaps shake Pollard's hand or touch something inside the shop."

They walked to the door of the shop and Hadrian knocked. Pollard answered, his mouth twisting into something between a frown and a grimace. "Why have you come again?"

"We have a few more questions," Hadrian said amenably. "I promise we won't take too much of your time."

"I will hold you to that," Pollard said as he opened the door for them to move inside.

Tilda immediately noticed a woman standing near an empty case with a glass top and recognized her as the woman who'd been sitting beside Pollard at the inquest.

Pollard closed the door and walked around them. "This is Mrs. Pollard. Joanna, I believe you will recognize Lord Raven-hurst and Miss Wren from the inquest. They've come to bother me again with questions about Louis. You may recall that Miss Wren is working for Mrs. Chambers as an *investigator*." His tone seemed to indicate that he didn't approve.

"Why does she need an investigator?" Mrs. Pollard asked. She was taller than average, nearly as tall as her husband, but with a far more curvaceous figure. She had dark-blonde hair and small brown eyes. "Aren't the police investigating Louis's death?"

Tilda smiled patiently. "They are. However, I have been employed to conduct an investigation." She did not bother mentioning that Hadrian had hired her.

"Seems unnecessary," Mrs. Pollard said with a tsking sound. "But then the Chambers like to spend money."

There was another knock at the door, and Pollard went to open it. He returned a moment later with a card which he handed to his wife. "The funeral is on Wednesday."

Mrs. Pollard perused the card and made a moue of distaste. "I suppose I should go with you."

"You needn't bother, if you'd rather not," Pollard said. "I know you aren't particularly fond of Mrs. Chambers."

"Why is that?" Tilda asked.

Mrs. Pollard sniffed. "She doesn't care much for the shop. I think she believes it's beneath her husband to be so involved in the direct management. She thought he'd just give money to Edgar, and we'd run things. How I wish she'd been right."

"Come now, dear," Pollard said cajolingly. "None of that matters now that Louis is gone." He shook his head. "I am sorry about that. We may have fallen out somewhat, but I would never have wished him dead." A wistful expression passed briefly over the man's features. "We had some good times together in the beginning. I hadn't known then that he was such a wastrel."

"Are you referring to his financial problems?" Hadrian asked. "Or his behavior with women?" He glanced toward Mrs. Pollard. "Pardon me for asking such a question in your presence."

Tilda watched Mrs. Pollard closely. When Hadrian had asked about Chambers' behavior with women, her nostrils had flared, and her lip had curled ever so slightly. Tilda was convinced the woman knew something. But would she volunteer the information?

"Both," Pollard replied. "He was not content to remain faithful to his wife, as I am to Joanna." He sent her a warm smile, and his love for her seemed evident to Tilda.

Joanna returned his gaze but didn't respond in kind.

"Mr. Pollard, you mentioned Chambers didn't want a wife," Tilda recalled. "Was that because he did not wish to commit himself to just one woman?"

Pollard shrugged. "I am not sure of his reasons, but I suppose that could have been why."

"I don't suppose you were aware of any of his paramours?" Hadrian asked. "He didn't tell you of a mistress?"

"No one specific." Pollard wrinkled his nose. "He liked to visit brothels, but I never accompanied him."

Tilda moved on to her next line of inquiry. "Louis's death has allowed you to accept Oliver Chambers' investment as a partner."

Mrs. Pollard came toward them, her eyes blazing. "Don't you dare insinuate Edgar had anything to do with that man dying."

Pollard sent his wife an appreciative glance before returning his attention to Tilda. "I would have found a way to persuade Louis to permit his brother to invest. The man wasn't making his payments, and I'd planned to speak with the solicitor."

"Louis Chambers wanted so badly to be a successful business-man, but the truth was that he was terrible at managing financial matters. He was a prideful fool," Mrs. Pollard said with consider-able vitriol.

"Are you very involved in this business, Mrs. Pollard?" Tilda asked.

Mrs. Pollard lifted her chin and met Tilda's gaze, her eyes glit-tering. "I am the head designer and oversee all the seamstresses. Furthermore, my husband wants me to be."

"I am very impressed," Tilda said, meaning it. "I admire an enterprising woman—and the man who supports her."

Mrs. Pollard appeared to relax, her features softening slightly and her body losing a measure of stiffness that had been present since their arrival.

"Did either of you have occasion to visit the Chambers' home?" Tilda asked.

The Pollards exchanged a brief look, which gave Tilda her answer.

"On occasion," Pollard replied. "Louis often hosted dinner parties. We attended one a few weeks ago."

Tilda inclined her head. "Who else was in attendance?"

Pollard shrugged. "A couple of gentlemen from the club and their wives."

"Thank you, Mr. Pollard," Tilda said with a benign smile. She looked over at Hadrian. "Do you have any questions?"

Hadrian inclined his head, then fixed his gaze on Pollard. "You've known Louis for quite some time. Can you tell me why he despised me? I truly have no idea as to the cause."

Pollard blinked. "I can't say that I recall. He was clear in his dislike of you—hatred, really—but I don't know that he ever said why."

Tilda was sure that answer disappointed Hadrian and shot him a sympathetic glance. Taking a step to her right, she looked about the shop. "How close are you to opening?"

"I'm not sure," Pollard said on a frustrated sigh. "We don't have enough inventory to sell yet."

Mrs. Pollard sent him a heated stare. "That's because there hasn't been enough money to buy the supplies I need to sew. With Oliver investing now, I hope we can open within a few weeks."

"I thought you were finished with your questions," Pollard said curtly, though Tilda had not said that. "Neither my wife nor I had anything to do with Louis's murder."

"I didn't say you did," Tilda said patiently. "However, I'd say his demise worked out well for you."

Pollard scowled, and Mrs. Pollard took a few steps toward Tilda. "Louis Chambers was most definitely a problem, and no, I can't say we're sorry that he will no longer cause us distress or financial hardship. We will open the shop of our dreams, in spite of him." She sent her husband a confident look, and he nodded in response, his eyes crinkling with emotion.

"Thank you for your time," Tilda said. "I'm sure we'll see you at the funeral." She pivoted and noticed that Hadrian had moved toward the case where Mrs. Pollard had been standing. His fingertips were pressed along the top edge.

Then he removed them and brushed his hand along his temple. He turned and bid good day to the Pollards before opening the door for Tilda.

Outside, she asked, "How is your head?"

He narrowed one eye at her briefly. "Aches a bit, but it should ease soon, I think."

She paused before they reached the coach, so they were not within Leach's hearing. "What did you see in the shop?"

"Something that will probably make you want to learn all you can about Joanna Pollard."

~

"*J*'ll tell you in the coach," Hadrian said.

Tilda's eyes gleamed with anticipation. This was how she looked when her mind was turning over information and the thrill of investigation had a firm hold on her. "If what you're going to say will prompt questions about Mrs. Pollard, we should see what we can learn about the woman. Do you recall Flanders mentioning that Mrs. Pollard had worked for someone called Madame Ousset?"

"I do," Hadrian replied with a nod, delighting in Tilda's excitement. "Shall we stop in at the millinery and ask where we can find her?"

Tilda grinned. "Precisely what I was thinking."

They proceeded to the coach where Hadrian informed Leach of their next stop.

Once they were inside the vehicle and moving, Tilda looked eagerly toward Hadrian, waiting for him to describe his vision in the shop. It was moments like these, and the one outside the coach, that he enjoyed the most with her—the shared excitement of new information, the partnership of them working toward the same goal.

"As soon as I touched the display case, I felt overwhelming frustration and outrage. Then disgust." He stopped. "I'm getting ahead of myself. The disgust came with something in the vision. I saw Louis Chambers—in the shop. His expression was seductive, similar to what I'd seen in the visions in his bedchamber."

"I am very sorry you keep seeing *that*," Tilda said sardonically.

"As am I. Thankfully, this time it didn't last long. He was

advancing on the person whose memory I was seeing, but he stopped and his expression turned to anger. He said something, but of course I couldn't hear him. Then he was pushed."

"By you?" Tilda asked anxiously. "Rather, the person whose memory you saw."

"Yes. I glimpsed the hands, and they were feminine. I did not see any rings on her fingers, but that doesn't mean there weren't any, for it all happened very quickly. Chambers moved toward her again, his features menacing. Then he abruptly turned and left in a huff."

"Who could that have been?" Tilda asked.

"Since this happened in the shop, I suspect it was Mrs. Pollard. That's why I thought you'd be even more interested in her."

Tilda sat back against the squab, her expression contemplative. "I don't want to assume it's her, but it seems likely. I wonder what was happening. Was he trying to seduce her?"

"That is certainly something we can expect from him at this point," Hadrian said wryly.

A shudder passed through Tilda, and she made a face. "What a horrid man. It's bad enough he took advantage of his employees, but to attempt to seduce his partner's wife? The man had no scruples whatsoever."

Hadrian hadn't possessed strong feelings for the man when he was alive, but he did now. He was sorrier than ever that poor Beryl had fallen for his charm, not that he'd ever seen the man display any. "More and more, it seems any number of people would have good cause to wish him dead."

"I think Mrs. Pollard has now joined that group. She certainly seems to detest him, and I can see why. Not only had he caused disruption to their livelihood, but he also likely made advances toward her." Tilda's lip curled.

"Does this not also increase Pollard's potential as the murderer?" Hadrian asked. "If I learned my business partner had tried to seduce my wife, I would be very angry."

Tilda arched her brow at him. "Angry enough to kill?"

"I can't say, for I do not actually have a wife."

"You had a fiancée, and someone *did* seduce her," Tilda pointed out. "And no, I am not saying I suspect you of murdering Louis Chambers. I am merely pointing out that there is a line between being angry and wanting to kill someone."

"You make a valid point. There is a line, and I wasn't even close to it. Perhaps that is because I didn't love Beryl. If I had, would I have been closer to the line or even over it?" He couldn't answer that. He hadn't ever been in love. He'd yet to meet a woman who provoked such a visceral emotion within him.

Or had he? He recalled the ferocity of his need to protect Tilda when a murderer had lunged for her just over a week ago. There had been no line to cross. Hadrian simply would have done whatever was necessary to keep her safe.

"Pollard seems to love his wife," Tilda said. "Perhaps that is motivation enough."

The coach stopped in front of Flanders Millinery. Hadrian didn't wait for Leach to open the door. He did so himself and climbed down, then helped Tilda to the pavement.

They were able to see Flanders and learn that Madame Ousset had a shop just a little farther down Regent Street.

"Shall we walk?" Tilda asked as they exited the milliner.

"It is no longer raining, so why not?" It had rained right up to when he'd arrived at Tilda's house earlier. Hadrian informed Leach of where they were going, and the coachman said he would move the carriage to their location whilst they completed their errand.

"Do you suppose she's as French as her name?" Tilda asked as they made their way along Regent Street.

"Probably not. At one time, a French modiste was all the rage for the aristocracy, even though we supposedly despised the French."

"You upper-class types are strange," she said with a laugh.

"Some of us even have odd, inexplicable powers." He waggled his brows at her, and her mirth continued.

They reached Madame Ousset's shop, and Hadrian held the door for Tilda. The interior was most elegant with bolts of fabric on display and a few seating areas where ladies sat perusing fashion plates.

A young woman approached them, and Hadrian summoned his most charming smile and demeanor. "May we please speak with Madame Ousset? It's a matter of some importance."

The woman, who was beautifully attired, looked Tilda over from bodice to hem. "I can see that. I am not sure Madame Ousset has an appointment today, however."

Hadrian darted a glance at Tilda, hoping she was not offended by the woman's perusal and comment. Whilst Tilda's wardrobe was out of date, it was in good condition. To him, she always looked lovely.

"Perhaps Madame Ousset can find time for the Earl of Raven-hurst," Hadrian said with the barest hint of a smile.

Bobbing a curtsey, the woman said, "Of course, my lord." She hurried to the back of the shop, and Hadrian noted a pair of patrons looking in their direction.

"I think they heard you playing your earl card," Tilda said with a lively look.

"I felt it was necessary," he said in his defense.

"Oh, I agree. And I am grateful for it in these instances."

The young woman returned and ushered them to a private sitting room. "Would you care for tea?"

"No, thank you," Hadrian replied.

After dipping into another curtsey, the woman left.

Tilda looked at the closed door. "I believe she thinks we're here to purchase a gown for me."

Hadrian wasn't sure how to respond. "Does that bother you?"

"Not particularly. My grandmother has been insisting I update my wardrobe, but it simply isn't in our budget to do so."

Whilst Hadrian wasn't aware of the specifics of their financial situation, he'd thought she might be able to purchase a gown or two with the income she'd made from their last investigation along with the funds he'd supplied to her grandmother's long-lost account. "Perhaps you'll be able to do so after this investigation."

"Grandmama says I ought to look like a successful investigator if I want to encourage people to hire me."

Hadrian thought that argument would make sense to Tilda. "*Should* you order a gown then?"

She shook her head. "Not here. I could never afford a place such as this."

Their conversation ended as the door opened, and a woman nearing fifty entered. She wore a simple but elegant day dress, and her mostly dark hair—there were some gray strands here and there—was swept atop her head and adorned with a gold comb.

"Good afternoon, Lord Ravenhurst," she said with a curtsey and, as Hadrian had predicted, without a French accent. Her gaze moved to Tilda. "Lady Ravenhurst."

"Pardon, but I am not Lady Ravenhurst," Tilda said firmly. "I am Miss Wren. I am a private investigator, and Lord Ravenhurst is my associate. We'd like to speak with you about Joanna Pollard."

The modiste hesitated as she gave them a dubious look. "Why?"

"We are investigating the murder of Louis Chambers," Tilda replied.

Madame Ousset's eyes rounded briefly. "I read about that. I didn't know him at all, but I knew he was Pollard's partner in that new store. Did someone really kill him in his bed?"

"Yes," Tilda replied.

"Do you think the Pollards are responsible?" Madame Ousset asked with a gasp. "I don't know Pollard well, but he could be somewhat aloof. Joanna, on the other hand, is easily agitated. But to kill someone?" The modiste made a sound as she shook her head.

Hadrian looked to see Tilda's reaction. She was watching Madame Ousset closely.

"Do you think she is capable of such a thing?" Tilda asked.

"I wouldn't think so, no." Madame Ousset pursed her lips. "Though Joanna left my employ some five years ago, and I have not kept in close contact with her. I couldn't tell you what she is like now."

Tilda continued to study the modiste. "Why did you not remain close with her?"

Hadrian was probably too focused on Tilda, but he couldn't help himself. He loved to watch her work.

The modiste shrugged. "Joanna is exceptional with a needle and has a keen eye for fashion. However, she is not terribly friendly and has a short temper. At least, that was true when she worked for me. Honestly, it was a relief when she resigned her position," Madame Ousset said, her shoulders dipping briefly. "She always wanted to be more than a seamstress. Her father was a tailor, and her mother had been a seamstress, though she died relatively young, leaving Joanna to care for her four younger siblings."

"That is a great deal for someone to bear," Tilda said. "Am I correct in assuming she and Mr. Pollard do not have children?"

"Not that I am aware of, but as I said, we have not maintained a friendship. I am happy to see her achieve what she dreamed of —that shop her husband is opening on Oxford Street. I hear she is designing the ladies' garments."

"I hope you won't find this question indelicate, Madame Ousset," Tilda said gently. "Mrs. Pollard married Mr. Pollard later than most women typically wed. Was she married before that? Or did she have any other sort of romantic relationship?"

"She was not wed prior to Pollard." Madame Ousset cocked her head. "Indeed, I was surprised when she married him, as I'd always thought she preferred to remain a spinster. As one myself, I usually recognize a kindred spirit. However, I think Pollard offered her the life she wanted." As Tilda had pointed out in the coach, Pollard also seemed to love his wife. Hadrian had sensed that too, though Mrs. Pollard had been harder to read.

Madame Ousset continued, "When Joanna resigned her position here, she set up her own business and a few of my clients chose to use her services."

Tilda offered the modiste a warm smile. "Thank you for your time, Madame Ousset. If you think of anything else that may be helpful about Mrs. Pollard, or even Mr. Pollard, please let us know."

Hadrian handed the modiste his card. "Thank you."

He escorted Tilda back into the main area of the shop, then outside onto the pavement. "I think it's time you have cards printed," he said.

"That is not an expense I can afford at the moment." She looked at him and quickly added, "Nor will I accept an offer from you to purchase them for me."

"Not even as a loan?"

She pursed her lips at him. "No. I know you can't possibly understand what it means to be frugal, but I do not purchase things I can't afford."

"Nor do I."

Arching a brow at him, she gave him a sardonic stare. "*Is* there something you can't afford?"

She had him there, and he found it unaccountably irritating. Not her question, but the fact that he truly couldn't relate to what she was saying. He used humor to mask his frustration. "I am fairly certain I couldn't purchase Buckingham Palace."

Tilda laughed. "That's because the Crown wouldn't sell it to you."

"Probably not." He helped her into the coach as Leach opened the door. "Any other errands today?"

"Not that I can think of," she replied.

"It's best we are done earlier today," Hadrian said. "I've meetings I ought to attend at Westminster."

Tilda arched a brow at him. "I have been wondering about your primary occupation in the Lords. You mustn't let helping me with my investigations interfere with your responsibilities."

"I won't." Though he sometimes did, if he were honest. He couldn't help himself. He enjoyed working with her.

And perhaps it was a little more than just that.

After instructing Leach to return to Marylebone to take Tilda home, Hadrian joined her in the coach. "Did you find Madame Ousset helpful?"

"Yes, though I need to think through what we've learned today. It does seem as though Joanna Pollard might have had motivation to kill Louis Chambers, along with all the others."

"I noticed you asked the Pollards if they'd been to the Chambers' house," Hadrian said. He'd meant to ask her about that when they'd left the Pollards' store, but he'd been focused on his vision.

"I wondered if they may have had access to poison something. But it would have had to have been something only Chambers ingested since no one else was ill."

As they neared her grandmother's house, he offered to convey her to the funeral tomorrow.

"I would like that, thank you," she replied. "Now, if I don't invite you in for tea, I will be scolded. But don't feel you must."

"I wouldn't miss it," he said with a grin. "Your grandmother's stories as the wife of a magistrate are most engaging." She would relay tales of cases her husband had heard, mostly colorful characters that appeared before him repeatedly for disturbing the peace.

Tilda chuckled. "I've told her to write them down as I daresay they would make an interesting history. I'm glad you enjoy them. I know she enjoys sharing them with you."

As he escorted Tilda toward the door, he found himself wishing they could continue like this, even if they weren't investigating something. So far, murder had drawn them together, and he would hope that their deepening friendship would ensure their association continued—whether they were solving a crime or not.

CHAPTER 17

"I am very glad you let me convince you to purchase that gown yesterday," Tilda's grandmother said as she came down the stairs on Wednesday just before Hadrian was due to arrive.

Tilda hadn't told her that being in Madame Ousset's shop as well as the reaction of the young woman who'd greeted them had finally persuaded Tilda that she needed a new gown. "Thank you for going to the shop with me to choose it. Mrs. Acorn did a wonderful job with the alterations." The housekeeper had insisted on making sure the dark-gray gown fit Tilda "to perfection."

"I'm just so pleased to see you in a gown from the current decade," Grandmama said with a mischievous laugh.

Tilda couldn't help smiling as she moved toward her grandmother. "My wardrobe isn't *that* old." Still, she hadn't had a new gown in years. That didn't include the evening gown she'd had to purchase for her last investigation with Hadrian when they'd gone to Northumberland House. Tilda hadn't possessed anything remotely appropriate for such an auspicious occasion. And she'd no idea when she'd wear that extravagant garment again. "I do appreciate that you care so much, Grandmama."

Her grandmother took her hand and gave it a squeeze. "I know how important your investigative business is to you. I only want others to see you as I do—and as you are, an extremely intelligent and capable woman. Your appearance must reflect that."

This gray gown was fashionable but sedate and would serve Tilda well in her profession, particularly if she were to attend funerals on a regular basis. It wasn't full mourning, but since she was not family or even a friend, the dark gray was quite suitable.

"You are right, Grandmama." Tilda pulled on the black gloves she'd also purchased. Her hat—also black—was not new, but she hadn't been able to bring herself to buy anything else.

"I often am, dear." Grandmama's blue eyes sparkled with mirth as she released Tilda's hand. "I only wish you could further expand your wardrobe. Perhaps after this investigation is concluded and you've collected payment, you'll be able to do so."

If Tilda spent any of the money at all instead of saving the lot, it would likely be to purchase cards, as Hadrian had suggested. However, she wasn't going to debate expenditures with her grandmother. It was one area where Grandmama was not right—financial matters were simply not her strong suit. "Hopefully, I will continue to find employment," Tilda said with a smile.

"Your father would be so proud." Grandmama missed her son almost as much as Tilda missed him.

"And my mother?" Tilda said with a faint chuckle. It was a rhetorical question.

"How would she even know?" Grandmama asked. "I wouldn't tell her anything, and I can't imagine you would."

No, Tilda would not. Her mother wouldn't care. And that was worse than if she'd objected.

Tilda heard the front door open and hurriedly bussed her grandmother's cheek. "I'll see you later."

But her grandmother followed her into the entrance hall where Vaughn held the door for Hadrian who stood at the threshold. Hadrian's gaze locked on Tilda. His lips curved into a smile, and butterflies flitted annoyingly in Tilda's belly. She didn't have time for such nonsense, nor did she want it.

Regardless, the butterflies persisted.

And Tilda smiled in return. She couldn't seem to help it. When she'd dressed for Northumberland House, she'd felt more feminine than ever before in her life. What was most surprising was that she'd liked it. But that didn't mean she cared a whit about having fancy clothing or wearing the latest fashion. It was just nice to look … nice.

Blinking, Tilda pushed her smile away.

"Good afternoon, my lord," Tilda's grandmother said effusively. "It was such a pleasure to have you come for tea the other day. And last week too." She laughed softly. "May we expect you every week?"

"I would have no quarrel with that," he said with a gallant bow.

Tilda had plenty of quarrel with it. The Earl of Ravenhurst could not be a regular visitor. Yes, they were friends as well as associates, but that was all. There was nothing wrong with taking tea occasionally, but weekly was far too often. "We should be going."

"Good luck," Grandmama said as they departed.

"That's a new dress, isn't it?" Hadrian asked as they walked to the coach.

"Yes."

"Did you purchase that yesterday after we visited Madame Ousset's?"

"Yes." She darted a glance toward him, hating that she felt self-conscious because they'd discussed her purchasing a dress yesterday.

He smiled at her. "Well, you look marvelous."

"You do indeed, miss," Leach said in agreement as he held the door to the coach.

"Thank you, Leach." Tilda climbed inside with the coachman's help. How quickly she'd become accustomed to this manner of travel. She thought of what her grandmother had said about her father being proud. What would he think if he saw her gadding about with an earl?

He would have liked Hadrian, she realized. And her father wouldn't have given a fig about Hadrian's rank, so long as he was kind and had integrity.

Hadrian sat beside her, and the coach started forward.

Tilda looked over at him to share the most recent developments in the investigation. "I received a note from Mr. Forrest earlier. A pawnbroker called on him yesterday regarding the list of Beryl's missing jewelry I published. He has a shop located just off the Strand. He recognized the description of the pearl necklace and ring. Unfortunately, he'd already sold them, so Mr. Forrest wasn't able to confirm the pieces specifically. However, I don't think that's necessary because the pawnbroker identified Louis Chambers as the man who sold him the items."

Hadrian met her gaze. "So Louis stole multiple items from Beryl that we know of. He gave one item, the brooch, to Martha and sold some others."

"It certainly supports the idea that he was short of funds or out of them entirely."

"And spending lavishly on his mistress," Hadrian mused.

"Also on those monthly dinner parties which included expensive cakes," Tilda said. "Multiple people have said Louis liked to spend money, and it appears he did so quite recklessly."

Hadrian nodded. "It's not difficult to see why his brother cut him off."

"I do wonder why he wasn't yet selling everything he could. But since there is still jewelry in Beryl's possession, not to mention other items in the household, perhaps he just hadn't become that desperate." Tilda would never want to be in that position, which was why she was so careful with her grandmother's finances. "Though I'm sure he was close."

Hadrian glanced toward her. "Did you inform Teague of the pawnbroker's information?"

"Not yet, but I will. I don't imagine he'll be at the funeral."

"We can stop in at Scotland Yard afterward, if you'd like," Hadrian offered.

She sent him a smile. "Thank you."

They were quiet a moment before Hadrian said, "I hope I didn't imply yesterday that you needed to buy a new dress."

"No." Tilda smoothed her hand over her skirt. "As I said, my grandmother has been pressing me to do so. However, I confess that our visit to Madame Ousset's may have persuaded me to finally spend the money." She hadn't intended to tell him that, but she felt comfortable doing so. Perhaps because he'd broached the subject. She didn't want there to be awkwardness between them.

He grimaced faintly. "I hope you didn't feel bad. About your wardrobe, I mean. You always look nice."

"But incredibly outdated," she said with a laugh. "I will replace the lot as I can, but it will take me a while—and a steady stream of clients."

"I shall do my best to support you in your endeavors."

"Do you mean in attracting clients or with investigating?"

"Both," he said eagerly. "If you'll allow it."

Tilda could never have imagined becoming a private investigator with an earl as an assistant. But he was quite helpful. "Your investigative skills are developing nicely."

"We make an excellent team. In my opinion."

"I cannot disagree." Tilda met his gaze, and it was a long moment before they each looked away. "Although you must ensure you have adequate time to devote to your duties in the Lords. I daresay they need a man of your intelligence and integrity."

Hadrian grimaced and wiped a hand over his brow. "I would agree after yesterday. Too many of them are unserious too much of the time."

"Did something happen?"

He sent her a look of frustration. "Several had read the reports of the inquest and asked me about Chambers—and Beryl. It was incredibly irritating, if I must say. Then my mother called this morning. She'd also read the papers and was concerned about me. It's as if I've been transported back four years." He rolled his eyes and blew out a breath.

Tilda turned toward him. "I'm so sorry. I didn't want any of that to happen. I promise we'll find the killer soon."

He smiled faintly. "You can't promise that, but I appreciate your support. Don't let my complaints interfere with your investigation. You'll discover the truth of everything, I have no doubt."

The coach arrived in Catherine Place, where several other coaches were queued or parked. They stopped a few houses away from the Chambers' and climbed out. The day was gray and dreary, perfectly suited for a funeral.

Hadrian offered Tilda his arm, and she took it without hesitation, thankful the butterflies from earlier had moved on. As they approached the house, she saw the milliner, Flanders, and his daughter enter.

The butler, Oswald, greeted them somberly. Chambers was on display in his coffin in the parlor whilst refreshments had been laid out in the dining room. There was not enough room for everyone to sit, for there were quite a few people in attendance. Tilda saw Louis's brothers standing near the coffin.

"I'd prefer to avoid the parlor for now," Tilda murmured. She longed to speak with Daniel Chambers, but that would not happen today. Thankfully, there were other avenues to pursue.

"The dining room then?" Hadrian suggested.

"Wherever we may find the housekeeper—*if* we can find her. I realize today is not the best day to query any of the retainers, but

I would like to ask them about how a killer may have accessed the house."

The corner of his mouth ticked up. "I expected nothing less than for you to use the funeral as an opportunity for further investigation."

"That is what you're paying me for," she said wryly.

They walked through the dining room but did not see the housekeeper. Clara was busy ensuring the buffet remained presentable.

Tilda approached the maid with a smile. "Good afternoon, Clara. I'm sure you are all very busy today, but I am hoping to speak with you and the other retainers later, if possible."

"We are busy, Miss Wren, but I always wish to be helpful."

Oliver Chambers appeared in the dining room to announce that the funeral was starting.

Hadrian escorted Tilda to the parlor where the furniture was arranged so that the family was seated near the coffin whilst the rector spoke. Tilda could only see them from the back and in profile, depending on how they held their head, but she recognized Daniel Chambers. He was flanked by women— one older and one who looked to be near his age. His wife and mother, perhaps? Oliver sat down next to the older woman, and Beryl was on his other side. Mrs. Styles-Rowdon sat beside Beryl.

"Did no one from Beryl's family come?" Tilda whispered to Hadrian.

He glanced about the room. "Not that I can see."

"How sad." Tilda also saw the Pollards, Mr. Flanders and his daughter, and even Massey was present, though he stood in a corner as he'd done at the inquest.

The rector's remarks were thankfully short, after which Daniel Chambers rose to deliver a eulogy. When he was finished, he announced they would convey the body to the cemetery in a while.

"Will you be going?" Tilda asked Hadrian as people began to talk and mill about once more.

"I don't think so, unless you'd find it helpful to your investigation?"

Tilda considered that for a moment. What was the likelihood Hadrian would observe something useful? She doubted he'd have a chance to speak with Daniel Chambers about Louis's finances.

"I can't think of a reason for you to go." Tilda saw Beryl looking toward Hadrian. "I think Beryl wishes to speak with you," she said softly.

"I see that." He pressed his lips together, then looked to Tilda. "Pardon me for a moment or two."

Tilda watched as he threaded his way to Beryl. She hugged him and said something. When they parted, he guided her from the parlor, past where Tilda was standing just inside the doorway. She exchanged a look with him as they left.

Curious, Tilda stepped into the entrance hall and watched them walk toward the back of the house. They stepped into the sitting room and moved just out of view.

Tilda followed their trail, progressing slowly, until she was in a position to see them. Her vantage point allowed a clear view of Beryl standing on her toes, her hands on Hadrian's arms, as she pressed a kiss to the corner of Hadrian's mouth.

Her breath trapped in her lungs, Tilda tensed. Hadrian stepped back from Beryl, his expression grim. He said something, then smiled faintly as he shook his head. Beryl nodded, and they spoke for another moment before she turned and departed.

Tilda quickly spun about and hurried into the dining room lest she be caught spying. Whilst she couldn't say for certain what had happened, it appeared as though Hadrian had rebuffed Beryl's advances—whatever they were.

Though it was none of Tilda's affair, she could not deny that she was glad to see his reaction. Beryl had treated him poorly in the past, and he didn't deserve the grief his association with her was now causing. Tilda was just glad she was here to help him.

The protectiveness she felt for him jarred her. But why should it? They were friends, and they'd demonstrated they cared for one another during their last investigation. Of course, Tilda didn't want him to be hurt. That was what friends did for one another.

~

*H*adrian watched Beryl walk away and in doing so caught sight of Tilda hastening into the dining room. Had she seen Beryl kiss him? He hoped not.

But why should it matter? There was nothing between him and Beryl—and he'd made that clear to her.

Beryl had thanked him—again—for his support. Then she'd shocked him when she'd pressed her lips to his. She'd seen his reaction and apologized. Still, Hadrian had backed away from her while telling her there would be no going back to their former relationship. She'd said she understood and that she didn't really want that. Apologizing again, she'd then turned and left.

The episode left Hadrian feeling discomfited, and not just because he'd no interest in rekindling *any* kind of romantic attachment with Beryl. He suspected she was carrying on with Oliver Chambers. Why would she, then, offer Hadrian a kiss? Either Hadrian—and Tilda—was wrong about Beryl and Oliver, or Beryl was up to something distasteful. All Hadrian could think was that she was pondering her future as a destitute widow. She could not have a future with Oliver, for the law prevented her from marrying her husband's brother. That she may think Hadrian would accept her again pricked his ire. But he would not make that assumption. Not today, anyway.

He stalked from the sitting room with the intention of speaking to Tilda, but he came face-to-face with Daniel Chambers and decided he didn't want to miss the opportunity to speak with him.

"That was a fine eulogy," Hadrian said.

"Thank you." The man, who was a few years Hadrian's senior, appeared and sounded skeptical. "I know Louis could be difficult to like. I'm sure you had no love for him at all."

"I hardly knew him. And I bore him no ill will for things that happened long ago." Not until the man's death had revealed the true darkness of his character.

Chambers' thick brows shot up and his hairline, a widow's peak like that of his deceased brother, also moved with his surprise. "You are more forgiving than he was."

Hadrian wondered if he could finally discover why Louis had despised him so greatly. "Am I? I confess, I do not understand your brother's dislike of me."

"Dislike is a mild word for what he felt." Chambers' hazel eyes narrowed slightly. "You truly don't know? Or perhaps you don't remember."

Hadrian lifted a shoulder. "I've no notion whatsoever."

Chambers cocked his head. "Do you even remember Louis from Oxford?"

"I knew everyone in my college, and I can assure you that Louis was not in it."

"He was not," Chambers replied definitively. "Do you recall a woman you were … friendly with for some time?"

Hadrian had been "friendly" with plenty of women when he'd been at Oxford. "I'm afraid you'll have to be more specific."

Chambers waved his hand. "Doesn't matter. Forget I said anything."

"No, I should like to know why your brother hated me." Hadrian decided to dispose with gentler words that weren't true.

"He hated you because you stole a woman from him," Chambers replied, sounding almost stiff. "At Oxford, he'd planned to woo someone, but you got there first. It's asinine, but my brother never met a grudge he didn't grasp with both hands."

Hadrian thought of what Pollard had said about Louis not wanting to marry. "Are you saying he stole Beryl away from me because of whatever happened at Oxford?"

"He said it started that way but that he decided he wanted to marry Beryl." Chambers exhaled. "But I knew my brother. I don't know that he would have married her if he didn't have to. He was an incredibly selfish person."

Words failed Hadrian for a moment, both because the reason for Louis's hatred of him was astonishing, and for the vulnerability Daniel Chambers was showing—on the day of his brother's funeral. "You loved him anyway, and that is a wonderful gift."

"I tried to love him. He made it very hard." Chambers shook his head. "Despite that, I am committed to finding justice for him." He met Hadrian's gaze. "I don't believe you killed him. It just doesn't make sense that you would."

"Thank you." Hadrian was surprised but glad to have the man's support.

"I understand you hired Miss Wren to find my brother's murderer. I've also hired someone."

"I saw you with Padgett at the inquest," Hadrian said.

Chambers nodded. "You know him?"

"I was stabbed in January, and he investigated the crime." *Poorly.* Hadrian kept the latter to himself.

Chambers' eyes rounded. "I'd no idea. I'm sorry. How are you now?"

"Well enough, thank you." Hadrian considered telling him that Padgett was corrupt but didn't want to broach that topic today. Instead, he preferred to glean what he could from Chambers. "How do you feel about Oliver investing in Pollard's shop?"

"He can do what he likes with his money. Unlike Louis, he has a head for financial matters. I did try to dissuade Louis from investing, but he was insistent that he needed his own enterprise." The man's features darkened. "I feel badly for Beryl. She will pay the price for his recklessness."

"In what way?"

"Financially. My brother was out of money. There is a fund from which he draws a modest income, but he has borrowed against it extensively. There will be little to nothing for her to inherit, aside from what's inside this house."

Though Hadrian didn't want to continue his association with Beryl once the murder was solved, he did not want to see her suffer. "Were you aware Louis was stealing Beryl's jewelry?"

Chambers' brows rose. "Was he really?"

"According to a friend of his, he gave some items, which he showed to the friend, to his mistress. And it appears he sold some items to a pawnbroker." Hadrian hoped he wasn't disclosing information he should not. He took the chance in case it prompted Chambers to share more about Louis.

"I hadn't realized Louis was that despicable. Though I will say that Beryl's spending habits rival that of my brother."

Hadrian stared at the man. "Are you saying she deserved to lose her heirlooms?"

"She is not blameless in her own financial situation," Daniel said blithely. "She can't think her dowry lasted this long into the marriage, not with the way they spent money."

Hadrian could well imagine what Tilda would say—that Beryl wasn't in a position to even know her financial situation. He began to truly understand why Tilda was so careful with her own finances. She had to be.

"What did they spend their money on exactly?" Hadrian asked.

"Fripperies, mostly. They dressed in the latest fashion, and they liked to be invited about town, though I've seen their invitations diminish over the past year or two. They also like to entertain. They have dinner parties about once a month. I confess I stopped attending about six months ago, as I could no longer bear to watch their hedonism."

Oliver Chambers approached them. "Sorry to interrupt, but it's time to proceed to the cemetery."

Daniel glanced at Hadrian. "I don't suppose you will be coming?"

"I will not." Hadrian offered them a bland smile. "I don't think your brother would want me there. I am only here today for Beryl."

The brothers departed, and Hadrian looked about for Tilda. She stood in the small anteroom before the dining room. Before he could make his way to her, a parade of women moved out of the parlor led by Beryl. Mrs. Styles-Rowdon brought up the rear, but she stopped in front of Hadrian.

"You are such a dear friend to our Beryl," she said. "Fetching her sleeping tonic and mourning accessories and sending lilies for the coffin." She batted her lashes at him, and he wondered if she was purposely flirting or if that was simply her demeanor. She seemed the type of woman who was always aware of her appearance and its effect.

Hadrian looked past her at the coffin as it was carried foot-first from the parlor. The men carrying it, including Oliver Chambers, passed through the entrance hall and outside. The butler held the door.

Mrs. Styles-Rowdon turned and watched the spectacle with him. She put her hand on his sleeve. Hadrian glanced down at her black glove against his black coat, wondering why she would feel so informal with him.

She took her hand away abruptly. "Will you be going with them? You should hurry."

"No. As you said, I am a friend to Beryl. Not to Chambers."

"No, I suppose you weren't." Mrs. Styles-Rowdon tucked her hand under his arm and clasped his sleeve. "Let us join the ladies then."

Hadrian allowed her to tug him toward the dining room where Tilda and the others were standing about. The housekeeper was pouring tea at one end of the table.

Mrs. Styles-Rowdon released Hadrian's arm, and he exhaled with relief.

"Beryl, your hem is coming loose." She moved toward Beryl with a slight frown. "I'll have words with my maid."

"I've pins in my reticule," Joanna Pollard said, whipping a few from the depths of her bag before removing her gloves and kneeling.

"It's one of my old gowns," Mrs. Styles-Rowdon said. "My maid took up the hem."

Mrs. Pollard looked up, her face pinching briefly. "I could have made you a gown, Beryl. I still can, if you like." She finished pinning the hem. "That will hold for now."

She started to stand, and Hadrian moved to help her up. The moment he clasped her hand, a vision rose in his mind. He saw the same blonde woman he'd glimpsed in Louis's bedchamber, the one who'd appeared to be a maid. Except the vision was odd. It was hazy, as though he were looking through something.

Such as a veil.

Was he seeing Mrs. Pollard's memory? He was now confident the maid was Martha Farrow. Was Mrs. Pollard the veiled woman who'd visited Martha?

Hadrian took care to notice everything he could. They were standing in the lodging house in Spitalfields on the landing from which Martha had fallen. He clung to Mrs. Pollard's hand, hoping he would see what happened next. She took a step toward Martha.

Mrs. Pollard released his hand and thanked him for helping her up. The vision was gone, leaving a searing headache and a lingering sense of rage—not his, but Mrs. Pollard's.

Of course, it had been her memory, for he'd been touching her hand. Had she pushed Martha? She'd advanced on the young maid as anger coursed through her. If only Hadrian had seen what had happened next.

He was eager to leave. And to tell Tilda what he'd seen, as well as what he'd learned from Daniel Chambers.

Alas, that was not to be as Clara appeared in the doorway. She was extremely pale, and her eyes were round as dinner plates. "Miss Wren, you must come see what I've found in Mrs. Chambers' bedroom."

Tilda, her forehead creased, moved toward the maid. "What's that, Clara?"

"A knife."

CHAPTER 18

"There's no knife in my chamber," Beryl said crossly.

Tilda didn't spare a glance for Beryl as she gestured toward Clara. "Show me, please."

Clara turned, and Tilda looked toward Hadrian, who gave her a slight nod. She followed Clara and knew that Hadrian would be behind her.

On the stairs, he moved up alongside Tilda. "Wouldn't the constables who searched the house the other day have found this knife?"

Tilda lifted a shoulder. "I would hope so, but it's possible they missed it."

When they reached Beryl's bedchamber, Tilda saw that a dresser drawer was open.

"It's in the drawer," Clara said, but she did not go to the dresser.

Tilda moved toward it, and Hadrian joined her. Lying at the back of the drawer, partially obscured by handkerchiefs, was a knife such as one would use in a kitchen.

Carefully, Tilda moved the handkerchiefs so she could see the knife more clearly. The blade was long and thick—and clean.

Tilda turned her head to look at Clara. "You just found this today?"

"I didn't notice it before. There are usually stacks of handkerchiefs, but Mrs. Chambers has been going through them rapidly the past several days."

"Move," Beryl said loudly as she elbowed her way past Clara into the bedchamber. "What is this about a knife?"

Mrs. Styles-Rowdon followed Beryl into the room, whilst Clara had moved just inside the doorframe, her expression still one of fright or disbelief. Or both. The others who'd been in the dining room, including the housekeeper and Joanna Pollard, loitered outside the bedchamber.

Beryl moved to the other side of Hadrian and looked into the drawer. "Where on earth did that come from?" She turned and glared at Clara. "Did you put that there?"

Clara gasped. "I did not."

Tilda fixed her attention on Beryl. "Are you saying you did not put this knife in your drawer?"

"Of course not."

"And why would you think Clara did?" Tilda asked.

Beryl threw up her hands. "Who else comes into my room?"

"You must consider that people who are not expected to be in your bedchamber may have been. Just as you must consider that someone outside this household may have come into this house to both poison and stab your husband." Tilda looked around at everyone, her gaze lingering on the housekeeper. "Is there any way someone could gain access to the house without anyone noticing?"

Mrs. Blank pursed her lips. "Sometimes the back door is left unlocked. I told the detective inspector about that, just as I told him I don't know if it was unlocked the night Mr. Chambers died. May I look at the knife? To see if it is from the kitchen."

"You can tell?" Tilda asked.

Mrs. Blank nodded, and Tilda gestured for her to come to the dresser. Peering into the drawer, the housekeeper frowned. "That is definitely Mrs. Dunning's missing knife. There's a chip in the blade down near the handle. It's why she didn't use it as often as the others."

Tilda surveyed the knife and saw the chip to which Mrs. Blank was referring. "Thank you, Mrs. Blank. Would you mind fetching Mrs. Dunning so that she can confirm? I would also ask that you or Oswald ask his lordship's coachman to inform Detective Inspector Teague of what we've found."

Nodding, Mrs. Blank left—after casting a look of derision toward Beryl.

Beryl waved her hand toward the dresser. "I did not put that knife there, nor did I kill my husband."

"I think it's time you tell us the truth about your marriage," Tilda said evenly.

"I don't know what you want to know," Beryl said somewhat defiantly. "I've told you everything about our marriage." She looked at Tilda as she crossed her arms over her chest. "You saw the bruises Louis gave me."

Mrs. Styles-Rowdon moved to stand beside Beryl and lightly touched her arm.

"I did," Tilda replied. "However, I did not see the injuries you gave him."

Beryl gasped. "Who told you such lies?"

Tilda resisted the urge to roll her eyes at Beryl's obvious dissembling.

"We understand you hit Louis on occasion," Hadrian said softly but firmly. "With your hairbrush."

"And with his walking stick once," Mrs. Styles-Rowdon said, which provoked another gasp from Beryl who sent her friend an accusing glance. Mrs. Styles-Rowdon gave her friend a sad look. "I'm sorry, Beryl. It is the truth." The woman looked back to Tilda and Hadrian. "You must know that Louis was a beast. Beryl was only defending herself."

Tilda wasn't sure she believed it was only that, but she did think that Beryl and Louis's marriage had been most contentious.

Hadrian locked his eyes with Beryl's. "You must realize that you are the primary suspect in Louis's murder. Withholding information will not help you, and I must say that the presence of this knife in your bedchamber will only make matters worse."

Tilda agreed with everything Hadrian had said. Indeed, she wondered if Teague might arrest Beryl when he arrived. She had plenty of motive and opportunity, and the evidence against her was mounting.

"I don't know where the knife came from," Beryl insisted. "Someone had to have put it there." She glowered toward Clara.

The maid looked at Tilda. "Do I need to stay?"

"Not in here, no. But the inspector will want to speak with you when he arrives," Tilda said.

"Thank you." Clara hurried from the room without looking in Beryl's direction.

Tilda glanced toward the dresser. She didn't plan to disturb the knife. Teague could collect it when he arrived. Before that, however, she needed Hadrian to touch it.

Turning her back to Beryl, she motioned for Hadrian to step closer to the drawer with her. "You must touch the knife before Teague arrives," she whispered. "You may not have another chance."

"Of course."

Tilda shielded him as best she could as he reached into the drawer. He closed his hand around the handle. Frowning, he moved his fingertips to the dull side of the knife and slid them along the blade.

After a moment, he withdrew his hand. "Nothing," he muttered.

"That's unfortunate," Tilda murmured.

The housekeeper returned with the cook who said, "Mrs. Blank said Clara found my missing knife."

"It's in the drawer here," Tilda said. "We are not going to remove it until the detective inspector arrives. Can you verify it's yours?"

Mrs. Dunning came to the dresser and looked inside. "That's mine. I chipped the blade a year or so ago when I dropped it." She shook her head. "I was not pleased with myself."

"And how long has this been missing from your kitchen?" Tilda asked.

"Since Friday when the inspector asked me if anything was missing. I can tell you what I told him, that I used it on Wednesday. I remember because I only use it for certain things, one of which is cutting bone. I had to do that last Wednesday."

"Thank you, Mrs. Dunning," Tilda said. "You can go back downstairs, though the inspector may wish to speak with you when he arrives."

The cook sent a nervous glance toward Beryl on her way out the door. The housekeeper accompanied her.

Teague arrived a short while later with a pair of constables. He retrieved the knife from the drawer and confirmed that it belonged to Mrs. Dunning. He then questioned Beryl about how the knife may have come to be in her dresser. After that, he spoke with Clara.

Ultimately, as Tilda expected, he took Beryl into custody.

She wept as the constables led her from the house.

Tilda told Teague they would come to Scotland Yard, as she still needed to tell him about Louis Chambers selling Beryl's jewelry to the pawnbroker.

As Hadrian guided her to the coach, he said, "I had quite a conversation with Daniel Chambers."

"I can't wait to hear about it on the way."

"I also need to tell you about the vision I saw when I helped Joanna Pollard to stand."

Tilda nearly missed the step as she climbed into the coach. How had she failed to notice Hadrian having a vision?

~

*H*adrian sat beside Tilda in the coach and removed his hat, tossing it on the opposite seat. He wiped his hand across his brow.

"I'm so sorry I didn't notice your head was bothering you," she said. "My investigative skills are failing me."

"I don't believe that for a moment. There was a great deal happening today." He gave her a faint smile. "My headache is fading."

"Good." She sounded relieved. "Now tell me about the vision."

He laughed softly, glad that it didn't hurt to do so. "Because I was touching Mrs. Pollard, I know that what I was seeing and feeling was her memory. She was at the lodging house in Spital-fields with Martha Farrow."

Tilda's eyes rounded briefly. "Joanna Pollard is the woman in the veil?"

"I believe so because Martha looked as though I was seeing her through a film. She advanced on the maid, but that was all I saw before Mrs. Pollard released my hand."

"You didn't see if Mrs. Pollard pushed her?"

"I did not, unfortunately."

"Did you feel anything?" Tilda asked.

"Rage. Mrs. Pollard was most definitely angry with Martha. I've no idea why, of course." Hadrian exhaled with frustration. "I wish I could hear the thoughts that go along with a memory and not just the emotions."

"Still, this is significant. We must speak with Joanna Pollard again. I'd like to call at the shop tomorrow."

Hadrian's brows arched briefly. "Am I invited?"

"Of course. What happened with Daniel Chambers?"

Hadrian leaned back against the squab. "I finally know why Louis Chambers despised me. Apparently, I stole a woman he was interested in when we were at Oxford." His lips twisted into a brief smirk. "I barely even remember him from Oxford—we did not attend the same college. I certainly don't recall whatever woman I 'stole' from him. He never forgot, however."

"All this time, he's held a grudge against you for something of which you were not even aware?"

"So it seems. The worst part is that he stole Beryl from me as an act of revenge. You recall Pollard saying Louis didn't really want to marry."

"I do." Tilda gave him a stony look. "Just when I thought my opinion of Louis Chambers could not sink any lower, it does."

"Quite. Daniel Chambers confirmed what his brother said about Louis being terrible at managing his finances. Both he and Beryl were spendthrifts."

"Was he aware that his brother had a mistress?"

"I'm not sure, but I did inform him that Louis had stolen Beryl's jewelry and given it to his paramour. I hope that was all right. I wanted to see his reaction."

Tilda's brows dipped. "And what was it?"

"He wasn't surprised, just disappointed, I think. He said he attended their dinner parties until about six months ago when he could no longer watch Louis's financial recklessness. I have the sense he hoped his brother would change."

"After all we've learned about their spending habits, I am surprised their house isn't more lavishly decorated. It's nice enough, but compared with your house … well, there's no comparing." She glanced away, and he wondered if his house intimidated her. Their experiences were quite different, particularly in how they lived day to day. However, he did not see that as something that divided them. He hoped she didn't either.

"You can't compare Ravenhurst House to the Chambers' residence or to very many others. It's been in my family for generations and is filled with items collected over those generations. And there are substantial coffers to ensure it is elegantly appointed, as every countess has endeavored to ensure."

"I should hate for that to be my responsibility," she said with a faint shudder. "I'm quite content with a house my grandmother's size—and with its amenities and decor. Or lack thereof," she added with a smile.

Hadrian had his answer. Tilda absolutely saw them as coming from distinctly different places. Perhaps this was why she bristled against him paying her to conduct business. She would hate knowing that he'd replenished her grandmother's fund after her grandfather's cousin had carelessly used every shilling for himself.

Which was why he would never tell her.

They fell quiet for a short while. Finally, he brought up the question that was most bothering him at the moment. "Do you think Beryl is lying about putting the knife in her drawer?"

"Are you asking if I think she stabbed Louis after all?" Tilda leaned her head back and looked at the ceiling of the coach a moment. "Whilst she has maintained her innocence and speaks convincingly, I remind myself that I have been sympathetic to her since I was hired to help her." She turned her focus to Hadrian. "You and I both are inclined to believe she did not kill her husband, and if she did, that she may have been justified. But murder in the manner Louis was killed cannot be rationalized. She was not actively defending herself. She likely poisoned him and then, frustrated that it took too long, stabbed him."

Hadrian couldn't disagree with any of that. "I hate thinking she did that, but it does seem most likely. Yet you remain interested in investigating Mrs. Pollard."

Tilda smiled. "Because I have unanswered questions, particularly why she would visit Martha Farrow. How did she even know the maid?"

"You are incredibly thorough," Hadrian said. "Anyone would be lucky to hire you."

They arrived at Scotland Yard and departed the coach. Inside, they were shown to Teague's office, but he was not there. They were assured he would arrive shortly.

After a few minutes, the detective inspector joined them. "I appreciate you sending for me. I thought today would be for mourning. My mistake."

His office was large enough for his desk as well as a small seating area with two chairs near a hearth. There was a third chair positioned near the desk, which Teague dragged to the other two. He motioned for them to take the two chairs whilst he sat in the one that he'd brought.

"Is Beryl being charged with Louis's murder?" Tilda asked.

"Not yet, but probably. The cook is certain the knife that was found is the one that went missing from the kitchen." Teague frowned. "Its presence in Mrs. Chambers' dresser drawer is rather damning."

Tilda arched her brow at Teague. "Your constables didn't find it the other day?"

"No, in fact they are insistent it wasn't there. I am inclined to believe them, but then where was it and why was it moved to the drawer?"

"Someone could have put it there since your constables searched," Tilda said. "You already know that the back door to the house is sometimes left unlocked."

"That would mean someone is trying to ensure Mrs. Chambers is blamed for the murder," Teague replied. "Who do you think that would be?"

Tilda clasped her hands in her lap. "I can't answer that yet. Our investigation is ongoing. We did learn why Louis Chambers was holding a grudge against Hadrian." She turned her head toward him.

Hadrian explained what Daniel Chambers had told him.

"Did Mrs. Chambers know about this? Was she aware her husband married her out of spite?" Teague shook his head. "That does not help her case."

No, it did not. *If* she knew. "We have not discussed the matter with her," Hadrian said.

A knock on the door prompted them all to look in that direction.

"Come," Teague responded.

The door opened to reveal a constable in a blue uniform. He was young and tall, his expression earnest. "Detective Inspector, there is a man here who wants to see you. Says his name is Oliver Chambers."

Teague looked over at Hadrian and Tilda, his brows arching. "Wonder what this is about." He stood. "Bring him here."

Teague moved the chair he'd been sitting in back to where it had been, then went to stand behind his desk. A few moments later, Oliver Chambers came in carrying his hat, his face lined with worry.

"Good afternoon, Mr. Chambers," Teague said. "What brings you here on the day of your brother's funeral?"

Oliver Chambers straightened, pushing his shoulders back as he faced the inspector. "I came to confess to Louis's murder. I killed him."

CHAPTER 19

Two things were evident to Tilda in the moment immediately following Oliver Chambers' confession. First, he was lying. He'd no more killed Louis than Hadrian had. Second, he was trying to save Beryl. She'd already deduced that he was likely Beryl's lover, but now it was certain.

Tilda looked up at Oliver. "How long have you and Beryl been having an affair?" She felt the stares of all three men in the room but did not move her gaze from her subject.

"We weren't having an affair," Oliver said quickly. "At least not like you may think." His face burned crimson, and Tilda recalled that she was speaking to a former curate. His morals were perhaps slightly more intact than those of his degenerate, deceased brother.

"Please explain," she urged with a patient smile.

"I love her. I have for some time." His shoulders slumped, making him appear as defeated as he sounded.

"And does she reciprocate your sentiments?"

Oliver rotated his hat in his hands. "I believe so." He didn't sound completely convinced.

Tilda wasn't sure Beryl was all that trustworthy, particularly after the way she'd behaved with Hadrian earlier.

"You realize you can't marry her," Teague pointed out.

Since Beryl was Oliver's brother's widow, they would not be permitted to wed. It was a ridiculous law.

"I know. That is why we have tried to stay apart."

"But you haven't been entirely successful, have you?" Tilda prodded. "Do you enter your brother's house through the back door to visit Beryl?"

Oliver's eyes rounded. "No, we would usually meet somewhere and then go for a ride in my brother's coach." His neck flushed, and he looked away.

"Has this been going on since you returned to London?" Tilda asked.

Again, Oliver blushed. "It started during a visit last autumn. I came to see my mother on her birthday."

"Why did Louis give you twenty pounds in December?" Hadrian asked.

Oliver snapped his gaze to Hadrian. "How do you know about that?"

"The payment is recorded in the household ledger," Hadrian replied. "Were you in need of funds? Since you are now investing in your brother's drapery shop, it seems you were not."

Oliver shrugged. "He assumed I needed help. He and I inherited less from our father than Daniel did. And I inherited the least of all. Louis felt bad about that. I gave it to Beryl as I knew he'd decreased her pin money."

Tilda arched a brow at Oliver. "How ironic since it seems Louis sold some of her jewelry, and the funds from that likely went to you and then on to her. I wonder if she would prefer to have her jewelry back instead."

Oliver clutched the hat to his chest. "That is why I gave her the money," he said quietly. "She told me that Louis had been stealing her jewels."

Teague crossed his arms and fixed an expectant stare on Oliver. "If you indeed killed your brother, why would you put the knife you used to stab him in Beryl's dresser? Surely you would know that would make her appear guilty."

Blanching, Oliver sputtered.

"And were you also poisoning him?" Teague asked. "How and when did you administer the poison? How did you gain access to the house?" When Oliver said nothing, Teague uncrossed his arms. "You didn't kill your brother, did you?"

"No." Oliver made a sound rather like a whimper as he cast his gaze toward the floor. "I can't watch Beryl go to prison."

"If she killed her husband, she will hang," Teague said darkly.

Oliver twitched, and Tilda felt a rush of sympathy for the man. No matter what she thought of these people, it would be difficult to watch someone you cared about swing from the end of a rope in front of a jeering crowd. It was such a barbaric way to die, in Tilda's opinion. She hoped the current push to eliminate public executions was successful.

"You may go, Mr. Chambers," Teague said. "Though if you think of anything else that will be useful to my investigation, please let me know immediately. It may be the information that sets Mrs. Chambers free."

Oliver's features brightened. "I hadn't considered that. I'll try to think of anything helpful."

After Oliver departed, Teague frowned at the door. "I took Mrs. Chambers into custody hoping she might confess. Instead, I provoked her paramour. She maintains that she is innocent." He moved from behind the desk and situated the chair near them once more before sitting down. Looking at Tilda, he asked, "Who is your primary suspect?"

"Beryl, for the reasons I stated earlier. But we must also consider the Pollards, who had a motive to protect their business from Louis Chambers' financial woes." Tilda could not tell him what Hadrian had seen—that Joanna Pollard had visited Martha

Farrow and that Louis Chambers had likely made a seductive advance upon her.

"What about the Chambers' retainers?" Teague asked.

"They don't seem to have liked him much, but their motives are not as strong as the Pollards' or Beryl's. With the exception of Massey," Tilda said. "Chambers knew his secret and was not above threatening the valet about it. I was curious as to why the coroner didn't question him about that at the inquest."

Teague cleared his throat. "Massey explained to me that he visits the Cock and Hen because he meets his lover there. It is not a situation I wanted to draw attention to at the inquest. I am aware of it, however, and acknowledge that Massey does have a motive to kill Chambers. Furthermore, I will pursue him as a suspect as the evidence indicates."

"We must also consider Martha, even though she too is dead," Tilda pointed out. "She was carrying Chambers' child, and he forced her to resign."

Teague squinted faintly at his desk. "After cleaning the knife she used to stab Louis, she stole into Beryl's room and put it in her dresser drawer? That assumes my constables are mistaken about it not being there."

Tilda inclined her head. "She did know the house very well and would have known that Beryl was unlikely to wake due to her sleeping draught."

"Excellent points," Teague said. "Still, I think Beryl is the likeliest candidate." He looked to Hadrian. "I know that isn't what you want to hear."

Hadrian met Teague's gaze. "The truth is what matters. Will Beryl be staying here tonight?"

"Yes," Teague replied. "I am still hopeful she might decide to reveal more than she has."

Tilda rose. "And what if she's telling the truth?"

"That's always impossible to know, isn't it?" Teague stood and opened the door for Tilda and Hadrian. They agreed to share information if they learned anything.

When they were in the coach on the way to Tilda's house, Hadrian shook his head. "That was not how I expected the day to go."

"Nor did I," Tilda said. "I am not surprised, however, to have confirmation of Oliver and Beryl's association."

"Though it is sad that they have no future together," Hadrian remarked.

"I'm not convinced she would have wanted one." Tilda glanced toward Hadrian. "When Oliver said he believed Beryl reciprocated his feelings, he didn't seem certain. And her behavior leads me to believe she may be interested in someone else."

"What behavior is that?" His eyes focused on her in the dim light of the coach. When Tilda didn't immediately reply, he asked, "Did you see her kiss me?"

Tilda's heart knocked about in her chest as her pulse sped. "I didn't mean to spy. I was curious. That's my job."

He smiled softly, and the blue of his eyes was especially arresting—rich and deep, like the sky just outside London after the sun has dipped below the horizon before it turned dark. Tilda had found him handsome when they'd met, but she'd avoided thinking of him that way since. Mostly. Right now, she could not deny that he was attractive, nor that she was drawn to him. Or would be—if she was interested in any sort of romantic entanglement.

Which she was not. She *could* not.

"I was surprised when she did it," he went on. "I did not appreciate her overture, nor do I want that to happen again. I told her so. I've no romantic interest in Beryl."

Why was he telling her this? "That's probably for the best since she is currently in the custody of the Metropolitan Police."

Hadrian smiled again, a bit more widely, and the butterflies he sometimes stirred in Tilda's belly returned. He sobered as he brushed his hand over his thigh. "There is only one woman I would consider kissing, and it isn't Beryl." He held her gaze.

Tilda's heart beat a staccato rhythm. Was he flirting with her? And not in the superficial way that was expected when men and women socialize. She wasn't sure she knew how to flirt back.

"Why haven't you kissed that woman?" The question tumbled from her mouth. Was that her attempt at flirting, or was she actually thinking of what it might be like to kiss him?

She swallowed. Perhaps he wasn't even talking about her. Indeed, it was likely he wasn't. Why would he want to kiss her of all people? They were associates. Friends, at best. Tilda was not someone the Earl of Ravenhurst would consider kissing.

"I'm not sure she wants me to."

The coach stopped in front of Tilda's grandmother's house. She still couldn't be sure he was talking about her. Regardless, she was now thinking of what she would do if he did kiss her.

She'd kissed precisely one man. A boy, really. He'd been seventeen, and she'd been fifteen. It had been an experiment on her part—an investigation.

With Hadrian, she somehow knew it would be quite different. And she could not deny it intrigued her.

Leach opened the door, and Tilda once again spoke without thinking. "You may find the woman wouldn't mind if you did." She stepped out of the coach with Leach's assistance and called back to Hadrian, "See you tomorrow."

"I'll pick you up at eleven to go to the drapery shop," he said.

Hopefully by then Tilda would have stopped contemplating what it would be like to kiss him. She simply could *not* indulge such fancy.

∾

*H*adrian stepped out of his coach in front of Tilda's grandmother's house the following morning. The narrow terrace was neat and simple, a perfectly respectable home. But after his thoughts yesterday regarding what Tilda must think of his house, he was looking at hers in a new way.

Or perhaps it was the flirting they'd done yesterday.

He made his way slowly to the door, wondering how she would receive him. He feared he'd overstepped when he'd said there was only one woman he wanted to kiss. But he hadn't thought about what he was saying. The words had shot from his mouth, a direct truth he'd never intended to share.

Because he hadn't realized he wanted to kiss her until that moment.

Since then, the idea had occupied far too much of his mind. He needed to push it away and focus on their investigation.

Except she'd told him she wouldn't mind him kissing her.

But had she, really? Perhaps she hadn't even realized he was talking about her.

Hell, he was woefully out of practice with this sort of thing. He'd completely denied the potential for romantic entanglement since Beryl. This situation—allowing Beryl back into his life even for a short time—was making him think of things he'd buried for years, namely whether he truly wanted to forego marriage or if he was merely avoiding the possibility of another disappointment. Of humiliation. Of wondering what he lacked and someone like Louis Chambers possessed.

Vaughn greeted him at the door just as a light rain started. Hadrian stepped inside to see Tilda waiting for him. She was back to wearing her regular wardrobe, which, after seeing her in yesterday's new, extremely flattering gown, seemed lackluster. Still, regardless of what she wore, Hadrian found her beautiful. Perhaps even distractingly so after yesterday's flirtation.

But he wasn't going to think about that.

Tilda's grandmother stepped into the entrance hall from the parlor and bade Hadrian good morning.

"Good morning, Mrs. Wren. I trust you are well."

"Exceedingly, thank you." She beamed at him.

Hadrian returned her smile. "I hope you don't mind me taking Tilda away from you again."

Mrs. Wren shook her head before looking upon her grand-daughter with unabashed love and pride. "We shall never tire of your presence or your association with Tilda."

Tilda drew on her second glove. "I'll see you later, Grandmama." She kissed her grandmother's cheek before moving across the entrance hall.

Hadrian stepped aside as Vaughn opened the door. "It's raining. I've a pair of umbrellas in the coach."

She cocked a brow at him. "A pair?"

"Leach is always prepared," Hadrian said with a chuckle.

"Well, they do us no good at the moment." Her mouth curled into a grin. The expression was brief, but it lit the dreary day.

"I didn't say good morning to you," he said as they hurried to the coach. "Good morning."

"Good morning," she replied as Leach opened the door and helped her inside.

Hadrian considered sitting opposite her. However, things did not seem to be awkward between them. Perhaps they were just going to ignore their conversation from yesterday.

"I hope you slept well," she said. "We must prepare ourselves for a difficult assignment this morning with the Pollards."

"How so?" Hadrian asked as the coach moved toward their destination on Oxford Street. It seemed she preferred to avoid discussing yesterday's flirtation. Which was fine. It was better that they focus on the investigation.

"My goal is to discover why Joanna visited Martha," Tilda said. "However, we can't explain how we know that she did. She was veiled, after all. It's not likely that someone would have recognized her or even been able to describe her."

"You've an idea to provoke her to confess?"

Tilda lifted a shoulder. "I have some thoughts. I do think we must divide and conquer with Mr. and Mrs. Pollard, and our stated purpose ought to be shopping."

"Shopping?"

"I will begin with Mrs. Pollard by asking her for a gown."

Hadrian's admiration for Tilda's intellect somehow grew. It had already been quite high. "That's brilliant. You'll have her talking about something she loves. She'll relax, and who knows what she will reveal."

"Exactly," Tilda replied with a nod. "Can you do the same with Pollard?"

"I will endeavor, though I am not sure what he is passionate about. The store, I suppose?"

"He also seems to like his club," Tilda noted.

"True. I'll do my best to befriend him. Or appear to, anyway." Hadrian still hadn't warmed to the man, though their interactions had been limited.

After a few minutes of silence, Tilda asked, "Have you been worried about Beryl?"

Hadrian had wondered how she'd spent her night incarcerated. "I hope it wasn't too uncomfortable. I actually found myself wondering what will happen to her when this is over—*if* she is innocent."

"It seems her family won't help her. She may need to marry again." Tilda wrinkled her nose. "It's a shame she'd have to relinquish her independence as a widow."

Hadrian smiled. "I imagine that independence would appeal to you."

"Indeed it would, though the 'becoming a widow' aspect does not."

"Because that would mean losing your spouse?"

She inclined her head. "As well as taking one to begin with."

Yes, she was staunchly against marriage. Another reason, perhaps the primary one, he needed to not think of kissing her. It was one thing for a widow to carry on with a gentleman but quite another for an unmarried woman, even someone who considered herself a spinster.

"Is there no circumstance in which you would marry?" he found himself asking. "Not even love?"

"Not even love," she said, her gaze moving toward the window. "We have arrived."

The coach slowed and came to a stop. And that was the end of their intriguing conversation.

They departed the coach, and Tilda took his proffered arm. It was a short walk to the door of the shop. She took her hand from Hadrian's sleeve as he knocked.

A moment later, Pollard answered, his brows immediately pitching into a V. "Why have you come again? The murder is solved. Mrs. Chambers has been arrested."

"She has indeed," Tilda said. "We have come on another matter. I am in need of a gown, and I was hoping Mrs. Pollard might help me."

"I decided to accompany Miss Wren," Hadrian said with a smile, warming to his new role. "I couldn't help noticing the men's gloves that were stacked on a case during our last visit."

Pollard appeared nonplussed. "But we aren't open for business."

"As I understand it, you should be," Hadrian replied. "If you would prefer we went elsewhere, perhaps you can recommend an alternative."

"No, no, come in." Pollard opened the door more widely.

Hadrian escorted Tilda inside. She cast him a surreptitious but clearly approving glance. Hadrian felt a rush of pride. Perhaps he had achieved novice investigator status.

"We do hope to open in a fortnight now that we have partnered with Oliver Chambers," Pollard said in an animated tone. It was the most pleasant he'd ever sounded since Hadrian had met him.

"How marvelous," Tilda said. "Where is Mrs. Pollard?"

Pollard glanced toward the central staircase. "She is upstairs. I can take you up."

Tilda waved her hand and gave Pollard a warm smile. "No need. I'll find my way. Lord Ravenhurst is keen to buy new gloves. And perhaps a neckcloth or two." She waggled her brows at Hadrian before moving toward the staircase.

Hadrian smiled after her, his gaze lingering on the alluring sway of her hips before recalling that he must not look at her in that way or think of her as anything other than a friend and business associate.

Pollard gestured for Hadrian to accompany him. "The gloves have been placed in their case, which is back here. The front of the shop will have ladies' items as they will be our primary customers. Men aren't as inclined to shopping, in my experience." He glanced toward Hadrian as they passed near the staircase and into a corner where the men's gloves were located. "Indeed, I'm surprised you would think to come to my shop, my lord. Do you purchase your own clothing and accessories?"

"I confess I have a tailor in Saville Row, and I typically leave the accessories to my very capable valet. However, I saw your stack of gloves and thought it might be nice to try some on for myself for a change."

"Certainly, my lord. Is there something in particular you are looking for?"

"Not really. Why don't you show me what you think is best?" He gave Pollard an encouraging smile as he removed his gloves. At last, he would have the opportunity to touch Pollard.

The gloves were arrayed in the case from white to black with an array of colors in between. Pollard stepped behind it to open the back.

"What a pleasing display," Hadrian remarked.

"Joanna's work," Pollard said with a measure of pride. "She has an eye for such things." He pulled a dove-gray pair from the case and slid them over to Hadrian.

Hadrian masked his disappointment. He would much rather have had Pollard hand them to him so he could at least try to see a vision from the man. But the moment Hadrian picked up the gloves, he was transported to another time and place.

He recognized it immediately—Beryl's bedchamber. He stood before the dresser and watched as a dark-gloved hand opened the drawer ... and tucked a long kitchen knife behind neatly stacked handkerchiefs. The vision came with an accompanying sense of nervousness and excitement. There was also a distinct rush of daring and risk.

Had Pollard put the knife in Beryl's drawer? Or had it been his wife since she'd also handled these gloves? He watched as the hand closed the drawer. It was small, feminine.

It had to be Joanna Pollard. But why? And when had she done this?

Her glove was black, which meant it was likely the funeral yesterday.

The vision dissipated. Hadrian's head began to ache as he pulled on the dove-gray gloves.

"Those are quite nice, if you don't mind my saying," Pollard noted.

"They are," Hadrian said vaguely as he pulled them off and set them atop the case. "What about the darker gray?"

"An excellent choice," Pollard said as he pulled them from the case.

Hadrian put his hand out this time, hoping for even a scintilla of contact with Pollard. He was not disappointed—until he was. Though Pollard's fingertips grazed Hadrian's palm, it wasn't enough to spark a vision or even a feeling.

But as Hadrian pulled on the first glove, he once again found himself in the Chambers' house. This time he was in Louis's bedchamber. It was dark, but someone carried a lantern. Hadrian strove to see their face. It was the blonde maid—Martha Farrow, certainly. She handed the lantern to whoever's memory Hadrian was seeing. It had to be Joanna Pollard, didn't it?

Joanna took the lantern in her left hand as she handed something from her right.

The knife.

She stood with the lantern on one side of Louis's bed, whilst Martha walked around to the other. Joanna set the lantern on the table beside the bed and reached down to shove at Louis's shoulder. He stirred.

Louis blinked as he fixed on Joanna, then turned his head toward Martha. She looked angry. No, furious. She waved the knife in front of his face. Fear gripped his features. He nodded.

Joanna's hands, including the one holding the lantern, moved wildly. She was just as furious as Martha appeared. But it was more than that. There was rage but also a violent urge.

Suddenly, Martha plunged the knife into Louis's chest. Joanna slapped one hand over his mouth and held his arm with the other as he began to flail.

The vision faded, and Hadrian hastily pulled on the other glove, his head throbbing. He wanted to see what happened next.

But what he saw next was not that. He was now at the lodging house, the veil making his vision hazy. Though he could still make out Martha. She held something that she thrust toward Joanna. The item lay in her palm—it was the brooch they'd found in Martha's bedroom at the lodging house.

Joanna knocked the brooch from Martha's hand. Then she stepped forward, putting her hands out toward Martha.

Hadrian felt the connection of Joanna's fingertips with Martha's shoulders, then her palms as Joanna shoved the poor maid. Martha stumbled backward and hit the railing. She tried to grasp the wood, but it gave, just as it had when Tilda had touched it. Wobbling the barest moment, Martha's mouth opened in a silent—because Hadrian couldn't hear her—cry as she fell over the railing.

Hadrian had never felt such agony in his head. He put his hand to his temple as the vision disappeared, leaving him with a sense of diminishing rage and escalating fear.

"Are you all right, Lord Ravenhurst?"

The question sounded as if it were coming from far away. Hadrian blinked hard, which made pain shoot through his forehead. "I'm fine," he managed, taking a deep breath. Or trying to. The effort made his head hurt more if that was possible.

He'd never had so many visions in rapid succession. In truth, he felt queasy in addition to his head aching.

"You look a bit pale, if I may say," Pollard said. "Would you like to sit down?"

He would, in fact, but what he'd seen in the visions came back to him. "I would like to find Miss Wren, actually." *Immediately.*

She was with a killer.

CHAPTER 20

*T*ilda climbed the staircase at the center of the drapery shop. It ascended in a circular fashion and on the first floor, a gilt railing ran around the edge where one could look down onto the ground floor. It was incredibly elegant and gave the store a sense of sophistication.

Joanna Pollard was busy near the top of the staircase where a wooden figure stood. Crouched down, she was pinning the hem of a gown that was draped over the form. She glanced at Tilda as she approached.

"Good morning, Mrs. Pollard. I am sorry to disturb you when you are so hard at work."

Mrs. Pollard's small blue eyes darted toward Tilda but didn't linger. "I am indeed. I can't imagine why you've come to bother us when Beryl Chambers has been arrested for killing her husband. Surely your investigation is concluded."

"I'm not here about that," Tilda said with a careless wave of her hand. "When you offered to make a gown for Beryl yesterday, I wondered if you might be interested in making one for me. I realize the shop isn't open yet, and I suppose I could wait. Still, I couldn't resist coming to ask." She flashed a smile. "I confess I was also hoping to see more of the shop. Mr. Pollard said you'd be able to open in a fortnight since Oliver has joined as an investor."

Rising to stand, Joanna rolled her shoulders back. Her gaze was wary, as if she wasn't sure she trusted Tilda. "You want a gown?" Her gaze dipped over Tilda's garment. "I can see why."

"My wardrobe is rather outdated." Tilda bristled slightly at the woman's judgment. She'd liked how she looked yesterday—and how it made her feel. It hadn't occurred to her that the right garments could instill confidence and pride. That didn't mean Tilda ought to purchase another gown. This was nothing more than a ruse.

Joanna gave her a dubious look. "The frock you wore yesterday was from this year, I'd say."

Tilda nodded. "It was, and after seeing myself in it, I decided I ought to have another."

"You would look lovely in burgundy, I think, with an ivory sash." Mrs. Pollard wrinkled her nose. "You really must dispose of the wide crinoline. It's almost vulgar, if I am honest."

Though Tilda wasn't at all interested in debating the amount or shape of the crinoline in her petticoat, she resented Mrs. Pollard calling it vulgar. Did Tilda really look that bad? She was suddenly very self-conscious about how she might appear when she was out with Hadrian. She would not want to reflect poorly on him.

"I would hate to be vulgar," Tilda said tightly. "Can you help me?"

The faintest smile passed over Joanna's thin lips. "I can. I've just the wool in a lovely shade of burgundy that would look splendid on you. I will need to take your measurements. Would you like to do that today so I may get started?"

"Certainly," Tilda said. "But first, tell me about this wooden figure and what you're doing."

"These figures are quite dear," Mrs. Pollard replied. "We only have two for now. One will be downstairs in the main window, and I wanted this one up here so people coming up the stairs or looking up from the ground floor would see it straightaway. I'm adjusting this gown to its best effect, which is more difficult than I'd anticipated. The wooden figure isn't as close an approximation to a woman's body as I would have liked."

"I see." Tilda searched for a way to turn the conversation to her purpose. "Forgive me for saying so, but looking down over this railing reminds me of the death of the Chambers' maid, Martha Farrow." She met Joanna's gaze, keeping her expression serene. "You knew her, didn't you?"

Joanna's left eye twitched, and her nostrils flared slightly. She turned and fidgeted with the sleeve of the gown on the wooden figure. "I did not."

"Really? When Ravenhurst and I visited her lodging house in Spitalfields to investigate her tragic death, one of the occupants said you visited her."

Joanna snapped her attention to Tilda, her eyes sparking with agitation. "They were mistaken."

"I don't think so," Tilda said blithely. "They said Martha mentioned her friend Joanna who was opening a drapery store on Oxford Street. I understand that you wore a veil, so perhaps you thought they didn't know who you were. Why *did* you wear a veil?"

Returning her attention to the wooden figure, Joanna's hand appeared to shake as she gripped its waist. It was then that Tilda noticed the ring on her finger—garnets. The woman Hadrian had seen in the vision with Martha Farrow in Louis Chambers' bedroom.

Suddenly, the wooden figure came toward Tilda. She moved to avoid it, her body hitting the railing. Gasping, Tilda recalled the railing at the lodging house when it gave way and the terror that had streaked through her. Until Hadrian had grabbed her close to him.

What she wouldn't give for that sense of security right now.

"Tilda!" Hadrian's voice carried up the stairs as Tilda clung to the railing, which—thankfully—hadn't moved.

Joanna pushed at the figure again, but Tilda shoved it back. With an angry cry, Joanna came around the wobbling figure. She reached into the pocket of her apron and pulled out a long pair of scissors.

Before Joanna could lunge forward as Tilda entirely expected her to do, Hadrian leapt at her, tackling her to the floor. Tilda gasped again whilst her pulse sped impossibly fast. Heart pounding, she heard Joanna's cries. The end of the scissors nicked Hadrian's neck, drawing blood.

"Joanna!"

That had to be Mr. Pollard, but Tilda didn't hesitate. She dropped to her knees and clasped at Joanna's wrist, enclosing it in her grip and squeezing as she wrested the woman's arm away from Hadrian.

"Joanna, stop!" Mr. Pollard pleaded.

Tilda glanced up to see him standing near his wife's head. "Joanna, please listen to your husband. You don't want to kill anyone else."

"I didn't kill *anyone*!" Joanna shrieked.

"*Kill?*" Mr. Pollard sounded horrified.

Hadrian's hand wrapped around Joanna's wrist next to Tilda's. His gaze met hers, and in the blue depths she saw safety—and promise. "You can let go," he said softly. "I've got her."

Tilda released Joanna and exhaled, her heart still hammering. She noted that the cut on Hadrian's neck had clotted quickly so that he only looked as if he'd been cut shaving. "We need to send for Teague."

"Leach can do it," Hadrian said.

"Get off me!" Joanna cried.

Hadrian moved his attention to her, his expression turning

hard. "So that you can try to stab me again? Release the scissors and give them to Tilda."

Grunting, Joanna loosened her hold on the would-be weapon. They fell to the floor, and Tilda scooped them up.

Pollard knelt next to his wife's head. "You tried to stab the earl?"

"She did," Tilda replied. She was not going to give Joanna the chance to lie. "And she tried to push me over the railing, just as she did to Martha, I presume."

"Don't bother lying," Hadrian said, his gaze locked with Joanna's. "You will already be charged with attempting to kill Miss Wren and me. Perhaps if you tell the truth about pushing Martha, you will avoid hanging."

The woman's face paled. "I couldn't risk Martha telling anyone what happened to Louis Chambers. She killed him!"

Pollard looked on his wife in abject misery. "Oh, Joanna. Why didn't you tell the police?"

"Because I was there," she said quietly. "I met Martha the night of the dinner party. We commiserated about our hatred of Louis. We decided we would scare him into giving her money because she was carrying his child and me the money he'd promised for the store."

That had to have been the conversation Hadrian had seen in Louis's bedchamber. Joanna, with her garnet ring, had been speaking to Martha.

"How did you plan to scare him?" Pollard asked, aghast.

"Martha said we could steal into his bedchamber the next night that his valet was gone. We planned to threaten him with a knife. But then Martha stabbed him. I don't know what came over her."

"Did you help her in any way?" Hadrian asked darkly, his features set into grim lines.

Tilda realized Hadrian must have had a vision downstairs. Perhaps more than one. He seemed confident that Joanna had pushed Martha. And now he was asking if Joanna had helped with Louis's murder. What had he seen?

"I—" Joanna closed her eyes. "He began to make noise. We couldn't have him yelling the house down."

"I am going to stand now, and your husband can help you up," Hadrian said. "Do not try to run. We are going to fetch the police."

Hadrian rose and stepped back from Joanna who opened her eyes. She appeared defeated.

Pollard took his wife's hand and helped her to stand, his features a mask of disbelief and distress. "What have you done?" He dropped her hand as if he'd touched a hot iron.

"Louis Chambers was ruining everything," she snapped. "How were we to launch this store when he couldn't pay what he'd promised?" She fixed on her husband, her eyes wild. "He would have bankrupted us, and you were content to let it happen."

"I was *not*." Pollard's bushy brows pitched in anger. "I was working to bring Oliver into the business."

"You allowed Louis to forbid it!" she shrieked. "I had to try to convince Louis. Did you know he even attempted to seduce me? Disgusting, lecherous jackanapes."

Pollard's shoulders slumped. "I didn't know."

"Because I didn't tell you." Joanna exhaled. "What would have been the point? I knew you wouldn't stand up to Louis. He needed to be stopped." She glowered at her husband.

"So you visited Martha to ensure she kept your secret?" Tilda asked.

"She asked me to come, said she needed money. She wanted to exchange a brooch for money." Joanna scoffed. "I told her to see a pawnbroker, but she said she'd tried, and he accused her of stealing the brooch. I have to agree with him. Can't imagine why a chit like her would have something as expensive as that."

"So instead of just refusing her, you pushed her?" Hadrian said, his tone slightly elevated. He briefly pressed his hands to his temple, and Tilda assumed his head ached from whatever vision he'd seen downstairs.

Pollard gestured toward Hadrian. "My lord, you still haven't sat down. Are you still feeling ill?"

He'd felt ill? Tilda's pulse had calmed in the last few minutes, but it picked up speed again as worry for Hadrian coursed through her. She moved to his side, angling herself toward him, and gently touched his back. "Do you need to sit?" she asked softly.

"Not at the moment, but thank you." His gaze met hers briefly, and she saw the agony behind all the emotion simmering in his eyes.

"Why don't we go downstairs?" Tilda suggested. "Mr. Pollard, do you have a seating area where we may await Detective Inspector Teague?" She would dash out to Leach and ask him to fetch Teague.

Joanna released her arms and turned on her husband. "You can't let them send for the police! He'll arrest me. I haven't done anything wrong! I've only tried to protect our business, our livelihood!"

Pollard appeared anguished. "Joanna, I think you need to sit down. Or lie down."

As he moved to take his wife's arm, she jerked away and darted toward the stairs. Tilda followed in pursuit. But a third of the way down the circular staircase, Joanna slipped. Her arms flailed as she pitched forward and tumbled down several stairs until she hit the railing. If it had been a straight staircase, she would have fallen all the way to the ground floor.

"Joanna, my love!" Pollard rushed to his wife's crumpled form.

Tilda descended to stand just above them. "I think she hit her head."

Pollard rotated his wife so that her face was revealed. Her eyes were closed, and she appeared unconscious.

Hadrian joined Tilda. "That seems almost poetic," he whispered.

Tears fell from Pollard's eyes onto his wife's cheeks, and Tilda felt rather sad for him. He seemed to have been completely unaware of his wife's underlying violent nature.

Joanna's eyelids fluttered open. "Edgar?" she rasped as she focused on her husband.

"I'm here, love. Are you hurt?"

She nodded but winced. "My head. And my ankle."

"I'll carry you downstairs," Pollard said.

"I'll help you," Hadrian offered.

Tilda put her hand on his arm. "Is that wise? Are you well enough?"

"He needs help. I can manage."

Hadrian and Pollard worked together to lift Joanna from the stairs and carry her down to the ground floor and then made their way to the back of the store where there were several chairs. They set her down in one of them, then Pollard moved another chair so that Joanna could elevate her feet.

Pollard looked to Hadrian. "When you send for the police, will you also find a physician, please?"

"I'm going out to speak with Hadrian's coachman," Tilda said. "Do not let Mrs. Pollard leave."

"I can't walk," the woman said, lifting her skirt to her calf. "Edgar, will you remove my boot? It pains me terribly."

"Come, let us send Leach on his way," Hadrian said, touching Tilda's arm.

They turned together and hurried toward the door leading to Oxford Street. Tilda looked over at him as they walked. "Are you all right? Truly? You must have had a vision or even two."

"I had three," he said, grimacing faintly. "In fairly rapid succession. I have never felt so poorly afterward, but I'm doing better now." His eyes locked with hers briefly as they reached the door, and he opened it. "There is nothing like a terrible fright to allow one to put their pains aside."

Tilda hesitated. "What do you mean?"

"As soon as I knew Joanna was a killer—she pushed Martha to her death—and that you were alone with her upstairs, I *had* to reach you. My headache and queasiness be damned."

The queasiness was new, but Tilda wasn't fixated on that. She was wholly mesmerized by the intensity of his stare and the vehemence of his words. He'd *had* to reach her.

"Leach!" Hadrian called as he held the door.

Shaken from her ridiculous musings, Tilda hastened outside. Leach strode toward them.

"You must go to Scotland Yard and fetch Detective Inspector Teague," Hadrian said.

"Tell him to bring constables," Tilda added. "He will be arresting Joanna Pollard for the murders of Martha Farrow and Louis Chambers."

Leach's brows shot up. "Right away." He paused a moment as he studied Hadrian. "You all right, my lord? You look a bit pale."

"I'm fine," Hadrian replied. "A physician would also be helpful —not for me. Mrs. Pollard fell and has an injury."

"Yes, sir," Leach said with a definitive nod before dashing back to the coach. He was already pulling into the street when Tilda and Hadrian walked back into the store.

"Promise me that you will sit when we return to the back of the shop," Tilda said sternly.

"I promise, especially since you are using that authoritative tone." He flashed her a smile. "I'm glad to see your concern."

"Of course, I'm concerned. I care very much about you, Hadrian." She hadn't intended to say that. In fact, the words somewhat surprised her, but she knew them to be true.

His features softened. "And I feel the same about you."

He offered his arm, and she took it—to provide him support

should he need it. And perhaps because she simply wanted to touch him. Yes, that felt … right.

~

*H*adrian hadn't suffered such a terrible headache since he'd struck the pavement when he'd been stabbed two months earlier. This one, however, was not due to hitting his head but a direct result of the successive visions he'd had. Though he didn't regret them since they'd prompted him to reach Tilda before Joanna Pollard had inflicted any physical harm upon her.

Thankfully, Teague had arrived relatively quickly with a pair of constables. He'd questioned Joanna, and she'd told him everything she'd already said to Hadrian and Tilda. She'd also confessed to putting the knife Martha had taken from the kitchen and used to stab Louis into Beryl's drawer the day of the funeral. She'd hoped Beryl would be blamed for the murder.

Teague had arrested Joanna and asked Hadrian and Tilda to meet them at Scotland Yard so they could provide official statements.

Once they were in the coach, Hadrian had detailed the visions he'd seen whilst Tilda had hung on every word. He'd sat beside her, glad for her proximity and warmth. She'd positioned herself toward him and given him her fullest attention.

Whilst it hadn't eased the ache in his head, her focus certainly made him feel good.

"Beryl will be released now that Joanna is in custody," Tilda said as they neared Scotland Yard. "I suppose you should take her home."

"I was going to offer," Hadrian replied. "I confess I'm not too keen on helping her any longer. I'm glad this affair is concluded." He met her gaze. "Are you?"

"I will be, though for me it is not finished quite yet. There are still missing pieces of jewelry that she hired me to find."

They arrived at Scotland Yard and were shown to Teague's office where they waited for a short while. A young clerk brought them tea, which was most welcome. Hadrian's headache finally began to ease.

A constable came to take their statements. Teague arrived just as he was finishing.

The inspector poured a cup of tea and settled into a chair. "I must thank you both for your assistance today. I am rather shocked by Mrs. Pollard's confessions."

"Have you charged her with murder?" Tilda asked.

"At the very least, I expect to charge her with manslaughter, but I am still collecting evidence."

Hadrian was disappointed. He'd seen Joanna push Martha Farrow and hold Louis Chambers down. "Is that because she didn't stab Louis Chambers?"

Teague nodded. "Nor did she intend to push Martha Farrow to her death—at least not when she went to visit her initially. She says she panicked in pushing her. I'm inclined to believe her. Why would Martha tell anyone what happened? She would only implicate herself." He shook his head. "Anyway, it is difficult to know what happened without having a direct witness besides Mrs. Pollard."

Hadrian kept his face impassive whilst exchanging a look with Tilda. It was moments like these when his ability to see things was both a blessing and a curse. "What about Joanna's attack on Tilda?"

"And on you," Tilda added. "She nicked Hadrian's throat with her scissors. I saw that with my own eyes." She sent Teague an expectant look.

"She'll be charged for both those crimes as well—either assault or mayhem," Teague said.

"Will she also be charged for trying to blame Beryl for her husband's murder?" Hadrian asked.

"Perhaps, though there's still the matter of the poisoning. As you heard earlier, Joanna denies having anything to do with that." Teague had questioned her about that at the shop.

Tilda fixed her gaze on Teague. "Did you know that Beryl Chambers was ill in January for some time? She's recovered, however. Her symptoms were the same as what was mentioned at the inquest."

Teague frowned. "You think she was poisoned?"

"I think it's possible. But if she was, the poisoner stopped at some point."

"Perhaps they were mistakenly poisoning her instead of her husband?" Teague mused. "It's peculiar. I suppose I must turn my attention to the household staff. They had the ability to poison both Mr. and Mrs. Chambers. I just don't know what their motive would be."

"I believe none of them cared for Mr. Chambers," Tilda said. "But I don't know if they felt strongly enough to kill him."

Hadrian looked from Tilda to Teague. "Perhaps they were just trying to make him ill for a while, as they'd done with Beryl?"

Teague exhaled. "I don't suppose you could find a way to provoke the culprit to confess as you did with Mrs. Pollard?" He gave them both a sardonic look.

"We can try," Tilda said.

"I was joking, but I would greatly accept any help you can offer," Teague replied with a smile. "You are most helpful, Miss Wren. I think I must consider consulting with you in the future."

"Do you have support for that from your superiors?" Tilda asked drily.

He chuckled. "Not yet."

Tilda stood, and Hadrian joined her.

Teague also rose. "You're conveying Mrs. Chambers to her home?"

"If she's allowed to leave," Hadrian said.

"She is," Teague said. "The poisoning investigation will continue, but I don't have strong evidence against her for that crime. I'll have her meet you outside."

Teague left, and Tilda and Hadrian followed him from the office.

They waited a few minutes outside before Beryl came toward them in the company of two constables, having exited from a different door. She appeared tired, her clothing creased.

Hadrian gave her a warm smile. "Beryl, you look well."

"I do not," she said crossly and then exhaled. "Forgive me, I am quite ready to leave this place and hopefully never return."

"Of course," Hadrian said. "My coach is just there." He indicated where Leach was standing.

"Thank you." Her expression was filled with gratitude as she made her way to the coachman.

Leach helped her inside, and she took the forward-facing seat. Tilda climbed in next and sat opposite her. Hadrian settled beside Tilda, and they were shortly on their way.

Beryl looked at Hadrian and seemed puzzled. Was that because he'd chosen to sit with Tilda?

"I can hardly believe Mrs. Pollard sought to blame me for Louis's murder." Beryl clucked her tongue. "I am glad she will be charged with the crime. And with pushing poor Martha. It's all so shocking."

"Indeed, it is," Tilda murmured.

They were silent a few moments. Beryl looked at them warily. Finally, she said, "I know you are aware of Oliver and me, and that you probably think poorly of that … situation."

"It is not our place to judge," Tilda said evenly.

Hadrian was glad she'd spoken for him too since he felt the same. He also rather liked being included in her sentiments. It showed they were close partners and friends.

Beryl sniffed. "I was very unhappy with Louis. This marriage was not what I'd hoped it would be." She flicked a glance at Hadrian.

"I can't imagine it was," Hadrian said. He didn't think she knew the truth about why Louis had married her—as revenge against Hadrian, and he wasn't going to tell her. Perhaps she would find out at some point, but not from him.

"Thank you both again for your help." Beryl's gaze fell on Tilda. "What of my missing jewelry? I know my brooch was found with Martha's things, and I'll have it back soon, and that my pearl pieces were apparently sold." She frowned sadly. "But will you continue to look for the others?"

Tilda exchanged an uncertain look with Hadrian. "I learned that Louis gave your rubies to his mistress. He showed them to friends at his club. I'm sorry."

Beryl gaped. "The bastard! Have you no idea who she is?"

"I'm afraid not," Tilda said with a faint grimace. "And I doubt I can find your other missing pieces—not unless someone comes forward."

A lone whimper sounded from Beryl's throat. "What am I to do now? I wanted my jewelry back because it belongs to me and many of the items are heirlooms. But now I suppose I must sell them to live. Oliver says Louis had debts and that his quarterly income must pay for them. He says it will take years to satisfy them in full." She sent a forlorn look toward Hadrian.

Was she expecting him to offer assistance? He would not. "Perhaps you ought to write to your parents."

She crossed her arms over her chest. "I doubt they would help me."

They rode the rest of the way to Beryl's house in an awkward silence. Hadrian's head still ached, but it was mild now. Nevertheless, he looked forward to going home.

"Let us walk you inside, Beryl," Tilda offered, sending Hadrian a look that said this was important.

As they approached the front door, Oswald opened it. He

blinked at Beryl. "Mrs. Chambers, you've returned." He appeared surprised, and perhaps not in a positive way. At least, he wasn't smiling.

"Finally," Beryl said as she walked into the entrance hall. "I require a bath and tea."

"Right away, Mrs. Chambers." The butler took himself off.

Beryl removed her hat and gloves. She looked at Tilda and Hadrian, her expression morose. "I don't suppose you need to stay. Thank you for bringing me home."

A knock on the door prompted them all to divert their attention. In the absence of Oswald, Hadrian answered.

Mrs. Styles-Rowdon stood outside. She was not wearing a hat or gloves and appeared somewhat harried. "My housekeeper said she saw Beryl arrive."

Hadrian opened the door wider to reveal Beryl.

"I'm here, Gillian." Beryl looked at her friend with relief.

"My goodness, what an ordeal! Does this mean you're free?" the neighbor asked as she bustled inside. Her cherry-colored skirt brushed Hadrian's boots as she walked by him to embrace Beryl.

"They've arrested Joanna Pollard," Beryl declared as they parted. She went on to explain to Mrs. Styles-Rowdon how Joanna had helped to kill Louis along with Martha and then killed Martha.

Mrs. Styles-Rowdon put her hand to her chest. "How gruesome."

"Unfortunately, the detective inspector said I am still a suspect for poisoning Louis." Beryl made a face. "Why does it matter? The poison didn't kill him—Martha and Joanna Pollard did."

"It matters because it's a crime to poison someone," Tilda said evenly, though Hadrian could see a bit of fire in her eyes.

"Of course it is," Mrs. Styles-Rowdon said with a nod. "Beryl, you mustn't worry about that now. I'm sure you need rest. And a bath." She wrinkled her nose.

"Oh dear, do I smell terribly?" Beryl asked in horror. "I must." She turned to Tilda. "Would you mind walking upstairs with me? I want to ask you about this poisoning investigation."

"Certainly," Tilda murmured. She sent a look toward Hadrian, her eyes rounding slighting, before following Beryl from the entrance hall.

"I'll check on you later," Mrs. Styles-Rowdon called after Beryl. Then she faced Hadrian. "How wonderful that you and Miss Wren brought Beryl home. You and Miss Wren seem to spend a great deal of time together."

"We are business associates. I help her with investigating."

Mrs. Styles-Rowdon's wheat-colored brows arched elegantly. "Is that the only reason?"

"We are also friends." Hadrian had the distinct impression Mrs. Styles-Rowdon was trying to ascertain Hadrian's romantic availability.

"One can never have too many of those," she said with an alluring smile. "Beryl is lucky to call you a friend too."

They were not friends, but Hadrian would not correct the woman. He looked forward to when Beryl would be a memory once more. He merely nodded at Mrs. Styles-Rowdon.

"You must be relieved to have the murder resolved. I can't imagine you enjoyed being labeled a suspect." She gave him a concerned pout, her lips forming a perfect bow.

"I did not." Hadrian hoped Tilda wouldn't be gone too long. Mrs. Styles-Rowdon had moved closer to him.

She gasped. "What happened to your neck?" She reached out and brushed her fingers where Joanna Pollard had cut him.

Suddenly, Hadrian was no longer in the entrance hall. He was in a small kitchen. A feminine hand poured something into a bowl of soup on a tray. He was seeing Mrs. Styles-Rowdon's memory. She set the bottle down and looked out a window at the ocean in the distance. Then she picked up the tray and carried it into a bedchamber.

A man lay propped on a few pillows against the headboard. His eyes were tired, his face pallid. He managed a small smile as the woman whose memory he was seeing—Mrs. Styles-Rowdon —set the tray down on the table next to the bed. She then proceeded to feed the man the soup.

"My lord?"

Hadrian blinked, and Mrs. Styles-Rowdon came into focus once more. "My apologies. I fear it's been a trying day." His headache had improved but now returned with a vengeance. Tilda may be right that he ought to limit his visions if he could. Not that he'd provoked this one. Mrs. Styles-Rowdon had touched him. "Joanna Pollard cut me with a pair of scissors."

Mrs. Styles-Rowdon sucked in a breath. "You poor man. It's a pity you don't have a countess to take care of you. Why, I'd make sure you had a steaming hot bath and a large tumbler of brandy."

"That is precisely what I had in mind for myself when I get home. No wife necessary," he added with a smile.

"But those things would be more enticing with a wife, would they not?" Her eyes had darkened in an almost seductive manner.

Though he wanted nothing more than to put distance between himself and this woman who had perhaps poisoned someone, he would not disappoint Tilda. After the vision he'd just seen, he had questions, and he needed to ask them, headache be damned. "Did you often ensure your husband had a bath and a glass of brandy?"

Surprise and perhaps discomfort flashed across her features. "Of course."

"You must miss him," Hadrian said with an excess of insincere sympathy. "How long ago were you widowed?"

"Three years."

"Poor dear," he murmured, echoing what she'd said to him. He held her gaze, hoping she would keep answering his questions. "Was that here in London or somewhere else?"

"Portsmouth."

Unfortunately, Tilda walked into the entrance hall and disrupted their revelatory moment. Tilda's gaze lingered skeptically on Mrs. Styles-Rowdon, then shifted uneasily to Hadrian. He could well imagine how this looked.

Hadrian stepped away from the woman and looked eagerly at Tilda. "Ready to depart?"

"Yes."

"I should be going also." Mrs. Styles-Rowdon moved toward the door, and Hadrian hurried to open it for her. "Thank you." She inclined her head toward them and walked outside.

Hadrian continued holding the door for Tilda who preceded him from the house. They walked in silence to the coach. He waited until they were settled together inside before speaking.

Except she beat him to it.

"Was Mrs. Styles-Rowdon flirting with you?"

"Yes, and I was flirting with her." Hadrian rubbed his forehead, wincing. "She touched me, and I saw something."

"Another vision?" Tilda touched his arm. "Are you all right?"

"I'll be fine." He hoped—his head felt as though it might split in two. "I saw her pour something into a soup and give it to a man who was ill in bed. I believe it was her husband. They were near the ocean, and she said her husband died in Portsmouth."

Tilda's eyes rounded. "She poisoned him?"

"I think so." He closed his eyes briefly. That felt better.

"I'm worried about you," Tilda said softly. Her hand was still on his arm.

"I'll be fine," he repeated. "Let's assume she poisoned her husband. Why? And why would she poison Louis Chambers?"

Tilda took her hand from his arm, and Hadrian opened his eyes. She looked pensive.

Her gaze met his. "What if Mrs. Styles-Rowdon was Louis's

paramour? That would mean both men had something in common—their intimate relationships with her. That isn't a motive, however." She looked away and her expression became determined. "I'm going back to Scotland Yard after Leach takes you home. Teague should be able to send a telegram to Portsmouth. We can find out how her husband died and anything else that may be helpful."

"I want to come with you."

Tilda gave her head a firm shake as she moved her attention back to him. "Absolutely not. You need to rest."

Hadrian frowned, which made him wince again. "At least let Leach drive you and then take you home."

"All right." She sent him a stern look. "You must promise me that you'll rest."

"I will. I plan to drink some brandy, take a warm bath, have a light supper, and sleep this headache away." He hoped. The one thing he could expect from his power and the resulting headaches was that he should always be prepared for something unexpected, such as multiple visions in a short amount of time leaving him feeling as though he'd been tossed about in a boat crossing the English Channel.

"I hope you don't have to be at Westminster tomorrow," she said. "You should take it easy."

He leaned back against the squab and stretched out his legs so that his toes nearly touched the other seat. "I do not, in fact. I shall take your advice. But you must come tell me what you learn from Teague."

"Of course I will—if only to ensure you are well." Her eyes gleamed with a warm promise that sparked something within him. He enjoyed this familiarity they shared. And he was delighted that she cared so much about him.

"Don't forget to bring an invoice for me to pay."

"Given how much you've contributed to our investigation, it hardly seems fair for you to pay me."

He waved his hand. "You deserve to be paid for your work."

"And what of your work?" She arched a brow at him. "And I'm not just speaking of your visions. You've developed very good investigative skills. Just look at what you did with Mrs. Styles-Rowdon today."

Hadrian's chest swelled and his heart sped for a moment as the thrill of her praise raced through him. "That is quite a compliment coming from you. Thank you." His eyes met hers, and they simply looked at one another for a long moment. She broke the connection first, moving her focus to the other side of the coach. His gaze dipped to her mouth, and he recalled their conversation about kissing. He wanted to kiss her. Would she really allow it?

Today was not the day to find out. Between his headache and everything that had happened, he didn't think an attempted kiss would be appropriate. Not to mention how it might affect their friendship, which he valued very much.

Hadrian would content himself with simply sitting beside her —and allowing her compliment to repeat itself in his head.

"You should divert Leach to Ravenhurst House," Tilda said.

"Indeed." He knocked on the roof and Leach slowed the coach. They were soon on their way to Hadrian's house instead of Tilda's.

As they neared Curzon Street, Hadrian loosened his cravat. "I want to say how glad I am that everything turned out well earlier. And if I haven't thanked you for preventing Joanna from causing further damage to my neck, let me extend my sincerest gratitude."

"I am grateful you came upstairs when you did. She likely would have come after me with the scissors since she was unable to push me over the stair rail."

"Thank goodness for that," he said with a great sense of relief. "What did Beryl want to speak with you about?"

Tilda rolled her eyes. "She wanted to point out that she had likely been poisoned, so it didn't make sense that she would be the poisoner."

"Unless it was a coincidence," Hadrian said wryly.

"I think we know it was not. Now that we know Mrs. Styles-Rowdon poisoned her husband, *that* is too much of a coincidence to ignore. But would she have poisoned Beryl in addition to Louis?" Tilda's features shifted into deep contemplation as the coach stopped.

Leach opened the door, and Tilda jolted from her pensive state, smiling at Hadrian. "Please take good care."

Hadrian turned from her and climbed out of the coach. He wondered if thoughts of kissing her would keep him awake tonight.

CHAPTER 21

*H*ailing a hack outside Scotland Yard, Tilda directed the driver to Ravenhurst House. She'd much to report to Hadrian in addition to seeing how he was feeling today. She hoped he was recovered because they had work to do.

She was particularly glad for the information taking up space in her brain. It prevented her from thinking overmuch about the day before—particularly the charged moments she'd shared with Hadrian in the coach.

It was natural that she would feel a heightened sense of concern after all that had happened. Hadrian had suffered greatly from all the visions he'd seen, and he'd protected Tilda from being attacked by Joanna Pollard whilst sustaining an injury, albeit minor, to his own neck. Tilda reasoned they had both been caught up with worry and relief. It made sense that they'd felt a particular … closeness.

She would hope that was all it was.

The hack stopped on Curzon Street in front of Ravenhurst House, and Tilda climbed out. As she approached the front door, she wondered if she would ever feel at ease calling here. Though she'd done so a few times before, she still had a nagging sense that she was out of her element.

The butler, Collier, greeted her warmly. "His lordship has been expecting you. He is in his study."

"Thank you." Tilda followed the butler to the study, a thoroughly masculine room decorated in blues and greens. Bookcases lined one wall, and a mantel with ornately carved stags drew one's attention.

Hadrian stood from a chair near the hearth, setting a book down on a small table. "Tilda, you are here at last."

The butler left them, and Tilda moved to the seating area to join Hadrian. "I'd hoped to arrive earlier, but I have been at Scotland Yard with Teague."

"Please sit and tell me everything." Hadrian gestured to a chair opposite his.

Perching on the chair, Tilda smoothed her gloved hands over her gown—she'd worn the new gray one again. At least she looked as if she could almost belong here.

Tilda began to recount what had happened with Teague. It had been strange to conduct this work without Hadrian at her side, she realized. "Yesterday, at Scotland Yard, I told Teague that I suspected Mrs. Styles-Rowdon might be Louis's paramour and that she may have poisoned her husband."

Hadrian arched a brow. "Did Teague ask how you came to suspect those things?"

"I said she'd made a jest about there likely being a great number of wives who have poisoned their husbands, and no one has ever known." Tilda shrugged. "That could have happened."

"That she said it or the number of wives poisoning their husbands?"

"Both, probably." Tilda smiled. "I asked Teague to send a telegram to the police in Portsmouth to find out whatever he could about Mrs. Styles-Rowdon's husband. He would be Mr. Rowdon, I presume."

"Unless she changed her name to hide her identity," Hadrian said.

"She did not, as it happens. Teague said he'd let me know when he heard something. I received a note requesting my presence at Scotland Yard earlier."

Hadrian grinned. "I imagine you could not arrive fast enough."

Tilda inclined her head with the flash of a smile. "I went as soon as I could and learned that Mr. Frederick Rowdon died of gastrointestinal illness in September of 1865. His wife, Gillian Styles-Rowdon, was his sole heir and left Portsmouth soon thereafter."

"Sole heir ... Was there a considerable inheritance?"

"That is uncertain. Mr. Rowdon was in his fifties when he died and had served in the Navy. He owned a few fishing boats."

"Mrs. Styles-Rowdon was quite a bit younger than him."

"Yes. I have many questions, but Teague isn't sure he has enough evidence of anything to pursue. The man's death could have been caused by arsenic, but it could also have been illness, even cholera. Teague will inform me if he learns anything more." Tilda frowned slightly. "I wonder if we ought to take a trip to Portsmouth." They'd traveled to Brighton whilst investigating their last case.

Hadrian tapped his finger on the arm of his chair. "Perhaps. Though I should like to see what we can learn from Mrs. Styles-Rowdon." He lifted a shoulder. "I was able to ascertain where she'd lived with her husband and when he'd died."

"She seems to like you," Tilda mused, thinking of the way the woman had been looking at Hadrian the day before—as if he were a food to be devoured. "Though any vision you happen to see will not be evidence, unfortunately. Are you hoping to coax a confession from her?"

"That is my thought exactly. I am not above using her ... inclination for me to our advantage."

"You said you flirted with her yesterday, and you did obtain results." She gave him an approving smile. "You are becoming an accomplished investigator. I do hope you won't decide to take up the profession and steal my clients."

"Never," he said rather vehemently but with a glint of humor in his eyes. "I have learned to portray someone I am not from watching you. You are an excellent tutor in all things investigative."

"What do you propose with Mrs. Styles-Rowdon?" Tilda asked. "Could you invite her somewhere? I could use that time to steal into her house and look for Beryl's rubies. That would confirm she was indeed Louis Chambers' paramour."

"What of her retainers? How will you enter the house without being detected?"

"I'll have to do some reconnaissance as to how I may enter and how many retainers she has." She looked to Hadrian. "I suppose that means we need to return to Beryl's. I'm sorry. I know you'd like to be done with all this."

He flattened his palm on the arm of his chair. "On the one hand, I am eager to put my past with Beryl behind me once and for all. On the other, the poisoning crime has not been solved, and justice must be served."

She clasped her hands in her lap. "I'm so glad you think so."

"One of the reasons I enjoy my other occupation—serving in the Lords—is the opportunity I have to work towards justice for all."

"You see it as a noble calling."

He nodded once. "I do. It pleases me to know you understand that."

"Are you in support of the cessation of public executions?" Tilda suspected he was, but they hadn't discussed it.

"Most fervently. I have been speaking about it as often as I can. In truth, I would rather we didn't execute people at all."

"Even in the case of murder?"

"To take a person's life is no small thing," Hadrian said softly. "Murders happen for a variety of reasons. However, for the state to murder someone takes many people, all of whom must carry that burden."

"That includes you." Tilda met his gaze. "And me. We played a role in bringing Joanna Pollard to justice. If she hangs, I don't know that I'll feel burdened. I am not troubled by the death of the man we recently caught."

Hadrian scowled. "He was truly horrible. He had raped and murdered. And would have done so again. However, lifelong imprisonment would ensure he did not."

"So does death," Tilda replied, enjoying their debate.

"You are in favor of capital punishment then?"

"I am undecided," she said. "You have given me pause to think about it. Thank you. Now, where were we with our plans to further investigate Mrs. Styles-Rowdon?"

"We decided we needed to call on Beryl. I'll ring for the coach." Hadrian stood and went to the wall where he pulled a cord.

"You pull that and somehow Leach magically appears with the coach?" she asked with a smile.

He laughed as he returned to his chair. "If only it worked like that. That rings a bell downstairs, and Collier or Mrs. Kenworth will come see what I need."

Collier appeared in the doorway, and Hadrian asked him to have the coach brought round.

Hadrian returned his attention to Tilda. "Our plan then is for me to occupy Mrs. Styles-Rowdon so you can search her bedchamber for Beryl's missing rubies. What will you do if you find them?"

"I don't plan to take them. I'll inform Teague that she is in fact Louis's paramour. That would mean she has a dead husband and a dead lover who were both being poisoned—potentially."

"But why would she kill them?" Hadrian asked.

"The obvious answer would be financial gain."

"If she inherits her husband's wealth, I see the motive. Though I wonder why she needed to kill her husband, unless she was seeking independence. Or she simply didn't like him." His brows drew together. "What would she gain with Louis's death?"

"That is a very good question. He was giving her jewelry and spending extravagant amounts of money on her. Though it seemed he was rapidly losing the ability to do that." Tilda leaned forward slightly. "Louis supposedly wanted to divorce Beryl. Had he planned to wed Mrs. Styles-Rowdon? Perhaps she realized he would not be the wealthy husband she'd thought him to be."

"I still don't understand why she would need to poison him."

Tilda arched a brow. "As you said with regard to Mrs. Styles-Rowdon, perhaps she, like so many others, simply didn't like him."

Hadrian chuckled. "*That* I would believe."

~

A short while later, they arrived at Beryl's house. Oswald admitted them and said Beryl was in the parlor.

Beryl welcomed them from the settee. "Join me for tea. Oswald, please have Mrs. Blank bring more cups."

The butler disappeared, and Hadrian waited for the ladies to sit before taking the chair next to Tilda's. They sat across from Beryl.

"Forgive me," Beryl said. "I'm afraid I've just finished the last of Gillian's delicious cinnamon biscuits. I have missed them so. There is lemon cake, however."

Tilda's brow creased. "Mrs. Styles-Rowdon brought you those biscuits?"

Hadrian now recalled that she had done so. The neighbor had brought a tin the day the inquest had been postponed. His blood chilled. That was food from outside the house, and Mrs. Styles-

Rowdon was a known poisoner—if his visions were to be believed. And so far, they had not been wrong.

"Yes, she used to bring them frequently, but it's been some time," Beryl explained. "She says it's her secret recipe. It's the brandy that makes them so delicious. Or so Gillian told me the first time she brought them. Goodness, when was that?" Beryl thought a moment. "Ah yes, the day after Epiphany. We'd had a dinner party and invited Gillian. She brought the biscuits to thank me. That was the beginning of our friendship."

"But she stopped bringing you biscuits?" Tilda asked. "When was that?"

Beryl cocked her head. "I'm not sure."

"Was she bringing you biscuits whilst you were ill?" Tilda pressed. She leaned slightly forward, her gaze intensely focused on Beryl.

"No," Beryl said quickly. But then her eyes narrowed briefly. "Actually, it may have been."

The reason for their visit faded with this revelation—at least to Hadrian. Did Tilda feel the same? It seemed they had proof that Mrs. Styles-Rowdon was likely poisoning Beryl. But why?

Tilda looked toward Hadrian, and he had his answer.

Beryl, meanwhile, had gone white as cream.

Mrs. Blank entered then with the teacups for Tilda and Hadrian. She set them on the tray, which sat atop a table that had been moved near the settee and the chair where Tilda sat.

The housekeeper paused as she looked at Beryl. "Are you all right, Mrs. Chambers?"

"I don't know," she said softly.

"She's fine," Tilda said to the housekeeper with a smile. "It has been a trying week."

"Hasn't it just," Mrs. Blank said with a shake of her head before departing.

Beryl stared at Tilda and Hadrian. "Was Gillian poisoning me? I can't believe it."

"We can't jump to conclusions just yet," Tilda said. "Though it is suspicious that you were ill when she was bringing you biscuits."

"I've been eating them since Saturday." Panic flashed in Beryl's eyes. "Am I going to be ill? Am I going to … die?" She slumped back against the coach, and Hadrian feared she may faint as she had when Teague had said she was a suspect in Louis's murder.

"I think you'd already be ill if those biscuits were poisoned," Tilda said. "How quickly after Epiphany did you feel poorly?"

"Within a few days, I believe." Beryl put her hand to her forehead. "Why would Gillian poison me? We're friends," she croaked and seemed to be holding back tears. Shaking her head, she swallowed. "It doesn't make sense that she would. It's more likely her flour was bad. There is bad flour. I've read about how they put things in it to cheat people, and it makes them sick."

Poor Beryl looked very upset. Her eyes were wild, and she was still pale.

"We'll investigate that," Tilda said soothingly. "For now, please keep this to yourself until we learn more."

"Let us just ask Gillian," Beryl said. "I'm sure there's a reasonable explanation." She fell silent, her mouth drawn into a frown.

"I'm sure you're right," Tilda replied. "Please let Hadrian and me determine what that is. You've been through enough."

"What about Louis?" Beryl blurted. "Was Gillian poisoning him too? Why would she do that?"

Hadrian worried that Beryl was working herself into an agitated state. "Let's not worry about it now," he said gently, hoping to calm her.

"She thought Louis was awful," Beryl went on. "She was so eager to help me with the divorce. Would she have poisoned him to protect me?"

Tilda gave her a reassuring smile. "We'll look into that too."

"I need to know." Beryl blinked at him, then looked to Tilda. "We can just go next door and speak to Gillian. Now."

Hadrian and Tilda exchanged another look. "You can't do that, Beryl," Hadrian said, perhaps a trifle too sternly. "Promise me you'll let Tilda and me handle this. We don't know anything for certain." Except they did. He was more certain than ever that Mrs. Styles-Rowdon had poisoned Louis and perhaps even Beryl.

Tilda rose. "Beryl, I think you should rest."

Beryl shook her head. "I don't know if I can."

Hadrian also stood. He moved to offer his hand to Beryl. "Come. You'll feel better after you have a respite. Let Tilda work her investigative magic, and when you're refreshed, we may have all the answers for you." He smiled at her with encouragement.

Putting her hand in his, Beryl rose. "All right. But I want to know as soon as you've learned something."

Tilda nodded. "Absolutely."

Beryl left the parlor, and Tilda walked out after her into the entrance hall.

Hadrian followed, and together they watched as Beryl went into the staircase hall and up the stairs.

Turning to Hadrian, Tilda's eyes were wider than normal. "We need to find out if Louis ever received any biscuits from Mrs. Styles-Rowdon."

"Whom should we ask?"

"Whomever we can find." Tilda started toward the back of the house.

Hadrian accompanied her. "Are you going downstairs?"

"That seems the best place to start." Tilda moved into the sitting room where the door to the servants' stairs was located. But they didn't need to go any farther, for Clara was just coming from the stairwell.

She stopped short upon seeing Tilda and Hadrian. "My lord, Miss Wren."

"Good afternoon, Clara." Tilda sounded quite stimulated. That was precisely how Hadrian felt. "Do you know if Mr. Chambers ever received biscuits from Mrs. Styles-Rowdon?"

Clara's brow furrowed in confusion. "Do you mean like the tin of cinnamon biscuits she brought to Mrs. Chambers the other day?"

"Yes, exactly," Tilda replied.

"Not that I'm aware of." She blinked, her head tilting briefly. "On second thought, I do recall a tin on his bedside table recently. I can't recall exactly when. And I didn't look inside."

Tilda barely waited for her to finish before asking, "The tin didn't belong to this household?" Clara shook her head, and Tilda continued, "Where is the tin now?"

Clara shrugged. "I haven't seen it. I forgot all about it until now."

"Thank you, Clara." Tilda inclined her head toward the staircase hall where Beryl had gone upstairs. "You may want to check on Mrs. Chambers. She was feeling agitated. We thought she would benefit from a rest."

"She has been most distraught since returning from Scotland Yard." Clara's brow formed deep creases. "She cried all morning after writing a letter to her parents. She didn't want to ask for their help but decided she had no other choice since it seems there are no funds to run the household. I fear I will be shortly out of a position—and she said as much."

"It's possible you'll be able to accompany Mrs. Chambers to her parents' house," Hadrian said optimistically.

A flash of distaste passed over the maid's features. "I don't think I would want to go. I do feel badly for Mrs. Chambers, but it has been difficult to work for her since Mr. Chambers was murdered. But I don't really have a choice. I've nowhere else to go whilst looking for a new position, and I'm worried I won't be able to find one after what happened here."

Hadrian didn't want to tell Clara that she was right to be concerned. "Miss Wren and I will make sure you have somewhere to go and that you find a new position." He glanced toward Tilda who nodded.

"What of the rest of the staff?" Tilda asked. "Are they also concerned about future employment?"

"No. They've been at this house through three different sets of tenants. They seem confident that the landlord will keep them on with the property."

"There is no way you can stay here with them?" Tilda asked.

"I could try, but the new tenants may not require a maid. I can't risk not finding employment immediately." Clara's cheeks reddened. "But I don't think they really want me to. I confess it's rather lonely since Martha and Massey left."

"I'm sorry to hear that," Tilda said gently. "We'll do our best to ensure you're settled somewhere, Clara. Try not to fret."

"Thank you." The maid dipped a curtsey toward Hadrian before hastening to the staircase hall.

Tilda moved into the study, and Hadrian joined her. "I did not see a tin anywhere in these rooms when we searched them."

"Nor did I." He put his hands on his hips and surveyed the room. "Should we look again?"

"I suppose it wouldn't hurt." She glanced at his hands. "I'm glad you hadn't yet removed your gloves. I don't think it's necessary for you to try to see anything."

Hadrian went to a cabinet whilst she began with the desk. "Why do you think Mrs. Styles-Rowdon would poison Louis and Beryl?"

"That is what I'd most like to know. I think it's all but certain she is the poisoner. Let us also assume she was Louis's paramour. Perhaps she poisoned Beryl because she was jealous." Finished with the desk, Tilda turned to face him.

"And why did she stop?"

Tilda exhaled. "I've no idea. This is most puzzling." She moved into the bedchamber where they searched everything again. Then they did the same with the dressing room.

"Now what?" Hadrian asked.

"It may be that we *should* question Mrs. Styles-Rowdon. Or

have Teague do that. At the very least, we should inform him of what we know."

"Let's go to Scotland Yard." Hadrian gestured for her to precede him. They made their way back to the parlor but once again encountered Clara, this time in the entrance hall.

"How is Mrs. Chambers?" Hadrian asked the maid.

"You were right that she is upset." Clara appeared agitated herself. "She insisted she needed to go out, despite my efforts to convince her to stay. I even suggested she take her sleeping draught. I think the stress of everything has taken a toll."

Tilda slid a look at Hadrian before addressing Clara. "Where did Mrs. Chambers go?"

"To Mrs. Styles-Rowdon's." Clara lifted a shoulder. "I'm sure she'll be fine. At least she went to a friend's house."

Clara moved past them toward the back of the house.

Hadrian frowned as he turned toward Tilda. "I am not certain Mrs. Styles-Rowdon *is* a friend."

Tilda's eyes glittered. "On the contrary, I think we must consider that she is a killer."

CHAPTER 22

"We've no choice but to go next door," Tilda said. "It may be best if we send Leach to Scotland Yard to fetch Teague."

Hadrian moved to open the door for her. "He's becoming quite used to that, I think."

They stopped at the coach to speak with Leach before walking—quickly—to Mrs. Styles-Rowdon's.

A woman in her middle forties answered the door.

Once again, Hadrian used his status by handing her his card. "We're here to see Mrs. Styles-Rowdon. We're friends of Mrs. Chambers. We believe she's here?"

"I know who you are, Lord Ravenhurst," the woman, presumably the housekeeper, said. She looked to Tilda but said nothing. Perhaps she did not know who Tilda was. This amused Tilda as it seemed likely that Mrs. Styles-Rowdon would mention Hadrian but not Tilda.

The housekeeper opened the door wide so they could enter. "They are both upstairs. Mrs. Chambers arrived a short while ago and was most urgent in her need to speak with Mrs. Styles-Rowdon. She would not even allow me to fetch her."

"We'll just go on up then too," Tilda said with a smile. She'd no intention of asking, not when they needed to find out what Beryl was doing. She glanced toward Hadrian who gave her a faint nod.

"Thank you." Hadrian nodded at the housekeeper as he escorted Tilda into the staircase hall. The house was laid out much the same as Beryl's next door.

They made their way upstairs and paused at the landing. A moment later, they heard voices coming from the back of the first floor.

"I'm not going to allow you to ransack my things," Mrs. Styles-Rowdon said loudly.

Exchanging glances, Tilda and Hadrian moved in the direction of her voice. The door to her bedchamber was open. Mrs. Styles-Rowdon stood in the doorway to another room—perhaps her dressing chamber—whilst Beryl, her back to Hadrian and Tilda, was in front of her.

"If you've nothing to hide, just show me that you don't have my rubies," Beryl demanded.

Mrs. Styles-Rowdon's features were tight, her eyes fixed on Beryl. The woman's hands were braced on the doorframe, effectively blocking Beryl from entering.

Tilda considered the best course of action. They could force Mrs. Styles-Rowdon's hand, knowing Teague would be here soon. Unless he wasn't available. It might be best that they wait for his arrival, in which case they needed to convince Beryl to leave.

Opting for the latter, Tilda stepped into the bedchamber. "Beryl, you are distraught. Please allow Hadrian and me to escort you home."

Beryl whipped her head around. She appeared even more agitated than when they'd seen her a short while ago. "Of course, I'm distraught. Gillian is not my friend. She has been having an affair with Louis. And she poisoned me!"

"I did no such thing," Mrs. Styles-Rowdon said with a click of her tongue. "The stress of the past week has finally affected you, my dear. You know that I *am* your friend."

Keeping her attention on Tilda and Hadrian, Beryl went on. "After I told you about the Epiphany party, I remembered something. I saw Louis try to kiss Gillian that night. She pushed him away. At the time, I was glad to see her reaction and angry that Louis had tried that. But when I thought back to the event itself, I realize Gillian hadn't appeared upset. She'd been more … furtive, as if she didn't want to be caught. I know what that looks like because I did that with Louis myself when I was trying to hide our affair from Hadrian."

Tilda glanced over at Hadrian, but his expression was stony.

Beryl turned back to Gillian. "How could you do that? I thought we were friends. You were so kind to me, so supportive, especially when I said I wanted to divorce Louis." Beryl sucked in a breath. "Was that because you hoped to marry him?"

Gillian shook her head. "You've gone mad, Beryl. I didn't poison you, and I certainly didn't want to wed Louis. He was utterly despicable." She looked past Beryl at Tilda and Hadrian. "I have suspected that Beryl poisoned him. She was desperate to get away from him. I wondered if she may have stabbed him, to be honest, but since she apparently did not, I would wager she was responsible for the poisoning." She gave Beryl a sad look.

A primal sound erupted from Beryl just before she launched herself forward, pushing Gillian into the dressing room. Surprised, Gillian fell back, stumbling but not quite losing her balance.

Tilda rushed after them into the dressing room. Beryl was at the dressing table, grasping for the jewelry box. But Gillian had recovered and pulled on Beryl viciously.

With a cry, Beryl hit her head on the corner of a dresser and slumped to the floor.

Hadrian was also there. He grasped Gillian by the forearm.

His hand was bare, which meant he'd removed his gloves at some point. Tilda glimpsed them on the floor near the doorway.

Since he had Gillian, Tilda went to crouch next to Beryl. She appeared unconscious, but she was breathing. Hopefully, she would wake momentarily.

Tilda's heart crashed wildly as she rose and reached for the jewelry box.

"Don't!" Gillian cried.

Opening the box, Tilda easily found Beryl's rubies. "Not a very good place to hide jewelry," she said darkly as she looked back to Gillian.

It was then Tilda noticed Hadrian's face. His gaze was locked on Gillian, but he didn't seem to be seeing her.

Tilda knew he must be having a vision. "Hadrian?" She spoke his name loudly.

However, all that served to do was alert Gillian to the fact that he seemed lost. She wrenched her arm free and dashed into her bedchamber.

Putting his hand to his head, Hadrian blinked. "Where did she go?"

"Her bedchamber!" Tilda started toward the doorway, but Hadrian was closer.

Just before Tilda reached the bedchamber, she heard the report of a pistol. Hadrian recoiled, nearly hitting her as he fell back.

She caught him, but his weight pulled her down. Sinking to the floor, she cradled him.

And her heart stopped as she feared she'd lost him.

∽

The bullet struck Hadrian in the bicep, tearing through his flesh in a burst of agony. His first thought was that it was far too soon for him to be facing his mortality again.

His second thought was that it was just his arm, and he would be fine, despite the searing pain.

His third—and best—thought was that Tilda had come to his rescue.

"Hadrian!" She moved her gloved hands over his chest.

"It's my upper arm," he managed. "I'm fine. Go after her before she gets away."

Mrs. Styles-Rowdon had dropped her spent pistol and run from the room.

"I don't want to leave you," Tilda said, her voice quavering.

Hadrian pushed himself upright so that he wasn't leaning on her. He met her gaze. "*Go.*"

She hesitated the barest moment before leaping to her feet and streaking from the room in a flurry of gray skirts.

"Hadrian?" Beryl's query came weakly from the dressing room.

Wincing, Hadrian turned and used the doorframe to hoist himself up with his uninjured right arm. He stepped into the dressing room where Beryl lay next to the dresser. She lifted her hand and turned her head to the side.

He saw the blood on the floor and swore beneath his breath. Glancing about, he didn't see anything to press to the wound. Moving to the dresser, he opened a drawer and removed the first thing he saw. Lifting Beryl's head with his right hand, he put the cloth to her scalp using his left, grimacing against the pain. There was also a staggering throb behind his temples, courtesy of the visions he'd had whilst touching Mrs. Styles-Rowdon.

"Can you hold this?" he asked. "I need to help Tilda."

Beryl blinked at him. "But you're bleeding. Did I hear a pistol shot?"

"Yes. Your *friend* shot me. I really must ensure Tilda is all right. She's gone after Mrs. Styles-Rowdon." He stood. "I'll send the housekeeper to help you."

Hadrian turned and sprinted through the bedchamber. He ran

down the stairs, moving so fast he nearly tumbled down the last few.

The housekeeper stood at the bottom, her face white. "What is happening?"

"Where did Mrs. Styles-Rowdon go?"

"Out the front door." The woman gestured toward the entrance hall, her hand shaking. "Your … whoever followed her." She stared at his arm. "You're bleeding. Did someone fire a pistol?" The housekeeper's face lost even more color, and Hadrian feared she may faint.

Hadrian speared her with an intense stare. "You must remain calm. I need you to go up to Mrs. Styles-Rowdon's dressing room to help Mrs. Chambers. She hit her head and is bleeding. The police will be here shortly." Hadrian did not wait for the housekeeper's reply before dashing outside. He didn't even bother to close the door behind him.

He looked up and down the street, then froze for a moment as he saw Tilda sitting atop Mrs. Styles-Rowdon on the pavement just past Beryl's house. His arm ached fiercely, but he ran toward the two women.

When he reached them, he stood so Tilda could see him. "Are you all right?"

Tilda nodded. She was breathing heavily. "I've got her." Indeed she did. She straddled the woman's hips and held her wrists. Mrs. Styles-Rowdon lay on her back, moving angrily as she sought to free herself.

"Stop," Hadrian barked. "You're caught now."

Thankfully, the police wagon turned the corner onto Catherine Place at precisely that moment. Hadrian exhaled with relief. "The police are here now."

"Let me up!" Mrs. Styles-Rowdon fought harder as tears leaked from the corners of her eyes.

"No," Tilda replied calmly, though Hadrian could see her pulse hammering in her neck.

The police wagon pulled up alongside the pavement, and Hadrian saw that Leach was behind them. Teague jumped down from the seat, and two constables came from the wagon.

The detective inspector registered Hadrian's arm with a frown. "All right there, Ravenhurst?"

"I will be. Help Tilda up, please."

Teague nodded for the constables to grab Mrs. Styles-Rowdon. When they had hold of her arms, Tilda released her and allowed Teague to help her up.

Tilda immediately went to Hadrian and looked at his arm. "We need to staunch this bleeding." She whipped her gloves off and pressed them to the wound. "It's the best I have at the moment." Relief tinged her features.

Leach ran toward them. "My lord?" He appeared stricken.

"Fetch a physician," Hadrian said. "I've been shot, and Mrs. Chambers hit her head and is bleeding."

"Is she?" Tilda asked. "I should have stayed to help."

Hadrian shook his head and immediately regretted it. Tilda touched his cheek. The touch of her bare hand was both soothing and stirring. He could not look away from the tender concern in her gaze.

"Your head," she whispered. "It must be paining you along with your arm. I know you saw something when you grabbed Mrs. Styles-Rowdon."

"I'll tell you about it later," he said softly, giving her a reassuring smile. "I'll be fine."

As Leach left to find a physician, Teague turned to address them. "I gather Mrs. Styles-Rowdon is, in fact, our poisoner."

"Yes," Tilda replied. "She was baking cinnamon biscuits for Beryl back in January which coincided with when Beryl was ill. She brings them in a tin, and Clara says she saw a tin in Louis Chambers' bedroom recently."

Teague nodded. "As it happens, I was preparing to come here to speak with her when your coachman arrived, Ravenhurst. I received further information from the Portsmouth Police. It seems Mrs. Styles-Rowdon collected on an insurance policy on her former husband. What's more, she also collected insurance money on her first husband, Mr. Styles, and from her parents, all of whom died of gastrointestinal illness."

Mrs. Styles-Rowdon made a noise in her throat before her head lolled forward. She had not lost consciousness, but she'd gone limp in the constables' grip.

Tilda glanced about, and Hadrian realized several of the neighbors had come out of their houses to watch the spectacle. "Should we move inside?"

"I will take her to Scotland Yard, but I would like to speak with Mrs. Chambers first," Teague said.

"Then let us repair to Mrs. Styles-Rowdon's house," Tilda suggested.

As they passed Beryl's house, her staff stood on the front porch. "Where is Mrs. Chambers?" Clara asked.

"Come with us," Tilda said. "She hurt her head and will likely need care."

"I'll fetch some things from downstairs," Mrs. Dunning said sternly before hurrying back into the house.

They continued to Mrs. Styles-Rowdon's house with Beryl's retainers following behind.

Mrs. Styles-Rowdon's housekeeper was just helping Beryl into the entrance hall as they entered. Both women registered surprise as the constables brought Mrs. Styles-Rowdon inside.

Teague stepped into the nearest room, the parlor, which was situated exactly like Beryl's off the entrance hall. Everyone moved into the room, and Tilda made Hadrian sit on the settee where she joined him. She took over pressing the gloves to his arm, and he relaxed against the back of the settee, glad to be sitting down.

Beryl went to a chair and practically fell into it whilst the housekeeper said she would fetch some things to help Hadrian.

He didn't bother telling her that the cook from Beryl's house was already doing so.

Teague remained standing, as did the constables who were holding Mrs. Styles-Rowdon. "You may put handcuffs on her now."

One of the constables did so, securing her arms together in front of her. She was surprisingly stoic. Whilst she did not make eye contact with anyone, she did not appear as cowed as she had outside.

Teague turned toward the woman. "Mrs. Styles-Rowdon, you will be prosecuted for the crimes I mentioned outside."

"What are those?" Beryl interrupted.

He repeated the crimes against Mrs. Styles-Rowdon's parents and her two previous husbands. Beryl and her retainers gasped in near unison. "She's a murderer," Beryl said. "But why were you poisoning me? What would you have gained?"

When Mrs. Styles-Rowdon didn't speak, Tilda replied. "I believe she wanted Louis for herself. He'd been giving her lavish gifts, so I'm sure she thought he would make a fine third husband." Tilda looked toward the woman in handcuffs. "Do I have that right?"

"That was my plan, yes," Mrs. Styles-Rowdon said in a low voice. She briefly looked at Beryl. "However, I grew to like you and I felt sorry for you because of Louis. I realized he had no money and was an idiot. He also treated you terribly and wasn't at all faithful—not even to me, as I believe he was carrying on with the maid even after our affair began."

"You were his paramour then," Beryl said with a sniff.

Tilda nodded toward Beryl. "I found your rubies upstairs."

"You then went on to poison Mr. Chambers?" Teague asked Mrs. Styles-Rowdon.

She nodded. "It seemed the right thing to do. No one liked the man. His staff loathed him. They complained to my cook and housekeeper about him taking advantage of the maids and of his treatment of Beryl, not to mention his drunkenness and generally uncouth behavior."

Mrs. Dunning entered then and set a tray of medicinal items on a table. She hesitated, but Tilda motioned for her to come over.

Teague looked toward Clara. "You saw a tin in Mr. Chambers' room of late?" At her nod, he continued. "Did you happen to see what was inside?"

"I did not."

"I took him biscuits," Mrs. Styles-Rowdon spat. "But those other women killed him first. Honestly, they did everyone a favor. Can't we all agree on that?" She looked around the room.

No one debated her.

"Nevertheless, it is against the law for you to decide who ought to die for being a bad person," Teague said. He addressed the constables. "Take Mrs. Styles-Rowdon to Scotland Yard. I need to collect the rubies as evidence and will follow shortly."

The constables nodded and left with Mrs. Styles-Rowdon, who held her head high as they marched her from the room.

"We need to remove your coat," Tilda said, drawing Hadrian's attention.

"All right." He let her do most of the work, wincing as the pain renewed with his movements.

"I'll need to cut the shirt away," Mrs. Dunning pronounced. She fetched a pair of scissors from the tray and cut Hadrian's shirt at the shoulder.

Tilda then carefully peeled the sleeve away from his wound, whispering her apologies as he grimaced. Hadrian was glad she was there, for he found her demeanor and concern most soothing.

Mrs. Styles-Rowdon's housekeeper returned and tended to Beryl.

Teague stepped toward the settee. "Sorry you were shot, Ravenhurst. Do you know where I can find the weapon?"

"It's upstairs in her bedchamber," Tilda said. "The rubies are in her dressing chamber in her jewelry box. She didn't even bother to hide them somewhere special."

"Mrs. Styles-Rowdon has been a successful criminal for some time," Teague noted. "I'm sure she felt confident in her abilities at deception."

The cook dabbed a wet cloth on Hadrian's newly exposed wound. Pain shot up through his shoulder. "I don't suppose there's any brandy or other liquor about?"

"There's some in the dining room," Mrs. Styles-Rowdon's housekeeper replied.

"I'll fetch it," Mrs. Blank offered, hurrying from the room.

"Breathe," Tilda whispered, her gaze meeting his. "Does it hurt terribly?"

"Not much worse than my head," he said with a smile that was meant only for her. He held her gaze until her cheeks turned pink, and she returned her attention to Teague. "Shall I join you upstairs?" he asked the inspector.

Teague waved his hand. "No need. Though I require your description of what happened. Mrs. Styles-Rowdon will also be charged with shooting Ravenhurst."

"And attacking Beryl," Hadrian noted. "Mrs. Styles-Rowdon threw her against a dresser, and Beryl was knocked unconscious."

"She's going to hang, isn't she?" Beryl winced as Mrs. Styles-Rowdon's housekeeper cleaned her scalp.

"I would think so," Teague said.

"Good, she deserves to," Beryl said, her jaw tightening.

Mrs. Blank returned with a bottle of brandy and a pair of glasses. She gave one of each to Hadrian and Beryl. Hadrian swallowed half the contents.

Teague went upstairs, and Leach arrived with the doctor. Satisfied that Hadrian was in good hands, Leach returned to the coach.

Hadrian insisted the doctor see to Beryl first. He prescribed rest and asked Clara to keep a close eye on Beryl for the next few days.

"I may need to travel soon," Beryl said wearily.

"Not for at least three days," the doctor instructed before moving to care for Hadrian.

Tilda continued to sit beside Hadrian as the physician inspected and cleaned his wound. He then closed the flesh with several stitches.

Hadrian had finished his glass of brandy whilst the doctor tended to Beryl, then drank another at Tilda's insistence. The effects of the liquor dulled the prick of the needle moving through his arm.

The physician said he would call on Hadrian in a few days to review his healing progress and would remove the stitches at a later date—at least a week from now.

As he was packing up his bag to go, Hadrian asked Tilda to help him put on his coat. He would not be able to get his arm in the sleeve at the moment, but he could drape it over his bare arm instead of leaving it exposed.

Teague had returned whilst Hadrian was being stitched and now recorded their testimony, including Beryl's, of what had occurred.

"May I return home now, Inspector?" Beryl asked.

"Yes. I will be in touch regarding what happens next with Mrs. Styles-Rowdon."

Clara looked from Beryl to Teague. "What if Mrs. Chambers has left London?"

Teague's brows pitched together as he regarded Beryl. "Where are you planning to travel?"

"I wrote to my parents this morning. I asked if I could return home to Rutland. They may say no, in which case I've no idea where I will be. I can't afford to stay in my current home."

Mrs. Blank looked expectantly at Beryl. "Didn't Mr. Chambers say he would set an appointment with the solicitor as soon as possible to discuss your financial matters?"

"He did." She glanced toward Hadrian. "Oliver has promised to help me sort things and determine what is left for me to rely upon." Her expression was utterly morose.

"I'm sorry things have turned out this way, Beryl. I'm confident Oliver can help you."

"I'd thought to ask Gillian if I could stay with her for a while, as I will not be able to continue to lease the house next door. *That* is no longer an option obviously."

Hadrian could see she was quite upset. "I'm sure things will look better after a good night's sleep," he said optimistically. "I have faith in your parents." He'd liked them, particularly her father, when they'd spoken about the betrothal.

"I'm glad someone does," Beryl said with a faint pout.

Teague rose from the table where he'd sat to write down what everyone had said. "Mrs. Chambers, please inform me if you do leave London."

Beryl nodded.

"Come, you need to go home," Tilda said softly to Hadrian.

He nodded, his headache now gone, and stood. Tilda rose alongside him.

Oswald helped Beryl up, and she and her retainers began filing from the parlor. Tilda and Hadrian followed, accompanied by Teague.

"Thank you both again for your contributions to solving this bizarre case," Teague said in the entrance hall. "I hope the arm isn't paining you too badly, Ravenhurst."

"It's more of a nuisance than anything else," Hadrian replied. "Let us know how we can help with anything further."

Teague held the door while they left, and they walked together to Hadrian's coach.

"Do you need a ride to Scotland Yard?" Hadrian asked.

"I'll take a hack," Teague replied. "If you don't go directly home to rest, I fear Miss Wren will explode."

Was she worried? Hadrian turned his head toward her to see she was shaking her head at Teague. The inspector chuckled and took himself off to find a hack.

Leach helped Tilda and then Hadrian into the coach. Tilda asked him to take Hadrian home first. "He needs to rest as soon as possible."

"It won't take long to drop you at home first," Hadrian said.

"Nonsense. We're going to Ravenhurst House first, and I will walk you to the door."

Leach agreed with Tilda, and they were shortly on their way to Hadrian's house in Mayfair.

Tilda angled toward Hadrian on the seat. "You must promise me you will take good care. You were stabbed not that long ago, and you suffer regular headaches. Now you've been shot."

"I am fine," he assured her. "Aren't you curious what I saw when I grabbed Mrs. Styles-Rowdon?"

"You know I am. But I have been more worried about you. What did you see?"

"First, I saw her feeding those bloody cinnamon biscuits to a grinning Louis Chambers in his bed. And I am glad the vision ended there," he added with a chuckle. "Second, I saw her standing beside a coffin bearing an older woman who bore a resemblance to her. After hearing what Teague said about her parents, I assume it was her mother."

Tilda blinked. "It's shocking she killed so many people. I think you may have been her next target."

"I'm sure you're right. I am relieved I did not have to flirt with her today as we'd originally discussed. It was bad enough I had to grab her." He looked down at his hands. "I just realized I left my gloves in her dressing room. And I need to buy you a new pair after thoroughly ruining yours."

"I'm just glad you're all right." She exhaled. "When I heard that pistol fire, I feared the worst."

"I recall you checking my chest for a wound." That had felt rather nice actually. He wished he'd been in a better state to enjoy it more.

Pink flushed Tilda's cheeks. She looked very soft and feminine just now. "I didn't mean to overstep," she murmured.

"You did not," he replied. "You *could* not." His eyes met hers and silence reigned for a long moment during which a warmth curled in Hadrian's belly.

Overcome with gratitude and something far more primal, he leaned toward Tilda. Her lips parted the barest amount.

Hadrian didn't hesitate, nor was there anything in his mind telling him to do so. Closing his eyes, he kissed her.

CHAPTER 23

*T*ilda watched him lean toward her, but she hadn't entirely realized what he'd meant to do until his lips met hers. Surprise, mingled with a wonderful heat, raced through her with delicious speed.

It was over almost as quickly as it had happened. Their eyes met as Hadrian retreated. A few fine lines marred his forehead. Was he worried that he should not have kissed her?

Good. Because he should *not* have, no matter how lovely it had been.

And it had been *quite* lovely.

"Pardon me," he said softly.

Tilda settled herself back against the squab and turned her head toward the front of the coach. Her heart was beating madly, and she fought to control her breath. "That should not be repeated."

He didn't immediately respond, and when he finally did, she heard confusion in his voice. "I thought you said you wouldn't mind if I kissed you. We spoke of it the other day. I was talking about you. Did you not realize?"

She had realized, of course, and she'd responded saying she

wouldn't mind, which had been most foolish of her. What good could come of them kissing one another?

"I should not have said that," she said firmly. "I do apologize. We must maintain our professional association."

"But we are also friends."

She glanced at him, which was a mistake because he looked like more than a friend to her eyes. That was probably due to what had happened. She was naturally upset after he'd been shot. And he had to be too. That was likely why he'd kissed her. They were both shaken.

Which meant she could put the kiss from her mind. It had been the result of an overwhelming event, nothing more. Tilda was relieved, especially since she had no intention of indulging in any kind of romantic entanglement. That would lead to marriage, and she had absolutely *no* interest in that. Especially to an earl.

Thankfully, the coach stopped, and she saw they had arrived at Hadrian's house. "Today has been remarkably intense. I understand why you … overstepped. We needn't discuss it," she said just before Leach opened the door.

She climbed out and watched as Leach helped Hadrian from the coach. Leach waited for her whilst she walked Hadrian to the door.

"My apologies," Hadrian said. "I did not mean to offend." His tone had gone cool.

"I am not offended," Tilda rushed to say. "Kissing is just not something we can allow. That leads to … a different kind of attachment."

He turned his head toward her as they made their way to the door. His eyes were bright. "I would *never* expect you to behave inappropriately." He frowned slightly. "But I did when I kissed you, particularly without seeking your permission. I do apologize. It won't happen again."

His butler opened the door. His gaze fell on Hadrian's arm

and the awkward drape of his coat. "What on earth has happened, my lord?"

"I shall explain, Collier." Hadrian looked to Tilda. "Thank you for your assistance." He moved into the house, and Tilda accepted that she had been dismissed.

"Please let me know how you're doing," she called after him.

He nodded in reply. Tilda smiled at the butler, then she returned to the coach where Leach opened the door for her.

"Thank you, Leach," she murmured, her mind a tumult of thoughts and agitation.

How she wished he hadn't kissed her. Except …

She put her fingertips to her lips as she recalled the wonderful sensation of his mouth against hers. His lips had moved over hers briefly but with a sensuous purpose that she'd felt deep inside herself. It wasn't like anything she'd experienced before.

In truth, it had been terrifying.

Though perhaps not as terrifying as the idea of being married to someone like him. She could not imagine the responsibilities and expectations that would come with such a role. Actually, she could, and that was why she wasn't interested. She liked her life. It was compact and manageable, and she was on the verge of embarking on a new path of conducting her own investigations, something she'd only ever dared dream.

But one of the reasons it seemed possible and even probable was Hadrian's involvement. With an earl's recommendation and support, she actually had a chance for success.

Would he still provide that? Or had she completely ruined things?

No, it wouldn't be her fault. He'd kissed her.

Because she'd led him to believe she didn't mind.

Argh!

This was a complication she didn't need. She wanted things to go back to the way they were before he'd kissed her. No, before he'd talked about kissing her.

If they could do that, all would be well.

~

*T*hree weeks later, Tilda descended the staircase in a new gown and with a more intricate hairstyle than she was used to. Her grandmother smiled widely. "You look lovely, my dear. I'm so glad you saw fit to purchase another gown. The mulberry is very pretty on you. And Clara has made a masterpiece of your hair."

Clara had come to stay with them—temporarily—a few days ago after Beryl had gone home to her parents in Rutland. The house in Catherine Place would soon have new tenants, and as expected, they did not have need of Clara. In fact, they hadn't wanted any of the existing retainers to stay, and so they'd all needed to find a new situation. Clara would be looking for a position as a maid or lady's maid, but in the meantime, she'd had nowhere to go. So Tilda and her grandmother had taken her in, just as they'd done with Vaughn.

Now they had two additions to their household that they did not particularly need but who had ended up being quite helpful. Tilda could not have known that she would need someone to style her hair for a new client. The new client was also why Tilda had purchased a new gown. It was vital she looked her very best because today she was meeting with that client.

The dowager Countess of Ravenhurst.

Well, Tilda supposed Hadrian had been her first client and Beryl Chambers had been her second. This was the first client referred to her specifically for an investigation.

That it was Hadrian's mother was slightly bothersome, but only because Tilda was still caught up on the idea that she oughtn't be paid by him or his family for every investigation. He'd ended up paying for Tilda's time investigating Beryl's missing jewels, in addition to her invoice that covered the investigation to prove Hadrian hadn't killed Louis Chambers.

However, Hadrian wouldn't be paying for this investigation—his mother would. He was the reason behind it though, and whilst Tilda was grateful, she was also a bit nervous. She'd seen him just once since the Thing She Would Not Name had happened to ensure he was healing well.

During that meeting, Hadrian had reiterated his desire to help Tilda with her investigative work, which included referring people to her. He'd also ensured she paid a *very* fair price for the printing of her cards. Indeed, she wondered if he'd shared the expense without telling her. She hoped not, even as she told herself that she oughtn't let pride rule her decisions.

"Thank you, Grandmama."

Tilda's grandmother eyed her with concern. "Are you nervous?"

"Perhaps a little." Whilst Tilda had met the dowager countess previously, working for her would be a different kind of interaction.

"You will be splendid!" Grandmama assured her. "I only wish I could come along and watch your triumph."

"This isn't a social engagement," Tilda said, which she'd explained before. She realized it was somewhat difficult for her grandmother to fully comprehend that Tilda was a woman of business. That was just so far outside her grandmother's experience.

"I know, dear. I shall wait eagerly for the full report of what transpired."

Hadrian's coach arrived—he'd insisted on sending it to fetch her, and Leach helped her inside. "Good to see you, Miss Wren."

"And you, Leach," she replied with a smile.

When she arrived at Ravenhurst House, Collier showed her to the drawing room where Hadrian was already waiting. The dowager countess did not appear to have arrived yet.

That meant Tilda and Hadrian would be alone for a time. Tilda would do her best to ensure it wasn't awkward.

He greeted her warmly, with his usual smile that still set a few butterflies loose in Tilda's belly no matter how hard she tried to remain unaffected. She just had to accept that she had an attraction to Hadrian and would need to ignore that. In time, she presumed, it would pass. Especially after more time had elapsed since the Thing She Would Not Name.

His gaze lingered on her gown, and she knew he must recognize that it was new. She waited for him to compliment her as he often did, but he did not. That was probably for the best. After all, she'd said they needed to keep matters between them professional. Or something like that.

"You appear completely recovered from your wound," she said.

"I am, thank you. I resumed my morning rides in the park a week or so ago."

Morning rides in the park were an excellent reminder of why Tilda could have no future with Hadrian. She didn't know how to ride a horse, nor did she have any interest in learning.

"I'm glad to hear that," Tilda said. "Have you any idea why your mother seeks to hire me?"

He shook his head. "She is being rather guarded. She said she would reveal all today when she could meet with you in person. I only know she wishes you to make some inquiries on her behalf."

"I am happy to help. And thank *you* very much for recommending me to her."

"It is my pleasure. I hope to continue the practice."

"Are you planning to assist me?" she asked tentatively, unsure of what answer she was hoping for. "With your ability, I mean."

"If you require it, I would be delighted. I confess, I am somewhat jealous as I've developed an affinity for investigation. With you, anyway." He looked away abruptly. "How is your grandmother?" he asked quickly, as if he wanted to distract Tilda from what he'd said. There was no need, for she didn't want to think about how much she enjoyed investigating with him too.

"Good afternoon!" Hadrian's mother sailed into the room in a flurry of dark-yellow silk. "Miss Wren, you are here, how lovely." She smiled broadly, and Tilda saw the similarity in mother and son, primarily in the shape and color of their eyes.

Tilda dipped into a brief curtsey. "Good afternoon, Lady Ravenhurst. I am honored you would seek my services."

"It is a delicate matter, and since you have helped Ravenhurst before, I am hopeful you can help me too." She went to Hadrian and bussed his cheek. "Afternoon, my boy. I trust your arm is no longer paining you?"

"It hardly pained me at all, Mother," he said with a patient smile.

"What a nasty business to have been shot," the dowager countess said with a cluck of her tongue. "There shall be none of that with what I am hiring you to do," she said to Tilda before taking a seat at the table where tea had been laid out. "Do I need to pour?" She looked at Hadrian and then at Tilda.

"I can," Tilda offered, though she wondered why she'd felt the need. She wasn't the hostess here. Perhaps she thought an earl shouldn't pour tea, which was silly. As she poured into their cups, she had an eerie sensation, almost as if she were watching herself at the tea table. She didn't belong in an earl's drawing room pouring tea, for heaven's sake.

She added milk and sugar to their cups as they directed, then added a bit of sugar to her own before sitting. As Hadrian sat along with her, she belatedly realized she ought to have sat to pour. Further proof that she had no business in this environment. And yet, she needed to learn if she intended to have clients such as the dowager Countess of Ravenhurst.

Hadrian sipped his tea, then fixed his gaze on his mother. "I am on tenterhooks waiting to hear why you need Miss Wren's help."

"I don't want to hear any admonishment about any of this," she said sternly to him. "Do you understand?"

Appearing alarmed, Hadrian frowned slightly. "Of course, but such a warning does not herald a sense of comfort."

"I just don't want you to counsel me," the dowager added with a sniff.

"I will not, Mama."

Lady Ravenhurst turned to Tilda. "I have recently begun consulting with a medium."

Hadrian had taken a drink of tea and now coughed.

The dowager glanced at him with slightly narrowed eyes before returning her attention to Tilda. "She says she can communicate with Gabriel. Miss Wren, I want you to determine if she is authentic."

Tilda slid a look toward Hadrian and noted that his neck was red above his collar. His lips were pressed together as if he were trying very hard not to speak. Whilst she could understand his agitation—the notion of speaking with the dead was ludicrous—she also needed to listen to her client.

Unless she decided that she couldn't help the dowager. Just as Tilda didn't work for men who sought divorces, she wouldn't undertake an investigation she didn't think she could do. And authenticating a medium may very well fall into that category.

Except.

Except Hadrian saw visions that could not be explained. What if this medium *could* speak with the dead? Didn't Tilda at least have to try to find answers? Indeed, she was eager to.

Furthermore, Hadrian must help her. Perhaps this medium could even help *him* with his ability.

Tilda smiled at Hadrian's mother. "I will be glad to help, Lady Ravenhurst. Allow me to take notes whilst you provide the necessary details."

She risked another look at Hadrian who was glowering in her

direction. He was not happy that Tilda had accepted this challenge.

It would be up to her to convince him that it was necessary— for his mother and for him.

Don't miss the next book in the Raven & Wren series, A WHISPER AND A CURSE when Tilda and Hadrian are drawn into a deadly game where mediums across London are falling victim to the "Levitation Killer."

Would you like to know when my next book is available and to hear about sales and deals? **Sign up for my Reader Club newsletter** which is the only place you can get exclusive bonus books and material.

Join me on social media!

Facebook: https://facebook.com/DarcyBurkeFans
Instagram: darcyburkeauthor
Bluesky: darcyburkeauthor
Pinterest: darcyburkewrite

And follow me on Bookbub to receive updates on pre-orders, new releases, and deals!

I hope you'll consider leaving a review at your favorite online vendor or networking site!

I appreciate my readers so much. Thank you for reading!

AUTHOR'S NOTE

With the passing of the Matrimonial Causes Act in 1857, divorces became more common in the United Kingdom. Prior to this law, divorces could only be obtained through a private act of Parliament. After 1857, divorces were granted due to adultery, though a woman had to also prove a second reason such as desertion, cruelty, or bigamy.

Arsenic poisoning was not uncommon during the Victorian era. It was used as a pigment in green dye to make "Scheele's green" or emerald green. This color was very popular in the mid-nineteenth century and could be found in all manner of items including wallpaper and clothing. These items did great damage to people, making them sick or even killing them. I would likely have been afflicted since green is my favorite color! Of course, arsenic was also used to purposely poison people, as was the case with Mary Ann Cotton who, in 1873, was found guilty of murdering several of her children and husbands or lovers.

ALSO BY DARCY BURKE

Insatiable

Never Have I Ever with a Duke

A Duke is Never Enough

A Duke Will Never Do

The Untouchables: The Pretenders

A Secret Surrender

A Scandalous Bargain

A Rogue to Ruin

Love is All Around

(A Regency Holiday Trilogy)

The Red Hot Earl

The Gift of the Marquess

Joy to the Duke

Wicked Dukes Club

One Night for Seduction by Erica Ridley

One Night of Surrender by Darcy Burke

One Night of Passion by Erica Ridley

One Night of Scandal by Darcy Burke

One Night to Remember by Erica Ridley

One Night of Temptation by Darcy Burke

Secrets and Scandals

Her Wicked Ways

His Wicked Heart

To Seduce a Scoundrel

To Love a Thief (a novella)

Never Love a Scoundrel

Scoundrel Ever After

Prefer to read in German, French, or Italian? Check out my website for foreign language editions!

ABOUT THE AUTHOR

Darcy Burke is the USA Today Bestselling Author of historical romance and mystery and contemporary romance. Darcy wrote her first book at age 11, a happily ever after about a swan addicted to magic and the female swan who loved him, with exceedingly poor illustrations. Join her Reader Club newsletter for the latest updates from Darcy.

A native Oregonian, Darcy lives on the edge of wine country with her guitar-strumming husband, incredibly talented artist daughter, and imaginative, Japanese-speaking son who will almost certainly out-write her one day (that may be tomorrow). They're a crazy cat family with two Bengal cats, a small, fame-seeking torbie named after a fruit, an older rescue Maine Coon with attitude to spare, an adorable former stray who wandered onto their deck and into their hearts, and two bonded boys (a Russian Blue and a Turkish Van) who used to belong to (separate) neighbors but chose them instead. You can find Darcy in her comfy writing chair balancing her laptop and a cat or three, attempting yoga, folding laundry (which she loves), or wildlife spotting and playing games with her family. She loves traveling to the UK and visiting her cousins in Denmark. Visit Darcy online at www.darcyburke.com and follow her on social media.